THE MAN FROM
THE PLACE
OF CLAY

RIC LEONETTI

*To Elena
I love your passion
for the written word*

LUMINARE PRESS

WWW.LUMINAREPRESS.COM

The Man from the Place of Clay
© 2017 Ric Leonetti

Printed in the United States of America

Cover Design: Claire Flint Last

Luminare Press
438 Charnelton, Suite 101
Eugene, OR 97401
www.luminarepress.com

LCCN: 2017939164
ISBN: 978-1-944733-22-3

FOR ELLIS

Contents

PROLOGUE:
REVELATIONS

The New Spirituality Takes Hold in America

TAOS—What began with trespassing on sacred tribal land at the Taos Pueblo twenty years ago, has grown into virtually an unstoppable phenomena that has changed the way many Americans view God and the universe. And now, the movement is poised to spread across the globe.

Religious leaders from nearly every organized religion have come forward to challenge the validity of 'new spirituality,' but have struggled to win the debate in what is described as 'the undeniable truth.'

Based on a book of the same name, which was published nearly fifteen years ago, the 'truth,' as it is called, has defined religion versus spirituality.

Tens of thousands are expected to descend on Taos one week from today—in what is sure to be an explosive boon to the local economy—to hear several speakers, including the author of the landmark book, *The Undeniable Truth.*

JUNE 1990

A FISHER OF MEN

Proof that there is a supreme being, Cormick Proffitt scoffed to himself as he gently eased his new Mercedes 300 SL into his reserved parking space. *If there were a God, he would drive this car.* Though his promotion to Head of Psychiatric Medicine would not be official for a few more weeks, he had been granted a space on the east side of Vancouver Memorial that could be viewed from his office and would keep his new car out of the punishing afternoon sun.

Stepping out of the car, he drew in a deep breath of the fresh morning air and surveyed the scene around him. The early June sunshine bathed the hospital in a comforting, warm light as people quietly came and went through the hospital entrance. There were no sirens blaring and no commotion outside of the ER. Everything was exactly how he liked it: calm and orderly.

He grabbed his briefcase and stepped back to admire the fine German engineering that was now his. It was a work of art that would be envied by all who passed by. The glossy, silver color brilliantly reflected the sunlight like the precious metal it was named after. It was hard for him to freely spend money on items that were not necessities. But the upcoming and long overdue promotion had empowered him to spend for the sake of appearances.

Money was not, and never had been, an issue. Even though a trust fund and a significant inheritance had provided for his every need, he never spent money extravagantly. As far as he was concerned, the Mercedes was more than a status symbol, it seemed to him like a prerequisite for his new position. The purchase had been a rational decision, but he was surprised at how good it felt.

He strolled through the lobby, smiling proudly, but avoiding direct eye contact with everyone he passed. He was in a self-congratulatory mood. It was going to be a day of transition and new beginnings.

"Going up, Dr. Proffitt?" a voice called from the open door of the elevator.

"No thank you!" Cormick cheerfully called as he headed for the stairs.

The staff had operated for years under the misconception that Dr. Cormick Proffitt took the stairs every day for the obvious health benefits. But it was merely the lesser of two evils. Suffering from severe acrophobia and debilitating pathological height vertigo, he had trained himself to look only at the walls of the stairwell to avoid losing his balance. The daily battle he fought with himself on the stairs was nothing compared to the demons he would be at war with in the cramped, airless elevator. His claustrophobia was paralyzing. He could not risk anyone seeing a respected psychiatrist fall victim to the very fears he sought to ease in others. Climbing the five flights of stairs was a small price to pay for his peace of mind and the continued respect of the staff.

"Do not look down," he whispered to himself as he climbed the stairs. "Eyes up. Do not look down." He stayed close to the wall for the entire journey upward, verbally reassuring himself that he would survive the climb. "You can do this," he reminded himself.

He stepped into his outer office, running his fingers through his graying, light brown bangs to lift them from his forehead and to discreetly wipe away any sweat from the fearful ascent to his office. He had to look his best when he entered. Nurse Paige would certainly be at her desk, and every work day began with making a good impression on her.

She was sitting at the reception desk, her head tilted slightly to hold the phone against her shoulder. Her light brown hair was pulled back, and her bright blue eyes lit up as she made eye contact with him. Their first glance at each other in the morning was the highlight of his day. His senses were bombarded; the sound of her voice, the sight of her beautiful face, and the smell of her perfume tugged on his stomach. He dreamed of her touch and the taste of her warm kiss. This was his moment, and he inhaled deeply to breathe it all in.

But Dr. Cormick Proffitt was a consummate professional. Under no circumstances would there be a workplace romance in his life. He had considered the potential complications many times and had chosen to keep his work life separate from his nearly nonexistent personal life. She was half his age, and at forty-two, he was filled with self-doubt and anxiety when he imagined having to keep up with someone so young. He moved toward his office, giving her a wave and a smile as he started to pass.

"Good Morning, Dr. Proffitt," Nurse Paige called from behind her desk as she rose to her feet. "Dr. Carlson is waiting in your office. He's pretty upset about something."

"Bob? What is he still doing here?"

"He wouldn't say," she replied, "but he's really upset." She smiled, "I like your new tie."

He had purchased the tie over the weekend. He had been captivated by it from the moment he passed it in the case at Nordstrom's. The soft blue hue reminded him of her eyes, as well as the imaginary songbirds that flitted joyfully in the air every time he saw her. It was not something he would dare to admit to anyone.

"Thank you, Allison," he said and fell silent. Today—like every day—would be another missed opportunity for them to say the words that the other longed to hear. "Well, I had better see what Bob wants."

Cormick entered his office and found Bob Carlson staring out the window into the parking lot.

"Admiring my new car?" Cormick asked. "I imagine it looks beautiful from up here." He would not dare look himself. It was a full five stories down, and his disabling fear of heights always kept him a safe distance from the window. He would have to take his friend's word for it. "And Bob, the smell of the leather is…well, it is borderline erotic."

Carlson said nothing. He stood with his back toward Cormick, staring out the window. Cormick shot a quick glance at him as he laid his briefcase on the table then turned and moved toward the corner.

"We can take it for a spin later. Who knows, maybe I will even let you drive it. Do not tell anyone, but I named the car Klaus," Cormick said as he hung his jacket neatly on the coat rack. His small talk was met with silence. "I just had the office painted," he continued. "Studies show that mauve calms agitated patients, making them more receptive to treatment."

He turned and looked toward Carlson, who had not moved from the window. Cormick put his hands on his hips and cleared his throat.

"Bob, what are you still doing here? I thought you had the graveyard rotation in the ER last night. I assumed you would be powering through the fifth hole by now," he laughed.

Dr. Carlson continued to stare through the glass. "Do you believe in God?" he asked in a hoarse whisper.

"Pardon?" Cormick asked, caught off guard by the question. "Rough night downstairs?"

"You heard me," Carlson replied in a low monotone voice.

"Well…no," Cormick replied after a moment of hesitation. "No, I do not. Not anymore at least."

"Cormick…I'm going to tell you something," he began, talking to the window, "and you're not going to believe me. But you have to." He turned from the window and faced his friend. "Jesus, Cormick, I don't know what's happening."

"Okay, Bob. I want you to sit here on the couch and take a deep breath," Cormick said. "We can talk through this."

"I'll try," he said. "I feel like I'm going to have a panic attack. Every time I calm myself down, I start to freak out again."

"I can write you a prescription for Valium," Cormick said calmly. "That will help take the edge off."

"That's a good start. Maybe Thorazine…"

"Bob…really?" Cormick answered with a look of disapproval.

Carlson quickly made his way past Cormick and threw himself down on the couch. He let himself fall backward, with the palms of his hands covering his face. He was motionless for a moment, then sat up and stared at the floor, shaking his head.

"Bob, I really need you to take a deep breath," Cormick

said. He was worried about his friend. Bob Carlson was one of the best ER physicians around, known for his ability to keep his cool under pressure. As a decorated former Army Captain with the 95th Evac Hospital in Da Nang, it was universally accepted that he could not be rattled.

"Okay. You're right." Carlson drew in a deep breath and began his tale. "Okay. We got word last night that Life Flight was on its way with an accident victim from Kalama. They didn't expect him to make it. But they got him here." Carlson looked up at Cormick. "But, Christ, Cormick…I don't know how."

Cormick walked around his desk and sat down. "Well, Life Flight…they are the best at…"

"You don't understand Cormick," he said, shaking his head again. "He shouldn't have made it. I saw guys in 'Nam blown to fuck by grenades that looked better than this guy. Skull fracture, traumatic aortic rupture, tracheobronchial tear, pneumothorax…we were plugging holes as fast as he was springing leaks! Every single limb had at least one compound fracture. I swear to God, if you had seen what was lying on that table, you would never have guessed that he was alive."

"But you saved him, Bob, right?" Cormick said with his hands in the air. "That is not a miracle from God. That is your skill and your talented team…"

"Cormick, shut up and listen!" Carlson said as he jumped to his feet. "Jesus Christ, Cormick, you're a fucking psychiatrist, do I have to pay you a hundred dollars an hour to just shut the fuck up and listen?" He walked over to the widow again and stared out at the sky.

Cormick sat quiet in his chair. Instinctively, he wanted to tell Carlson to take a deep breath, but he thought better of it. "I apologize, Bob. I should not have interrupted. Please, go on."

"Anyway," Carlson continued after a moment of staring in silence, "he should have been DOA, but we managed to get him on life support. How…I…I just don't know. Even though he made it through the first hour, there just wasn't enough of him there. I mean, a human being cannot lose that much blood and flesh and survive. It's not possible. It's just not fucking possible!"

Cormick nodded in agreement from his chair, without a word. *Bob is exhausted and over-worked,* he thought. He quietly reached in his desk drawer for his prescription pad.

"We rush him into surgery. The new Trauma Unit guy is there…what's his name? You know…the Mexican guy with the German accent…Hess? I think it's Hess. Anyway, I'm going to leave it in his hands, you know? I go to change my scrubs, get cleaned up, and Hess is calling me from the OR. He's yelling and cursing me out, telling me I wasted his time by calling him in. So, I figure the patient coded. I mean, it made sense. He told me to come get my patient. I told him to call the morgue."

"I am sorry, Bob," Cormick said. "Losing a patient is tough…especially when you have worked so hard to save him."

"That's just it, Cormick," he replied. "I didn't lose him." Carlson turned and walked back to the couch. "He was alive," he said as he sat down. "I went back up there and…his chest…Jesus, Cormick…there was no evidence of trauma to his chest. Hess is fucking screaming at me, demanding to know where my patient is, and all I can do is stand there like an idiot."

"What happened to your patient?" Cormick asked.

"That was my patient!" he yelled. "Fucking pay attention, Cormick! And don't start any psychobabble bullshit with me, either. I had this same fucking conversation with Hess! That Nazi prick."

"Clearly there was a mix up," Cormick said calmly.

"No, Cormick. It was my patient. Do you understand? My patient. The compound fractures in his arms and legs were still there. But his chest…" Carlson shook his head from side to side in disbelief. "Anyway, Hess calls for an orthopedic surgeon and orders up a set of pictures. So I take the guy to X-ray. There's no way he's leaving my sight. When I get down there, I tell the tech to forget the extremities and get me a CAT scan on his chest. We run a series of films, and I can see broken ribs and a cracked sternum. Nothing else. Nothing!" he exclaimed as he threw his hands in the air. "I tell him to run the series again. Do you know what I find? His rib cage is intact. There isn't even a hint of damage, Cormick. We had just seen multiple fractures and then there's nothing!"

Cormick got up from his desk and walked over toward the couch. He sat next to his friend and offered him the prescription he had just written.

"Bob," he began, "you have the toughest job in the hospital. The stress is…"

"Dammit, Cormick!" he said. "It's not stress! His chest cavity was mush! I saw it! And he healed himself! Do you hear me? His ribs healed in the time it took to run two series of films down there. I mean, I don't know what I've got, but there's a good goddamned chance it's not from Earth! I realized he couldn't leave my sight, so I personally took that patient to run additional films on his chest, arms, and legs. And I saw it, Cormick. I stayed there while they took those X-rays. That man…that thing healed itself. I saw it!"

"Bob, I need you to listen to me for a moment. That is simply not possible. Let us look at this rationally for a moment. A man comes into the ER, succumbs to traumatic injury, and is taken to the morgue. Meanwhile, the OR techs come in and grab the wrong patient. I am confident that *together*, we can go downstairs and clear this up in a matter of minutes."

"No, Cormick," Carlson said as he began to laugh. "We can't. He's not downstairs. He's on six. He's lost sight in both eyes, but other than that, he is alert and talking."

"Well, what is your miracle patient talking about?"

Carlson reached out and snatched the prescription from his grasp. "He's asking for you, Cormick."

—————

Cormick stood outside of room 632. Carlson was a few paces from the door, shaking his head.

"Come in with me, Bob," Cormick said. "We will get this mess sorted out and you can go home and get some rest."

"You go in," Carlson replied. "I'll wait here."

Cormick reached out and placed his hand on his friend's shoulder to gently urge him in. Carlson didn't budge.

"He's waiting for you, Cormick. If you start to freak out, just, uh… 'take a deep breath.' Isn't that what you tell everyone?" And with that, Carlson turned and walked away. "I'm going to the pharmacy to fill this prescription," he called without turning around. "I won't be in tonight."

Cormick placed his hand on the door and paused. He watched Bob walk down the hall and get in the elevator. *There is a simple explanation,* he thought. He pushed the door open and walked in.

The miracle patient was silently sitting in bed, propped up by pillows. His shoulder length jet black hair and beard were a stark contrast to the white bandages wrapped around his head covering his eyes. Cormick assumed he was around thirty, about ten years younger than him, but without seeing his eyes, he wasn't sure he had guessed correctly.

"Hello, Cormick," the man called from the bed.

"You have me at a disadvantage. Do we know each other?" Cormick asked.

"We do now," he smiled. "I'm Angelo. Angelo Taranto."

"It is nice to meet you, Angelo," Cormick said as he approached him. He held his hand in front of Angelo's face and waved it in front of his eyes. "You have caused quite a stir here today."

"Can't imagine why," Angelo smiled. "You should have been here when Dr. Carlson asked me if I was from Earth! Man, I have to tell you, if I could have remembered the name of any planet from Star Wars…" he laughed.

"Bob—that is to say, Dr. Carlson—is not quite sure what to think of you."

"What do you think of me, Cormick?" Angelo asked.

"Well, at first glance, I would surmise that you are a patient who was in the ER last night who heard everything that was happening around him and thought it might be fun to play the part of a prankster," Cormick said. "However, I assure you that hiding a body in the hospital and assuming the identity of that body falls far short of being a prank and well beyond being a felony."

"I didn't hide a body, Cormick," Angelo said, smiling, as he slapped his chest. "I am the body! Look, I'm sure you have a lot of questions, and we do have some time before we have to go, so pull up a chair."

"Go?" Cormick asked incredulously. "Where is it exactly that we are going?"

"Santa Fe," Angelo answered very matter of fact.

"Tell me, Mr. Taranto," Cormick said as he pulled up a chair to the side of the bed, "what makes you believe that there is a scenario in which the two of us would travel to Santa Fe together?"

"God told me it would be so," he replied.

"I see. And God talks to you often?"

"Oh yeah, man," Angelo laughed. "He talks to me all the time."

"And God mentioned me…by name. Is that correct?"

"That *is* correct," Angelo replied. "You're much better at this than Dr. Carlson." Angelo paused for second. "Ah… Alderaan! Dammit! I could have told him I was from Alderaan!"

"Mr. Taranto…" Cormick started.

"Angelo," he interrupted. "Cormick, I want you to call me Angelo. We're going to be spending a lot of time together, so let's be friends, okay? Now go ahead, ask me anything."

Cormick paused for a moment to plan his line of questioning. The patient was fully immersed in his fantasy, but was it a delusional perception, hallucination, or some sort of game?

"Are you currently on any medications, prescribed or otherwise?"

"No. And I don't do drugs," Angelo replied. "I'm not on acid, I didn't eat any mushrooms, and I don't take pills. I know what you're thinking. I'm not hallucinating."

"What about work?" Cormick asked. "Do you have a lot of stress at work?"

"I own a crab boat in Alaska," Angelo replied. "I guess I

stress out sometimes. I have to make sure my guys are safe, I've got quotas…nothing I can't handle."

"I see. How often do you drink?"

"Whenever I'm in a bar," Angelo laughed. "How often do you drink, Cormick?"

"Do you find yourself in a bar often?"

"Cormick, I drink. Sometimes often, sometimes not," Angelo said. "I'm not schizophrenic, I'm not a drug addict, and I'm not having alcoholic hallucinations. God spoke to me on the ocean. It wasn't the wind. It wasn't my imagination. It was God. I know you don't believe me. But you will," he assured Cormick. "It was God, Cormick, and he sent me here for you. Do you understand? I am here for you, Cormick."

"Okay, Angelo," Cormick said, "I want you to take a deep breath and start from the beginning. When do you think God first spoke to you? What were you doing? And please, be as specific as you can."

"I was in the wheelhouse," Angelo began. "We had just laid some pots to soak, and the guys had gone below for supper. I heard someone call my name, so I turned around, but no one was there. I blew it off…you know? Thought I was hearing things. But then it called me again. I got up and looked around, but I was alone. As soon as I sat down, I heard my name a third time. So I went downstairs into the galley, and everything was normal. The guys were eating…talking," he trailed off.

Cormick stood up and walked to the foot of the bed.

"And then what happened?"

"I went out on deck to shake it off. I'm not gonna lie, man, it was eerie the way I heard my name. I could hear and feel it," he said shaking his head. "I could feel my name kinda echo in my body. It called to me and pulled at me at the same time. Anyway, I go up on deck. You know…maybe I had been cooped up too long, right? Some fresh air would clear my head, I thought. So, I'm standing at the railing, and I hear my name again…but it's different this time. It's like the Bering Sea calling me.

"No one was on deck, but I yelled anyway…telling whoever it was to knock it off. But no one was there. I looked back over the railing, and suddenly, it was like I couldn't hear anything else. Not the ocean or the creaking of the boat…nothing. And this voice calls out to me and tells me that I am to be a 'fisher of men.' Like the Bible, you know?"

"Yes," Cormick said. "Like the Bible. And then what did you do?"

"I ran to the galley, but none of the guys had heard anything. Hell, they thought I was the one pulling their legs!" Angelo said. "But the voice kept calling me. I thought I was losing it, man. I ignored it, but it called to me every day. After our final offload, we headed back to Dutch Harbor, and I got drunk at the Elbow Room to try to drown it out. But it wouldn't stop. A week or so later, I'm taking the boat back home to Seattle and decide to answer it. I mean, I'm at the end of my rope at this point. I figured if I was going crazy, I'd just surrender to it, you know? Embrace the madness. So, I said, 'What do want from me?' And that's when I became aware that it was God…it was amazing! He tells me again that I am to be a 'fisher of men.' And that's when his plan was revealed to me."

"I see. What was it that God revealed to you?" Cormick asked.

"That I'm not alone. That there are others," Angelo said. "But that it starts with me. He told me I am the Angel Messenger, charged with bringing everyone together. That I had to go to Santa Fe."

"If, in fact, that is true," Cormick began, "why would God allow you to get in an accident that would almost certainly kill you? Why not see you safely to your destination if that was his will?"

"By the time I got home to Seattle, I was ready to go, Cormick. I became a believer. I had a message to deliver…a mission. So, I just packed up and left. I figured I could be in New Mexico in a day and a half, maybe two at the most… so I was gone, man," he replied. "I'm heading south on I-5, making good time, and out of nowhere, God tells me that I have to stop for you." Angelo let his head drop as he shook it from side to side. "But I wasn't going to. I wanted…I had to be in Santa Fe. I needed to be with the others like me. I guess I should have listened."

"It is your assertion, then, that God crashed your car so you could drive me to Santa Fe?" Cormick asked.

"Cormick, I know it sounds crazy, but I wasn't going to stop. I guess it's true that you should obey the will of God, huh? Stop or he'll stop you," he laughed.

"For the sake of rationality, let me ask you this: Do you not think it possible that the long days on the ocean, the stress of work, and the binge drinking that followed, coupled with the urgency you felt to get to New Mexico had anything to do with the accident?" Cormick asked, offering up a rational explanation. "What about road conditions, driving in the dark, or a lack of familiarity with the freeway?"

"I really don't remember the accident. But I remember the light," Angelo said. "There was a bright light that appeared and stopped me." Angelo's voice grew quieter as he spoke. "And this is where it gets a little strange. The light…I drove into it, but once I was in it, I wasn't in my car. It was like I was floating, or being held…kind of both in a way. I was completely bathed in warmth and light. I have never been so at peace. In that moment, God told me that you were here, Cormick. God told me you would not believe me. But he told me that I had a job to spread the word. And that you would listen. He told me that enlightenment is right around the corner, Cormick. Anyway, next thing I know, I'm talking to Dr. Carlson."

"Angelo, I want you to take a deep breath and clear your mind," Cormick said as he paced at the foot of the bed. "Try to remove any emotional component from your situation. In fact, I want you to think from the perspective you maintained prior to hearing the voice for the first time. Now, put yourself in my shoes, as if I was relating the account of the accident to you. Would you not hypothesize that the bright light was oncoming traffic? Would you not assume that you were not in your car because at the point of impact you were thrown free of the collision? And that your alleged near-death experience in the warm light was just that? A near-death experience not unlike what has been documented by dozens of people before you? Perhaps your knowledge of those documented cases had an impact on your memory."

"No, Cormick. There were no other cars. And I don't think I had a near-death experience like dozens of others because—at the risk of damaging your ego—I don't think God talks about you to everyone near death. God intervened when I wouldn't stop and revealed to me the next part of his plan. He revealed you, Cormick. So, here I am."

"Why has God left you without your vision?" Cormick asked. "And how are we going to get to Santa Fe, you and

I? You can no longer drive a car. Are we flying?"

"You're driving," Angelo responded. "And it isn't just us." He drew in a deep breath. "Wow, man! That's it! Don't you see? God took my sight to force you to drive! How could I have been so…if you'll pardon the pun…blind?"

"I see," Cormick replied. He turned and took a couple of paces from the bed. "Why not hold off on the Santa Fe vacation and spend a couple of days here with me? We could talk at length about your relationship with God and anything else you wish to discuss."

"It's not going to work out that way, Cormick," Angelo replied. "I'm sorry. I know you don't believe me, but we're going. And you're driving."

"I hate to disappoint you, Angelo…"

"God gave me a message for you, Cormick. He told me that you would have doubts. He told me that you've had those doubts since you lost your parents," Angelo said sympathetically. "I'm sorry."

Cormick turned quickly to see Angelo facing in his direction. Though his eyes were covered, Cormick could feel his stare cut right through him. He stood still, unable to respond. He rarely thought about his family and certainly never spoke of them publicly.

"And Cormick, I'm supposed to tell you that you are the Charioteer and that you will 'ride to glory.' God said you'd understand."

ENLIGHTENMENT

Dawn Gallagher stood in front of her class, hands on her hips, shaking her head. Her thick red hair danced playfully on her shoulders. It was the last day of school at McLoughlin High, and only she and the final bell stood between her students and the city of Portland. Before her sat twenty-four seniors who were mere hours from entering the world of responsible adults. It was a prospect that both thrilled and worried her.

"Okay guys, any questions?" she asked.

A relative hush fell over the classroom. She scanned the faces of her students looking for the opportunity to interact in the little time they had left together. After an awkward pause, a student's hand raised slowly at the back of the room.

"Yes, Patrick…what's your question?"

"Will you marry me?"

The class erupted in giggles and laughter. Dawn laughed, too. Even though he was making a joke, Patrick's puppy-dog eyes had betrayed his true feelings the entire semester, and now the world knew. But the idea of marriage to anyone always drew laughter from Dawn.

"Let me rephrase that…are there any questions regarding Native American culture," she replied. "Ask now…I know this is devastating to all of you, but it's your last chance to talk about the indigenous people of the American Southwest this year." Once again there was silence. Either they had learned so much they were now experts, or they had reached the point that they never wanted to discuss the subject ever again.

"Okay, how about this…who is doing something great this summer before they leave for college or start a career? Who is going to have an adventure?"

A wide variety of answers erupted amid laughter as Dawn looked around the room, amused by the excitement.

"What's your adventure, Ms. Gallagher?" asked a girl in the front row.

"I don't have any adventures planned this year," she laughed as she turned and walked around behind her desk. "But if I did, it would be an old-fashioned road trip with no scheduled stops, no plans…just a destination and whatever comes to me on the way." She looked up at the clock. There were thirty minutes of high school left for these kids. "I'm going to give you all a graduation present…Go home!"

The students looked at each other with uncertainty, then back at her. They had clearly heard the words, they just seemed incapable of processing the command, like she had suddenly started speaking in a foreign language.

"Go! Go!" she exclaimed sweeping her arms forward as if to shoo them out. "It's not a joke! Get out!"

The silence gave way to a cacophony of excited laughter, screams of joy, and chairs sliding across the floor, crashing into desks. She knew the surrounding classrooms could hear the clamor and would catch on. She pictured all the other teachers following suit, sending waves of students flooding into the hallway like a dam breaking. And she giggled as she pictured the Vice Principal—or *acting administrator* as he referred to himself—having a second nervous breakdown.

Dawn looked around the classroom that would sit empty in the coming months. She had already removed the maps and other materials from the walls.

As she wiped down the two chalkboards behind her desk, her thoughts turned from the unhappy staff in the main office to the coming summer. Oregon was beautiful enough. There were mountains just ninety minutes to the east, and the coastline was the same distance to the west. While both offered a variety of activities and fun, neither provided real adventure.

I don't need any more adventure, she thought. There was something to be said for the slow, easy pace of a relaxing summer. At the end of every school year, she usually transformed herself into what she called a tourist extraordinaire, traveling to foreign countries, drinking in every bit of their culture as if she were dying of thirst in the desert. This year was different. There had been no overwhelming inspiration or deep desire to go anywhere since her last vacation.

She sat at her desk, letting out a heavy sigh. Another school year had drawn to a close. It was only a matter of hours until the Class of 1990 walked the halls for the final time. She turned her attention to the jumbled mess of empty desks, picturing the faces of the various students who had occupied them during the past year. She gave some thought to who would be going to college, who would end up in the military, and who would be seeking a career in Portland's food service industry. *Someone has to make my fries*, she thought as she spun herself 360 degrees in her chair.

As the chair came to a stop in its original position, she suddenly felt uneasy. She slowly spun the chair back around and turned her head toward the chalkboards. There, written in large capital letters, was the name *SANTA FE.*

She bit down on her lip and stared at the board. She was sure she had just wiped the boards clean, and no part of her lesson plan involved the city of Santa Fe. *Probably a student's summer vacation*, she thought.

Pushing herself out of her chair, she let out a sigh and reached for the eraser. With two broad strokes, the words disappeared into a cloud of chalk dust. She stood there for a moment, staring at the clean slate. The nonstop pace of the school year was over, and her summer, like the blank chalkboard, was full of nothing.

The previous summer had been an escape to Italy. Her original plan that summer was to explore the parts of the country that most travelers had never heard of. From the ruins of Alba Fucens to the abbey of Santa Maria Assunta in La Spezia, she'd been determined to immerse herself in the culture and history of the ancient land. She had learned early on that her journeys of discovery, while full of meaning to her, had little relatable information. So, as in trips past, Dawn had scheduled her first stop in a major city—Rome in this case—to fight her way through tourists in order to photograph the obligatory landmarks for her friends.

It was in Rome that she met Etienne, a poor French artist visiting Rome to find his muse and paint his way to a magnificent fortune. And it was then that all of her plans were instantly forgotten. Etienne was everything a woman wanted to find in a man while traveling across Europe. He was handsome and funny, artistic and intelligent. And he was very interested in her.

Like her life in Portland, traveling abroad did not involve romance. It was not something she desired or required. Dawn was comfortable with who she was and did not depend on a man for her self-esteem. But Etienne had been different. He had created in her overwhelming desire and a need to be near him every minute of every day. He had known exactly what to say to ignite an all-consuming passion inside her. And his touch had been gentle yet strong.

Abandoning her plans for the hidden treasures of Italy had been an easy decision. Just as easy as her decision to share her hotel room and pay for their meals. He was a starving artist, after all. For nearly two weeks they'd been inseparable. Days filled with laughter and nights consumed by a sexual intensity she had never known.

The morning she awoke to find herself alone had seemed surreal. He had been there every morning, presenting her with breakfast in bed, quietly delivered by room service, complete with champagne and strawberries, and sex in every conceivable position. No man had ever eroticized a meal for her before Etienne had come along. But that morning she awoke alone. No breakfast, no Etienne, and no money or credit cards.

Dawn shook herself out of the past and looked at the ebony surface in front of her. It was her job to teach lessons, not to learn them. *This summer will be different*, she thought. *I've learned everything I need to know.*

"Dawn…"

She looked back over her shoulder and turned. She was alone. She took a step forward and leaned to the side to peer under the desks for good measure. There was no one. Shaking it off, she righted herself and turned to put the eraser away. Surprised, she jumped back as if she had stepped on a live wire. Staring her in the face were the words *SANTA FE.*

She placed her hand in the middle of her chest as she took a step back. She could feel her heart begin to race. Dawn closed her eyes briefly and exhaled slowly to calm herself. She stepped up to the board and touched the chalk letters, her hands smearing the words.

"Dawn…"

Dawn did not turn around. She raised the eraser and methodically wiped the words from the board once more. She reached down for the single piece of chalk, removed it from the tray, and slid it into her pocket.

"Dawn…"

The voice was hushed, like a hoarse whisper. She couldn't make out if it was male or female. She continued to face the chalkboard trying to recognize the voice of her mysterious prankster. The voice felt closer but did not get any louder.

This is going to end one of two ways, she thought. *I'm either going to punch someone in the face, or the psycho clown hiding in my classroom is going to kill me.* She took in a deep breath and turned around, coming face to face with a vacant classroom.

She walked slowly and quietly toward the back of the room. Her eyes darted back and forth searching for the slightest movement on either side. As she reached the door, her right hand grasped the knob and turned. Taking in a deep breath, she quickly pulled the door open and lurched forward to startle whoever was having fun at her expense. The hallway was completely empty.

Dawn closed the door and paused to collect her thoughts. She realized it was possible that she was hearing things. She also conceded that it was possible she had been distracted when she first tried to erase the words from the chalkboard and had missed them entirely. She decided to pack up her things and head home for the day. As she began walking to the front of the classroom, she dropped the eraser and stood horrified at what she saw.

Both boards were covered—hundreds of times—with the words *SANTA FE*. The words were written at different angles and in many different sizes. She stood motionless, transfixed by the sight.

"Okay!" she yelled. "Enough! You got me!" She raised her hands as if to surrender. "You win! I'm scared!" She hoped she was calling to a person but feared she was talking to a ghost.

"Dawn…" the voice called to her again. "Enlighten them…"

She turned around and walked toward the door, her pace quickening with each step. She threw open the door and immediately collided with the vice principal, knocking him to the floor.

"Oh my God…I'm so sorry, Loony…um, Larry. Are you okay?" she asked as she reached her hand out to help him up.

Refusing the assistance she offered, Larry Loomis scowled at her from the floor. He understood some members of the staff referred to him as Loony Larry but never thought that Miss Gallagher would be one of them. Hurt and angered by her comment, he pushed himself up, straightening his glasses and tugging on the sleeves of his sport coat to cover his cuffs.

"I'm fine," he replied as he reached up and pushed his combed over wisp of long hair from his forehead. "Now, what's the big emergency? Why aren't you in there with your students?"

"There's no emergency," Dawn answered. "Why would you think there's an emergency?"

"Miss Gallagher, you came running out of your room fast enough to knock me to the floor. Do you really expect me to believe everything is just hunky-dory?" He leaned to the side to look through the window in the door. Dawn countered his move to block his view.

"Larry, everything is fine," she said. She placed her hand on his shoulder and gently turned him around. She began to walk down the hallway, guiding him beside her. "I just have to step out for a moment," she said in an exaggerated whisper. "I have a female emergency. You understand."

He stopped in his tracks, and she felt his body shudder. She stepped around to face him and noticed he looked very uncomfortable listening to her fabrication. She had him right where she needed him.

"I just need to use the ladies room," she continued. "After all, I'm teaching history not biology." Dawn turned her head from side to side, pretending to see if anyone could hear her. She bent down and put her lips very close to his ear and whispered, "You wouldn't, by chance, have an extra tampon, would you?"

He pulled himself away and glared at her. His lips were so tightly pressed together they were turning white. He shook his head and brushed past her on his way back to the office.

Dawn immediately ducked into the restroom and locked herself into the stall farthest from the door. Pretending to have a class full of kids was easy. Pretending to be on her period was easy. But pretending the poltergeist in her room didn't exist was not. She felt trapped. She couldn't hide in the teacher's lounge. Loomis would certainly find her in there, and she couldn't go home. Her car keys were still in the classroom.

She took in a breath and stood up. *Be strong*, she thought. *A ghost can't hurt you.* She slid the lock free and slowly opened the door just enough to peek out. The bathroom was empty. She stepped out of the stall and walked to the mirror. She slid her hands to her hips to smooth out her skirt then reached up to toss her hair back over her shoulders. *I can do this*, she thought.

⸺ ⁓⁓ ⸺

Dawn stood at the door to her classroom and stared through the window. The possessed chalkboards were directly ahead, completely blank. She carefully surveyed the scene. The desks were no longer the jumbled mess the students had left in their wake. Every desk was perfectly lined up, every chair neatly pushed in, and no sign of anyone. *I'm going to get my keys and get the hell out of here*, she thought.

Pushing open the door, she stepped into the classroom without making a sound. She cautiously sneaked toward her desk, wary of waking the spirit that held her classroom hostage. When she got to her desk, she leaned down to reach for her bag.

"Dawn...enlighten them."

Dawn spun around quickly toward the back of the room and fell back against her desk. As her open palms hit the surface she instantly pulled herself atop the desk and perched herself there on her knees. She could feel her heart rapidly pounding in her chest as she tried to control her breathing and stay calm. Looking to the exit, rows of empty desks were the only thing between her and the door. She calculated the time it would take her to make her escape. She knew she could make it.

"Dawn...enlighten them...save him."

Dawn began to feel nauseous. Leaning forward on the desk, she reached her trembling hand down for her bag and grabbed the handles. She pulled it close to her chest and held tight. The plan was simple. She had watched enough football to know how to pull it off: cradle the ball, keep your head down, and run as fast as you can.

"Dawn…" the voice called from behind her. She turned her head quickly and saw *SANTA FE* on the boards again. She closed her eyes tight. "Please God," she prayed, "protect me."

"Miss Gallagher!" Loomis yelled from the doorway and made his way into the classroom. "What is going on in here?"

Dawn jumped off the desk and ran to him. At 140 pounds and a full three inches shorter than her, he would be little help in a fight for their lives, but he would have to do. She grabbed his hand and started making her way to the door, nearly pulling him to the ground.

"Miss Gallagher, please!" Mr. Loomis exclaimed.

"Larry, we have got to get out of here!" she said forcefully. "There's something in here."

"I can tell you what should be in here. Students!" Loomis said as he yanked his hand from her grasp and looked around. "Did you let your students leave school grounds? What were you doing on the desk?"

"Write me up later Larry. Let's just get the hell out of here, okay?"

"You aren't going anywhere until you explain your behavior," he said sternly. "Or, is this another 'female emergency?'"

"Larry, look at the chalkboards…" she began as she motioned to the front of the room. Unable to finish, Dawn froze in midsentence. The prolific slates were completely clean.

"Look at what? The chalkboards?" he snapped. "Why don't we look at your students? Oh, wait, we can't. Because, for some reason, they're not here."

"I let them go Larry. Okay? It's the last day of school. Get over it," she said. Her attention turned from the chalkboards to Loony Larry. She was conflicted. His timely appearance in the classroom had thankfully chased away whatever was haunting her. But the nasal tone of his voice and his snotty attitude made her want to punch him.

"Allowing students to leave school grounds without parental permission opens us up to serious liability. As acting administrator…"

"Of course," she interrupted. "You're absolutely right." She wanted to defuse Larry without explaining what was happening and get to the safety of her home. The frightening minutes she spent with her ghost had exhausted her. Once she got home, she would have two months away from school to forget about Larry and her maniacal poltergeist.

"I'm sorry, but I'm going to have to put this in your file."

"I understand," she nodded. "I just wanted to let the kids have a little fun. It won't happen again. Now, can we please go?"

"Why were you on your desk? If you had fallen on school property, the district would be facing a…"

"Serious liability," she said, finishing his predictable sentence. "I climbed up on my desk because…I thought I saw a mouse. But I was imaging things, I suppose."

"Dawn…" the voice called.

Startled, Dawn dropped her bag and grabbed hold of Larry's arm, squeezing tight. Her eyes darted around the classroom.

"Did you hear that?" she cried.

"Hear what?" he responded. "Miss Gallagher, please let go of my arm." He didn't want to say it out loud, but her grip was so strong it hurt his frail bicep.

"Dawn…enlighten them…save him…"

"That, Larry!" she yelled. "That voice! Are you seriously going to stand here and tell me you can't hear that?"

"I don't hear anything," he responded. "Grab your bag and come with me." He pulled his arm back and stomped to the door. Dawn scooped up her bag and quickly followed him out the door and down the hallway to his office.

Dawn was scared, but she maintained her composure as she passed the secretaries and volunteers in the office. Her face betrayed her anxiety. To the people in the office, it meant little. Nearly everyone who was called into the office of Loony Larry Loomis had the same look.

"Have a seat," he said as he closed the door. He walked around his desk and sat in his chair. He leaned back and clasped his hands together. Extending his two index fingers, he brought them to his lips and exhaled. Loomis began every serious conversation this way. It was meant to convey superiority and deep contemplation. Dawn thought he looked like an idiot.

"I've seen this before," he started. "Educators become overworked, the stress of lesson planning, unruly children…" He leaned forward and spun through his rolodex. "I'd like you to see someone. Someone who could help you get through this tough time."

"Are asking me to see a shrink?" she asked. "That's not happening Larry," she said as she watched him scribble down the information.

"Miss Gallagher, as acting administrator, I can hardly ignore what I've witnessed today. Your erratic behavior, coupled with imaginary voices in your head, presents me with quite a dilemma. The liability here…"

"I'm not you, Loony!" Dawn stood up and threw her

bag into the chair. "I'm not crazy. And I'm not imagining things. Someone or something was talking to me in that classroom." She placed both hands firmly on his desk and leaned forward. "I'm not going to your psychiatrist."

"You are going if you wish to continue teaching here," he said as he placed the paper in front of her. He leaned back and resumed his pose of smug superiority. He was not giving in, especially since she had called him Loony.

"You can't fire me, Larry. The union would be all over this."

"Hmmm…you may be right," he said sarcastically. "Let's review, shall we?" He got up and slowly paced behind his desk. "A teacher releases students from school property, talks to invisible people and demonic chalkboards while sitting on her desk, and blames it on menstruation. Did I leave anything out?"

"Look, Larry…"

He reached across the desk and picked up the note he had written. Smiling he held it out for her to take. The two stared at each other, each waiting for the other to back down. Without breaking eye contact she snatched the piece of paper from his hand.

"Vancouver Memorial? Are you kidding me?" she exclaimed as she read the note. The traffic would be a nightmare. "Fine." She grabbed her bag and turned to leave.

"I want a report this week," he said. "I expect this to be addressed immediately."

"Fine," she said as she stormed out of his office.

"Dr. Proffitt did wonders for me," he mumbled to himself. "I can't wait to see what he does for you."

THE MYTHOLOGICAL TRIANGLE

Dawn sat on the couch, glaring at Nurse Paige. After the incident in her classroom, the confrontation with Loony, and the ridiculous afternoon traffic, she was quickly growing impatient with the young nurse, who had kept her waiting for nearly thirty minutes. She let out an audible sigh of disapproval, but it failed to get the attention of Nurse Paige. She reached for a magazine on the table, pulling it toward her, and began turning pages forcefully to get attention. Undaunted, Nurse Paige continued looking down, transcribing Cormick's notes into their corresponding files.

Dawn sized the young woman up. Was she even old enough to be a nurse? And what was she writing? Was she one of those girls who wrote their fictional married name repeatedly with little hearts? Maybe it was her diary. That must be it. *Dear Diary*, Dawn imagined, *Today I made a perfect stranger wait two hours just to prove that I can control the lives of others.*

"That does it!" Dawn exclaimed as she stood up, tossed the magazine on the couch, and marched toward the reception desk. "I have been waiting here, patiently, for half an hour. Now, I am—by nature—a very patient woman. But I've had a remarkably frustrating day, and all I want to do is see the shrink so I can keep my job and go home and unwind with a nice glass of wine. So, I just want to know, is the doctor going to see me today or not?"

"Dr. Proffitt is a very busy man," Allison replied. Timid by nature, she rarely engaged in confrontations of any type. But the outside office was her domain. She kept it orderly with the same passion in which she protected Cormick. "As I said when you came in, I can't make any promises. Now, if you had made an appointment in advance, none of this would be an issue." She forced a condescending smile at Dawn that conveyed her intention to not bend to her will.

Dawn straightened up and took in a deep breath. Not one to have a screaming match, she squinted at Allison to let her know she was lucky they were in a professional setting. She turned to head back to the couch but spun suddenly and bolted for Cormick's door. Allison jumped up to stop her, but she could not make up the distance in time. Dawn threw open the door, startling Cormick, who was sitting quietly at his desk.

"I'm sorry, Dr. Proffitt," Allison said as she hurriedly entered his office. "I tried…"

"It is okay, Allison. I am wrapping up here." He stood up, straightening his tie. "And how may I help you, Miss…"

"Gallagher, Dawn Gallagher. I was sent here by Larry Loomis."

"Well, you have me at a disadvantage, Miss Gallagher. I do not believe I know anyone named Larry Loomis. Is he your psychologist?"

"Why does everyone think I need a shrink?" she cried, throwing her arms in the air.

"Do you want me to call security, Dr. Proffitt?" Allison said in a surprisingly serious tone.

"Listen little girl…" Dawn growled.

"There is no need for that, Allison," Cormick said as he raised his hands as if to halt the action. "I have some time to talk to Miss Gallagher." He politely motioned to the chair in front of his desk. "Please, sit down."

Dawn turned toward the young nurse and stuck her tongue out at her. Allison said nothing as she watched her turn and walk toward the chair. Allison slowly pulled the door closed. Cormick could see she looked hurt by his unwillingness to follow her protocol, so he gave her a smile and a nod in an effort to quietly show his solidarity.

"Interesting color palette," Dawn observed as she looked around the office. "Was pink your first choice?"

"The color is mauve, actually."

"Isn't that French for light pink?"

"I apologize, Miss Gallagher," Cormick said abruptly, "you are going to have to refresh my memory regarding Dr. Loomis."

"Doctor?" Dawn laughed. "More like escaped mental patient."

"I see," Cormick said, even though he clearly did not. "Are you his caregiver?"

"Look, I'm going to make this easy on you. My boss is crazy. And ever since his nervous breakdown, he thinks he's Sigmund Freud," she said exasperated. "So, I have to see you to keep my job. All I need from you is a note saying that I'm sane and that he's a douche bag, and I'll be on my way."

"I would feel more comfortable if I left the douche bag part out of the note."

"Suit yourself," she quipped.

"Miss Gallagher," Cormick said as he leaned back and brought his folded hands to his lips, "before I 'write a note,' we should discuss the circumstances that put these events in motion."

"I told you. My boss is crazy," Dawn said as she shrugged

in mock disbelief. "Throw up some ink blots, ask me about my father…do whatever it is you do that proves I'm not schizophrenic so I can start my summer vacation."

"Perhaps I could just give your boss a call," he said as he reached for the phone, "and get some insight on…"

"Wait," she said as she leaned forward and placed her hand on his, "let's leave him out this." She pulled the chair forward and leaned on his desk. "Look…something strange happened today, and…it shook me up a bit. That's all."

"Take a deep breath and start from the beginning," Cormick said calmly. "Think of this as a safe place."

Dawn stared at the desk for a moment then lifted her eyes to meet his. Was this a safe place, she wondered? If she told the truth, would she still be able to teach? What would people—including the person in front of her—think of her if she admitted she was hearing voices? Resigned to her fate, she sat back in the chair and shook her head.

"Okay. I was in my classroom today, last day of the year, uh…I teach high school in Portland…and it was a day like any other. I mean, nothing seemed odd." She paused for a moment and laughed. "And then there was…well, things moved around. Desks moved, um…writing appeared on the chalkboards. Did you ever see *Poltergeist*? It was a little like that."

"To be clear, you believe you were contacted by spirits?"

"Look Dr. Proffitt, I'm not a big believer in the paranormal," she said, making the case for her sanity, "but I know what I saw and heard. The desks moved themselves and words appeared on my chalk boards."

"You saw the desks move?"

"Well, not exactly," she replied. "They straightened themselves up when I was looking at the chalkboards."

"Allow me to suggest a very simple and rational explanation," he began. "It is the last day of school, a tired teacher turns her back, and her students play a little prank. The teacher gets a little frightened, and the students get a big laugh."

"And this is why people think shrinks are a big scam," she fired back. "There was no one else in that classroom. I erased those chalkboards only to see words reappear. And those desks moved without a sound. And I heard someone—or something—talk to me."

"I see," he said reaching for a legal pad and pen. "Are you currently taking any medications?"

"You don't believe me," she said. "I thought the point of therapy was to listen and understand your patient."

"Well, in the first place, it is incumbent upon me to stress to you that our conversation today should not be mistaken for therapy. You showed up here, out of the blue, seeking help. I am merely taking the prerequisite information needed to refer you to a member on my team."

"You're not going to help me?" she said in disbelief. "Do you know how difficult it was for me to open up to you? To tell a perfect stranger that I'm hearing voices? My job could be on the line here."

"Please do not worry about anything that you have shared here today. And, do not mistake my referring you to a subordinate as a lack of empathy or compassion," he said trying to reassure her. "I am a department head. These matters are handled by the junior members of the staff, all of who are quite capable of helping you cope with your situation. Have Nurse Paige get you in to see Dr. Williams, she will be able to get you into a weekly session that will do wonders for you."

Dawn sat there for a moment staring at Cormick. She was taken aback by his careless dismissal of her. She watched, without a word, as he continued to write on his notepad. She stood up, straightened her skirt, and took a few steps toward the door. She reached for the doorknob but stopped just short of grasping it.

"You know what?" she said as she turned back to him. "No. I'm not going to be dumped on some junior member of your staff. I was sent here to see you, and my boss expects proof that I did exactly that," she said as she took a step toward the desk. "I don't have the time or the desire to spend my summer or my money sitting in therapy with a junior member of your staff." She folded her arms and defiantly stood her ground. "I'm not leaving here until you give me a letter or note or whatever the hell it is that you give normal people to prove they're not crazy."

"Miss Gallagher," Cormick said as he leaned back into his chair, "I am not giving you anything until you meet with Dr. Williams and we consult on your issues. It is simply how things work. Now, I can assure you that Dr. Williams…"

"You are a pompous ass," she interrupted.

"That may well be, but I am not putting anything in writing until you have had a chance to discuss your case with Dr. Williams. Now, if there is nothing else…"

"There is something else," she fired back. "This is bullshit. You're a doctor. You're supposed to help people not brush them off."

"I am trying to help you, Miss Gallagher. There are steps in this process that must be followed. Step one is my referral to Dr. Williams." He leaned forward, resting his arms on his desk. "Now, let us look at this logically, shall we? You can go back to your boss and tell him that I have arranged for therapy sessions for you, or you can tell him that you refused the assistance offered to you. The choice is yours."

Dawn stood silent in defeat. Arguing any further seemed pointless. She knew she wasn't crazy, but she also knew that disagreeing with him would probably add words like *combative* and *defensive* to the notes Dr. Proffitt had already taken.

"You win," she sighed as her shoulders slumped a bit. "I'll see Dr. Williams. Could you at least jot something down that I was here?"

"Of course," Cormick replied. He flipped the page on his pad and began writing. "I will have Nurse Paige type this up on my letterhead. It will only take a few minutes." When he finished writing, he stood up and walked around his desk and past her to the door. "Please, follow me," he said as he opened the door for her.

As they stepped into the reception area, Cormick caught sight of Nurse Paige sitting behind her desk, clearly unhappy that a patient managed to get past her. Her pouty face betrayed everything she felt without her uttering a single syllable. He had overridden her authority, and her feelings were hurt.

"Allison," he said as he walked over to her desk, "would you be kind enough to type this up on our letterhead for Miss Gallagher, please?"

"Certainly, Dr. Proffitt," she said as she glanced at the paper. "I'll have it ready in a few minutes." Without acknowledging Dawn, she set to work on her task.

"Also, could you see if Dr. Williams has an opening today?" he asked. He turned to Dawn and smiled. "Allison will take it from here. Listen, I do not wish to appear unsympathetic, it is simply the proper procedure. After you have had a couple of sessions with Dr. Williams, I promise to consult with her and review your case." He held out his hand to shake hers. "Now, if there is nothing further…"

She reached out and unenthusiastically placed her hand in his. She was uncertain where the events of the day would lead her. Dawn was keenly aware of the stigma associated with teachers who needed therapy. Larry Loomis had been proof of that. His nervous breakdown from years earlier had followed his career. Though he never actually suffered professionally, he had become a social pariah.

"Dr. Proffitt," Dawn said, "I'm not crazy."

"Well, I never said that you were," he said reassuringly. "And we do not use that word. People are not crazy. There are any number of environmental, personal, and professional stresses that can adversely affect the psyche. Perhaps your subconscious is trying to tell you something. But as I said, you can explore that with Dr. Williams." He turned and headed toward his office.

"I should have just done what the chalkboards said and headed to Santa Fe," Dawn sighed.

Cormick stopped dead in his tracks. He turned back and looked at Dawn. His mouth hung open slightly, and for a moment he considered that he had misunderstood her.

"Excuse me," he said as he took a step toward her. He paused again as his head rolled to a forty-five-degree angle to his shoulder. "Did you say, Santa Fe?"

"Yes," Dawn replied as she took the paper Allison was offering. "My chalkboards were practically screaming it."

"Dr. Williams has a ten o'clock tomorrow morning," Allison said.

"Hold off on that, Allison," Cormick said, never taking his eyes off Dawn. "Miss Gallagher, can we step back in my office and chat for a few minutes? I just want to be sure I have all the details I need."

Momentarily surprised by his request, Dawn realized that she had hit a nerve on the arrogant doctor. In a twist she didn't understand, she had gained the upper hand in the situation, and her knowing smile broadcast it to the world.

"If it's all the same, I'd feel better if I met with Dr. Williams," she said as she turned back to Allison.

"Me, too," Allison mumbled under her breath. "Okay, I have you in for tomorrow morning at ten o'clock."

"Allison, cancel that appointment, please," Cormick insisted. "Now, Miss Gallagher…"

"If I wasn't worth your time five minutes ago," Dawn said, "why am I suddenly worth your time now?"

"I…um…" Cormick stammered. "Perhaps…I was too hasty in…I feel some remorse in the way that I initially handled this situation. Compassion for patients is…"

"Oh, come now, Dr. Proffitt," Dawn said coyly as she moved in close, "do you expect me to believe that you just suddenly developed compassion for me? Or was it something I said?"

Allison watched warily as Dawn invaded Cormick's personal space. Dawn was way too close for her comfort, but she fought back the urge to speak up. Allison could feel her face flush with jealousy and within two seconds had already run through a dozen scenarios in her head in which she was victorious over Dawn in hand to hand combat for Cormick's affection.

Cormick was overcome by the wave of anxiety that washed over him as Dawn abruptly dominated him and the conversation. His pulse quickened as her face slowly neared his. She was beautiful. Their eyes met only for a second as her cheek lightly brushed past his. As she slowly moved in, he remained motionless, his eyes drinking in every inch of the supple skin on her neck. Her perfume was intoxicating, and as he breathed her in, he was completely disarmed. She stopped, her full, red lips just a kiss away from his ear and breathlessly whispered, "Santa Fe."

Cormick quickly straightened up and backed away. Her whisper had made the hairs on the back of his neck tingle. Catching his breath, he looked at the two women. He felt the need to apologize to Allison, and the desire to have Dawn breathe in his ear one more time. He tried to speak. His lips moved, but he uttered only intelligible sounds.

"Knock-knock," Angelo called from his wheelchair in the doorway. "Did somebody say Santa Fe?"

Cormick stood behind his desk as Dawn took a seat in the chair facing him. Allison entered his office, pushing Angelo in his wheelchair. Angelo's eyes were still covered in gauze that was wrapped around his head, and his inside-out robe indicated he had probably dressed himself. She maneuvered him around Dawn and parked him in front of the desk. Cormick silently stared at the two of them as Allison left the office, closing the door behind her.

"I guess you're wondering why I've called this meeting," Angelo said breaking the silence. His attempt at humor fell flat as Dawn looked back and forth between the two men. "Man, you have no idea how hard it is to wheel around in one of these things when you can't see. I hope I didn't run over someone's air hose or something!"

"Well," Cormick said as he sat down, "remarkable timing, Angelo. I suppose you know Miss Gallagher."

"Not exactly," Angelo replied, "but I knew she was here." He turned toward her. "Hi, Dawn, it's nice to finally meet you."

"Finally? I'm sorry," Dawn interjected, "what's going on here? How do you know my name?"

"God told me," Angelo smiled. "Didn't Cormick tell you?"

"Tell me what?" She asked as her eyes darted between the two men.

"We're going to Santa Fe!" Angelo exclaimed. "We're going to meet God!"

"Hold on," Cormick said as he raised his hands. "*We* are not going anywhere."

"Oh, but we are, Cormick. And sooner than you think."

"Okay boys," Dawn interrupted, "I like games just as much as anyone else, but you're starting to creep me out."

"Dawn," Angelo began, "you're not alone. The voice you heard was God. He is calling us…"

"Everyone take a deep breath," Cormick said. "There is a perfectly reasonable…"

"How do you know I heard a voice?" Dawn asked. "How do you know about Santa Fe?"

"I'm just like you, Dawn. I heard him call my name. And just like you, I was scared and confused when he called me. I fought it, at first. But when I answered, God revealed to me part of his plan. He revealed you to me, just as he did when he showed me Cormick. And now…"

"Can we just take a deep breath and start at the beginning?" Cormick pleaded. "The insinuation that a supreme being…"

"Quiet!" Dawn said, motioning to Cormick without taking her eyes from Angelo. "I want to hear what he has to say."

"I was on the Bering Sea when he called me, Dawn. Like you, today…in your classroom, I was afraid. But now I know that we are part of a bigger plan. God's plan."

"Angelo, please," Cormick implored, "Miss Gallagher has not indicated that she…"

"Can you quit interrupting?" Dawn snapped. "For a psychiatrist, you sure don't do much listening." She turned back to Angelo. "Go on, Angelo."

"You're here to bridge the gap for us, Dawn," Angelo smiled. "You are one more piece of the puzzle. You're here to help us see the big picture…to enlighten us."

His words left her speechless as a shiver went through her body like a small jolt of electricity. It was surreal to her. He spoke as if he had been in the classroom with her and heard every word.

"Okay," she nervously laughed. "What are you, a psychic? Am I on TV or something?"

"No, Dawn," Angelo said calmly as he reached out and rested his hand on hers. "We all have a role to play. I carry a message from God. An evolving message that guides me on the path he has laid out for me. And Cormick is the one who will carry us to our destination."

"Please," Cormick spoke up, "I am not…"

"And me?" Dawn asked. "What am I doing here?"

"You are here to enlighten us…to give Cormick the facts that he needs to accept this." He pulled back and righted himself in his chair. "You're a teacher. Teach us."

"Miss Gallagher," Cormick began, attempting to gain control of the conversation, "Angelo is a patient under our care here at the hospital. It was not my intent to involve him in your case. I merely…"

"No…I want to know more," she said. "I think I believe

him. I mean, how else would he know my name or what happened today?" She turned back toward Angelo and studied his gentle, smiling face. "What do you want to know?" she asked.

"Cormick doesn't believe in God," Angelo stated sympathetically. "He's our doubting Thomas, I guess. I delivered the word of God to him, but I'm not enough to make him believe," he said sadly. "But now that you're here, you can tell him about Santa Fe, convince him that, as crazy as this all sounds to him, we are right."

"Well, let me see," she began, "it's the oldest state capitol in the US, founded by the Spanish...but the area was originally inhabited by indigenous Pueblo tribes dating back before 1,000 AD." She looked back and forth at the two men. "I'm not sure..."

"Well thank you, Miss Gallagher," Cormick said as he rose to his feet. "That truly was enlightening. I think we have all had enough excitement for today." He smiled, satisfied that he had all the information he needed to move forward. "Now, if there is nothing further..."

"Wait," Dawn said, "there's something else." She could feel the excitement build in her chest. "Can it be?" she questioned. "If it's real...I mean..."

"Miss Gallagher," Cormick said, "while I appreciate the brief history lesson, I sincerely doubt that there is anything..."

"The Mythological Triangle," she interjected. "In college, I wrote a paper on the Mythological Triangle of the American Southwest." She turned her head to the side and stared quietly at the wall as she recalled her work.

"And what exactly is that?" Cormick asked.

"Several centuries ago, the indigenous tribes in New

Mexico faced the full force of the Spanish conquistadors as well as Roman Catholic missionaries," she said as she stood and began to lecture the two men. "The seat of the colonial Spanish government at the time was in Santa Fe. The Pueblo people had a cultural hero—a Christ-like figure who went by various names in different pueblos."

"Miss Gallagher," Cormick said, "once again, I doubt…"

"Did you raise your hand?" she asked.

"Pardon me?" Cormick responded as Angelo let out a laugh. "Raise my hand?" he asked incredulously.

"Yes, that's what you do when the teacher is talking," she stated in no uncertain terms. "Listen up and take notes, because there's going to be a test." She took a few paces and began again. "Now…around Santa Fe, this figure was known as *Poseyemu*, and he was favorably compared to the Aztec emperor Moctezuma II, another native hero who faced Spanish imperialism. As the conversion efforts intensified in New Mexico, the Pueblo people attempted to reconcile the stories of Jesus as told by the missionaries with the legend of Moctezuma from Central America (as well as their own ancestral beliefs)."

"I see," Cormick said. "However, while fascinating, that appears to have little to do with what the two of you have experienced."

"No, Cormick," Angelo said, "God is calling us to Santa Fe. Dawn is here to explain it to us. It all makes sense. You have to be open to this."

"There's more," Dawn said. "According to the legend, Poseyemu was the child of the Sun God and a virgin mother. The similarities to the stories of Jesus are striking."

"I must interject," Cormick said forcefully. "This discussion is best left for philosophers or theologians. I am a psychiatrist, not an anthropologist." He let out a deep breath. "In the interest of expediency, albeit against my better judgement, I will offer my diagnoses and recommendations for both of you. Miss Gallagher," he said as he sat down, "I believe you have some work-related stress that led to your specific set of circumstances, and you are simply in need of a little rest and a few counseling sessions to work through this difficult time. And Angelo, if it is not severe brain trauma from your accident, then—considering your long days on the ocean—it is most likely akin to a mirage one would see in the desert. The human brain has…"

"The ability to process information and reach a logical conclusion," Dawn said, finishing his sentence. "Look, Dr. Proffitt, this is worth exploring. I know what I saw. I know what I heard. It's so clear. I feel it. I'm supposed to go to Santa Fe!"

"Yes!" Angelo said as he catapulted himself from his wheelchair.

"You can walk?" Dawn asked, taken aback.

"Sure. Can't you?" Angelo responded.

"I just thought…uh…the chair…never mind," she shrugged. She turned back toward Cormick. "Can't you feel it?" She asked him. "Even a little bit?"

"I feel it all right," Cormick responded. "It feels like you two are trying to pull me into your delusion driven by little more than coincidence and conjecture."

"I'm not delusional," Dawn said, "and I'm not imaging things. In fact, Dr. Proffitt, I consider myself to be a pragmatic person. Just because something seems impossible, it doesn't mean it's improbable."

"Enough," Cormick said as he raised his hand. He sat in his chair and looked at his patients. It was a beautifully ornate tapestry of illusion the two were weaving. Now that they had each other, he knew they would build off one another, constructing a more complicated fantasy that would require more attention from his staff.

"Angelo, Miss Gallagher," he forced a smile as he exhaled through his nose, "I, too, consider myself to be a pragmatic person. After taking into consideration everything I have heard so far, I suppose you leave me no other option."

"You're taking us to Santa Fe?" Angelo asked excitedly.

"No, I am placing both of you in the care of my staff," he said firmly. "Miss Gallagher, I will set you up with six weekly sessions with Dr. Williams, and Angelo, once I receive the go ahead from your doctor, I am going to place you on ward 1D for observation."

"Cormick," Angelo asked quietly, "are you committing me?"

"Angelo, you almost killed yourself listening to this voice. For your own safety and well-being…"

"Oh, that's bullshit," Dawn said.

"Call it what you will, Miss Gallagher. But the fact remains that Angelo could have killed others during his high-speed pursuit of the voice he heard."

"Think about it, Dr. Proffitt," Dawn implored. "Angelo and I have never met. One in Alaska, one in Oregon. But both called to Santa Fe. You've got to admit that this is more than coincidence."

"For the sake of argument, if I follow your stream of consciousness down the rabbit hole, would it not make sense that I, too, would hear this calling? If, as you two say, I am an integral part of this, why do I stand here so blissfully ignorant?"

"That may be overstating it," Dawn said. "I don't find

your ignorance blissful at all."

"I think we are done here," Cormick said as he walked to the door. Opening it, he called to Nurse Paige. "Allison, can you get someone from six down here to collect Mr. Taranto, please?" He turned back to the two in his office. "Miss Gallagher, Nurse Paige can help you with Dr. Williams."

"I'll take Angelo to his room," Dawn said. She grabbed the handles of his wheelchair and pushed him toward the door. She stopped just short of the doorway and glared at Cormick. "You know, I used to make fun of Larry Loomis, but after meeting his psychiatrist, I feel nothing but sympathy for the poor bastard."

"Cormick," Angelo said as he reached for his hand, "time is short. We're leaving in two days. We have to get to the others."

"Others?" Dawn asked as she pushed the chair through the outer office. "Tell me more!"

THE OTHERS

The old Zenith console spilled forth a pale blue light into the darkened room, eerily illuminating the motionless figure passed out in the recliner. While images of national monuments and soldiers faded in and out on the screen, the national anthem played, barely audible over the drunken snoring coming from the chair. The light flickered as images of fireworks accompanied the music's climactic end. There was a brief pause as the Channel 12 test pattern took over the screen, and the music was replaced by a high-pitched tone. It was now 2:05 am. The broadcasting day had come to an end.

Horace Jordan awoke to screeching from the set. He abruptly sat up, forcing the recliner to lurch forward. The metal framework inside scraped against itself as if it were going to break into pieces. He squeezed his eyes tightly shut to block out any light that could force him into consciousness.

His head bobbed back and forth. The shrill tone from the television bore into his temples and reverberated inside his skull, which already felt two sizes too small for his brain. Dehydrated, he reached back and to the left toward the side table for something to drink. As he blindly grasped in the self-imposed darkness, his fingers danced their way through a mountain of cigarette butts piled in the ashtray. He shook the ash from his hand, and in doing so, knocked over his bottle of Jack Daniels.

"Goddammit," he growled.

He realized he was fighting a losing battle. He was going to have to get up. He slowly opened his right eye first and stared at the black and white image of a Native American in a feathered headdress in the middle of the screen. Though he had seen the test pattern hundreds of times, he never understood why that image was chosen. It was only a moment before he realized he didn't care.

"Who gives a shit," he mumbled as he opened his other eye. He pulled himself forward and out of the recliner. A belch erupted from deep inside his gut, forcing his head back. For a moment, he thought he was going to vomit. He took two steps forward and turned off the volume on the set. With the noise gone, he was free to use the dim light to quietly find the path of least resistance to the kitchen.

He stumbled out of the living room and into the small dining area. Shuffling along, he slammed his toe into the leg of the table. He let out a muffled cry as he backed away from the table. Resisting the urge to launch a torrent of profanity, he took in a deep, labored breath and continued toward the kitchen.

Using the sink for support and holding on tightly, he reached for a glass in the cupboard. He filled it with cold water and guzzled every drop. He filled it again and turned to leave the kitchen. His first step landed his bare foot in the litter box.

"Fucking cat," he mumbled as he lifted his foot from the box. He had been at odds with the cat since his younger brother brought him home eight years earlier, and somehow, the cat always seemed to have the upper hand. He shook the pellets from his foot, convinced the cat had pushed the box into his path.

He made his way to the dining table and slid into a chair. He reached into his shirt pocket and removed his pack of Marlboro cigarettes. He flipped open the top of the box with his forefinger and discovered a single broken cigarette. He shook his head in disbelief. This was clearly the work of the diabolical cat.

Undaunted by the setback, he removed the hanging shreds of tobacco and lit the stub of the cigarette. He inhaled deeply and blew a cloud of smoke into the darkness. He leaned forward with his elbows, anchoring him to the table, and stared at the cigarette. It had a good six or seven drags in it. That was six or seven more than his doctor had allowed him to have.

In the six months following his diagnosis, he had done nothing to stop the spread of the stage 2 cancer in his lungs and lymph nodes. He was only forty, but he had spent the last two decades slowly dying. Never able to recover from his time in Vietnam and the loss of the life he felt should have been his, he lived every day in a cloud of smoke, drowning in a pool of alcohol. He couldn't hide the smoking and drinking, but the cancer was a secret he would never share.

He stared through the smoke into the darkened living room. He had more important things to consider than cancer: How much alcohol had he spilled when he awoke? Was there still a pack of cigarettes on the side table? Where was that fucking cat? He crushed out his cigarette in the ashtray and got up from the kitchen table. His eyes had adjusted to the night. Navigating his way to his pack of cigarettes was going to be free of painful obstacles.

As expected, the red and white pack was on the side table. He scooped it up and knelt to pick up the bottle of

Jack Daniels lying on the floor. He held the bottle up in front of his face, using the illuminated test pattern to see what he had lost. He shook his head. Looking did no good. He had no idea how full the bottle had been before he knocked it over. He brushed his hand across the carpet and gauged his carelessness had cost him five shots of quality Tennessee sour mash.

He slowly stood up and let out an exhausted sigh. He took a swig from the bottle and set it on the table. Lighting a cigarette, he walked around the TV to the open windows overlooking the Pacific.

He had listened to the Huntington Beach tides from these windows nearly his entire life. From this familiar vantage point he could hear that the tide was going out, doing everything it could to fight back against its natural ebb. It was all he could hear, and it was still the most beautiful sound he had ever known.

He flipped through the pages of his past as if he were paging through a book looking for just the pictures: a boy running through the waves, a teenager riding the waves, a young man holding hands with Elaine. The first chapters of his life read like an all-American-boy story. But the novel of his life got darker. The next chapters included a bloody tour of duty in Vietnam, the death of his mother, alcohol, and cancer. He took in a long drag and blew the smoke into the darkness. He watched as it slowly dissipated in the night air.

"Horace…"

He turned slowly and peered into the empty room. He was alone. It was nothing, he thought. He turned back to the window and continued listening to the waves lap at the shore in the distance.

"Horace…"

Once again, he turned and stared into the dimly lit room. He was sure he had heard it this time. It was a faint whisper that seemed to quietly echo in the house.

"Sayer," he called for his younger brother, "is that you?" His call was met with silence. "Fucking cat," he mumbled.

"Horace…"

He flicked what remained of his cigarette out of the window and took a step toward the middle of the room. That was no cat, he was sure of it. He walked quietly through the room toward the hallway. The light from the Zenith was too far away to be of any use, but he navigated through the dark easily. He stopped at his brother's open bedroom door.

"Sayer, goddammit," he began as he flipped on the light switch.

Sayer's bed always looked the same: a massive pile of pillows, sheets, and blankets lumped in a nearly indistinguishable mass atop the mattress. The sheets were covered with images of Garfield and Odie. In every fold, it seemed the cartoon characters were staring at him, mocking him.

"Fucking cat," he said as he started toward the bed. "Sayer!" he called as he pushed his hand into the pile of linen. The bed was empty. Sayer wasn't home. He stood for a moment and looked over his brother's room.

The bedroom was not much different than the room Horace had when he was younger. Both brothers excelled in surfing and had the trophies on display to prove it. Like Sayer, Horace had once taped his favorite pictures to his wall, and both had maintained an impressive collection of vinyl. There were differences, too. The smell of stale bong water hung in the air—something that their mother would have never allowed—and Sayer's bedroom played host to significantly more female guests than his ever had.

Horace turned and walked back toward the door. He stopped short of entering the hall and listened for his name to be called again. But there was only silence.

He walked slowly down the hall, looking over the family photos hanging in the narrow corridor. Apart from his brother and himself, all the faces smiling at him were the faces of ghosts.

He walked quietly through the house, lost in memories. *Elaine should be here*, he thought. Though two decades had passed since they were together, she had been his one and only love. She had married Russ Hanrahan, and Horace remained alone. And now, both Horace and Elaine were damaged goods.

"Horace…"

He froze where he was standing. Using the light from the television, he carefully scanned the living room. Just as before, no one was there. The only movement came from the open window as the sheer curtains danced in the soft ocean breeze.

"Horace…"

He cocked his ear toward the console. He was sure he had turned the volume off. He walked cautiously toward the set and knelt in front of the screen. The test pattern was still there. He leaned in and listened carefully.

"Horace…"

He leapt backward from his kneeling position, falling into the recliner with enough force to tip the chair backward. He fell—seated in the chair—and hit his head on the floor as he landed. He scrambled out of the chair, kicking his legs frantically toward the TV until he had moved a safe distance away.

He rolled over onto his stomach and crawled low over

the back of the recliner, using the upended seat as a protective wall between himself and the television. He reached up and grabbed the cushion with both hands. Steadying himself, he slowly raised his head above the seat of the recliner until he had a line of sight to the television.

It had spoken to him and called him by name. He slid back down into the recliner and rolled into a sitting position.

Okay, he thought, *let's be reasonable. TVs can't hold a conversation. On the other hand, if they could, why wouldn't the set know my name? It has sat in the living room for years listening in on every conversation. Wait, that's fucking stupid. It's a TV. Why am I afraid of a TV? I've seen combat. Wait, that's it! I'm having a flashback. No, I'm asleep. This is a dream.*

He spun himself over again onto his knees and slowly raised his head to peer over the cushion. The test pattern was still on the silent screen, flooding the room in an almost supernatural glow.

"Horace…" the voice called from the TV. He watched in disbelief as the profile of the Indian turned to look directly at him. "They are coming, Horace."

Not taking his eyes off the screen, he grasped for the table to his left and grabbed the remote. He moved slowly behind the protection of the cushion. He reached over the seat and carefully aimed the remote toward the console. Taking precise aim, he pressed the power button, simultaneously silencing the set and plunging himself into darkness.

He continued staring at the set as his eyes slowly adjusted to the darkness. The two faced off in the night, neither of them moving or making a sound. The standoff seemed to last forever for Horace, though only seconds had passed. He slowly got to his feet, aiming the remote like a handgun at the blank screen.

Horace walked cautiously toward the console. He knelt in front of the set and reached out to touch the screen. As his fingers gently touched the screen, a white aura appeared and then faded beneath his fingertips. He brushed his fingers across the screen and trails of phosphorescence followed his hand like shooting stars in the night.

He stood up and walked to the outlet behind the TV. He yanked hard on the cord then dropped it to the ground. *That oughta do it*, he thought. He tossed the remote toward the couch and walked back toward the kitchen. As he neared the kitchen table, the kitchen was slowly illuminated by pale light from behind him. He stopped dead in his tracks.

"Horace…"

He turned slowly toward the television as his pounding heartbeat echoed in his ears. The Zenith once again displayed the familiar test pattern. In the faint light, he could see the unplugged power cord lying on the floor exactly where he had dropped it just seconds before.

"What the fuck?" he mumbled breathlessly as he walked hesitantly toward the set. Once again, he knelt in front of the screen. He extended his index finger and poked the Indian. He ran his palm across the screen as it crackled with static electricity. He watched as the test pattern slowly faded to black.

As he watched the screen, letters formed and slowly grew brighter. *TIME TO QUIT SMOKING* appeared in bold white letters then slowly faded to black once again.

"Fuck that!" he said as he placed a cigarette between his lips. "I'm already dying."

He lit his cigarette and watched as letters once again slowly grew brighter with a message he had heard from the Indian in the test pattern. *THEY ARE COMING* illuminated the screen briefly and slowly faded to black.

"Who is coming?" he growled at the television.

THEY ARE COMING appeared again on the screen growing bright enough to light the whole room. The words pulsated on the screen. Horace sat completely still, transfixed by what he was witnessing.

The phone rang, startling him out of his near catatonic state. He turned quickly toward the kitchen as adrenalin exploded into his system. He spun back to the screen which had gone dark. The phone rang again.

"Goddammit," he grumbled as he got to his feet. "What the fuck is going on?" He picked up the phone on the fifth ring and, skipping the customary greeting, barked, "Who the fuck is this?"

"Horace…they are coming," a voice echoed into the receiver.

"Who is this?" he yelled into the phone. "Who's coming?" After a brief silence, he heard the dial tone.

He yanked his cigarette from his mouth and leaned over the counter, deftly flicking it into the litterbox, where his cat sat quietly in the dark relieving itself. The animal sprang from the litterbox, hissing, and abruptly disappeared deeper into the darkness.

As he reached forward to hang up the phone, the television set emitted a bright, white light. He could feel his pulse quicken as he held his breath. The light seemed to blaze from the screen, lighting every detail of the messy home. He stood his ground, determined to face whatever was happening head on.

The phone rang again. He pulled his hand up and stared at the receiver in disbelief. He put the phone to his ear and listened.

"It's time to quit smoking," the voice said.

With the phone still to his ear, he turned back to the brilliant light in the living room. The light was so intense that he had to raise his hand to shield his eyes. Squinting hard, he fought to keep his eyes on what was happening in the living room.

"Horace," the voice called, "they are coming." The voice reverberated inside him as if it was emanating from him. He could feel it more than he could hear it. He dropped the phone and covered both of his eyes.

"Time to quit smoking," the voice called out once again.

Unable to see through the light radiating from the television, he backed away toward the kitchen table. His foot landed on the receiver, forcing him to lose his balance, throwing him backward. He reached out to grab the countertop but fell to the floor, hitting his head on the yellowing linoleum. As he lost consciousness, the light slowly faded into darkness.

Horace awoke to morning sunlight streaming through the windows. He opened his eyes and stared up at the cracked plaster ceiling, which was peeling in random spots. He groaned as he thought about the work involved and closed his eyes to ignore the problem.

The sharp pain in the back of his skull stabbed at his neck and down his spine until it became a dull ache in his lower back. He slid his hand under his head and ran his fingers through his hair. Relieved there was no blood, he let his arm slide across the linoleum until it came to rest at his side. He had nowhere to be, so lying on the floor until the pain subsided suited him just fine. He lit a cigarette and blew a cloud of smoke toward the ceiling.

Then it hit him. He rolled his head toward the old Zenith. The set was off and the cord was lying on the floor exactly where he had dropped it just hours before. The cat was investigating the tipped over recliner as if it were something it had never seen before.

"Oh shit," Horace grumbled as he sat up. "My fucking back." He rolled to his side and pushed himself up from the floor. He stood there, momentarily off balance. "What the fuck?" he murmured to himself as he recalled the events of the early morning.

"Good morning, sleepy head!" a shirtless Sayer called from the kitchen table, startling his big brother. "Want some Cap'n Crunch?" he asked as he lifted the spoon from his bowl. "It's got crunch berries! Yummy in your tummy, bro." Sayer brushed his long, blonde hair from his face, and eagerly put the spoon in his mouth. "Mmmm," he smiled as he rubbed his stomach, "they're delicious." He was trying not to let the milk spill from his mouth.

Horace watched quietly for a moment as his brother smiled at him with his mouth full of cereal. At twenty-four, Sayer was sixteen years his junior, but their relationship was as strong as if they had grown up together. Horace had acted as both brother and parent since the death of their mother.

A professional surfer, Sayer spent his days on the beach impressing girls with his surfing prowess. But the girls on the beach were interested in more than just his ability to ride the waves. His lean, toned body, deep brown tan, and piercing blue eyes caused girls to all but throw themselves at his feet.

"Have you been here all night?" Horace asked as he pulled out a chair and sat across from his brother.

"Nah, dude," Sayer smiled. "We spent the night under the stars," he said as he scooped another mound of cereal into his mouth. "Hey, why were you sleeping on the floor, dude? I don't think that's good for your back."

"I wasn't sleeping," Horace replied through a cloud of cigarette smoke. "I fucking fell."

"I don't think that's good for your back, either," Sayer replied as he dug into his bowl for the last few bits of cereal.

"No shit," Horace replied.

"Ya know dude, you need to get healthy again," Sayer said. "Come surf with me, man! C'mon, you know you want to!"

"It's been a long time, Sayer. Besides, what could be more pathetic than a forty-year-old man falling off his board? Christ, I'd probably wipe out on the jetty. There has to be a safer way to get healthy."

"Then how 'bout this…exercise, drink less, and most of all…time to quit smoking," Sayer responded.

"What did you just say?" Horace asked.

"Which part?"

"Smoking…that's what the TV said last night. 'Time to quit smoking.' Are you sure you weren't here last night, fuckin' with my head?"

"No way, dude! You're my big bro," Sayer exclaimed. He got up and placed his bowl in the sink. He stopped for a moment then turned to Horace. "Wait! The TV said that? What else did it say?"

"Sayer, I'm sure it was a commercial," Horace said. "Bring me some water and aspirin. My fucking head is killing me."

"Dude," Sayer began as a broad smile spread across his face, "that was no commercial." He quickly grabbed the aspirin and water and sat back down with his brother. "What else did it say? Did it tell you that the others are coming?"

"Goddammit Sayer, it's too early for this."

"You heard his voice, didn't you?" Sayer stood up with his hands on the top of his head. "This is totally awesome! God wants you, too! Do you know what this means? We're in this together, Horace!"

"Jesus, Sayer," Horace began as he placed his palm over his face, shaking his head from side to side, "it was just a commercial."

"No way, dude. It's God! And he needs our help! How cool is this?"

"Sayer, you need to stop saying that shit," Horace warned. "People are talking. They're gonna think you're crazy." He crushed the cigarette in the ashtray.

"Dude, I totally don't care what people think. I know I'm not crazy. God needs me—I mean, us. How cool is it that he wants us both?"

"God already had his shot at me, but he sent me back," Horace sighed. "Look at my life, Sayer. If God hasn't taken any interest in me so far, why does he need me now?"

"We can ask him when we see him!" Sayer exclaimed as he threw his arms in the air. "He's waiting for us in Santa Fe!" He turned and headed down the hall. "So awesome!" he exclaimed as he disappeared into his bedroom.

"Shit," Horace said in a frustrated whisper. He pushed his chair from the table and followed Sayer into his room. He found his brother changing into a pair of white board shorts. "Sayer, please listen to me. These things you hear… not everyone is going to understand."

"Oh dude, they will understand," Sayer replied with a reassuring smile.

Horace stared at his brother, shaking his head. It had been more than a week since his brother started preaching on the beach. Though Horace strenuously objected, there was no stopping his brother. Giving up yet again, he plopped down on Sayer's bed and sat on something hard.

"Oooo…" a muffled voice said from under the pile of cartoon-covered linen. The sheets began to stir, and Horace felt a foot being pulled from under him. A few seconds later, a girl emerged, smiling.

"Hey, Horace!" she exclaimed.

"Hey, Sunny," he replied. He watched as she sat up, immodestly letting the sheets fall to her waist. "You wanna…" he said as he motioned with his fingers for her to cover up.

"You're silly, Horace," she said as she pulled the sheets up just enough to cover her nipples. "You are, like, the only guy in town who doesn't want to see my boobs."

"I'm not sure your mother would be too happy about me seeing them as often as I do."

"Daddy would kill you if he knew," she laughed.

"He could try," Horace replied. "Sunny, it's not a good idea for you to be here. Not that I don't enjoy knockin' the shit out of your daddy once in awhile, but I don't want any more problems for your mom."

In the two decades since her mother, Elaine, had married Russ Hanrahan, the two men had fought more times than either could remember. The three of them were caught in a vicious cycle of violence. Horace would beat Hanrahan, who would take it out on Elaine, which made Horace beat him again. Though Elaine had been the love of his life since he met her more than two decades earlier, she had married Hanrahan, and now her daughter was seeing his brother.

"I should get going," Sunny said as she sprang from the bed wearing only panties. She wrapped her arms around

Sayer and nestled her head on his chest. "Wanna hang out later?" she asked.

"No can do, babe. I have the grommets this afternoon, and those little munchkins turn into rabid squirrels if I'm not there teaching them how to shred."

"Sunny," Horace said, "please put on some clothes."

"What about later?" she asked, ignoring Horace.

"Babe, I gotta get some solo time in," he said as he gently pulled her arms away. "Have you seen my wettie?"

"It's in my car. I'll get it!" she said enthusiastically, as she started out the door to retrieve his wetsuit.

"Can you put some clothes on first?" Horace asked.

"Whatever," Sunny said as she smiled and dove into the sea of sheets. A moment later she surfaced with her bikini top around her neck. As she fastened the snaps, she searched the floor for her cutoffs and flip-flops. "There they are!" she exclaimed as she scooped up her shorts and slid into them. "I'll be right back!" she said lyrically as she disappeared into the hallway.

"Sayer, what are you doing?"

"I'm trying to figure out which sled I'm gonna use today," he replied. "Good ol' Wayne…" he said as he reached for his favorite board. "My trusty daily driver."

"No…I meant what are you doing with Sunny? C'mon man, she's just a kid, and she's clearly in love with you. And you, well, you're not exactly a one-woman man. You have to put an end to this before her parents…"

"Dude, those are your hang-ups," Sayer said. "Sunny can date whoever she wants. She just wants me, that's all." He walked over to the bed and placed his hand on his brother's shoulder. "You worry too much."

"If you won't listen to me about Sunny, at least hear me

out about the voice you've been hearing," Horace implored. "I was in the bar last night, and Vic called you the Surfboard Savior. It's getting embarrassing."

"I'm sorry, bro," Sayer said as he sat down next to Horace. "This may be hard for you to understand, but I can't stop. God is reaching out to me, dude, and I have to spread the word. It, like…totally overwhelms me." He looked at his brother and saw the concern on his face. "Try this…you know when you pour just the right amount of soda into a glass, but it fizzes up and overflows? That's me and God. I'm the glass and the spirit of God is, like, overflowing me."

"Sayer, have you ever even read the Bible?"

"Dude, the Bible is, like, a hundred years old. It's not even relevant."

"Jesus, Sayer! The Bible is the word of God!" Horace yelled. "Can you imagine what Mom would say if she heard you talking like this? She'd call a goddamned exorcist!"

"Here it is!" Sunny shouted as she appeared in the doorway with Sayer's wetsuit. "Can I drive you to the beach?"

"Babe, seriously," Sayer said as he stood up. "This hombre needs some one-on-one time with Wayne." He walked over to the door and kissed her on the cheek. "C'mon, I'll walk you to your car."

Horace got up and followed the couple into the kitchen. He stopped and watched as they walked to Sunny's car. He could see by her body language that she was more invested in the relationship than his brother. "This won't end well," he mumbled.

CONSEQUENCE

Cormick emerged from the stairwell onto the fifth floor and let out a discreet sigh of relief. He had survived yet another perilous morning climb to his office. He brushed his bangs to the side, simultaneously mopping up the small beads of sweat from his forehead. Looking his best every morning for Allison was part of his daily routine.

He opened the door to the outer office with a contrived nonchalance and, as always, caught sight of her diligently working at her desk. He looked forward, each day, to the fleeting moments when he could watch her just being herself before she knew he was watching. Even as she performed the most mundane tasks in the office, Cormick thought she did them with unrivaled beauty and elegance.

"Good morning, Dr. Proffitt," she said melodically as she smiled at him.

"Good morning, Allison. How was your evening?" he asked as he walked up to the reception desk.

"Oh, it was alright," she replied unenthusiastically. "Dr. Blanton wants to talk to you." Her voice was strained, and the forced smile on her face betrayed the concern she felt.

"I will call him in a few hours," he said as he leaned over the desk and glanced at his schedule. "Let me see," he began as he checked his watch, "it is nine o'clock here, which means the sun is just coming up in Hawaii...please set a reminder for me to call him in two hours."

"He wants to see you in person," she replied.

"Well, he returns on Sunday. Clear my schedule for Monday morning and…"

"He's waiting in your office," she replied in an exaggerated whisper as she pointed toward the door.

Cormick turned and stared at his office door. If John Blanton had returned from his trip five days early it had to be for something important. In his heart, Cormick knew that important and unpleasant were more than likely synonymous in this case. He took a deep breath and opened the door.

John Blanton was sitting in the leather chair facing Cormick's desk. His head was down and moved slowly back and forth as he paged through a recent copy of *Psychology Today*. Cormick knew he was not actually reading anything; the behavior was merely one of the several ways he communicated the importance of his thoughts over anything else that was going on around him.

"John! This is a surprise," Cormick said as he carefully slipped out of his sport coat and hung it neatly on the coat rack. "I was not expecting you until next week." Cormick recognized the anxiety in his voice and paused a moment to regain his composure. "How was Maui?"

"Maui was Maui, Cormick," he said as he closed the magazine and carelessly tossed it on Cormick's desk. "Cocktails, palm trees, and five hundred doctors with their six hundred mistresses…same as last year. It's hard to go to these things when they hold them in tropical locations." He leaned back as if he were aiming his face directly at the sun he was imagining. "My mind wanders when I'm in paradise, Cormick. It's hard to focus on lectures and panel discussions when all you can think about is lying on the beach with a cocktail."

"I suppose it is," Cormick answered. "But you did not fly back days ahead of schedule to tell me how much you love paradise, did you?"

"Interesting design choices…" he said as he looked around the office. "Especially the paint. I'm not sure I would have chosen pink. To each his own, I suppose."

"The color is mauve, John. Studies show that mauve tends to calm agitated patients. In fact, police departments around the country use this color to reduce the risk of outbursts from detainees. It seemed the logical choice."

"That's what I've always liked about you Cormick," John laughed, "always so sane."

"Well, John, that is what they taught us at Georgetown. Rule number one was to be more sane than those you are treating." Cormick paused for a moment. Blanton was not making eye contact with him. He was looking around the office, fixating on nothing in particular. "John, why are you here?"

Blanton turned and sighed. "I was called back by the board. We have a…situation that needed my attention."

"How can I help?" Cormick asked as he leaned forward, resting his elbows on his desk.

"Cormick, let me get right to the point. I terminated the hospital's relationship with Bob Carlson this morning."

"What?" Cormick fell back into his chair. "Why?" he asked. He knew the answer somehow involved Angelo, but he chose to remain silent.

"Cormick, you were the first person I hired when I became the administrator of this hospital," he said as he rose from the chair and began to walk around the office.

"What struck me most during that interview, and you have reinforced this in the subsequent decade, is that you were so…so…sane."

"John," Cormick began as he leaned forward, "where is this going? And why do you keep using that word *sane*?"

"Perhaps that's the wrong terminology. Let me rephrase. I was taken not only by your rational approach to the treatment you provided patients but by your entire logical outlook on life and your career." He reached out and ran his finger down the wall. "Even though you sit in a pink office."

"It is mauve, John," he interrupted. "Where is this going? What happened with Bob?"

"Maybe you should tell me Cormick. He's your friend, after all. The two of you are thick as thieves. Using your trademark rationality, it isn't a stretch to assume that anything Bob Carlson does, you'd be aware of."

"Stop right there," Cormick ordered as he rose from his chair. "These conversation fragments must form some cohesive thought. Take a deep breath, collect your thoughts, and tell me what in God's name you are talking about."

Nodding, Blanton returned to his chair. As instructed, he took a deep breath and stared directly into Cormick's eyes.

"You're right, Cormick. It seems Dr. Hess has filed a complaint against Bob Carlson. And in that complaint, he alleges that Dr. Carlson caused the death of a patient in the ER two days ago due to negligence. He further alleges that Dr. Carlson took extraordinary measures to cover up his incompetence by falsifying and destroying patient records, scheduling unnecessary procedures for patients that don't exist, and finally disposing of the body and substituting another patient—most likely from your ward of nut jobs—for the deceased. Now, since you two are such good friends, I can't help but be curious if you were aware of Dr. Carlson's actions."

"You are out of line, John," Cormick said sternly.

"Funny, that's what Dr. Carlson told me when I asked him about *you.*"

"Why were you asking about me?"

"Did you write Dr. Carlson a prescription for Xanax?" he asked pointedly.

"Yes, John, I did," Cormick responded. "Not unlike the one I wrote for your wife, if you remember. There is nothing unethical about my decision. Bob was suffering from anxiety that…"

"Why was he so anxious?" Blanton fired back. "Was it because he believes a spaceman was nearly killed in a car accident but then healed himself?" Blanton shook his head and laughed. "You two really need to work on your alibis."

"I do not require an alibi, John. I have done nothing wrong. Neither has Bob Carlson."

"What are you going to tell me, Cormick? That you knew nothing about this? That you believe that an alien traveled light years in a sophisticated ship only to be nearly killed by a primitive automobile? And then was saved by his mystical powers of rejuvenation?" He leaned back in his chair and took another deep breath. "You two are going to have to do better than that. I mean really, Cormick. Why would aliens want to attack Vancouver?"

"John, I do not for an instant believe that there is an alien in the hospital. This whole thing is being blown out of proportion."

"We're missing a body, Cormick. There's no way to blow this any further out of proportion."

"John, there is no missing cadaver," Cormick said reassuringly. "Bob's patient is on six, alive and well."

"You mean Mr. Taranto? Your patient with the Christ complex? Why isn't he in the Psych Ward, Cormick?"

"I have not finished my evaluation, John. The man was just in a near fatal car accident. I am not going to commit someone unless I determine that they are a threat to themselves or others. Additionally, I would never jeopardize the well-being of a patient in this hospital by moving them to the Ward without a clean release from their physician."

"You won't have to worry about that, Cormick. I released Mr. Taranto this morning."

"Let me get this straight. You released a blind man, who may or may not be suffering from mental illness, into an unfamiliar city, and you want to lecture me on ethics?" Cormick shook his head in disbelief. "John, you had no right to…"

"I have every right, Cormick," Blanton said as he rose to his feet. "I have a responsibility to this hospital," he said as he forcefully tapped the desk with his index finger. "You three and your goddamned shenanigans have opened this hospital to significant legal liabilities!" Blanton stood straight and placed his thumbs in his vest pockets. "Now, I want to know everything you know about this shit sandwich!"

"John, listen," Cormick said as he stood and walked around the desk, "Mr. Taranto was in an accident which robbed him of his eyesight. He was airlifted here and we discovered he was suffering from mild delusions. Bob was shaken up by the things Angelo—Mr. Taranto—was saying. It is just that simple."

"This is what I think, Cormick. I think Dr. Carlson was

negligent—whether from exhaustion or an addiction to the pills you supplied him—and he lost a patient. I further believe that you went to the aid of your friend and out of misguided loyalty to him, or to hide your own culpability in the matter, helped him dispose of the cadaver and used one of your patients to assume the identity of the dead man."

"You think my story is farfetched?" Cormick asked in disbelief. "Did you and Hess come up with this fairy tale over breakfast this morning, or was it just pillow talk last night?"

"You had better watch your step, Dr. Proffitt," Blanton warned. "Guillermo Hess has only the highest level of integrity. And this fairy tale, as you call it, is the preliminary conclusion I've reached at this point of the investigation."

"Investigation?" Cormick asked incredulously. "There is nothing to investigate, John. What about my integrity? I do not *supply* pills to anyone. Bob Carlson is not a drug addict, and he most certainly would not dispose of a body. Frankly, John, if you persist, I will call my attorney, and we will take your ridiculous allegations to the board and…"

"I'm going to stop you right there, Cormick. I've met with the board. They agree with Dr. Hess and me. You've sealed your fate. I just want the body."

"John, there is no body," Cormick said firmly. "There is no cover up. You want to say I am opening us up to legal liability? You wrongfully terminated not only a good surgeon, but a good man. You then compounded *your* gross incompetence by discharging a blind patient who was receiving ongoing medical and psychiatric care into a city that he has never been to prior to two days ago. And, because the sheer stupidity of your careless and reckless actions had not yet reached an inevitable and absurd conclusion, you decided to concoct a wildly unbelievable and irresponsible fable about Cormick the drug dealer!" Cormick turned away shaking his head. He walked back to his chair, and sat down. "Maybe you should be the one in therapy." Cormick paused briefly to collect himself. "Now, if there's nothing further, please get out of my office."

"I'm afraid I can't do that, Cormick," Blanton said as he pulled his right hand from his vest pocket and twirled his finger on the desk. "Effective immediately and until further notice, you're on paid administrative leave."

"What?" Cormick exclaimed as he rose to his feet.

"You heard me. And don't make any trouble, Cormick. We're trying to handle this in house to avoid a public relations nightmare." He lifted his finger and pointed directly at Cormick. "Be clear," he said through squinted eyes, "you cause any trouble for this hospital and we will go to the authorities. We will drop this whole fucking mess in your lap: the body, the prescriptions, and blind Space Jesus. I mean it, Cormick."

Cormick stood motionless, his mouth agape. He wanted to speak, but he was too stunned to form a coherent argument.

"This is bullshit," he said, even though he did not approve of profanity.

"Call it what you will, Cormick, but my bullshit smells a whole lot better than the pile of pig shit you dropped this hospital into." He paused and looked around Cormick's office. "I need you to pack up anything personal and leave the premises. Considering your tenure here, I'll give you thirty minutes before I send security up to escort you out. Neither of us wants that, now do we?" he asked as he headed to the door. He reached for the knob. Grasping it firmly, he turned to Cormick. "I'll be honest with you, Cormick. You're the strangest psychiatrist I've ever met. Afraid of heights, afraid of small places, afraid of the dark...I doubt you've truly ever helped anyone. You hide from the world in your little pink office, where your undeserved sense of superiority shelters you from any real responsibility. You spend your whole life as a shrinking violet, and now is when you choose to do something risky? What did you do...use your little pill pad to write yourself a prescription for a pair of testicles?" He looked down at the floor and shook his head. "I'd have this paint checked out if I were you. Maybe pink paint fumes affect your brain." He opened the door and left without closing it.

"Mauve..." Cormick began as he hung his head and stared at his desk. "It is mauve, you pernicious piece of shit."

——〰〰——

Slumped down in his chair, Cormick sat silently in his office, blankly staring at the wall. He was unsure how much time he had left to leave the premises, and he did not care. He had never been one to make waves, but he imagined himself barricaded in his office while one of Vancouver's finest tried to negotiate through a bullhorn five stories below.

He imagined Allison calling upward to him with tears in her eyes, pleading with him to leave it all behind and run away with her. He smiled as he thought of how enraged John Blanton would become at his act of defiance. And then he considered what it would look like to the rest of the medical community when a distraught psychiatrist locks himself in his office with no weapon and imaginary hostages. His reputation was far too important to him to jeopardize with such a rash act.

As Cormick looked around his office, he realized the order to remove his personal belongings would be an easy one to follow. There were no pictures of friends or loved ones hanging on the wall and no frames neatly arranged on the shelves. Not that there was a lack of space for such things, their absence was due to a lack of friends and loved ones in his life. And now, without his beloved hospital, there would no longer be any friendly acquaintances.

Leaning against the bookshelves, three large frames sat on the floor. Cormick slowly walked over to them and knelt for a closer look. They were his diplomas and the only items in his office that were not hospital property. He was a psychiatrist and MD from Georgetown, and a psychologist from Johns Hopkins. He nodded, trying to quietly comfort himself that credentials such as his could get him a job wherever he wanted. Unfortunately, he was leaving the only place he wanted to be.

"Dr. Proffitt?" Allison called from the door. "Is everything okay?"

"It will be," Cormick responded as he stood up. "I am having a rough week," he added, staring at the floor.

"Dr. Blanton…what he said…" she struggled to put the words together as if saying them out loud would cause her to completely break down.

Cormick lifted his eyes to meet her gaze. She was so beautiful. Even as her eyes welled with tears, he compared their soft blue hue to the spring morning sky. She had stopped talking, and the two stood motionless unable to speak.

Cormick felt his heartbeat accelerate. It was one of those life-changing moments. She was standing in front of him, vulnerable and afraid. This was the moment he could finally take her in his arms, a moment when a tender, reassuring embrace could lead to the kiss he had waited an eternity to share with Allison.

They stood a mere ten feet apart, but it may as well have been a mile. Cormick could not take the first step toward her. Even though he was sure that just taking one step would cause her to come running to him, he stood still, trying to say something to make them both feel better. As he began to speak, he felt the moment slip away.

"Allison, I am truly sorry." He hung his head and walked back to his desk. "I will, of course, write you a letter of recommendation."

"You're really leaving? But Dr. Proffitt, I…" she wanted to tell him that she loved him, but thought better of it. *If he felt the same way he would have held her*, she thought. "I don't know what I'll do without you."

"You will be fine without me," he said, knowing full well he would not be fine without her. "Bosses are a dime a dozen."

"But Dr. Proffitt…" she turned away when she heard the door to the outer office open. "Please don't leave yet," she said as she left the office.

Cormick slowly walked past his desk, dragging his fingertips gently across its high gloss surface. Keeping a safe distance from the window, he stared into the distance. The mountains to the east were bathed in morning sunlight. Beyond the mountains, on the opposite end of the country, was his family home in Maryland. He wondered if this was the impetus he needed to return.

"Hey, Cormick!" Angelo shouted from the doorway, arm-in-arm with Nurse Paige. "No fair hiding from the blind guy!"

"Angelo!" Cormick shouted, "You are safe!" The relief in his voice made him sound joyful at the sight of his patient. He moved quickly to him and helped Allison walk him to one of the wingback chairs.

"Thank you," Angelo said as he sat down. The leather beneath him was not forgiving, and the chair let out a sound that made everyone stop in their tracks momentarily. "That wasn't me," Angelo said as he blushed anyway. Allison put her hands to her lips to hide her giggle as she left the office.

"I heard you were released this morning," Cormick said as he sat behind his desk. "I apologize for that. We here at Vancouver Memorial strive to provide…"

"Save it, Cormick. You sound like a commercial," he laughed. "Listen, I know you would never kick me to the curb. Heck, you want to spend time with me so bad, you were going to commit me!"

"While I do take some comfort in finding you safe, it does not negate the fact that you are in need of professional help."

"That's why I'm here, my friend! You are my professional help!" Angelo exclaimed as he threw his arms in the air. "I need a driver!"

"That is not going to happen," Cormick responded. "But I do need you to tell me what Dr. Blanton talked to you about this morning."

"Now *that* guy is crazy," Angelo said. "You want to lock me up for my story, but you work with one of the most delusional men I've ever spoken to. Cormick, get this…he thinks you gave me drugs in exchange for pretending to be a dead man."

"Did he say anything else?" Cormick asked.

"Oh, yeah. Man, he talked forever," Angelo said shaking

his head. "And he had another doctor with him…someone with a German accent."

"Hess," Cormick said through clenched teeth.

"Yeah, that's it! Hess! Man, Cormick, that guy really has anger management issues."

"It is just his accent," Cormick responded before changing the subject. "When John…um, Dr. Blanton, released you this morning, what did he say?"

"Good luck and get lost," Angelo laughed. "But seriously, he seemed pretty anxious for me to leave. He kept asking me my name, but when I told him, he just said, 'That's not possible.'"

"Yes, well, John Blanton has never missed an opportunity to impress people with his bedside manner."

"Cormick, he wouldn't give me my wallet because he said it belonged to the dead man," Angelo said in disbelief. "I told him to look at my license, but that only made things worse. I forgot that I was clean shaven and sporting a Mohawk when I renewed my license. I laughed about it, but that Hess guy didn't think I was very funny."

"Historically, the Germans are not necessarily known for their sense of humor," Cormick responded. "I will have Nurse Paige track down and retrieve your wallet."

"Thanks, Cormick, you're a good friend."

"Angelo, I am your doctor not your friend," Cormick responded. "The things I do for you, I do because you are in my care. It is just that simple."

"Aww, Cormick…you like me. You just don't want to admit it," Angelo smiled. "Listen, if I wasn't sitting here, I'd still be sitting on the bench next to the ashtray out front, right where Dr. Blanton had security drop me. I sat down there, no money, nowhere to go…but I knew I would be safe with you. And I hate to tell you man, but I heard the sound of your voice when you saw me. You were happy. C'mon… admit it. You like me. And, like I said before, we're going to be good friends."

"Angelo, I was merely concerned for your safety," Cormick answered. "The thought that this hospital would throw a blind man out on the street without his wallet is obscene."

"You didn't say I was crazy. You only said blind," Angelo stood up and danced a little circle in front of his chair. "I'm winning you over! C'mon, Cormick, no one can resist these dance moves."

The door opened as Allison entered, followed by two security guards. The three stopped at the entrance and watched as Angelo danced in his little circle. Aware of their presence, Angelo slowly wound down and took his seat.

"Excuse me," Cormick said sternly as he got to his feet. "I am in the middle of treating a patient. Could you give us a minute?" He stared intently at the two men until they looked at one another and started to back out.

"Ten minutes," one of them called from the doorway.

"Hey, I smelled Drakkar Noir," Angelo said. "I smelled it on the rent-a-cop that plunked me on the bench downstairs. And one of those guys farted. Man, my senses are alive!"

"Angelo, our time here is short. I will have Nurse Paige locate your wallet and call around to some nearby churches to see if there is a family that can put you up until you can get back to Alaska."

"Man, God's not gonna like that," Angelo laughed.

"I finally see the roadblock in our communication. I have been unsure how best to approach you. The psychologist in me believes that this is an underlying emotional issue that can be addressed by intervention, while the psychiatrist in me wants to prescribe this problem away. But it is clear to me that I should have faced this head on with the truth, no matter how unpleasant. So here it is: There is no God," Cormick said very matter-of-factly. "There is no logical basis in fact…no evidence whatsoever that some…one of a kind *super being* created everything or even anything and even less evidence that he wants me in New Mexico."

"In that void that you call a lack of evidence," Angelo said, "is where faith exists, because faith is evidence of things that cannot be seen. And God wants us to have faith, Cormick. Faith is the point where fear and hope meet, and it gives us the strength to go on when we can't take another step. It's being sure of what we hope for but can't see. Faith is what bonds us to God—and to each other—and brings salvation."

"Salvation from what?" Cormick snapped. "Salvation from each other? You can have faith in what you believe is God, but when it comes to your fellow man, faith…well, faith is a luxury that often comes at a great price."

"What happened to you, Cormick? What great price did you pay for your faith in mankind? When did you become such a cynic?"

"I am not a cynic, Angelo. I am a realist," Cormick replied. "Now, if you would excuse me, I have a busy day ahead."

"Now, Cormick," Angelo began, "you and I both know that you don't really have a busy day."

"What makes you say that?"

"It was revealed to me by a higher power," Angelo said, smiling.

"God revealed my schedule to you?"

"Actually, it was your receptionist," Angelo replied.

Cormick looked up and smiled. "Nurse Paige does have extraordinary powers."

"Look, Cormick, we don't have a whole lot of time here. We have to be on the road by tomorrow. The others are waiting. They don't know it yet, but…"

"Angelo," Cormick said as he leaned back in his chair, "I am not going to Santa Fe with you tomorrow. I could not drive you if I wanted to. My car only has two seats, and I am certainly not going to hitch a trailer to a brand-new Mercedes."

The office door opened again, and the two security guards stepped inside the door immediately followed by Allison. One of the men tapped his watch, signaling to Cormick that it was time to go.

"Well, that does it for today, Mr. Taranto," Cormick said as he got to his feet. "Please be sure to follow up with Nurse Paige on those other matters we discussed." Cormick started to walk to the coat rack to grab his jacket when Angelo suddenly reached out and grabbed his wrist.

"I'm sorry, Cormick," he said quietly.

"Sorry? Sorry for what?" Cormick asked, just as a thunderous crash echoed up the side of the building from the parking lot. The noise from the collision below was punctuated by the sound of metal scraping along the pavement, followed by an abrupt silence.

Allison and the two guards ran to the window and looked down at the scene in the parking lot. She had both palms firmly on the glass as she stood frozen at the window, flanked by the men in uniform. Cormick stood motionless as Angelo slowly released his grip.

"Oh shit…" uttered the watch-tapping guard.

"Oh my…oh, Dr. Proffitt…" Allison began as she slowly

turned her head from the window. "It's…it's Klaus!"

"Klaus!" Cormick shrieked in horror as he ran to the window. There below lay what was once the model of advanced German engineering and now was all but unrecognizable as an automobile. The semi that had plowed squarely into the back of his beloved new car looked unscathed.

Cormick began to waver as his paralyzing vertigo took control of his mind and body. The ground five stories down seemed to rush upward and down again as his breathing grew shallow and waves of panic washed over him. He tried to retain his equilibrium as the room seemed to spin and rock out of control. His vision blurring, he stepped backward to catch himself but lost his balance. His legs gave out as he fainted and fell to the floor.

"For that," Angelo said as he sat back in his chair.

VOYAGER

Cormick stood speechless in stunned disbelief beside the twisted heap of metal that was once his beautiful car. The smell of diesel hung heavy in the air, and he could see the fuel dripping from the tank like tears of sadness. The truck that had destroyed his status symbol had since been towed, leaving no evidence of how poor Klaus had met his end.

Angelo sat quietly on a bench facing the wreck. His dark Ray-Ban sunglasses hid his eyes, and his face was completely emotionless. He wanted to speak but thought better of it. There were no words to comfort Cormick Proffitt.

"Do you see this mess?" Cormick asked. His arms were stretched forward as if he were about to hug his injured car.

"Actually, I can't see that mess," Angelo said quietly.

"But you saw it coming!" Cormick said angrily as he turned to face him. "You all but warned me that it was about to happen. How did you know this was coming?"

"You already know the answer to that, Cormick," Angelo replied. "Just be thankful that no one was hurt."

"Thankful? I should be thankful that a parked truck just mysteriously rolled down the hill and destroyed my car?" Cormick asked. "There is fifty thousand dollars of junk in my parking space!" He turned back and stared at his car. "I think I am going to be sick."

"Cormick, it's just a car, man…an inanimate object that can be easily replaced."

"Easily replaced?" Cormick shook his head and laughed. "Is that a joke?"

"It's no joke, Cormick. God is telling you what he wants from you, but you refuse to listen."

Cormick looked at the gnarled wreck, glanced up to his office window, then turned to Angelo. "That is where you are wrong," he said after a moment. "I *am* listening. Today your God told me that I do not need a job and that he hates cars."

"Oh, Cormick, that's not the message at all," Angelo said sadly. "What's it gonna take, man? What more do you need to see your destiny?"

"My destiny?" Cormick questioned. "Until you came along, I could see my fate, and let me tell you, it was wonderful! But now…now I have nothing." Cormick walked to the bench and stood directly in front of Angelo. "In less than three days there have been two car accidents, two men have lost their jobs, and you have lost your sight. You are not the messenger of the Almighty, you are a one-man wave of loss and destruction!"

Angelo patted his left hand on the bench. "Sit down Cormick. You've had a rough morning."

Dumbfounded by the lack of a suitable response, Cormick stared down at him. Angelo continued to face forward with a slight smile. Cormick did not want to sit but realized that there was little else to do while he waited for the tow truck.

"Good man," Angelo said as Cormick relented and sat down next to him. "Listen, Cormick, fate and destiny are two completely different things. Think of yourself in a poker game. Fate would be the cards you're dealt, but your destiny is how you play those cards. Understand? Losing your job and your car is fate, my friend. What you do with that is your destiny." Angelo paused for a moment and reached out to place his hand on Cormick's shoulder. "You may not believe me, but you're going to find your destiny on the very road you want to avoid taking."

Cormick leaned forward and stared at the sidewalk. He had barely heard a word Angelo said. Instead, he was remembering how good he felt when he bought his car and how miserable he was without it.

"You think your job and your car define you?" Angelo continued. "They don't, Cormick. You're defined by how you live your life not by material things. You can get another car and, when the time is right, another job. But right now, you've got more important things to do. God needs us, Cormick. God needs you."

Wallowing in self-pity, Cormick shook his head and sighed. There was no more important title, no big office, and no more Allison. Unable to see beyond what he considered the ruins of his life, he remained silent.

"I know you feel bad now, but what lies ahead of us…" Angelo paused and took in a deep, cleansing breath. "Cormick, God doesn't want you unemployed, and he certainly doesn't hate cars."

Still hunched over, Cormick turned his head to Angelo. "Then your God hates me," he said. "It appears he enjoys my suffering."

"Oh stop it, Cormick. You're not suffering," Angelo replied. "I hate to say it like this, but you're kind of being a pouty baby."

"Is that right?" Cormick retorted. "People need time to process loss and come to terms with grief. And the only cure for grief is to grieve. I am not an infant. You would be best served by leaving the psychology to me."

"Whatever you say, Cormick. But don't be such a pessimist, man. These little hardships are not obstacles, they're opportunities. God has freed you from your excuses. Since you don't have to be at work anymore…"

Cormick stood up and let out an exasperated sigh.

"I do not know how to phrase this any better or how to make my point any clearer. You say I do not listen to God, but I say you do not listen to me. There is no God. The idea of a supreme being was created by uneducated people who lacked the ability to understand the natural phenomena around them. That was fine for ancient man, but we have science. We know how the world and the universe work."

"That sun up there…that is not a god, it is a big ball of gases and nuclear fusion that one day will expand and obliterate this solar system. When it rains, it is not the mercy of some unseen deity who is responding to a human sacrifice, it is the result of condensed water vapor that falls to the Earth when it is too heavy to stay aloft." Cormick walked over to his car.

"And this mess—this fifty thousand dollar mess—was not caused by God freeing me from anything. It is the result of a failed parking brake and nothing more."

"You're wrong, Cormick," Angelo replied. "You told me that you couldn't drive us to Santa Fe because your car only had two seats. So God removed that excuse. Now you can drive Dawn and me to New Mexico in a bigger car!"

"I am not driving anyone to Santa Fe, and I am not getting a bigger car," he countered.

"Don't be so sure," Angelo said smiling.

"Excuse me," a man called as he neared them. "I'm looking for Dr. Proffitt."

Cormick turned and raised his hand to identify himself. As the man neared, he wiped the sweat from his forehead and extended his arm for a handshake. Instinctively, Cormick began to reach forward but, unnerved by the sweaty hand, slowly brought his hand to his mouth and cleared his throat.

"Good morning!" the man said boisterously as he looked at his clipboard. "I'm Tom. Tom Jones. Not that Tom Jones. But that would be nice, huh? To be Tom Jones? I get that a lot. But it's a common name. Tom…and Jones, of course. Tom Jones. It's a common name, and people remember it. You know, because of Tom Jones."

Cormick stood silent as the perspiring man walked over to examine the Mercedes. He noticed the man was sweating through his undershirt, creating damp stains on his dress shirt. The temperature was only in the mid-seventies, certainly not hot enough to cause such a sweat.

"Are you okay?" Cormick asked, concerned the man was about to have a heart attack. "Do you need to sit down?"

"Yeah, yeah, yeah. You doctors are all alike," he laughed. "The sweat, right? Tom Jones sweats, too. Ever seen him on stage? Moist. Sweaty. Soaked to the skin. But he's dancing and singing. That makes him moist. I guess I just have moist genes. Sometimes my moist genes give me moist jeans," he laughed.

"Could you not say moist so often?" Cormick asked as he grimaced. "And who are you?"

"I'm Tom. Tom Jones," he said smiling.

"Yes, we have covered that," Cormick said. "What I mean is, what do you want?"

"Wow! Is this your car? What did you do? Drop it from the roof of the hospital?" Jones laughed again. "Nah, I know you didn't. I mean how would you get it up there? Right?" he gave a little snort as he laughed again. "Car on a roof. Funny. Am I right?"

Cormick shot a glance toward Angelo who was shaking a little as he tried to control his laughter. He turned back to Jones who was flipping papers on his clipboard.

"Are you with Northwest Insurance?" Cormick asked.

"Ugh! Insurance? No! Can you imagine? Being an insurance agent? Boring, am I right? Big words like indemnity. Premiums. Annuities. I mean, what's an annuity? I don't know." Jones talked fast and gave Cormick no time to respond between his fragmented sentences and pointless questions. "Sorry. Off track there. I'm Tom, Tom Jones, with Vancouver Dodge." He walked to Cormick and removed a damp business card from his shirt pocket.

Cormick hesitated, momentarily uncomfortable about touching the card. He used his thumb and forefinger to grab it. The card read, Tom Tom Jones. Confounded by what he read, he looked up to speak but could not get a word out before Jones started talking again.

"I know what you're thinking. Tom Tom, right? Funny story. I'm on the phone ordering cards. They ask my name. I say my name is Tom, Tom Jones. The cards come and bingo-bango they say Tom Tom. You know. Like the Indian drum. Funny right? Anyway, wow. Your car. Looks new. Was it new? Looks new. What a shame. I sell cars. Not Mercedes, though. Can you imagine? Lots of money in that I bet. But I'm about American cars. Dodge has a great history. Well, Chrysler, I should say. And Plymouth. But I love Dodge. Are you a fan of muscle cars? Charger? Challenger? That's muscle!"

"I apologize, Tom Tom, uh…sorry, Tom," Cormick

began, "did my agent send you here?"

"Agent? What are you, a movie star?" Jones snorted again. "No. I know what you mean. Insurance. It's boring, but gotta have it. Am I right? Life, home, auto. But yeah. Got a call from Northwest. Looks like I beat them here. Well, wasn't hard. I'm, like, right across the street. Well, not really. Actually, same side of the street. But, you know. Close."

"Take a deep breath, Tom," Cormick said. "I am having difficulty keeping up. To be clear, Northwest Insurance sent you here to provide me with a car?"

"Yeah, yeah, yeah," he quickly replied. "A loaner. But wow. Your Benz. Ouch. You don't need a tow truck, you need a crane!" he exclaimed, snorting again.

Cormick dreaded the snort. Each time Jones did it, a little bead of sweat on the end on his nose was vacuumed into his right nostril only to slowly drip out again. Watching it made him queasy.

"I am sure there are papers to sign, so why not let me get started on that while you bring my car around."

Jones handed him the clipboard and a pen from his soggy pocket. Cormick took them from his clammy grasp and looked them over. Jones reached across and tapped the bottom of the paper, leaving a wet spot. "Just sign there!" Cormick complied with the order and handed the paperwork and the pen back to him.

"Keep the pen! Free advertising for me," Jones said as he snorted. This time the droplet of perspiration fell from the tip of his nose and landed on the paperwork.

"I will pass on that," Cormick said as he forced a smile and handed the pen back. "Trust me, I will remember you."

"It's the name right? Tom Jones. Who could forget? Sometimes, when women come car shopping, I say, 'What's new, pussycat?' Get it? Like Tom Jones? They love it. I give 'em a deal if they're foxy. Know what I mean? I like blondes. Who doesn't, am I right?" he snorted again. "Never had a redhead. Kinda scary. I don't know any redheads. They seem scary. My buddy calls them gingers. Weird, right? Ginger isn't red. It's brown. Wait! Gilligan's Island! Ginger Grant! Hey, did they do that on purpose? Whaddaya think?"

Exhausted by the lopsided conversation, Cormick nodded but did not respond. He was sure that any comment he made would send the salesman off on another tangent. He thought of Dawn and silently agreed that redheads were scary.

"Perhaps you could just show me to my car?"

"I can bring it around. Wait here. I'll be right back!"

"No!" Cormick exclaimed. "I mean…no, thank you." He dreaded the thought of the diaphoretic man drenching the driver's seat with his bodily fluids. "Why not just take me to the car?"

"Sure thing! Is your friend coming? Wow! Nice sunglasses. Ray-Bans? I'm a Vuarnet man, myself. They look good though. Nice beard. You don't see a lot of full beards any more. Kind of a seventies thing. They may come back. Who knows? Am I right? I can't grow one. Good thing, though. Might make me sweat more. Moist genes, you know."

"Yes, I know," Cormick responded. "My friend is staying here. Now, if you would be so kind as to show me to my car."

"It's more than a car!" Jones said as he snorted. "Follow me. Are you excited? It's like Christmas, right? I mean you won't be unwrapping it or anything, but it's a surprise! So exciting! Man, I love selling cars. Maybe you could give your doctor friends my card. Doctors are good customers."

Cormick followed Jones quietly, anxious for the conversation to end. The man talked so fast Cormick felt dizzy. As
he walked behind him, he realized that he had stopped listening to the long-winded salesman. Jones stopped abruptly
and threw his arms out.

"Ta-dah! Here it is! What a beauty. Am I right?"

Cormick stood there, unable to utter a single syllable.
He stared at the car in front of him then looked in every
direction for a luxury sedan he had been expecting. It
dawned on him that the car in front of him was what Jones
had delivered.

He turned and made eye contact with Jones as he
pointed to the car. "There must be some mistake," he said.

"No mistake!" Jones replied. "This is what the order said.
Other doctors see you in this and BAM! Jealous! Before
you know it, this parking lot will be full of them! She's a
beauty. Am I right?"

Cormick turned and faced the powder-blue minivan in
front of him. He closed his eyes tightly and counted to three.
When he opened his eyes, the van was still there.

"It's a Voyager! Awesome. Am I right? Awesome. Seats
six comfortably, but you can squeeze eight in here if you
need to. More than that if it's kids. Not enough seatbelts
for that, though. Who cares? Am I right? Got kids? I don't.
Can't find the right woman. I'm picky. Gotta be blonde."

"I am not taking this car," Cormick said. "I am not driving a minivan. There must be some mistake."

"No mistake!" Jones repeated. "Listen, this is the king of
minivans. Chrysler invented the minivan. 1983. Did you
know that? They know what they're doing when it comes
to minivans. Women will love you in this! You know what
this says? Stability. Confidence. Ready for kids. All things

women love. Am I right? Power windows!"

"I want a different car. I do not want a van, mini or otherwise," Cormick said calmly but firmly. "I want a car. Do you understand? I realize that Chrysler is not known for luxury automobiles, but I want you to take this back and, at the very least, return with a New Yorker."

"Yeah, yeah, yeah. I hear what you're saying. I get it. I read you loud and clear. But this is it. Last loaner on the lot. Saved the best for last, though. Am I right? Huh? Give her a chance. She's a beauty! Your chariot awaits! Ride her to glory!"

"What did you say?" Cormick demanded.

"Your chariot awaits!" Jones repeated as he tossed the keys to Cormick. "Listen, show your friend. He'll love it! Little secret…this is a chick magnet! Roomy enough for you and your buddy to pick up four chicks! Keep redheads in the back. They're scary. My buddy says they have no souls." Jones snorted and laughed. "Listen, I gotta go. You've got my card. Trust me. Drive this today, you'll come to me begging to buy one!"

Jones reached out and patted Cormick's upper arm, leaving a wet palm print behind as he turned and left. Cormick looked at the keys in his hand and shook his head. Looking back at the bench, he could see Angelo sitting quietly. Cormick hung his head and walked to the driver's side.

He got in the Voyager and put the key in the ignition. The van had the smell of an Ozium air freshener, unlike the smell of soft leather to which he had grown accustom. The blue-on-blue cloth interior was a far cry from the rich black leather interior he loved so dearly. He looked down at the stereo that played cassettes and shook his head. It was just one more indignity.

Overcome by guilt, he drove to Angelo who had not moved an inch. He got out and walked over to him.

"Do you have a place to stay?" he asked. "I cannot leave a blind man stranded on the sidewalk."

"I thought you'd never ask! I hope dinner is included!" Angelo said as he jumped to his feet. "Hey, how much coke do you think that guy snorted on his way here? Am I right?" Angelo asked, mocking Jones. "Wait, we can't leave. What about the tow truck?"

"I do not even care," Cormick said dejectedly. "I will just wait for the check in the mail. Oddly, I take some comfort in knowing I am leaving that mess for Blanton to clean up," Cormick said as he carefully helped Angelo into the passenger seat and handed him the seat belt.

He shut the door and turned to glance up to the fifth floor, hoping to see Allison gazing down at him. The windows reflected the morning sky and nothing else. He knew that his administrative leave was just a formality that would ultimately lead to his termination. Dejected and depressed, he let out a mournful sigh as he walked around the van and crawled into the driver's seat.

"Smells brand new in here. What is it?" Angelo asked.

"It is a nightmare," Cormick said as he guided the van out of the parking lot, leaving Vancouver Memorial in the rearview mirror.

⁓⁓

Cormick unlocked the door to his condo and reached in to flick on the light. He turned back toward Angelo and gently grabbed him by the upper arm to lead him inside to the sofa.

"I would show you around," he began, "but…"

"Cormick! Did you just make a joke?" Angelo laughed.

"It's good to hear you're loosening up."

"I do not know if I am loosening up or giving up," Cormick said as he walked to the kitchen. "I do know, however, that I could use a glass of wine. Would you like one?" he asked as he twisted the corkscrew into the bottle.

"I don't need to be asked twice!" Angelo exclaimed.

Cormick filled each wine glass and walked to the leather chair adjacent to the couch.

"Reach forward," he said, and Angelo eagerly complied. He placed the glass in his hand and sat back. "There is a table to the right of you if you need to put the glass down. Please be careful. The couch is white."

"Maybe I should have sat in the leather chair," Angelo said as he took a drink.

"How did you know...?"

"I heard you sit down. I hear everything! Man, Cormick, all of my senses are heightened!"

"What about your sense of reality?"

"Was that another joke?" Angelo said with a smile. "I knew you had a sense of humor. You just hide it under your doctor clothes."

"I hate to disappoint you, Angelo. I find there is little to laugh about right now," Cormick said as he stared into his glass of Cabernet. "I have lost everything." He was relieved Angelo could not see the look on his face. He wanted to blame him for everything. His life had been perfect until this fisherman appeared to turn it all upside down.

"Look, Cormick. I don't want to be a dick, but you have to stop your whining. Believe me, I know how you feel. I thought I lost everything, too. But now I have something to believe in...something greater than myself."

"I do not believe in God," he said firmly. "Perhaps you are

clinging to this notion of God because of just that. People tend to seek out religion when they are at their weakest." He noticed that Angelo had hastily emptied his glass. "More wine?" Cormick asked as he stood to pour.

"First of all, I'm not seeking religion," he said. "Second of all, just bring the bottle over here." Angelo reached his glass forward. "You know Cormick, you lost a job and a car. Both of those can be replaced easily by a guy like you."

Cormick held Angelo's glass as he poured the wine.

"And you?" Cormick asked as he returned to his chair. "What have you lost?"

"I'm losing income every day that I'm down here. I've lost a lot in life, just like every other guy out there. I've lost my parents, I've lost my sight, hell, I've even lost my heart. I was married once, you know." Angelo began. "Man, she was so beautiful. She had silky blonde hair, eyes that were blue as the ocean but looked as green as emeralds in dim light. She always smelled like springtime. Man, Cormick, I was so in love." Angelo paused for a drink, but the lump in his throat made it difficult to swallow. He shook his head slowly.

"We had a house in Seattle. The mortgage was insane so I let my best friend Donny rent out the basement. Almost immediately he hurts his back on the job and can't work. There were some delays in workers comp, so there I am, paying his rent. It was tough. I had to pay his bills along with mine. Not exactly what I signed up for."

"And you lost the house?" Cormick interrupted.

"I thought you guys were supposed to listen to people," Angelo said with a slight smile. "Anyway, I came home early one day and called for my wife. She came out of the basement in just her robe. It was surreal, man. I asked her why she was down there half dressed with Donny. She told me he needed a backrub because of the pain, and she had gone down to give him a massage. I called her out on that bullshit, and man…she tore into me! Made me doubt what I knew was true. Man, was I blind."

Angelo paused and a moment passed before they started laughing.

"Little has changed," Cormick pointed out.

"Yeah…" Angelo said as his laughter quieted. "But then, I woke up one night, and I was alone in bed. I walked downstairs, and I could hear them through the vent, talking in the basement. She was begging him to be with her. I heard her tell him that she was in love with him. He had found a girlfriend, but my wife wanted him to stay in our house so she could have it all. Man, Cormick, it ripped my guts out. I never confronted her. I lived the next several months knowing that my wife didn't love me. Sex became nonexistent for us. We were practically newlyweds, and all of her passion and emotion went to another man."

Cormick remained silent as Angelo paused. He noticed a tear slowly fall from behind his dark glasses. He said nothing.

"Turns out, every time I left Puget Sound for Alaska, he not only lived in my house, he ate my food, drove my car, and made love to my wife. It had been going on for almost a year." He let out a mournful sigh, and wiped his cheek. "And one day she tells me she wants a divorce. Tells me that she thinks I'm cheating when I'm out crabbing. You know what I did? Nothing," he said as he slowly shook his head from side to side.

"I never said a word about what I knew to be true. I still loved her. As pathetic as that sounds, I loved her too much to hurt her with the truth. I couldn't eat or sleep. The images haunted me in my dreams. It was a slow torture I couldn't escape."

Cormick had not noticed, but Angelo had managed to finish his second glass of wine as he spoke. Angelo reached his empty glass forward, and Cormick filled it for him.

"She got everything. The house, the car, the guy…hell, she even tried to get my boat. She claimed emotional distress for my infidelities. But I never strayed. I wanted to cheat, don't get me wrong. But my heart just wouldn't let me. I kept my boat but lost my dignity. It was humiliating."

"Angelo," Cormick began as he leaned forward, "I am so sorry."

"Yep…me too. It gets better, though. She flew up to Dutch about a year or so after the divorce to tell me he had left her for another woman. Seems he had been sleeping with someone else the whole time they were together. And as I sat there listening to her heartache, watching her wipe the tears from her eyes, I actually felt bad for her. How ridiculous is that? My heart was literally breaking for her. I wanted to cry because I never, ever wanted her to shed a tear. Even with everything that had happened, I felt sorry for her.

"She asked me to get back together. The one thing I wanted most in life—even after everything that had happened—was to be with her. So, I agreed. I went back. Within a year, she had found another man, and the cycle repeated itself. Man, I am so fucking pathetic."

"No, no you are not," Cormick replied. "Your reaction is not uncommon in relationships. Often times…"

"Cormick, I'm not telling you this for psychoanalysis, I'm telling you because I know what loss is. I know what heartache is. It's not like losing a car or a job." Angelo sat back and aimed his face at the ceiling. "I've lost a lot in thirty-one years, Cormick, but I've never lost hope."

"I am going to open another bottle of wine," Cormick said as he poured the last drop into Angelo's glass.

Neither man spoke a word as Cormick looked for a wine he could properly pair with the Cabernet they had just finished. Finding a suitable vintage, he grabbed two new glasses and headed to the living room. A fresh bottle required clean glasses. That was non-negotiable.

"I know heartache," Cormick said as he set the glasses down and poured the wine. "I understand pain and loss. It is why I am where I am today."

"Tell me, Cormick. Tell me about your pain," Angelo said quietly. "You're off the clock. You can come out from behind that rigid facade of yours."

"I do not share my pain. It is my burden to bear," Cormick said as he sipped from his glass.

"It's time, then. It's time to unburden yourself," Angelo said. "What would a psychologist say about the need to purge the poison from your brain? Maybe we could find one and ask."

Cormick looked at the stranger on his couch. He was confident Angelo needed emotional help, perhaps even antipsychotic medication. But there was something about him. Cormick had never seen his eyes and wondered if they were as kind as his face or as comforting as his voice.

"Granted, the cathartic effects of a patient…"

"Stop it, Cormick. Just stop. Neither one of us is a patient right now. We're just two guys…two friends getting to know each other and talking about their past. There is no analysis or judgement. We're just two friends, sharing stories and a damn good bottle of wine." Angelo smiled and tossed back what was left in his glass.

"My story is very dark, Angelo. The pain I carry cuts very deep and is not isolated to one circumstance. I have locked it all away. I have successfully accepted and dealt with it."

Angelo leaned forward with his hand outstretched.

"Give me your hand," he said.

Cormick stared at his calloused palm. Angelo had several old scars on his hand from years of working on the Bering Sea. They were a stark contrast to Cormick's soft hand and perfectly manicured fingers.

"Give me your hand, Cormick," he repeated. "Trust me."

Cormick grudgingly reached forward and grasped Angelo's hand. He made it a point to avoid human contact, especially with a patient. He was uncomfortable at first but slowly relaxed.

"Take a deep, cleansing breath, Cormick," Angelo said as he held his hand. "Clear your mind. I want you to think about your pain. I want you to open up to me and share your feelings. You spend every day asking others to reveal themselves to you but you reveal yourself to no one. You must be so lonely. But you don't have to be lonely anymore."

Cormick was disarmed by the experience, unable to understand the sudden need to reveal the scars on his soul. His secrets had been buried for decades. He had never sought professional help or openly shared the trauma he had suffered when he was young. Instead, he became what he needed most in his own life. But holding Angelo's hand and listening to his compassionate plea, he began to weaken.

Without warning, he quickly pulled his hand free.

"You are asking me to do something I cannot do." He stood up and took a drink from his glass. "Please believe me, I do not wish to minimize anything you have gone through. My past is disturbing, even frightening. I have spent years studying so that I could heal myself. Is that not how the old saying goes? Physician heal thyself?"

"Cormick, I'm not a doctor, I'm just a fisherman. I'm not here to heal you, I'm here to help you. This is part of the plan. God wants you to release your pain."

"There is no God!" Cormick yelled. "If there was, he would have intervened." Cormick reached for the bottle and refilled his glass. He emptied it into his system just as quick as he had poured it, and filled it again. "I believed in God once," he said as he began to slowly pace in front of the couch. "I was a good Catholic boy. God turned his back on me."

"That's not true, Cormick. Everything happens for a reason," Angelo replied. "Everything we do, every decision we make, brings us to this moment. Without your pain…"

"Without my pain, I would probably be a priest. I would have devoted my life to God at one point."

Cormick sat back down and hung his head. He had come too far to stop talking now. The memories battered his brain like a fierce storm. He tried to hold back, but he was at an emotional breaking point.

"When I was twelve, I told my priest that I felt the spirit of the Lord moving through me," Cormick began. "I told him I was willing to devote my entire life to the service of the Lord. He asked me to his room to discuss what that meant. It was then that this man of God, the man I looked up to most and respected, who should have been there to nurture and protect me, did unspeakable things to an innocent child. I learned then that there is no God."

"Oh, Cormick…" Angelo whispered.

"I am lucky, I suppose," Cormick sighed. "I came to terms with it immediately. I have treated men my age and older who have suffered in their relationships and careers because of such trauma. Most victims battle one form of addiction or another." Cormick stared at the floor. "Yes, I am the lucky one."

"Cormick, I'm sorry, man," Angelo said tenderly. "But God didn't hurt you. A man hurt you."

"I am aware that it was a pedophile, not God, who harmed me. He was a servant of the Lord, and I was in the house of God. At twelve years old, it was impossible to distinguish the difference." Cormick reached for the wine bottle and refilled their glasses. "I lost my faith that day. And God lost me."

"You never told anyone?" Angelo asked.

"I told my mother," Cormick began, "but one of the other things I didn't understand at twelve, is what bipolar-type Schizoaffective Disorder means." Cormick sipped from his glass and paused for a moment to collect his thoughts.

"I'm not sure I understand what it means at thirty-one," Angelo said.

"In lay terms, it means my mother needed help that simply was not available in 1960," Cormick said sadly. "She was prone to manic episodes and wild mood swings. She struggled everyday of her adult life, swinging wildly from violent anger to deep depression. In the blink of an eye she could go from being the life of the party to a suicidal monster."

"What did she do when you told her about the priest?"

"She blamed me, of course," Cormick said. "She told me that I had given myself over to Satan and that I had seduced Father Thomas. In her state of mind, he was the victim."

Cormick got up and began to methodically pace once again as he replayed his childhood in his mind.

"When I refused to go back to Saint Peters, she held me by my feet from the third floor balcony and shook me to try to scare the devil out of me. When that failed, she locked me in a small crawlspace with no light. None of the servants were allowed to feed me or help me in any way. The result was crippling claustrophobia and paralyzing acrophobia."

"What about your Dad?" Angelo queried. "Where was he?"

"My father owned businesses in several countries. I remember seeing him every Christmas and at odd times during the year," Cormick smiled as he reminisced about him. "He was a kind man—a good and decent man. Unfortunately, he was also a very busy man. When he finally witnessed just how disturbed my mother was…" he trailed off as he stopped pacing and stared at the carpet.

"What happened?" Angelo asked eagerly.

"It was Christmas morning in 1960. My father and I were listening to Bing Crosby as we sat together on the couch… and my mother entered the room with a gun. She told my father that I was possessed by a demon and that the only way to save me was to kill me and release the demon. She called me the Charioteer and said the bullet would allow me to 'ride to glory.'"

Cormick sipped from his glass as he moved to the couch and sat next to Angelo.

"My father stood in the line of fire. He was willing to take that bullet for me. I cannot recall a single word the two of them spoke after that. I do remember my mother screaming and my father talking calmly until he saw his moment and disarmed her."

"Thank God," Angelo said, letting out a deep breath. "I was afraid that was going to end a lot differently."

"It eventually did," Cormick said. "That night a doctor came to the house and sedated my mother. From what I understand, he and my father made arrangements to have my mother committed to a sanitarium. The next day he put her in the car and told me he would see me in a few hours. He promised me that I would never feel pain ever again," Cormick said as his voice began to quiver. "He hugged me and kissed me on the cheek and drove away from the estate. I never saw either of them again."

Cormick swallowed hard to force the lump in his throat downward. He rubbed his eyes with his thumb and forefinger, setting free the tears welling in his eyes.

"What happened? Why didn't he come back?" Angelo pleaded for an answer.

"According to the Maryland State Police, my mother shot him in the head while he was driving outside of Annapolis. She died shortly after the accident," Cormick said stoically as he regained his composure. "I am a product of my childhood. I work every day to prevent tragedy. I try to be the voice of sanity and reason, but I fear I am little more than a frightened, broken man."

The two men sat quietly and drank their wine. Angelo searched for words of comfort but found none. Cormick replayed memories of his beloved father in his mind but could not remember more than a dozen interactions.

"I have never shared that much with anyone," he said, breaking the silence. "I do—as you so astutely indicated— have a rigid facade. It is important to approach the issues my patients face in a logical and analytical manner. Therefore, to be the strength my patient's need to heal, I keep my pain hidden."

"What about empathy, Cormick? Don't you think your

patients would benefit more if you related to them with your experiences?"

"I do have empathy," Cormick said, "or you would still be sitting on the bench outside the hospital. And my experiences are my own. I may not have had a demon inside of me when I was twelve, but I am haunted by my demons at forty-two. No one can benefit from my pain."

"That's not true," Angelo said. "I've benefitted. I've learned something. That's what it's all about, right?"

"I do not understand," Cormick said wearily.

"Think about it, man," Angelo said excitedly. "I've learned that I can survive if you can, because, wow, you have fought battles that, before today, I could have not imagined. I've learned about you, and—like I told you when we met—we've become friends. I'm honored to know you, man. You have to feel better letting go of that burden. No one should face all of that alone. And I'm not sure, but I think I just learned that you're rich!"

Cormick felt light headed. He looked over at the wine bottle and realized they had finished it.

"I believe I have had a little too much to drink," he said. "I should make us some dinner." He got up and headed to the kitchen. He pulled his apron from the pantry hook and tied it tight in a perfect bow. "I have some very nice cuts of filet mignon. I hope that is acceptable."

"Honestly, man…I'm a burger-and-fries kinda guy, but I can make the sacrifice just this once," Angelo replied as a broad smile spread across his face. As it slowly faded, he changed the subject.

"You're coming with me tomorrow, Cormick. We're going to find our answers. There's nothing holding you back any more."

Cormick placed his hands on the counter and let his head fall forward. Shaking his head, he let out a frustrated sigh. "Angelo, while it is true that our conversation has provided me with some abreaction, it has not suddenly changed my views on God."

"Fine, then don't do it because it's God's will. Do it because we're friends, and I need you to drive me. C'mon man, I'm blind, for the love of God!" Angelo stopped and laughed. "No pun intended."

Cormick stared into the living room at Angelo. The man was wearing him down. He was defeated and exhausted.

"I will make you a promise," he said. "You say that God talks to you, and he gives you signs. You tell him that I need a sign. I am not going to instantaneously change who I have been for three decades because we shared some wine and heartache."

"What more do you need, Cormick?" Angelo asked incredulously.

"I do not know," he replied. "But I need a reason to drive two thousand miles. You told me there are others, why are they not here with us right now? That would be a good sign." He turned and opened the refrigerator and reached for the beef he was about to prepare. Before he could turn around, the doorbell rang.

Cormick walked to the door to open it but stopped just short. He looked back at Angelo, who was smiling on the couch. He turned back to the door and opened it to find Dawn Gallagher standing there with a large brown bag cradled in her arms.

"Who wants Chinese?" she asked boisterously.

THE CHARIOTEER

Horace wiped the oil from his hands as he walked out of his garage. Ten years earlier, he had added on to the structure and, ever since, had managed a modest living working on cars. But today he was in it for himself.

The 1965 Galaxy 500 convertible had been his pride and joy when he was a teenager. It was a gift from his father, given to Horace in anticipation of his sixteenth birthday, though his father would not live the next six months to celebrate the milestone. The car had been parked in the garage the day before Horace shipped out for Vietnam and had lain there, hidden, for more than twenty years.

He walked to his backyard and looked out over the calm Pacific. Tucking the rag into the left back pocket of his coveralls, he lit a cigarette and exhaled into the ocean air. The sands below were filled with bodies bronzed by the early summer sun, and the beach was littered with surfboards that brought back memories of his youth. A slight smile curled one corner of his lips.

He reached into his right back pocket and pulled out a pint of whiskey, which contained more air than liquid. He looked at what was left and knew he could finish it quickly. Using only his thumb, he deftly spun the cap off, sending the screw top flying into the grass. He pressed the bottle against his lips and with two large swigs, swallowed half of what was left.

He sat down in a weathered Adirondack chair, one of two his mother had purchased after his father's death. She placed the chairs in the back yard facing the ocean. His mother would spend every evening she was physically able to, watching the sunset and talking to the empty chair. Roy Jordan had been the love of her life, and she was determined that not even death would take their sunsets from them. Now, Horace sat in his father's chair and, on occasion, spent sunsets talking to his mother's empty chair.

He let his head fall backward so the afternoon sun could bathe his face in warmth. He had imagined Elaine sitting with him in those chairs one day, but it was too late for that now. He gulped the last drink of whiskey, dropped his spent butt into the bottle, and let it fall from his hands to the dry grass below. He considered his options for the afternoon and decided that a short nap would be the best way to start.

"Dude!" Sayer laughed as he stepped in front of his brother, eclipsing the sun. "Are you sleeping?"

"No…I'm napping," he replied, not moving or opening his eyes. "There's a difference. Sleeping is what you do at night, napping is what you do before you go to the liquor store."

"Gotcha," Sayer said as he looked around at nothing in particular. "You know bro', you totally oughta blow the dust off your board and shred some waves with me. You are like a legend!"

Horace let his head slowly roll to the side to face his brother and opened one eye.

"We go over this every day, Sayer," he said wearily. "I'm too fucking old. There's no way I could maneuver out there anymore. They would call me a fucking Grey Belly! I'd do a fucking rock dance for chrissake! I'd go from legend to laughingstock in a matter of seconds."

"Why do you do that?" Sayer asked. "You always take a big dump on anything positive I say."

Horace let out a long and labored sigh as he sat up and turned to face his brother.

"I don't, Sayer. I believe in you. I'm just tired, man."

"No, dude…you've given up," Sayer replied. "You can't keep hurting yourself like this. You're gonna die, bro'. You drink way too much. You smoke more than anyone around. You're always in fights. You gotta chill out…you're all I have left."

Horace slapped his palms on his knees and stood up.

"Sayer…" he began as he placed his hand on his brother's shoulder. He thought for a brief moment that this might be the time to tell him about the cancer but thought better of it. "You're all I have, too. C'mon…let me show you something." He put his arm around his brother and walked him toward the garage.

When the two men reached the entrance, Horace let his arm slip from Sayer's shoulder. He walked toward the Galaxy, running his hand across the front fender as he passed by the car like he was caressing a woman. After a brief pause, he turned to face Sayer, who was still standing in the doorway with his mouth open.

"Dude, your car!" he exclaimed as he walked in the garage. He placed his hands on the hood. "You're fixing the Galaxy! This car is totally bitchin'."

"Yeah, the body's still straight, the paint is in great shape. I figured, what the hell? Right? I can get her running again," he said proudly. "Of course, I'll have to find a new home for the fucking squirrels that live in the air cleaner."

"This is amazing! When I was little, I used to peek under

the tarp, and sometimes, I would even sit behind the wheel and pretend to be cool like you."

Sayer walked around to the passenger side and looked in. The gold interior, beneath the dust, was undamaged.

"I can't wait to see you drive this baby around. Hey, promise me the first ride!"

"You'll get the first ride," he said smiling. "I'm fixing it for you. It's your car now, little brother."

Looking his own mortality in the face, Horace was working to make sure his brother would be taken care of after he was gone. With sixteen years separating them, Sayer was not only his brother and best friend, he was like a son to him. He had cared for him when his mother was no longer able, and he was worried about leaving him alone. Sayer wasn't the most intelligent person he knew, and he wondered if he had given him all of the necessary life skills to do more than surf and screw.

"Dude, no way," Sayer said as he took two steps back with his hands in the air. "I can't take this. It's from Dad. It's your car."

"You can and you will," he replied. He walked around to the passenger side of the car and leaned back against the front fender as he folded his arms. "Dad may have been gone before you were born, but he loved you, Sayer. Dad was excited about teaching you how to ride a bike, play baseball…he talked about you with tears in his eyes before you were even born. He would be proud of you today. And since he can't be here to give you your first car, I can give you a car he bought for his kid."

"Dude, that's so awesome," he said as he embraced his big brother. The two men held each other tight. "I love you, bro.'"

Horace nodded but did not respond. He had said the

words a thousand times to his brother, but he feared that saying them now would reduce him to tears. He really wasn't sure how long he had left, but he was sure he wanted as many moments like this as he could fit into his remaining time.

Sayer released his grasp and stepped back to look at the car again.

"I guess it'll be a while, though," he said. "Not just because we gotta do stuff for God. People bring their cars here all the time."

"Business has slowed a bit," Horace replied. "People are kind of avoiding us right now."

"What? Dude, you are, like, the best mechanic around!"

"Sayer, it's about the stuff you say about God. People… people think you're a little out there. They're nervous about coming by."

"Whaddaya sayin'?" he asked. "People think I'm crazy? Do you think I'm crazy? 'Cause, I'm not, Horace. And the people on the beach don't think so either. They believe me. They know that God is speaking to me." He looked at his brother with a pleading look in his eye. "Do you think I'm crazy, Horace?"

"Sayer, you are my brother, and I love you," he said as he approached him. "Honestly, I'm a little uncomfortable with all this God stuff. But I don't think you're crazy. I've got your back. I will do whatever it takes. If you want me to go to Santa Fe with you, I will."

Sayer shot a sad glance to his brother and slowly walked toward the door.

"I'm sorry about the business, bro'. I really am," he said staring out into the yard. "I'm not trying to hurt you."

"I know, Sayer," Horace said quietly. "It isn't in you to

hurt another person. And I don't care if business slows. I say fuck 'em. I'm just worried that…"

"That I'll get hurt?" Sayer asked as he turned to face his brother. "I won't. God needs me, dude. He told me that I am the Carpenter. I'm totally God's woodworker! And no one can hurt me. I have a mission. And so do you big brother. He's reaching out to both of us. Nothing can harm us until we have completed our mission for God."

"Sayer, I'm with you no matter what," Horace replied as he walked toward him. "If there's no work here, then I guess all that means is I have more time to be with you." He smiled at him, and nodded his head reassuringly. "But God's gonna have to give me a little free time to fix your new car here."

Sayer walked over to the car and ran his fingers across the fender just as Horace had done.

"God will give us time. But not right now. The others… they're coming, bro'. We have to get ready. They'll be here tomorrow night."

"Who's coming Sayer? Huh?" Horace asked. "Who are these people? Where are they coming from?" Horace said as he looked around the garage.

"Dude, I don't know who they are or where they're at now. But they are following God's voice, and they will be here tomorrow." Sayer looked up toward the ceiling and stared. "It's gonna be huge. God hasn't told me everything yet, but it's gonna be bitchin', man."

"How will they find us?" Horace asked. "If you don't know who they are, how do they know who we are?" Horace walked around the car to his brother. "Look," he said gently grabbing him by the upper arms, "we can leave right now. We can pack our bags, drop a dozen bowls of cat food down, and head to Santa Fe. Just you and I. The Bonneville will make the trip."

"That sounds cool, big brother, it really does. But that's just not the plan," he said with a pleasant smile. "We should pack tonight. Tomorrow morning the waves are gonna be crankin', and I'm gonna shred the shit outta them!" He slapped Horace on the back and started to walk toward the house.

"Wait!" Horace called. "Are they meeting you on the beach tomorrow?"

"I don't know, bro," he answered as he continued forward. "God says they'll find us if we do like we do. You know, just lead a normal life!"

Horace watched his brother walk to the porch. He thought about it for a minute and ran to the garage door and called to Sayer.

"What the fuck is a normal life?"

—⁓⁓—

Cormick watched from the kitchen as Dawn and Angelo laughed and joked while eating their takeout food from white and red cartons. The idea of eating to-go Chinese food nearly brought him to the point of nausea. Watching a blind man eat with chopsticks while sitting on his white sofa did not do his stomach any favors, either. The thought of an uninvited guest in his home unnerved him almost as much as the MSG-laden toxic waste they were shoveling in their faces.

"Excuse me," Cormick said. "I hate to interrupt your party, but how did you know where I lived?"

"Ever heard of the phone book?" Dawn quipped. "I just looked up Mr. Pretentious and *voila*! Here I am." She looked over at Cormick. "Now, come over here and get a bite to eat. We have a lot to talk about."

"I cannot eat that food," Cormick said.

"Here," Dawn said as she threw a fortune cookie him. "Eat that."

Cormick cracked the dry cookie open and nibbled on it. It tasted stale, and he was sure the sweet aftertaste was not any form of natural sugar. His curled lip made his distaste obvious.

"What's your fortune say, Cormick?" she asked.

"It says I am about to make a big mistake," he replied.

"Oh for the love of God, quit pouting and get over here," she demanded.

Cormick unenthusiastically did as he was told. He looked at the mess they had made in his living room and stared at Dawn's suitcase. He realized events were spiraling out of his control.

"Are you moving in?" he asked.

"Oh, Cormick," she began, "may I call you Cormick? It really doesn't matter, because I'm going to anyway." She bit the head off of a deep fried shrimp and smiled at Cormick as she chewed. "It's really time to stop pretending this isn't going to happen. Angelo has told me everything. Now, you seem like an educated man; so tell me, what possible excuse could you have for not going to Santa Fe other than you simply don't want to?"

Cormick looked at her, his face completely expressionless. That was exactly his excuse. He knew that he could easily concede to her that there was enough circumstantial evidence to suggest something beyond a coincidence, but he refused to openly take that leap with them.

"Okay," Dawn said after a sustained silence. "Easier question…is this a condo or a monastery?"

"I am sorry," he replied, "what did you just ask me?" He looked around at the uncluttered walls and his tastefully expensive furniture, then back to her. He heard Angelo trying to suppress his laughter. "Do you, as an uninvited guest, take exception with the decor of my home?"

"What decor?" she asked. "There are no pictures, knick-knacks…Cormick, do you even own a TV?"

"I do not," he responded. "I believe that television plays to the lowest common denominator of the populace. I have a very nice stereo and an extensive collection of record albums."

"What do you do, man?" Angelo asked, bewildered by what he had just heard. "I'm being totally serious. What do you do when you're relaxing at home?"

"I read, listen to classical music, review notes from sessions…" he trailed off as he looked at their faces.

"What?" he asked. "The both of you act is if one could not survive without the aid and comfort of a situation comedy filled with adolescent sexual tension or some ridiculous soap opera in which lonely housewives live vicariously through the exaggerated dramatic fantasies created by an actress who gets married every year to a different rich man on the program. And no, I do not know this first hand. I am forced to follow the exploits of afternoon television as I stand in line for groceries at the market."

"Cormick, man…what do you do for fun?" Angelo asked.

"Why, exactly, are we here today?" Cormick asked. He was noticeably agitated. "Did you come here seeking my assistance or to insult my taste in interior design?"

"We're sorry, Cormick," Angelo said. "We need your help."

As Angelo raised his chopsticks to his mouth, the greasy, orange piece of sweet and sour chicken slipped from the grasp of the sticks. Cormick watched it fall in slow motion to the white cushion between Angelo's legs and bounce to the carpet below. Dawn saw the whole thing as well, watching wide eyed and mouth agape as the poultry splashed and stained everything it touched on the way to its final resting place. She shot a quick look at a horrified Cormick and flashed a devilish smile.

Angelo guided the chopsticks to his mouth and bit down on the wooden ends.

"Huh…I thought I had some food. I guess I'm not as good at this as I thought," he laughed as he buried the sticks back into the box for another piece of chicken.

"No…no you are not," Cormick said as he lowered his head and shook it slowly from side to side.

"Cormick, like I said before, it's time to get going," Dawn reminded him. "You can't deny this any longer."

"Miss Gallagher, Dawn," Cormick began, "I do not believe in God. Therefore it is difficult for me to accept that God is speaking directly to the both of you. I have heard no voice. I feel no compulsion to go to Santa Fe. I can assure you, whatever you may believe is down there waiting for you, it is not God."

"But doesn't it strike you as odd that there is a fusion of cultural and religious beliefs centered in and around the area that we're being called to?" asked Dawn. 'Jesus and Poseyemu exist in cultures that are worlds apart. Yet, both were born after their virgin mother was mystically impregnated. Both were exceptional children who matured intellectually and spiritually at rapid rates and begin debating religious tenets with their elders. And both left their followers with a promise to return, offering all the rewards of God. There simply has to be something to this, Cormick."

"I understand everything you are saying," he replied. "The similarities are striking. Nonetheless, two questions still remain: how can you be sure this confluence of beliefs was not a result of the Spanish incursion, and what does it mean for us?"

"The legend predates the arrival of the Franciscans, and I don't know what it means for us," Dawn said. "But I want to find out. Where is your intellectual curiosity?"

"I hate to interrupt," Angelo interjected, "but is there any more General Tso's chicken?"

Dawn searched the containers and handed him the chicken.

"You might want to hold the carton under your chin. You know, just in case."

"Just in case of what? I've done alright so far, haven't I?" he confidently asked.

Dawn looked at the stains that dotted his jeans and the cushion and leaned toward Angelo to look at the orange puddle on the floor.

"You're doing just fine, honey," she laughed.

"Listen," Cormick said, "I have intellectual curiosity. I do, in fact, believe that the myth you describe bears a striking resemblance to Jesus as an historical figure. That being said, I believe any anthropologist would be better suited than I to accompany the two of you on your journey."

"No, Cormick," Angelo said while chewing a mouthful of spicy chicken. "It has to be you. You know I'm right. Do you think it's merely coincidence that Dawn and I end up in your office at the same time saying the same thing? Was it coincidence that I knew you before I met you? Is it coincidence that suddenly you don't have to be at work and you have a bigger car?"

Cormick leaned back in his chair and stared at the ceiling. He had little fight left in him. For reasons he could not fully understand, he did not want to disappoint Angelo. They were a formidable pair, presenting a case both intelligent and intangible.

"I just cannot leave everything behind," he said.

"You don't have to go to work," Dawn said. "It doesn't look like you have any pets. What would you be leaving behind?"

Before Cormick could respond, they heard a quiet knock on the door. The three of them looked at each other like they were criminals, and the police were attempting to gain entrance to their lair. Cormick calmed himself and went to the door.

"Allison!" he happily exclaimed as he opened the door. Seeing her face breathed new life into him. The smell of her perfume embraced him, and her captivating blue eyes held him hostage.

"I'm so sorry, Dr. Proffitt," she apologized. "I would normally never think of bothering you at home, but you forgot your things." She held out his diplomas and made intermittent eye contact.

"Thank you, Allison. It is so good to see you." He took the diplomas from her. "Please, come in."

"Oh, I shouldn't," she said as she was halfway across the threshold. "I know this isn't appropriate, but…" She stopped in midsentence when she saw Dawn. "What is *she* doing here?" Her voice and temperament changed immediately.

"Um…Allison, you remember Dawn…uh, I mean, Miss Gallagher, and of course, Angelo Taranto," Cormick stammered.

He set the frames down and gently placed his open palm against Allison's back. It was the first time he had touched her, and it immediately caused him to catch his breath.

"Please, sit down," he said as he regained his composure. "Have a bite to eat."

Allison first glanced down at the open cartons scattered on the table then at both of the guests. Dawn offered an insincere smile, and Angelo, still chewing a mouthful of chicken, nodded and waved. Allison raised her hand to return the gesture, only to realize it was pointless to wave at a blind man.

"No thank you," she said politely as she turned to Cormick. "I just came by to…well, I had your things and…" She leaned forward and lowered her voice to almost a whisper. "Can we talk alone?"

"Well, I know when I'm not wanted," Angelo laughed as he stood up. "I'll go, but I'm taking the girl and the food with me!" He took a step forward and hit his shin against the table, knocking the carton of sweet and sour chicken to the floor. "Oops! Good thing I didn't trip over the table. That would have been a real mess."

Dawn quickly turned the box over and scooped the contents back into the box.

"That's going to leave a mark," she said as she futilely dabbed napkins into the carpet fibers. "I'll take Angelo and General Tso out to your patio to eat."

Dawn reached for Angelo's hand and started walking toward the sliding glass door. Leading the way, she didn't notice that Angelo had stepped into the spill and was leaving a trail of orange footprints on the beige carpet. Cormick placed his palms against his face and drew a deep breath as if covering his eyes could make it all go away. His life as well as his immaculate home had taken a beating from Angelo.

Allison reached up and grabbed his wrists to gently pull his hands from his face.

"Dr. Proffitt, I'm so sorry for what happened today. It breaks my heart."

He stood motionless as he realized that she still had hold of his wrists. He no longer thought about the stains or his job, he thought only of the soft touch of her hands. He looked into her sorrowful eyes and wasn't sure if he felt loss or love. The two had been so closely tied together for so long, he had trouble distinguishing the two feelings.

"Work won't be the same without you," she said through quivering lips. "Promise me one thing, Dr. Proffitt," she said as she moved closer to him. "Promise me you'll be careful when you're with these people. I know you have to go, but I have a very bad feeling that something terrible is going to happen."

Cormick heard everything she said but didn't listen to any of it. Immersed in the moment, he studied everything about her face. He noticed a small tear slowly drop from the corner of her eye. Without hesitation he tenderly wiped the tear from her face with the back of his fingers and, for the first time, felt the softness of her supple cheek.

He held his fingers there, caressing her face. He had not kissed a woman in years. On the rare occasion when the opportunity had presented itself, he was uncomfortable and awkward. But this time was different. It was as if gravity were pulling him to her. He cupped her cheek in his hand and leaned forward until his lips met hers.

Her lips were soft and warm, and there was nothing awkward about the moment. She nuzzled her nose against his as she pressed herself against him. As he pulled back to look into her eyes, he was only able to take short, staccato breaths. For the first time in his life, Cormick Proffitt understood passion.

"Oh, Dr. Proffitt," she said breathlessly, "you don't know how long I've waited…" She leaned into him and kissed him again.

Cormick ran his hands up the back of Allison's upper arms and pulled her close. His hands continued across the back of her shoulders, and he found himself in a tight embrace. He tried to pull away again, but she lovingly held his bottom lip in her teeth. She released it with a seductive smile.

"Allison, call me Cormick. I am not your boss any longer."

He stepped back and looked at her. After a moment, he tried to shake himself back into a reality he understood.

"I hope I was not too forward," he said as he regained his composure. "I guess I was swept up in the moment."

"Doctor…Cormick, I know you have to go to help these people. That's what makes you the incredible doctor that you are. But promise me that when you go with these people, you will come back to me. Promise me," she insisted.

He nodded at her and smiled.

"I promise," he said quietly.

Allison reached up and aggressively kissed him again. She turned her head from his lips and ran her cheek against his.

"Be careful."

With that, she turned and walked to the door. She looked back and smiled. She kissed the palm of her hand and gently blew the kiss at him. Though it was imaginary, when he closed his eyes, he felt the kiss land softly on his lips. When he opened his eyes, Allison was gone.

Unbeknownst to Cormick, Dawn had witnessed the entire spectacle from the patio and had given Angelo a complete play-by-play of the action. As Cormick turned to look at them, she quickly turned away, pretending she hadn't seen a thing. Cormick walked out into the sun to join the others. He walked past them with his hands in his pockets and stared out into the park beyond his yard. He took in a deep breath, closed his eyes, and smiled.

"Cormick, listen," Dawn said. "If you won't go on God's word, and you won't go for yourself, go for us. We're your patients. Don't you want to see us through this?"

He turned and looked at them. These two had invaded his life like a conquering army destroying everything in its path, but he was not angry, he just smiled at them. For the first time that he could remember, he felt no anxiety.

"Fine," he said. "While it is true that I may have nothing keeping me here, I believe I have something to come back to. We will leave tonight."

"What!" Angelo screamed as he jumped from his chair. "Yes! Cormick, you won't regret this, man!"

"I cannot say with certainty that you are correct," he responded.

"Wow! What suddenly changed your mind?" Dawn asked, aware that the kiss he shared with his young nurse had something to do with it.

Cormick looked down and kicked a small rock from his patio.

"I have decided that maybe it is time to live my life a little differently. It is possible that I may have overlooked some extraordinary opportunities in my life."

"Follow your heart, Cormick," Angelo said.

"I will, but I will take my brain with me," he replied.

CROSSROADS

Horace sat at the end of the bar silently staring at the clock that hung above it. He had stared at that same clock thousands of times over the past two decades quietly watching the minutes of his life slowly tick away through a veil of cigarette smoke. The dimly lit dive was almost as comfortable as home to him, and just like at home, an ashtray and whiskey were always within arm's reach.

Sayer was running behind, but Horace didn't care. Both brothers rarely adhered to the uncompromising constraints of the clock. There was no sense of urgency for either man to be anywhere. Life moved at a slow and easy pace for Sayer and Horace, and neither had any desire to change that fact.

He waved at the bartender.

"Yo, Vic…hit me again," he said, then tossed back a shot of Jack Daniels.

He lit a cigarette and leaned his head back to blow the smoke upward rather than directly in the face of the bartender.

"Fuck, Vic…when are you gonna paint the fucking ceiling?" he asked as Vic set down a double shot.

"When are you gonna shut the fuck up about the ceiling?" Vic responded. "You're the only asshole that ever looks at the ceiling. Jesus Christ!" He laughed for a moment then grew serious as he leaned on the bar. "Can I say that?"

"Can you say what? That I'm an asshole?" Horace asked,

as he blew a cloud of smoke in Vic's face. "I always figured that was your way of saying good morning."

"No, can I say Jesus Christ?" Vic whispered as he cautiously looked around the bar. "Shit! I did it again." He turned and surveyed the bar again.

"What the fuck, Vic? What are you looking for? The profanity police? Say whatever you want. It's your fucking bar." Horace took a generous sip of his drink. "I'm gonna need a beer back and a glass of ice water."

"Why ya bustin' my balls?" Vic asked. "I just didn't want to offend you, that's all."

"Vic, I've known you since we were kids," Horace replied. "In all that time, the only thing I've found offensive about you is your refusal to paint the fucking ceiling!" He laughed and took another drag. "And your breath. Seriously, did you have to have the whole bowl of garlic soup for lunch?"

"What I mean is, I didn't want to upset you by taking the Lord's name in vain."

Vic stepped to the side and poured a beer from the tap for Horace. He set it down and looked around again.

"So what is it? You two born again or what?"

"Are you fucking serious?" Horace asked. "Do I look born again?"

"I don't know," Vic shrugged. "What does born again look like?"

"How the fuck should I know?" Horace snapped. "Ask Jimmy fucking Swaggart!" He crushed the cigarette into the ashtray. "What about the ice water?"

"Forget it. That stuff will kill ya," he said as he dumped the ashtray into the coffee can under the bar. "Ya know, I haven't said anything because you're my friend from way back. But I gotta tell ya, people don't look at you two the same anymore."

"Who gives a shit what other people think?" he asked as he tossed back the last of the whiskey. He waved the empty glass in front of Vic and pulled another Marlboro from his pack and lit it.

"You know, Horace, a lot of people respect you around here. All I'm sayin' is some of those people don't understand."

"What's to understand? Huh?" Horace asked.

"It's easy to understand you finding God. You get shot up in 'Nam, almost die, hell, you live like a celibate monk out there…well, if monks can smoke and drink," he looked down for a moment wondering if they could. "But your brother, he's down there on the beach bangin' chicks three at a time and then talks about the word of God." He shrugged and grabbed the bottle of Jack Daniels and brought it over.

"My brother is a good man, Vic. Anyone who says any different needs to talk to me," Horace said as he tapped his glass.

"Hey, it ain't me," Vic said as he filled the glass. "But you can't beat up the whole town."

"Can we talk about something else, please?" Horace quietly implored. "Like maybe painting the fucking ceiling or some shit?"

"Let me take care of those guys shootin' pool," Vic said. "Then you can tell me all about the ceiling."

He walked away, leaving the bottle of whiskey on the bar. It was not an accident. Vic poured heavy for Horace and rarely collected money for his trouble. In exchange, Vic had all three of his cars fixed at no charge. Both men thought they were getting the better end of the deal.

The door opened, briefly flooding the bar with bright

light. The smoke became instantly visible, like a thick, white fog when headlights shine into it. The patrons all squinted as they turned their heads to watch the tan, lean figure enter the bar. The sign read, NO shirt, NO shoes, NO service, and those rules were strictly enforced by Vic, save for one customer. They all watched the shirtless, barefoot man walk to the bar.

"Dude," Sayer said as he patted his brother on the back, "you missed out again. When we get back, you're getting in the line up to ride some waves!" He laughed and nodded emphatically at his big brother. "Yo, Vic!" he called across the bar. "We need a tasty pitcher of ice cold suds!"

Horace discreetly glanced around the bar. Everyone was looking at them. Some were quietly whispering to each other, and Horace could imagine every word. He watched for a moment, waiting for someone to get up and walk toward them. But no one in the bar wanted to take on Horace Jordan.

"Sayer, listen," he leaned toward his brother, "let's not talk about the voice for a little while, okay? Let's just have a few drinks and talk about cars and girls and shit."

"Gotcha!" Sayer said, with an exaggerated wink to his brother. He smiled as his head bopped around on his shoulders to imaginary music.

Vic walked back behind the bar and put a pitcher under the tap. "I don't know about ice cold, kid…" he said as he poured the beer. "Hey, since you talk to God, maybe you could put a word in for my ex…get her a husband. Alimony is killing me!"

"Goddammit, Vic," Horace mumbled, "just pour the fucking beer."

"Hey! Can he say that?" Vic asked Sayer. "Is that allowed?"

"Dude, it's just words." Sayer grabbed the pitcher and filled his glass. "God has better things to do than get mad over words." He sipped from his beer. "God is preparing something as powerful as a groundswell."

"Yeah, Vic, so you better not pout, you better not cry…" Horace said sarcastically. "Can you give us a minute?" he asked as he motioned for him to go away.

"Dude, why did you do that?" Sayer asked. "Vic was totally asking me to share the word of God. I just can't refuse him."

"I know, I know," he replied. "Look, I think you might be disappointed about today. It's already after three, and we haven't heard from these *others* you keep talking about. I say we have a few here and then head to the beach."

"You don't look at the world right, big brother," he smiled. "It's not past three, it's only three, and there is plenty of day left for them to find us." He swallowed what was left in his glass and reached for the pitcher. "You're an empty glass guy," he said as he started pouring. "I'm a full glass guy."

Even though Sayer hadn't come close to the right metaphor, Horace understood what his brother was saying. He couldn't argue. Horace knew his glass had been half empty for a long time. The door opened and, once again, caused everyone to squint and peer through the smoky haze.

"Dude, it's like the land of the mole people in here," Sayer commented as he looked around. His eyes had not adjusted to darkness yet. "Why does everyone always turn away from what they're doing when the door…" He froze as the three backlit figures shut the door and looked around.

Horace was already focused on the beautiful redhead that led the way. The two brothers were seated closest to the door and could not see that every eye was on the trio, especially on Dawn. Horace turned back to the bar and lit a cigarette.

"Cowabunga!" Sayer said excitedly. "Are you seein' this?" He smacked his brother in the arm. "That chick has a bitchin' bod!"

Dawn led the way into the bar with Cormick and Angelo close behind. As she passed Horace and Sayer, she noticed that Sayer was smiling at her with a look she had seen on men's faces before. Horace turned and looked her over from top to bottom and back again, and when their eyes met, he knew he had been caught. She winked at him and smiled as she continued toward a booth near the pool table.

"Did you see that?" Sayer asked. "She totally winked at me."

"Sayer, I don't think…" Before he could finish, Sayer was already sauntering over to the booth. "Shit," he whispered.

Sayer stood at the end of the table slowly drinking her in like a glass of fine wine. Her white V-neck t-shirt was a perfect fit, and the direction of his stare made that obvious to everyone except Angelo. As Sayer slowly raised his eyes to meet Dawn's, he winked at her.

"Why don't you take a picture…" Dawn said.

"Babe, I don't need a camera to remember you," he said as he winked again.

"Is there something wrong with your eye?" She quipped. "My friend here is a doctor. Maybe he could help you."

"He better be a heart surgeon, babe, because you just stole mine," he said smoothly.

"Does that work?" Dawn asked as she looked at the three men at the table. "Do you guys honestly think a line like that works?" She noticed that Angelo was nodding and that Cormick had completely covered his face with his palms.

"Seriously…?" She stood up so Sayer could no longer have the privilege of staring down her shirt. "I am a woman. Not a high-school girl." She gave him the once over. "Are you even old enough to be in here? Where are your clothes?"

"Uh…" Sayer was stunned by the response. He had never encountered an obstacle like this before. He had always caught every woman he pursued. Now he just stood there, bewildered by her attitude and completely speechless.

"Everyone take a deep breath," Cormick said as he looked up at Sayer. "Look, we do not want any trouble. We are just passing through and—despite my emphatic objections—my companions felt this might be a good place to eat. Perhaps we can buy you a drink to show that there are no hard feelings."

"No, Cormick. He should buy *me* a drink for fondling my tits with his eyes!" She said as she placed her hands on her hips. "Well, blondie, what's it gonna be?"

"Chill out, Broadzilla!" Sayer said as he raised his hands to surrender and backed away. "I'm sorry." Embarrassed and confused, he walked back to his brother and noticed Vic laughing at him.

"Was that necessary?" Cormick asked as Dawn sat down.

"I didn't know you could fondle tits with your eyes," Angelo said. "I'm kinda bummed mine don't work right now."

"Can we please stop saying *tits*?" Cormick asked.

"Cormick, that guy was out of line," said Dawn. "I could see if it was a nightclub or something, but we're in a dive bar eating lunch. What was the point of that, anyway? Did he think he was going to sweep me off my feet and take me back to his van for a quickie?"

"Whatever his intentions, you must remember that we

are unfamiliar with our surroundings," Cormick warned. "We have no idea if he had a weapon or…"

"Stop it," she interrupted. "He was wearing a swimsuit. Where was he going to hide a weapon?" She leaned across the table and whispered, "Between you and me, he may not have had a gun, but he was packin.'"

"That is disgusting," Cormick said, over Angelo's giggling.

"Oh, grow up," she responded.

"We should not even be here," Cormick reminded them. "We should have taken Interstate 40. We are almost in Mexico! We are miles off course. That is what I get for…"

"Letting a woman drive?" Dawn asked.

"No. That is what I get for taking a nap," he retorted.

"Cormick, you have to sleep," she said, "We've been on the road nonstop for seventeen hours. What were you going to do? Give Angelo the keys?"

"Maybe after I've had a couple of drinks," Angelo said. "Can someone read me the menu? I can smell the cooked skunk already, so you can skip that part."

The door opened as two men entered.

"Well, well, well. Horace mother-fucking Jordan and his lesbian sister," Hanrahan said as he passed by. He gave the brothers a disgusted sneer as he wiped his hand across his bearded chin.

Russ Hanrahan and Horace had been in so many brawls over the past two decades that nobody could keep count. Though he rarely started a fight, Horace almost always came out on top, sometimes beating Hanrahan unconscious. He was the man who took the love of Horace's life. A fact Hanrahan relished and often used to provoke Horace. But today, he had other things to talk about.

"Hey, Russ," Vic yelled. "None of that shit today. You still owe me for the pinball machine you fell asleep in!"

Vic and the customers who had witnessed the event a week earlier laughed out loud. Hanrahan had not fallen asleep; he was knocked out cold when Horace threw him through the glass top of the machine.

Hanrahan sat down at the bar and ordered a drink. He talked with the man he entered with but would turn and glare at the two brothers. Horace knew Hanrahan wanted to fight, and this time it appeared he brought help. He didn't want Sayer involved, but he knew he couldn't take both of them.

"Excuse me," Dawn said to Vic as she stepped up to the bar. "Can I get a shot of Jack, two mugs of beer, and a glass of red wine?"

"Her wine is on me, Vic," Sayer said sheepishly.

"The wine is for my macho friend over there," she said, motioning to Cormick. "I'm the Jack and a beer."

"I'll get that round, Vic," Horace said as he looked over at Dawn. "I apologize if my brother offended you. I promise you, he means well. Beautiful women make him stupid."

"Thanks for the drinks," she said pleasantly. "Your brother is nothing I can't handle."

"Whoa!" Sayer said as he got up. "Ease up on the hostility, Big Red."

Dawn gave the men an obviously forced smile as Vic handed her a tray with her order. She got halfway to the booth and turned to look at the men who were sitting at the bar. They had all watched her walk away and immediately turned away once they realized they had been caught gawking. She shook her head and continued back to the booth.

Hanrahan got up and leaned against the bar. Horace carefully watched as Hanrahan started stretching. It was a clear sign that he was getting ready to start something. Horace looked up into the mirror above the bar and saw that Hanrahan was staring right at him.

"Sayer, sit down," Horace said in a hushed voice. "Listen to me very carefully. If that jackass comes over here and says anything, do not respond. Do you understand me? Keep your hands on the bar with your drink. If you have to turn to face him, just turn your head not your body. Understand? And whatever you do, do not mention Sunny."

"Yeah, dude," he replied. "You know, I'm not a little kid anymore. I can totally handle myself in a fight."

"That's good. Because I think you're gonna have to take care of his friend."

Hanrahan stopped stretching and stood up straight.

"You know, Vic, I hear they hold church outside now. Yeah…right here on the beach." He looked around at the other customers. "It's true. It's led by a surfing prophet who—get this—claims that God talks directly to him!" There was scattered laughter from the patrons, which emboldened him to go on.

"Now I ask you," he said as he walked to the middle of the bar, "if God was going to talk to someone in this bar would he choose that little bitch over there?" He pointed at Sayer. "Here's what I think. I think he was smoking a joint one day after jacking off to pictures of farm animals and thought that this God angle would be a good way to get laid. Let's face it, if you look like a girl, it's got to be hard to get a girl." He walked over to Sayer and leaned against the bar. "Ain't that right, sweetness?"

Sayer looked straight ahead and smiled. Nothing

Hanrahan said shook him. He was walking the path God laid out for him, and he wasn't going to do anything that could prevent that. He would defend himself if needed, but he was not going to throw the first punch.

"That's it? Nothing to say for yourself?" He looked up at Horace. "Go ahead, Jordan. Tell your bitch it's polite to speak when spoken to."

"That's enough," Vic said as he slowly lowered a baseball bat between Hanrahan and Sayer. "Russ, I warned you. I'm not going to warn you again. Now start drinking or start walking."

Hanrahan slowly raised his head to look at Vic, then turned back to glare at the brothers.

"Don't bring any of your God shit to my daughter," he warned. "If you even speak to her I'll kill you." He righted himself and headed back to his stool.

The scene had not gone unnoticed by Dawn, Cormick, and Angelo.

"Did you hear that?" Angelo asked. "Someone in this bar is one of us! We didn't go off course, we're exactly where we're supposed to be!"

"You're never going to believe who God has chosen down here," Dawn sighed mournfully as she slid down in the booth.

Cormick slid out of the booth and reached in to pull Angelo out as well.

"Come along, now. This is why we are here, is that not correct?"

Dawn got out of the booth and started walking up to the bar. Cormick put his arm around Angelo's shoulder and followed Dawn. She leaned against the bar and bent her head down to get Sayer's attention.

"We couldn't help but overhear your conversation," she said quietly. "Do you boys want to join us and talk about it?" She held out her hand. "My name is Dawn."

Horace leaned back on his stool to look at Cormick and Angelo, then righted himself and turned to Dawn.

"I'm not sure what there is to talk about. We're big enough to take a few insults."

Cormick and Angelo approached them.

"Hi! I'm Angelo!" He extended his hand, which was noticeably shaking. "And you are Sayer, right? God led me to you. You are the Carpenter!" He was so nervous, he was having difficulty breathing.

"Dude! No way!" Sayer exclaimed as he leapt off of his stool. He pushed Angelo's hand away and grabbed him in a big bear hug, lifting him in the air and knocking Cormick off balance. He stood with his arm around him and turned to face his brother. "Ta-dah! The *others*!"

Horace stood up and gave a half-hearted wave. "I'm Horace Jordan," he said. The afternoon of drinking had him a little off balance. "You're Dawn, you're Angelo, and who are you?"

"My name is Cormick Proffitt," he responded. He leaned into the group. "Taking into account what we have witnessed prior to this, I cannot help but feel we would be best served by having our conversation quietly in the booth, rather than here where we may inadvertently incite violence."

Horace stared at Cormick with a confused look on his face.

"I'm not sure, but I think you just said you're afraid of fights and don't want to talk in public." He grabbed a cigarette and lit it. "Let me guess," he said. "Talking like that you must be a teacher."

"No, I am a doctor. She is a teacher," he said motioning to Dawn.

"Hey babe," Sayer said as he reached out his hand. "Sorry about before. You're just totally hot. But now that I know… I'll be cool, I promise."

"Cormick! I told you, Cormick!" Angelo shouted.

Cormick looked cautiously around the bar. It was obvious that they had the attention of everyone, and for Cormick any attention was unwanted attention.

"Everyone take a deep breath and relax," he said in a hushed voice. "Once again—and I cannot stress this point enough—we should talk quietly elsewhere. At the very least, we should go back to the booth." He turned quickly and immediately slammed into Russ Hanrahan, spilling the man's beer. The beverage soaked Hanrahan from his beard to his shoes.

Cormick stepped back and looked in horror at the mess he had just made. He looked in Hanrahan's eyes and saw pure anger. He tried to apologize. Though his lips were moving, he was too terrified to utter a sound. He felt a hand grab his arm and pull him backward, unaware that Horace had just pulled him from the line of fire.

"Leave him alone," Horace warned. "It was an accident, Russ. Let it go." He could see Hanrahan's friend walking up to them. It was clear to him that they had planned for this moment in advance.

"Hey. Tough guy," Dawn said as she neared them. "Relax. It was just an accident like he said. I'll buy you another drink. Now walk away before someone gets hurt."

Hanrahan turned to look at Dawn and started laughing. He had no problem hitting women, a fact his wife could testify to. And he knew that the woman standing in front of him needed a lesson in how to talk to a man. He decided to save her for later and regained eye contact with Horace.

"Are you gonna let this bitch fight your battles?"

"Who are you calling a bitch?" Dawn demanded. "You're the bitch."

Hanrahan reached out and palmed her face, shoving her hard into Angelo, and the two fell to the ground. Horace stepped back and swung hard, landing a solid blow to Hanrahan's nose and cutting his hand on the man's front teeth. He immediately grabbed Hanrahan by the collar and swung again with enough force to knock him against the bar.

"Cormick! Cormick! Help!" Angelo cried as he flailed about like an upside down turtle.

Hanrahan's friend stepped forward to take a shot at Horace when, seemingly out of nowhere, Sayer leapt forward delivering a left cross with enough force to send the man sprawling to the ground. Hanrahan shook off the punch Horace had hammered him with and swung wildly at Sayer, who easily dodged the vicious onslaught of fists, laughing like he was having the time of his life.

With both hands, Horace grabbed the hair at the back of Hanrahan's head and slammed his face into the bar, breaking his nose. The man on the floor had gotten up and was running up behind Horace. Just a step from his target, he was stopped dead in his tracks by a roundhouse kick to the side of his head from Dawn, and he fell to the ground.

Cormick grabbed Angelo and tried to make his way around the melee to return to the safety of their booth. The man on the floor grabbed Cormick's foot as he passed, causing him to fall forward. The man stood up, rolled Cormick over, grabbed him by the shirt, and punched him in the eye with enough force to rip his clothing and knock his head against the floor. He raised his fist to hit Cormick again, but Dawn spun him around and with both hands clasped together—like she was returning a volleyball—delivered a brutal uppercut that stunned the man. She whirled around with another roundhouse kick to his face, knocking him unconscious. He crumpled and fell right on top of Cormick.

"Who's the bitch now?" she asked as she wiped her mouth.

Hanrahan broke free and swung at Horace's stomach. He landed several quick body blows with enough force to take Horace's breath away, knocking him to his knees. Towering over Horace, he made a move to kick him in the face. Horace quickly moved his head, grabbed Hanrahan's foot and stood up, forcing his attacker to fall backward.

Reeling from the rapid blows to his gut, Horace stumbled over to Hanrahan and looked down at him.

"Get up," he told him. He watched Hanrahan lying there, not making a move. "I thought so," Horace said as he turned to walk back to his barstool.

Sayer ran to Angelo and gently led him to the booth, while excitedly describing the epic battle to him. Dawn pulled the stranger off of Cormick and outstretched her hand to help him up.

"Where did you learn to fight like that?" he asked as he got to his feet.

"The school district made self-defense training mandatory," she smiled. "Most took martial arts, but I liked the sound of kick boxing. I never really thought I'd use it, though." She lightly touched his right cheekbone and the side of his face while studying his swelling eye. "Let's get some ice on that."

Horace grabbed his drink and effortlessly tossed back the whiskey.

"Sorry, Vic, but he put his hands on the lady."

He knelt down next to Hanrahan and studied his handy work. His nose was bent to the side a bit, and blood was trickling down the side of his face. Horace lit a cigarette and blew the smoke in Hanrahan's face.

"I've told you before," he said, "don't ever hurt a woman… any woman." He flicked his cigarette ash onto the man's bloody face and walked over to join the others.

Vic leaned over the bar and poured the contents of the spit pitcher down onto Hanrahan's face, rousing him to consciousness.

"Get out, Russ," he said. "You're eighty-sixed." Vic started to walk away but turned back and leaned over the bar. "Make sure you tell your tough friend over there that he got his ass kicked by a girl."

THE GATHERING

Cormick was sitting across the table from Angelo in the booth.
The bag of ice pressed to his eye was gradually beginning to thaw. A droplet of the cold water leisurely made its way down the right side of his neck and onto his shoulder. He knew that first drop was acting merely as a scout, blazing the trail for other, more irritating drops to follow. It was only a matter of time before the trickle would swell to become a river of icy water that would leave his shirt soaking wet. Rather than adjust the bag, he chose to stare at the nicotine-stained ceiling tiles, wallowing in self-pity.

"Someone needs to paint this ceiling," he said.

Angelo was uncharacteristically quiet. He had tried to comfort Cormick during the introductions, to no avail. After a sustained silence, he spoke up.

"I know you think your eye hurts, but it's probably just numb from the ice. I've always thought of pain as a state of mind."

"The bruising under this water torture device is called ecchymosis and is a direct result of trauma," Cormick complained. "That means there is bleeding into the surrounding tissue. Blood is often preceded or immediately followed by some level of discomfort."

"Come haul crab with me in Alaska some time. Then you'll understand discomfort," Angelo replied. "Besides, I just want to keep you from pouting in front of everyone. First impressions are everything."

Cormick squared his head and cut a sharp look at Angelo.

"I am not pouting," he explained. "I am however, disconcerted to discover that I had to drive a thousand miles to get beaten up in a bar, when I could have easily had this marvelous experience in Vancouver. Hold on…I probably could have gone another forty-two years without a beating from some drunken reprobate."

Cormick tilted his head back and continued staring at the ceiling. He was hurt that not even Angelo had sympathy for him. Dawn was off bandaging Horace's hand; she had said it more than likely had one or more of Hanrahan's teeth lodged in it. Cormick knew she would not offer the compassion he needed. *If Allison were here*, he thought, *she would offer the comfort I need.*

Sayer arrived at the table carrying a tray with two pitchers of beer. His face was beaming as he looked at his new friends sitting in the booth. God had told him they would come for him, and here they were. His faith in the voice grew stronger with each passing second.

"There were no clean glasses," he said as he set the tray in the center of the table. "So I thought, hey, let's just drink from the pitchers. If that's cool with you dudes, that is."

"Man, you bet it's cool!" Angelo exclaimed as he leaned forward, cautiously moving his hands on the table in search of a pitcher. "This is how we drink beer in Alaska," he said as he firmly grasped his beer. "Ever been to Alaska?"

"Dude, what's the surfin' like up there?" Sayer asked.

Angelo paused with his mouth wide open and his

pitcher only inches from his mouth. "Gee…uh…I don't think surfing is real big up there." He took a drink of his beer, leaving a foamy coating over his mustache.

"I am totally up for trying," Sayer replied.

He slid into the booth, bumping Cormick. The mild impact set free more water from the ice bag, which followed the same course as the first drop. It was so cold that Cormick could feel his chest hair tingle.

"I do not want beer, thank you," Cormick said.

"Ya know, dude, if you leave that bag there too long, it'll drip down your shirt." Sayer turned to Angelo. "Don't you hate that?" Angelo had no idea the conversation had been dropped in his lap. He tilted his frosty pitcher back and continued gulping beer.

Dawn emerged from the men's room with Horace following close behind. She carried herself with an air of satisfaction. Not only had she stood her ground in the heat of battle, defending her friends, she was the healer of their wounds. She thought Clara Barton would be proud. She fought the urge to point out that she was a modern woman of the nineties: confident, strong, and nurturing. Horace fought the urge to point out she had already made the men's room wall.

Sayer leapt from the booth.

"Here comes your babe!" he said excitedly. He would have been the first of the group to agree with Dawn on her woman-of-the-year status. In his eyes, she was everything a woman should be.

Dawn stopped short of sitting in the booth.

"Let's get one thing clear before we go any further. I am no one's *babe*. Are we all clear on that?"

All four men nodded in agreement.

Horace reached into his pocket and retrieved a cigarette. Lighting it, he took a long, slow drag and held it loosely in his wrapped hand.

"I think if you check your eye, you'll find the swelling has stopped," he said to Cormick.

"I appreciate your concern, but I am a doctor. I think I know how to treat an injury such as this." Though he knew Horace was correct, he remained adamant in his attempt to elicit some sympathy.

"You're not a doctor," Dawn laughed, "you're a psychiatrist. It's like a chiropractor saying he's a doctor. Now take that stupid bag off your face before it leaks down your shirt." She stood there with her hands on her hips, waiting for him to do as she directed.

"One must be a medical doctor prior to becoming a psychiatrist," Cormick said as he lifted the bag from his face to reveal a swollen, red cheekbone and a blackened left eye. "There, is everyone satisfied?"

"Shit, Doc. That looks like it hurts," Horace said.

"He'll be fine," Dawn answered for Cormick. "I have some Pamprin in my purse if he needs it. Now let's get down to business."

Cormick sat up and tossed the ice bag on the table.

"Just hold on a second," he said authoritatively. "There are several points we need to address regarding our journey to Santa Fe. So we need to take a deep breath and take this one step at a time. Only then can we even attempt to ascertain what direction we want to go with this."

"East," Sayer said.

"What?" Cormick asked.

"Santa Fe is to the east," Sayer offered, proudly smiling over his contribution to the planning.

Cormick glared at him. It was painfully clear that Sayer had not been cursed by the ravages of intelligence. *If it was God who brought us together,* he thought, *it was clearly a form of punishment.*

"What I meant was, we should follow a logical course of action…if that is possible."

Dawn eased herself into the booth next to Angelo. Horace pulled a chair from the neighboring table and, turning it backward, sat down. He scrutinized the four people in the booth and decided it was time for another drink. He signaled Vic to bring a round for the table.

Angelo could not stand the suspense.

"Has everyone here heard the voice?"

"I have yet to hear this voice," Cormick said. "What about you two?"

"Dude…it's, like, everywhere! God is totally happening!" Sayer said gleefully.

Cormick turned to Horace for a translation.

"What he's saying," Horace began, "is that the voice is in our TV, our telephone, and last night, I shit you not, I could have sworn it came from the fucking cat box." He flicked his cigarette indiscriminately as he spoke.

"I heard it in my classroom. It also wrote on my chalkboards," Dawn offered.

"Classroom?" Horace asked as his cigarette dangled from his lips. "Whaddaya teach? Assertiveness training?" He laughed, blowing smoke out of the corner of his mouth. He could see Cormick nodding in agreement in the corner of the booth.

"I heard it on the ocean. It's just like Sayer said." Angelo turned his face upward. "It's everywhere. It's God, man. Plain and simple."

"Angelo, take a deep breath. We do not know that this is God," Cormick said.

"Well, dude…what do you think it is?"

"I think that it is in our best interest not to assume anything in this situation. I will concede that the possibility exists that the four of you have experienced a shared vision—or delusion. But I, like the rest of the planet, am immune to this call to God; therefore, I—like the rest of the planet—find it hard to put faith in individuals who claim to have spoken directly to a supreme being."

"Well then, Doc, what the hell are you doing here?" Horace asked as the waitress returned to the table with three more pitchers of beer and two shots of Jack Daniels. "Don't you want to see God?" Horace smashed the butt of his cigarette into the ashtray. He reached into his pocket and removed a crumpled twenty dollar bill and tossed it on the waitress's tray. He raised his glass for a toast. "To God!" He threw back the shot and let out a grunt.

"I am here because I, apparently, am the only mode of transportation available…the only one who can get all of you safely to your destination," Cormick said. "I take the health and welfare of my patients seriously."

"My brother doesn't take this seriously," Sayer said.

"The hell I don't!" Horace closed his eyes and took in a breath to calm himself. "I take this shit very seriously. There is a fucking voice in my television set. It's on my phone. It's in my house." He turned directly to Cormick. "This voice has turned my brother from a surfer into fucking Billy Graham. So I just want to know one thing: what the hell are you doing here? And don't give me your 'mode of transportation' bullshit."

"Alright," Cormick said resolutely, "I admit that I want to

know what is happening. I want to help Angelo understand what is happening. I want to make sure that this man," he said, pointing at Angelo, "makes it to Santa Fe in one piece. I am not even remotely considering the possibility that God is speaking to people on earth. Furthermore, at the risk of sounding realistic—which I realize makes me the odd man out—I want to go on record as recommending that all of you exercise restraint in your judgement as well as your actions going forward."

"Dude, my brother is a war hero," Sayer said speaking on his brother's behalf. "When I was a baby, he was, like, fighting in Vietnam. He used to hear screams in his sleep and all sorts of stuff. God just has him kinda spooked."

"I'm not scared," Horace said as he pulled another cigarette from his pocket. "I just wanna live a normal life for chrissake." He lit the cigarette and blew the smoke into the center of the table just as Vic placed another shot in front of him. "And I'm no goddamned hero, either. And I'll tell you another thing. Sometimes I'm not even sure I believe in God. And judging from the past forty years, he sure as fuck doesn't believe in me." He emptied his glass and pushed it to the center of the table.

"Up in Alaska, when I first heard the voice, I fought it," said Angelo. "When I got back to town, I got drunk to try to drown it out. The main reason I went north in the first place was to escape life. Just like you, Horace, I needed to escape. But I was selfish. God has plans for me. God has plans for you."

"Hey bro', he's right," Sayer said. "We're being called to a gathering. We've been chosen."

"You may be chosen," Cormick said. "I have no calling. I have only what the four of you tell me."

"Dude, if you come to our house, you'll totally hear the voice."

"After a while, you'll be begging it to shut up," Horace grumbled.

Dawn raised her hand to silence everyone.

"Look boys, it's been a long drive and a thoroughly exhilarating brawl, and we should do it again sometime. But we aren't going to be able to make any sense of this sitting here getting drunk. I think it would be a good idea if we got some sleep and attacked this in the morning."

"You can totally crash at our house!" Sayer offered.

"Sayer, our house is a mess… I don't think…"

"I, for one, would like to see the talking litter box," Dawn said smiling. "I'll bet that's something most tourists don't get to see when they come to Huntington Beach."

"Yo, Vic!" Sayer called to the bartender. "Can we get some to-go cups for these pitchers?"

———— ⁄⁄⁄ ————

Horace hesitated as he inserted his key into the lock on his front door.

"I want everyone to keep in mind that this is the house of two single men." He pushed open the door and signaled for everyone to enter. He stopped Sayer, who was bringing up the rear of the procession. "You did finish washing your underwear, didn't you? I mean, they're not still soaking in the kitchen sink, are they?"

"Relax, bro," Sayer laughed, "I wouldn't leave my underwear in the kitchen. They're drying in front of the fireplace."

Horace dropped his head and followed his brother into the house. He looked up and watched the faces of his guests as Sayer turned on the lights in the living room. Cormick closed his eyes and slowly reopened them, unsure if he had seen the disaster correctly the first time. Dawn's face contorted to form a pained look of disbelief and apprehension.

Angelo breathed in deeply.

"So…it's just the one cat?"

"No wonder the litter box talks," Dawn whispered to Cormick. "It's begging for mercy."

Horace shut the door and walked past the group, careful to avoid eye contact with them. He made quick, discreet sniffs but found the house smelled the same as it always did.

"Here, kitty-kitty. Where is that fucking cat?" he asked.

"Asphyxiated…" mumbled Cormick.

"You guys thirsty?" Sayer asked. "We got milk, water, beer, and whiskey."

Dawn's face had relaxed since the initial shock of seeing the chaotic disorder that surrounded her.

"As tempting as that menu is," she said, "I'd rather get some sleep before we hit the road tomorrow."

"Sayer, show Dawn to Mom's room." Horace smiled nervously at Dawn. "It's the nicest room in the house."

"Did your Mom move out?" Dawn asked.

"She passed away," Horace said.

"Yeah," said Sayer. "Died in her bed. Don't worry," he said reassuringly, "we've totally changed the sheets since then."

Their mother's room had remained virtually untouched since her funeral ten years earlier. On that day, Horace had cleaned her room one final time. He would peak in from time to time, futilely hoping to see her there. He continued to place fresh lavender, her favorite flower, in the room every week to keep it smelling just as she'd liked it.

"Mom's room is upstairs," Sayer said. "My room is right

there. We can stop there first, and I'll show you my quiver. It's bitchin'."

Sayer led Dawn down the hall as he rambled on about his surfboards. As she followed him, Dawn looked at Cormick like it was the last time she would ever see him.

"Angelo?" Horace asked, hoping he got the name right. "You can have my room. I never sleep there. I usually crash in the recliner here." He turned to Cormick. "I'd give you Sayer's room, but I get the feeling you wouldn't be very comfortable there. So, if it's okay, I thought you could sleep on the couch."

"Sure. That would be…fine."

Cormick looked at what appeared to be the couch. It was clearly not used for sitting. Somewhere, beneath the pile of clothing, newspapers, and at least two pizza boxes, there had to be a couch. He didn't want to move anything without permission from Horace. He wondered if some creature, heretofore unknown to man, had evolved in the pile of debris and nested in the laundry.

Cormick was free to snoop around the house as Horace led Angelo down the hall to his bedroom. He walked past the fireplace, closely examining the pictures on the mantle. The first two pictures were of a woman who he assumed was the matriarch of the family. Her eyes were distant, and she looked sad and detached from her surroundings. He lifted the third picture from the mantle for closer inspection. Through the yellowing cracks of the old black and white snapshot, he saw someone who looked a lot like Horace. The boy in the picture was happy and joyful. Cormick knew that there were bound to be more lines on his face now, a few extra pounds on the waistline, but the Horace of yesterday seemed to be a hundred years in the past.

He stepped back to look at the odd banners hanging from the fireplace screen. At first glance, he assumed they were diving flags or some sort of thing a surfer would use on the beach. It took a moment before he noticed the open flies. He was staring at the most colorful collection of boxer shorts he had ever seen.

"Our dryer's broken," Horace said as he entered the living room. He awkwardly snatched the underwear from the screen and tossed them toward the corner of the room.

"Please, do not feel obligated to clean on my account. I, too, am a bachelor." Cormick smiled to help alleviate the embarrassment Horace was feeling.

"Want a drink?" Horace asked as he headed into the kitchen to pour himself one. "Whiskey okay?"

Wanting to keep his host at ease, Cormick followed him to the refrigerator, attempting to sound eager for a drink. "Considering the events of the past few days, I think a glass of whiskey is in order."

"Hey Doc, about my attitude in the bar…well, I'm sorry." Horace pulled the last two clean glasses from the cupboard and filled them with Jack Daniels. "I'm just not ready to see God again." He handed a glass to Cormick and took a long drink from his.

"Again?" Cormick asked. "I do not understand. You have seen God before?"

"Yeah…in 'Nam." Horace sighed and walked past Cormick. "C'mon." He took a drink and led Cormick back to the living room, carrying the fifth of Jack Daniels with him. He dropped into the recliner and lit a cigarette.

Cormick pushed some laundry aside and sat on the couch. He sipped from his glass, flinching as the alcohol burned its way into his system. He fought the urge to cough.

"So…you believe you saw God…during the war…" Cormick said. "Tell me about it."

"Not much of a story, really. The same story fifty thousand others could have told had they made it." Horace took a drag from his cigarette and flicked the ashes toward the ashtray. He let his head fall back into the cracked and peeling leather of the recliner. "Did you serve?"

"No, I was in college at the time. No other siblings, and my guardian…well, he had a Senator intervene and, like I said, with no brothers…" Cormick trailed off into uncomfortable silence.

He felt as if he had just severed the bond between them. What were once valid reasons seemed like cowardly excuses. He stared into his drink and felt ashamed. It was an unexpected feeling. He had always been thankful for his time in college, insulated from the brutal realities of Vietnam by the ivy covered walls. And now, this stranger, with no effort, made him discover his own guilt. He looked up and saw that Horace was staring past him.

"It was the perfect place for a war, Doc. God awful jungle that was just as dangerous as the NVA. Long periods of nothing punctuated by insane firefights. Anyway, one day, we went into this village, just to clear it, you know? Everything was fine, no VC. But some of the guys…well, some of the guys, they weren't satisfied just to clear it and leave. Ya know?" He sighed and shook his head slowly. "I just couldn't take part in that shit. I had a girl at home. Beautiful girl. Anyway," he continued as he took a drink, "I walked to the tree line for a smoke and came face to face with this kid. God, he looked scared. There we were, staring at each other, guns drawn…" Horace sat up in the recliner and looked at Cormick. "I didn't want to kill him. He was just a boy."

"I have counseled scores of veterans in my career," Cormick said. "I understand the impact taking a life has on a man. I understand that…"

Horace laughed.

"You don't understand shit, Doc. Not unless you've been there. Me and this kid…we just stood there, staring at each other. I smiled at him, ya know? To show him it was okay. He smiled back. I slowly raised my right hand and reached for my smokes…to offer him one. It was a peace gesture, ya know? He stepped forward and took one, and I lowered my gun to reach for my lighter. Can you believe it? I lowered my fucking gun, and he shot me." Horace crushed his butt into the ashtray. "I stood there, staring at him. He was still smiling when he fired the second shot. I felt that one. It burned like hell. Maybe I was too stunned to feel the first one. I don't know."

Cormick was riveted by the story. He sipped from his glass and let the whiskey burn its way through him again. He did not stop to analyze his symbolic act. The fire in his stomach helped him live the moment with Horace.

"Anyway…things were kinda fucked up after that. But there was this blinding light. A warm, forgiving light. And it called me by name. It embraced me…if that makes any sense. I have never before or since felt so loved. But it let me go. It told me that there was something I had left to do and that it was not my time. Next thing I knew, I woke up in a hospital."

"Based on your near death experience…" Cormick stopped himself immediately, concerned he was about to sound too clinical. "Let me rephrase. When the light called to you all those years ago, do you believe it was the same voice you heard here in this house?"

"When I heard it in the kitchen for the first time, I thought it was Sayer. It was familiar like that. But honestly, Doc, I don't remember the sound of the voice I heard all those years ago." Horace lit another cigarette and inhaled deeply. He exhaled, blowing a smoke ring that hung above his head like a halo.

"You are a lucky man," Cormick said.

"Yeah…real fuckin' lucky." Horace took two quick sips from his glass.

Cormick took a long drink to wash away his guilt. His deferment had kept him from the war, and he knew that made him the lucky one. His experience with veterans had been difficult for him. He feared many of the things that had made Horace and other veterans into the men they were now: guns, violence, death, and the unknown. He had given up counseling veterans a few years earlier because their stories and their sacrifice made it hard to look at himself in the mirror.

"We are not so different, you and I," Cormick said.

"Is that right?"

"Well, we are roughly the same age, we grew up at the same time—albeit on opposite ends of the social spectrum—we have grown to accept the world as it is and accept that our lives are shaped by events beyond our control. We are the only two expressing any reservations about what is happening."

"We're just old," Horace said.

"I am not old," Cormick replied indignantly. "I am only forty-two."

"Face it, Doc, those gray hairs on your head aren't gonna turn brown again any time soon. Even if you live to be eighty-four, you're already half dead."

Cormick glared at Horace, insulted by the comment.

"That is not a healthy attitude to have. Time should be regarded as precious, especially when there is less of it."

"There's nothing precious about time. It's a predator. It takes what it wants when it wants it, without care or concern, leaving us miserable bastards to deal with the loss and consequences." Horace rubbed his chest. "Time is a fire that consumes our souls, leaving only pain in its wake."

"I would disagree," Cormick replied. "Time is what brings us knowledge. Profound wisdom can only be gained with the passage of time. Time is a necessary component of relationships and love."

"Then maybe we're not so alike after all," Horace smiled. "But, hey, that doesn't mean we can't get along. Let's agree to disagree. More Jack?" Horace raised his glass toward Cormick.

"I should stick with what I have here," Cormick responded.

He rarely drank hard alcohol. There had been an occasional martini over the years, but that was done to keep up professional appearances. He was weary from the road, in a strange house, suffering a black eye, and emotionally exhausted. He longed for sleep.

"So tell me, Doc. If you don't think it's God...I mean, what do you honestly make of all this?"

Cormick took a drink.

"I feel like I am trapped in a bad dream."

"Yeah, Doc...that sums up my whole existence."

MORNING

In her dream, Dawn found herself standing alone in the desert.
There was no wind as the sun rose slowly to warm the dry, still air. She noticed a man lying on the ground in the distance. As she walked toward the motionless figure, she called out. There was no reply. Overcome by an uncontrollable feeling of panic, she began to run to the body. Her legs became heavy as her heart pounded furiously against her rib cage. She forced herself to continue forward until she reached the lifeless body. Painfully out of breath, she knelt down beside him. She was unable to focus on his face. It seemed clouded in her eyes. She felt he was someone she knew, but she could not make out his face.

She noticed dusty cowboy boots on the other side of the body and a figure backlit by the sun. She looked up to ask for help, but the face of the man was lost in the bright morning sun. She moved her head from side to side to see who stood before her, to no avail.

"Please…help him," she implored.

"Do not mourn, Dawn. His journey is over. Now that the sun has set, he can join the stars."

She woke suddenly to find herself in the bedroom of the late Mrs. Jordan. Mildly out of breath, she turned to face the four-paned windows that overlooked the beach. The beauty of the sun reflecting golden light off of the Pacific Ocean was lost on her as she struggled with the intensity of her dream.

Helplessness was not an emotion she was comfortable with. But she knew she was about to be helpless. *That was more than a dream,* she thought, *God is preparing me for the worst.*

She tossed the sheets aside and placed her bare feet on the floor, stretching her arms behind her back. She had not packed a robe. She considered going downstairs in her t-shirt and panties to show she was just one of the boys. She laughed, knowing Cormick would probably suffer a stroke.

She reached into the closet and removed a robe that had gone unused for more than a decade. Slipping it on, she started for the door. She stopped for a moment and looked out the window once again. It was a beautiful morning.

Dawn maneuvered past the piles of clothing in the hall to the top of the stairs. Making her way down the stairs, she was surprised to see neatly folded piles of boxer shorts. She was sure she would have remembered that from the night before. When she reached the bottom, she was even more surprised at what she found in the living room: carpeting. The mound of clothing and crumpled newspapers on the couch had been replaced by two souvenir pillows from the Grand Canyon and a patchwork quilt draped neatly over the back. With the exception of Horace, unconscious in the recliner, and the full ashtray beside him, the room was spotless.

She could hear the washing machine running and the sound of someone doing dishes. Rounding the corner into the kitchen she caught sight of Cormick at the sink. He was wearing grey sweatpants and a white t-shirt, accented with a knee-length, tie-dyed apron. He was using a screwdriver to scrape grease from an old skillet.

"You might try a scouring pad on that," Dawn offered.

Startled, Cormick turned to face her, revealing a giant

pot leaf on the front of his apron.

"I did try that, however, this substance appears to have the consistency of asphalt." He turned back to the sink. "I had hoped to finish before everyone woke up." He turned to her and smiled. "I do apologize. I have a problem dealing with disorder."

"Yeah, you're kind of a neat freak." Dawn surveyed the clean kitchen. "I don't smell the litter box anymore. What did you do…kill the cat?"

"I found the cat in the oven," Cormick sighed. "There is no telling how long it had been in there."

"My God! They cooked the cat?"

"No, it was alive…hungry and extremely grateful for its freedom." He shook his head, still unable to understand why the cat was in the oven. "I made some coffee. The mugs are in the cupboard to my left."

"I had the strangest dream," Dawn said, reaching for a mug. "But I'm not sure it was a dream. I think it was God." Dawn poured herself a cup of coffee. "You're a psychiatrist. Maybe you can tell me what it means."

"Dream interpretation is hardly my field of expertise," Cormick said, placing the pan in the warm, soapy water to soak. "The schools of thought on such interpretations are as varied as the color of Sayer's underwear." He wiped the dishwater from his hands and reached for a mug. "I suppose, from a strict Freudian point of view…"

"What does it mean when you dream about death?" Dawn interrupted as she sat down at the kitchen table.

Cormick poured himself a cup of coffee and leaned back against the cupboard. He took a sip of coffee, and after a moment of thoughtful consideration, said, "It usually means death."

"How many years of school did you have to go through to hone those deductive skills of yours?" Dawn asked. "I think you flunked the class on bedside manner."

"It is a matter of common sense, really," he responded. "Dreams about death usually mean the end of something: a job, a relationship…But sometimes, a cigar is just a cigar." He took another sip from his cup. "Was it your death?"

"I think it was one of you guys."

That got Cormick's attention. The thought of Alison warning him he would not return flashed into his mind. He felt a mild panic tighten its grip in his chest.

"Why not start from the beginning?" he asked. "Take a deep breath, and tell me everything you can remember."

"There was a dead man in the desert. I knew who it was, but at the same time, I didn't. Another man was there. I couldn't see his face, either, but I knew him, too. He refused to help me." Dawn shook her head and took a drink of coffee. "It was more than a dream, Cormick. It had that *dreamy* quality to it, but it was more than that."

"For the purpose of interpretation, we will assume it was a dream," he said. Despite his earlier indication, Cormick had studied dream interpretation. Dreams were once important to him, and he had spent years trying to unlock the cryptic answers revealed to him in his own dreams. Even more difficult, he struggled to find the questions he was asking.

"If memory serves," he continued, "being alone in the desert indicates isolation or a fear of being alone. Dreams about death are often misleading. It is my experience that patients experiencing such dreams fear a coming loss or disappointment."

"Maybe you're right. Maybe it just means one of you

guys will die," Dawn said as she got up. "I'm going to wake up Angelo."

Cormick sat at the table thinking about death. Just a few hours earlier, he had discovered that Horace, a man who had died and come back, was just waiting to die again. From the way he smoked and drank, it was obvious he was doing everything he could to extinguish his very existence. *Maybe Horace is the dead man in the dream,* he thought. It seemed to be what he wanted most. Perhaps it was Horace's destiny to be taken to Santa Fe to actually meet God again the traditional way: by dying.

"Dude, did your babe do this?" Sayer asked as he looked around the kitchen in amazement.

"I did it. And Dawn is not my…" Cormick looked up to find Sayer walking toward the stove wearing only a smile. "It would probably be a good idea to put something on before Dawn comes back."

"Dude, I'm just as God made me," he said.

Cormick got up to refill his coffee cup.

"There is more than enough clean underwear for you folded on the stairs. Please put on a pair before you do any further damage to my ego."

Sayer walked to the stairs and gave serious thought to his choice as he danced to the imaginary tune playing in his head. After careful consideration, he put on a pair of boxers covered with dancing ducks and headed back to the kitchen.

Dawn had led Angelo to the table, and Cormick was beginning to make breakfast.

"Good Morning," Cormick said as they entered the room. "There is a limited amount of actual edible items in the house, so I will have to ration out your meal."

"Whoa, even first thing in the morning, you're still a tasty bag of chips!" Sayer said as he winked at Dawn.

"Thanks," Dawn said. "I caught your act on the stairs. Nice." She topped off her cup. "Coffee?"

"No way! Caffeine doesn't cross these lips. But I'd totally love to help make breakfast! What can I do, dude?"

Cormick handed Sayer a can of fruit cocktail.

"Open this for the fruit cups." Cormick preferred fresh fruit for breakfast, but he found just one mummified banana.

Sayer stood there, staring at the can. "Which end do I open?"

"Maybe Dawn can help you with that," Cormick said shaking his head. "What time does your brother normally wake up?"

"Lately, he gets up when the voice calls him."

Angelo laughed. "Well Cormick, you might get to hear the voice after all!"

"I am not holding my breath," Cormick said as he pulled an egg carton from the refrigerator. "Do you have any bacon?"

"Dude, I don't eat pork!"

Horace appeared in the kitchen, squinting his bloodshot eyes. He was disoriented in the clean house.

"The house looks great," he said hoarsely. "You didn't have to."

"Cormick is a neat freak," Dawn and Angelo said, almost in unison.

"I am not as obsessive as they make me sound," he said. "After all, your ashtray is still full."

"Dude, that ashtray is always hitting terminal velocity!"

Cormick was impressed that Sayer had come up with such big words, even though he clearly was not using them properly. *Maybe there is hope for him after all,* he thought.

"Who wants scrambled?" he asked as he cracked the first egg.

———ww———

Cormick sat alone at the kitchen table, following the cat with his eyes. In turn, the cat slinked slowly through the kitchen, keeping a watchful eye on the oven. The cat was as unnerved by the feline-eating appliance as Cormick was by the prospect of actually meeting God in Santa Fe. But, with the breakfast dishes done and half of the trip behind him, Cormick was experiencing a momentary calm.

He walked to the living room window and gazed out at the ocean. The backyard was devoid of any species of flowering plant, and he assessed it was cared for as well as the house had been. He noticed Angelo was sitting alone in the patchy yellow grass. He had changed into a red flannel shirt and jeans, which seemed out of place in the California sun. Cormick removed the apron, folded it neatly, and went outside to join his friend.

He pushed open the screen door and stood on the porch for a moment to admire the Pacific. He had spent half of his life on the west coast but had taken the ocean for granted. This morning it seemed to have healing powers. He breathed in deep, filling his lungs with the fresh sea air.

"Hi, Cormick," Angelo said, still facing the ocean. "Come on over and have a seat."

"How did you know it was me?" Cormick asked as he descended the steps into the back yard.

"Like I said before, I don't need my eyes to see. Besides, I know the sound of your walk. It's kind of a heavy shuffle."

Cormick became immediately self-conscious and made an extra effort to lift his feet as he walked over to Angelo.

"I was just smelling the fresh air. After a night in that house, I had forgotten what it smelled like." He sat next to Angelo and stared out at the rolling waves.

"The air is a lot cleaner up north," Angelo said. "I didn't notice until I couldn't see."

"You must be nervous," Cormick said. "We are almost at our destination."

"I'm not nervous." Angelo continued to face straight ahead. "The closer we get, the more at peace I feel. But at the same time, I'm a little sad."

"What about it saddens you, exactly?"

"A couple of things, actually," Angelo responded. "Here we are, five strangers chosen by God for something that goes beyond our understanding. We're about to come face to face with God, Cormick. There are countless millions of people who pray for this every day, and we—five people who have never sought this out—are the ones chosen by God. I haven't spent a lot of time asking why because I've spent the last few days convincing you that this is what must be. But now I'm asking, why not all of those others?"

"There may well be others converging on Santa Fe from every conceivable direction as we speak." Cormick paused and waited for a reaction from Angelo. When there was no response, Cormick back tracked the conversation to Angelo's original point. "Are you distraught because more of the so-called faithful are not here with us? Does praying make any one of them more worthy than any one of you?"

"Or you?" Angelo asked.

"Or me, I suppose," Cormick answered.

"It's not just that. Before my mother died, she had so many questions about heaven." Angelo's voice softened as he stretched out his legs on the lawn. "I remember seeing her in the hospital, studying everything from the Book of Mormon to the Qur'an and several other books on reincarnation and New Age spirituality. We used to sit and talk for hours about what awaited her after death."

"I am sorry," Cormick said. "I understand how hard it is to be confronted with the mortality of a loved one."

"Cormick, she spent months searching in those books, but she never found the answer. And now, here I am, about to find out the one thing she needed most in her life, and I can't give it to her."

"Maybe those answers are for you," Cormick offered.

"What does that mean?" Angelo asked. "My mother didn't deserve the answers?"

"That is not what I am saying. What if your mother is a small part of a larger answer?" Cormick stood up and took a few steps in front of Angelo. "Her search to find the most basic answers about life and the afterlife created in you a desire to find the truth for yourself. She passed away, Angelo. She has those answers now. But it follows that, without her search for spiritual knowledge, you would not be here right now; you may not have been even the slightest bit receptive to this calling."

"Why, Cormick," Angelo let out a laugh, "are you saying this was all part of God's plan? You don't sound like a psychiatrist anymore. You're starting to sound like Sayer."

"I find that remark insulting."

"All I meant was, you sound less pessimistic than usual," Angelo replied.

"Do not misunderstand. I am not a believer. I have serious doubts about God speaking to any of you, let alone all of you. But there is evidence that something or someone wants us in Santa Fe. I have simply made a minor adjustment in my thinking to better manage the circumstances that surround me."

"If Dawn were here, she wouldn't let you off that easy," Angelo said.

"Fortunately for me, she is upstairs in the shower." Cormick turned to face the ocean. He raised his hands to shade his eyes. "Sayer is out there, somewhere, for a final ride before we go.

"Not any more, dude!" Sayer said as he rounded the corner of the house carrying his surfboard. He was dressed in a tight, black wetsuit that was cut off at the knees. "Man, I'm gonna miss those killer waves."

"That brings up an interesting point," Angelo said. "How long do you think we'll be gone?"

"I suppose we will be there until we discover the answers we seek. I am sure that at some point I will need to return to Vancouver. After that, you four will be on your own," Cormick said firmly. He had no intention of dragging this experience out.

"The way I see it," Sayer began, "at least six days but less than forty."

"Did God tell you that?" Cormick asked.

"Nah…but everything God does is between six and forty days. Six days…BOOM! Universe!" Sayer threw his hands apart to simulate the big bang. "Forty days…WHOOSH! Flood! Noah rides the biggest waves of all time." Sayer let his mind wander for a moment as he pictured all of the animals on the ark enjoying the ride of their lives. "Hey, has anyone seen my brother?"

"Yes, he went to the liquor store," Cormick said. "He said he needed supplies."

"Cool, so where's the babe?"

"Dawn is upstairs preparing for the trip. I suggest you follow her example," Cormick said. "I want to get back on the road as soon as possible."

"No problem, dude. Here," Sayer said holding out his surfboard, "tie my board to the van."

Angelo broke into laughter. "You're taking your surfboard? Sayer, do you even know where New Mexico is?"

"Um, yeah…next to Old Mexico."

"I believe what Angelo is saying is that there is no ocean where we are going, so surfing may be a bit difficult."

"Dude, where I go, Wayne goes. He's my daily driver." He walked over to Cormick and handed him the surfboard. "Wayne, this is Cormick. He'll take good care of you." He patted his board and walked into the house.

"You realize that Sayer is on drugs, right?" Cormick asked.

"Oh yeah. I caught a whiff of his room. It smells like bong water," Angelo said. "Hi Wayne, I'm Angelo. We weren't properly introduced." His introduction was followed by another short burst of laughter. "Man, this trip gets better every minute."

THE ROAD AHEAD

Cormick sat on the front porch, peeling the cracking paint from the railing as the shadows from the setting sun slowly enveloped him in soft darkness. He was too distracted to enjoy the beauty that surrounded him. Instead, he watched the road, waiting impatiently for any sign of Horace.

It had been more than eight hours since his departure for the liquor store, and Cormick began to wonder if it was going to be another eight hours before his return. There was a nervous tightness in chest, which he tried to ease by restructuring his completely unraveled travel schedule.

The Voyager sat poised for the trip in the gravel driveway with Wayne tied securely to the roof. The smiling lips painted on the board seemed to be smirking at him. Cormick suspected that since Wayne had been acquainted with Horace longer, he had probably seen this coming.

The aging screen door creaked behind him as Dawn stepped out onto the porch. He looked back over his shoulder, saying nothing. Her hair lightly danced about her shoulders in the subtle breeze, its color rivaling the best sunset the California coast could offer.

"Any sign of him?" she asked.

"No," he replied as he turned back to the road. "I guess I cannot blame him. Maybe he is smarter than the rest of us."

"Is he smarter because he's probably sitting in a bar?" she asked.

"Perhaps he realized how absurd this whole crusade is," Cormick answered. "In retrospect, I probably should have run away when I had the chance."

"Silly Cormick…you never had the chance." She sat on the steps beside him and placed her hand on his. "I've been listening to you, and I know you don't mean that. Deep down inside, no matter what you tell all of us, I know you believe."

"I believe that all people need to find answers to their questions. Take Angelo for example. For him, this is much more than being called by God. It is a continuing search for spiritual direction. It is a desperate need to understand what happens after death. And while I support that, I cannot help but feel that Angelo is setting himself up for a big disappointment."

"Cormick," Dawn said shaking her head, "we are not going to be disappointed. And God is going to give Angelo, and all of us, all the answers we seek."

"How can you say that?" Cormick stood up and took a few steps into the yard, careful to lift his feet to avoid his shuffle. "How can you even say that God is sitting in New Mexico waiting for us? Say the sentence out loud. It is absurd! Let us say that, for the sake of argument, the Supreme Being is in New Mexico. What is he doing there? Why not Vatican City? Jerusalem? And when we get there, what makes you think that God is going to reveal anything to us, let alone the answers we seek?"

"So, you are seeking answers," Dawn said.

"I meant you…the four of you."

"I got you, Cormick. I'm onto you," she said, smiling.

"You got me Dawn. There is no getting anything by you," he said. "I do need answers. I need someone to tell me what on earth I was thinking when I agreed to come along on this pilgrimage."

"It must have been hard for you to leave your girlfriend," Dawn said.

"I have not had a girlfriend since I was in college. The only thing I left behind was my sanity."

"C'mon Cormick. I saw the way you and that little nurse said goodbye."

Cormick pictured Allison in his arms. He could still hear her voice echoing in his head. Closing his eyes, he took a deep cleansing breath. He could smell her perfume as if it were carried on the breeze. He opened his eyes quickly, hoping Dawn had not seen his momentary lapse.

"Nurse Paige is not my girlfriend," he said.

"Oh, I see. So whenever you leave the hospital, you kiss the staff goodbye," she said sarcastically.

"How did this become about me?" he asked.

"We don't have to talk about God all of the time," Dawn said. "There's more to us than that. We're only human." She pulled a paint chip from the railing and tossed it into the yard. "So, do you miss her?"

Cormick slid his hands into his front pockets and shuffled back to the porch with his head hung low. He sat next to Dawn on the porch.

"I am not predisposed to discussing personal matters. I am actually quite uncomfortable discussing my private life."

"Hey, at least you have someone," Dawn said. "All I have is a cat, and it lives at the neighbor's house. It won't even eat at my house anymore."

"I do not have anyone, per se. Allison…Nurse Paige, that is…I think I have…" Cormick stammered.

"You love her."

"I cannot say it is love, exactly, as I have no frame of reference to draw from," he said.

"C'mon Cormick, you've been in love before," she said. "You're what forty-eight, forty-nine years old? Are you telling me that in half a century you've never been in love?"

"I am forty-two," he said through gritted teeth. "And no, I cannot remember a moment in which I was in love. I have had relationships, but I have not been in love. Not as I understand it at least."

"Oh you sweet talker," she began, "it's hard to believe that when you use such romantic phrases like 'not predisposed' and 'no frame of reference.' I can't believe women aren't throwing themselves at you."

"How would I know if I was in love?" he asked, looking for guidance.

"Well," Dawn perked up, eager to help, "how do you feel when you see her? What do you think about?"

"You know what, never mind," he said. "This is an exercise in futility."

"No, Cormick, tell me," she implored. "You built a career helping others find their way, let me help you."

"Look, this is extremely embarrassing. I do not want you to laugh in my face."

"Cormick, you've spent your entire career listening to people tell you their fears and their fantasies. You don't laugh at them, do you?" Dawn was eager to have him open up to her. "Everyone falls in love, and when they're in love, they do and say stupid things. But it's all for love, Cormick! Good ahead. I won't laugh, I promise."

"Okay," Cormick drew in a deep breath. "When I see her or hear her voice, I seem to imagine a small flock of little blue birds flying around her head."

Cormick slowly looked up into Dawn's eyes. She was biting down on her bottom lip hard as a broad smile slowly began to spread across her face. It was no more than three seconds before she burst into uncontrollable laughter.

Cormick jumped to his feet and stepped back into the yard, leaving Dawn laughing hysterically on the steps. He watched as she fell backward onto the porch. She righted herself twice, only to fall back each time she regained eye contact with him.

"Never again," he muttered.

Dawn sat up a third time, wiping tears from her eyes.

"I'm sorry," she said, trying to catch her breath, "but that bird thing…I've never heard anything like that before. It's really sweet. Funny, but romantic." She paused for a moment, then sang, "Why do birds suddenly appear, every time, you are near…"

"I knew I should have kept it to myself."

"So Cormick, I'm curious…what animal did you picture when you first met me?" she asked, giggling.

"Sharks," he sniped. "Now I do not want to discuss this any further. I want to find Horace and get back on the road."

"We could send Sayer out to find him." Dawn was still shaking a bit from laughter.

"And run the risk of losing another disciple?" He questioned. "No thank you. You four do not need a driver, you need a babysitter."

"Well, I guess we could send out a small flock of little blue birds to scout the neighborhood." Her eyes opened wide as she let go with another burst of laughter.

Cormick could not speak. He wanted the conversation to end permanently. He feared Dawn would tell the others and that he would become the butt of a tortuous, running joke. He was about to speak up when a car turned the corner and made its way down the street.

"If that is not Horace, I am going to get in the van and leave without him," he growled.

The road weary Pontiac Bonneville swerved and was set on a trajectory to collide with the deteriorating picket fence as well as Cormick, who was standing unprotected in the middle of the yard. He stood there terrified and unable to move, watching as the car jumped the curb and tore the mailbox from the ground.

Cormick bolted for the porch, almost running over Dawn who had thrown herself backward to escape the fury of the possessed vehicle. The runaway car careened off the corner of the house, causing Angelo to scream something incoherently from the living room. As the corner windows of the house exploded from the force of the collision, long daggers of glass flew indiscriminately into the yard. The car swerved sharply and clipped the front of the Voyager, shredding the driver's side fender before coming to rest against the garage. Sayer came running out of the house and stood between Dawn and Cormick, who were getting to their feet. No one said a word as they stared at the wreckage in front of them. Cormick took a few steps toward the van, his mouth hanging open in utter disbelief.

"I didn't see a driver," Dawn said, following Cormick down the steps.

"My van…" Cormick said in a pained hush.

"See, dude, I told you Horace would be here."

⸻

Horace was lying on the couch, watching the living room ceiling spin. The constant rotation created a gravitational pull on the bottom of his stomach and forced its contents toward his throat. He rolled to the side to throw up on the floor, but his stomach was empty. Its entire contents were covering the front seat of his 1977 Pontiac Bonneville. He saw Sayer out of the corner of his eye and tried to call out to him. He managed to form an unintelligible gurgle before he was overcome with dry heaves. Dawn appeared with a wet wash cloth and laid it on his forehead. She pressed it against his head, giving him a look of disapproval.

"Aren't we a little old for these games?" she asked without smiling.

Horace wanted to tell her to fuck off, but he could only offer a disgusted sneer and a burst of flatulence to add to his humiliation. He closed his eyes, hoping to make her disappear. As desperately as he wanted a mother, he was not ready for a stand-in just now. He felt the weight of her body lift from the cushions and opened his eyes to see her walking to the corner of the house he had just remodeled.

Sayer was holding sheets of plastic against the windows where panes of glass had once been. The whole room seemed crooked to Horace. He struggled to discern if it was caused by the damage to the house or the alcohol in his system. His head fell back against the cushion.

"It felt just like an earthquake. I know. I've been in plenty of them." Angelo was still shaken up. "Even if I could see, I would have sworn that was an earthquake."

"Dude, chill," Sayer said. "The Terminator won't do any more crashing tonight. Unless you count crashing on the couch," Sayer laughed.

Dawn looked toward the couch to see if Horace had indeed passed out. His left arm raised up then dropped to extend from the sofa at a right angle. He defiantly raised his middle finger.

"Your brother is a real charmer," Dawn said. She turned back to the task at hand. "Sayer, give Angelo a corner of the plastic. You hold this one and give me the staple gun."

The damaged corner of the house had once proudly displayed five four-paned windows: three across the front and two that ran down the side of the house. At present, only one window still held a pane of glass, but it was the general consensus among the group that this was to be a short-lived phenomenon. The corner of the fifty-year-old house had been nearly lifted from its foundation by the force of the collision that separated the porch from the south end of the house.

The Pontiac seemed none the worse for the wear. Cormick sat on its rusted blue hood, staring at the laceration in the front quarter panel of his once pristine Voyager. He was quietly working on his speech to Horace. He had to let go of the anger he felt but needed to be firm in making it clear that Horace's suicidal tendencies only endangered the others. And the van. There could be no more damage to his van. He was the Charioteer. His job was to get everyone to their destination safely. *But if God actually wants us to go to Santa Fe,* he thought, *why is he constructing so many roadblocks?* Cormick hopped off the hood and walked over to the van, running his fingers gently over the scarred fender. The diamond blue finish would never be the same.

"How am I going to explain this to the dealership?" he asked the Voyager.

He walked up onto the creaking porch, ready to jump if it gave way beneath him. *If God is going to save us in Santa Fe*, he asked himself, *who is going to save this poor old house?*

Suddenly, he realized that he had acknowledged God twice. *No more of that*, he thought. He feared that, if he thought it, he might actually say it in front of the others. It was a slippery slope.

When he walked in, the others went silent. He looked at them for a moment, nodded, and walked over to Horace. He knelt down and leaned in toward him.

"Can you hear me alright?" Cormick asked.

"Yeah," Horace grumbled. "Leave me alone."

"I am only going to say this one time, so I expect to have your undivided attention." Cormick was reserved and professional.

"Cormick," Angelo called from the corner, "I don't think he's in any condition to…"

"He is in the only condition we have seen him in since we met. He is a high-functioning alcoholic. I can only deduce that this is as good as it gets. Therefore, we will handle this right now."

"Look, Doc, I don't want to hear it," Horace growled.

"Well, you are going to hear it. You are going to listen, and you are going to understand." Cormick drew in a deep breath. "For some reason that I have yet to fully comprehend, we have been brought together. I have entertained the notion that each of us has something to learn from one another. You, I would imagine, being an example to the rest of us of what not to do. Your selfish and irresponsible behavior is not what anyone should emulate."

"Cormick…" Dawn called from the corner as she grimaced at his speech.

He shot a quick glance toward her. She was shaking her head. She thought he was being too wordy.

"But I digress," Cormick said turning back to Horace.

"My point is this: We are in this boat together. If you are not going to grab an oar and help row, get out of the boat. The waters are difficult enough to navigate without your self-destructive tendencies making tidal waves."

"Was that a parable?" Sayer whispered to Angelo.

Horace sat up, pressing his hands to the sides of his head. He was sure that if he let go his skull would spilt open and reveal an aching and throbbing brain.

"How 'bout I just shove an oar up your ass?"

"Enough!" Dawn exclaimed as she tossed the staple gun onto the table. "Now you look here," she stormed over to Horace, almost knocking Cormick to the floor as she brushed past him. "You are a drunken piece of shit and a total liability to all of us," she said, stabbing him in the chest with her index finger. "You could have killed us on that porch. But instead, you killed your house. If Cormick is right, and you *are* trying to kill yourself, just do it already. And do it away from us!" She righted herself staring down at him.

Horace let his head slip from his hands. His chin bounced off of his chest and caused him to bite his tongue. He stared at the floor, searching for something to say. "I'm sorry" was out of the question, and "bitch" would probably be followed by a size seven shoe mark on the side of his face. After sorting through his options in his cloudy brain, he chose to not say anything at all.

"I think I had the situation well in hand," Cormick said as he stood up.

"Blah, blah, blah…" Dawn said. "You didn't have anything in hand. But you did almost have an oar up your ass."

Sayer and Angelo were giggling in the corner.

"Yo, dude, she kills me," Sayer said.

"I'm not trying to be funny," Dawn said firmly. She turned back to Horace. "I don't care if God wants you there or not. In fact, I can't think of one reason God or anyone else would be interested in having you around. But here you are, and despite your best efforts, you're alive for some reason." She knelt down to be face to face with him. "Maybe my opinion isn't important, but I'm going to tell it to you, anyway. You're a poor excuse for a man. You're a drunk, and drunk and reckless is no way to live your life. So get off your ass, get in the kitchen, and get some coffee in you so we can get going."

"I'm not going," he said.

"Fine. Sayer, your brother can finish the windows while we're gone. You and Angelo get in the van."

"We'd better do as she says," Angelo said.

"Hold on," Cormick said. "Dawn, may I have a word with you in the kitchen?" He led the way.

"Cormick, I don't want to hear it. You have to know how to talk to these people."

"I am a trained psychologist. I think I know how to talk to people."

"You were getting nowhere," she replied. "You achieved nothing with your nonsense in there."

"The only thing *you* achieved in there was to alienate him further by brow beating him," said Cormick. "That man has serious problems. I can help him come to terms with that. I deal with patients like Horace all of the time. If I present matters from a rational point of view, I can lead him…"

"Cormick," she interrupted, "that asshole almost killed us out there."

"And chastising him is not going to change that. He is not one of your students."

"What is that supposed to mean?"

"It means he is an adult," Cormick explained. "You cannot lecture him in the hope that he will suddenly have a revelation that will turn his life around."

"If he's an adult, he does a damn good job of hiding it," Dawn responded. She took a step back and looked toward Horace, who was now lying on the couch. "Brooding Vietnam vets have been done to death. I get it. It was a bad war." She turned to face Cormick. "But the fall of Saigon was more than fifteen years ago. If he hasn't built some kind of life from the rubble by now, I don't see much hope for that poor bastard."

Before Cormick could respond, there was a knock at the door. *Police*, he thought as he nervously joined Dawn at the entry to the kitchen.

Elaine Hanrahan slowly pulled open the screen door and stepped into the house. She smiled briefly and nodded to Sayer. She turned and saw Horace lying on the sofa. She folded her arms and rubbed her thin biceps as if she were freezing from the chill of seeing her former love in such a poor state. She took a painful breath and stepped into the light to get a better look at Horace.

Cormick studied the woman carefully. At first she appeared frail, but he could see she had the classic signs of a timid and scared woman with no self-esteem. Her arms were folded so tightly that her shoulders were pulled forward. Her baggy sundress, with its faded floral design, hid any sign of her figure. Her graying blonde hair was pulled back into a ponytail, and her bangs hung lifelessly on her forehead just above her blackened left eye.

The house stood quiet as all eyes followed her every move. She said nothing. Standing in front of Horace, she stared down at him as if she were in a trance.

Sensing the shadow on his face, Horace opened his eyes. The spinning in his head had subsided, and he was able to focus on her face.

"Elaine?" He pushed himself up on his elbows. "Your eye… did fucking Russ do that?"

"You did it," she said fighting back the tears. "You just can't let it go, can you?"

"Elaine," he began as he tried to sit up only to fall back on his elbows.

"Just lay there. Let me get a good look at the man you've become."

"Elaine, if that son of a bitch hit you again…"

"Of course he hit me, Horace. He hits me every time you hit him." She choked as a tear fell down her swollen cheek. "I can take the pain from him, but I can't take this pain anymore…seeing you like this. It's breaking my heart, Horace. You drink to the point of drowning. You beat up my husband…look at you. You had it all. And now, now your legacy will be nothing more than a wasted life of drinking and fighting."

"Yo, that's not fair, Elaine," Sayer said.

"It's fair," she said turning to Sayer. "You were a baby. You don't know." She turned back to Horace, trying not to cry. A loving smile came across her face. "You were the greatest man I ever knew. I loved you, Horace. You could have done anything, but you pissed it all away. And now it's all this mess."

Horace felt his throat tighten. He tried to swallow in an attempt to avoid crying.

"I didn't piss it away. You walked away. You let Russ steal my future."

"I wasn't your future. If I was, we would be together now. What about the Olympics? Or your writing, Horace? Your beautiful words…"

"You were my inspiration, Elaine. You were my life," he said as he continued to fight back his tears.

"You made me go, Horace," she said as she burst into tears. "What was I supposed to do? You stopped writing. I thought you were dead. Was I supposed to keep waiting for a corpse?"

"I couldn't write. The hospital…the fucking war…"

"The war?" Elaine raised her hand, and Cormick feared she may strike Horace. Instead she dropped to her knees beside the couch and let her arms fall around his chest. "You're waging a war with yourself, and you're losing. I can't keep reliving this with you, Horace," she cried. "When you did come back, you wouldn't let me in. You never let me help."

"It was too much," he sobbed. "You couldn't…"

"Understand?" Her head came to rest in the middle of his chest. "I might have surprised you."

"What do you want from me?" Horace asked. He put his arm around her. He wanted to kiss her, comfort her, anything to make it better. Instead he just fell back on the couch.

"I want you to leave. Now." She raised her head and their eyes met.

"Where am I supposed to go, Elaine? What am I supposed to do?"

"Dude, we can go to Santa Fe!" Sayer exclaimed, bewildered that his brother didn't think of it first.

"I don't care where you go. But if you don't go, Russ will kill you."

"I hear that shit ten times a week." Horace imagined

that he was hitting Hanrahan. It always felt good, but the next time it would feel great. The next beating would be for Elaine.

"What if he kills me instead? He has a gun, Horace," Elaine warned, wiping the tears from her eyes.

"If there is a man out there with a gun," Cormick said, "we will leave."

"Look here, Doc," Horace started.

"No dude, you look." Sayer came at his brother fast, pointing his index finger to his face. "We are leaving. God wants you to go, but you don't listen. We tell you to go, and you say no. But now, dude, if you don't go, you'll die. Seriously, bro'…what's it gonna take?"

"I'm dying anyway, Sayer," Horace replied, taken aback by his brother's tone of voice. There had never been a cross word from his good-natured little brother, and he wasn't sure how to respond.

"I didn't know Dad, and Mom barely talked to me. You're it, dude. You are my only family…my whole life. This is big! That dick is going to shoot you!" Sayer warned. "Now, we are *going* to Santa Fe even if I have to pick you up and carry you to the van, dude!"

Horace cocked an eyebrow at his defiant little brother to show displeasure at his attitude. But Sayer stood his ground. His arms were folded across his puffed up chest to maximize the effect of his flexed biceps. It was a show of force he had used quietly to intimidate people on the beach.

Horace looked into the teary eyes of Elaine. He wanted to kiss her, but he knew she would push him away. He gently ran the back of his hand on her tear-stained cheek. She held his hand for a moment and stood up.

"Take care of him, Sayer," she said as she quietly walked out the front door.

Horace sat up and covered his face. He did not want anyone to see the tears welling in his eyes.

"Alright, dammit," he sighed, "give me some coffee and then somebody help me to the van."

THE KEEPER OF THE TORCH

Elaine Hanrahan sat alone at her kitchen table, staring into the cup of heavily creamed coffee that sat cooling in front of her. The rhythmic ticking of the grandfather clock in the entry way kept time with the labored wheezing of her drunken husband lying unconscious on the couch. She was oblivious to both. After years of hearing their monotonous tones, they had become little more than white noise. On this morning, all of her thoughts were with Horace, hoping he was safely on his way to Santa Fe.

The pathetic image of Horace lying in a drunken stupor on his mother's couch could not have been burned into her memory any deeper if it had been done with a branding iron. The man he had become, not unlike her nightmare of an alcoholic husband, was nothing like the beautiful boy she had fallen in love with in high school.

For the graduating class of Huntington Beach High, 1968 had begun with so much promise. The turbulence of the era had not yet scarred their lives. The fear and prejudice that had swept over most of the country seemed to dissipate in the cool ocean breeze. By summer, the whole world had changed.

The assassinations of Martin Luther King Jr. and Bobby Kennedy had rocked their worlds. The truth and horror of the Vietnam war, once an ocean away, had invaded their lives through the evening news and flag-draped coffins flown in from Southeast Asia. The graduates' innocence, and the invulnerability of their youth, could no longer shield them from what was to come.

Horace and Elaine had been a steady couple since meeting at a track meet two years earlier. Coaxed into going by her friends, she'd sat in the bleachers studying English while they talked only of the boys on the field below. The main topic of their conversation was the boy every girl desired: Horace Jordan.

Tanned and toned, Horace's surfing prowess was legendary on the beach. When he was on his board, he looked like Adonis, every muscle flexed and taut as he maintained perfect balance on his board. To everyone on the beach, his confident and sexy smile proved that the sport was his passion.

As a sophomore, he had already set records in both the 400-meter hurdles and the 400-meter dash. He trained every day in hopes of making the Olympics. Beyond his athletic ability, Horace was a solid 4.0 student and gifted writer, who spent off-days working at the newspaper.

But Elaine had no time for boy talk. Her parents had taught her early on that college was the only way to a successful future and that boys would be nothing more than a hindrance.

"Especially the bums that hang out on the beach," her father had warned.

But her parents hadn't counted on Horace Jordan.

He had spotted her in the bleachers, just one riser above the group of giggling girls. Some smiled and waved, and some hid their blushing faces. He had looked right through them. They'd faded from his view as he walked toward Elaine, his long, brown hair blowing majestically in the wind like the mane of a prized stallion. From that moment on, he would never notice another woman. Where Elaine was concerned, Horace had spontaneously developed tunnel vision.

They were inseparable for the rest of their high-school years, never missing a chance to dream out their happy-ever-after together. They spent night after night on the beach, staring into heaven, confident that they belonged together just as the stars belonged in the night sky. In Elaine's eyes, Horace shined brighter than any star above. He was the one. She knew the boy would become a man, and that man would be the father of her children. In turn, she would build her whole life around his dreams.

Russ Hanrahan had different ideas for Horace and Elaine. Unknown to Horace, Hanrahan had always envied him. After a decade of playing little league together and surfing the same beach, they were on the track team together. Year after year, in every sport, Horace had always been the better athlete. He simply did what came naturally to him blissfully unaware of the competitive hatred Russ harbored.

Hanrahan's father had built a trophy shelf for his son when he started playing baseball in 1957, telling the boy to fill it with bronze statues and blue ribbons. Eleven years later, the dusty shelf held only two small trophies, both of which were honorable mention. For each trophy Hanrahan hadn't won, Horace seemed to win two, and for each trophy Horace earned, Hanrahan earned a fierce beating from his father.

Elaine was the trophy that Hanrahan coveted most, but, once again, Horace Jordan had taken first place. He had done everything he could to separate the couple, and with each unsuccessful attempt, he had grown angrier and more desperate to extinguish the torch she held for Horace. But all he had had to do was wait. The United States Army had intervened on his behalf.

The answer to all Hanrahan's hopes had come in the form of an induction notice on July 24, 1968, addressed to one Horace Jordan. Horace's number had been drawn in the lottery months earlier, and time was up. Elaine would be alone, and Horace would be gone. Hanrahan had hoped he would never return.

—— ˜˜˜ ——

Elaine was wrenched back into the present by the slamming of her front door. Her daughter, Sunshine, came running into the kitchen. Her usually bright blue eyes were swollen and red, her face awash in panic as she confronted her mother.

"Sunny, sweetheart…" Elaine began as she rose to her feet to give a comforting embrace to her daughter. "What's wrong?"

"Sayer's gone, Mom!" Her voice was shaky. It was their secret and their curse. Both women had lost their hearts to a Jordan man.

"Shhh…you'll wake your father," Elaine warned.

Sunny sniffled and pulled her face from her mother's shoulder.

"But Mom, you don't understand!" she cried. Her lips quivered as more tears broke free and flowed down her face. "He was going to take me with him!"

Russ Hanrahan had awoken at the slam of the front door and had heard everything. He stepped around the corner, causing Elaine to give a startled gasp.

"Take you where?" he asked through gritted teeth. He stood there, clenching his fists menacingly, staring directly into the eyes of his young daughter. He would hit her to get the answer, and once she answered, Elaine knew that she would be next and that he would not be so gentle with her.

"Russ, you shaved of your beard. It looks nice," she said, desperate to change the subject.

"Shut up, Elaine," he barked without taking his eyes off of his daughter. "Goddammit, Sunny! Where!?"

Sunny turned back to her mother and stared at her black eye. She knew her mother would pay dearly for the truth. By slamming the door, she had set in motion a series of events that were now beyond her ability to control.

"Russ," Elaine began as she moved in front of her daughter to protect her, "let's have some coffee, and we can talk about it."

Hanrahan grabbed her left wrist, bending it backward until the pain drove Elaine to her knees. A gasp escaped from her as she collapsed on the linoleum.

"Daddy!" Sunny screamed as she backed up against the refrigerator.

"Tell me where…" he said with an evil smile as he twisted Elaine's frail wrist even farther.

"Russ, please…" Elaine pleaded from the floor. "Honey, you're hurting me," she cried.

"Shut the fuck up!" He raised his hand in the air and held it like a cocked trigger. "Still protecting him. Bitch," he said before turning his attention back to his daughter. "I swear to God, Sunny, if you don't tell me, your mom will get hurt. And it'll be your fault, Sunny."

"Daddy, please!" she cried out.

Hanrahan was unfazed by the tears of his nineteen-year-old daughter. To him, they meant nothing more than that she was about to give him the answers he needed. He only felt stronger as the women around him weakened. He cranked Elaine's wrist back one more time to make his point to his daughter. Even after he heard the snap in her wrist, he held a tight grip.

Elaine tried to cry out, releasing only a shallow breath as a wave of nausea washed over her. She crumpled to the floor, her limp wrist tightly held by her merciless husband.

"See what you did, Sunny? Are you happy now?" he asked. "Tell me!"

"The desert! They're in the desert!' she screamed. "Please Daddy, no more," she begged. "Please let her go."

Horace released his grasp and tossed Elaine's arm down on top of her, never taking his eyes off Sunny for a moment. He moved toward her, like a lion stalking its prey, ready for the kill. Sunny slid down the refrigerator to the floor, convulsing hard from crying. He matched her descent, moving slowly down to his hands and knees keeping his face level with his sobbing daughter.

"What desert? High desert?" he asked, knowing the drive to the Mojave would be a quick one.

"S-s-s-anta F-f-fe," she stuttered through the tears.

"Why were you gonna go?"

"I love him, Daddy," she whined, unable to look her tormentor in the face.

Hanrahan instinctively raised his hand to back hand her. He stopped in midair and clenched his calloused fist, except for his index finger, which he pointed directly into her tear-streaked face.

"You are never going to see that little fuck again," he said as his voice grew steadily louder. "Do you understand me?"

Sunny nodded in agreement.

Hanrahan turned back to Elaine. She was lying where he'd left her, in a fetal position, cradling her fractured wrist. The break had sent her into a state of shock. There were no tears, no cries of pain. Hanrahan crawled over to her and leaned over her head.

"I'm going to kill Horace Jordan," he whispered in her ear.

Elaine remained motionless beneath him. She was back in the summer of 1968, the last good year of her life. In front of her was Horace, fresh from the summer surf, carrying his board. His long brown hair was glued to his head from the ocean water, and he shook it free, never taking his eyes off of her. His graceful form was slowly running toward her, his bright smile reflecting the love in her eyes. "Horace..." she whispered.

THE MAN FROM THE PLACE OF CLAY

The Voyager shot through the desert like a bullet aimed directly at Santa Fe. Dawn had commandeered the driver's seat, allowing Cormick to get some much needed sleep after nearly a full night of driving. Cormick's strict adherence to the speed limit had made progress relatively slow in comparison to their current pace.

Dawn's view of driving differed from that of Cormick's, and if any member of the New Mexico State Patrol had been in the vicinity, they, too, would have vehemently disagreed with her interpretation of most traffic laws. But Dawn had luck and nearly nonexistent traffic on her side. She was in full command of the minivan, steering it powerfully along Interstate 40 at eighty-eight miles an hour.

With only a few miles to go before reaching the anticipated destination, Dawn rolled down the window to let the morning air blow some life into her matted red hair. She turned up the radio to compensate for the whipping wind that made the Temptations difficult to hear. Angelo, who had not surrendered the passenger seat once during the entire trip, sang along with the radio.

"Just my imagination once again…" he sang, trying to drown out Horace's snoring from the floor behind him. "Runnin' away with me. It was just my imagination runnin' away with me…" He laughed out loud.

"It's not your imagination, Angelo," Dawn said as she placed her hand on his knee. "But I wish that snoring was. It's beyond me how something so obnoxious could come from such a small opening in the face."

"Maybe we should wake him up before he swallows his tongue," Angelo said.

"Let him sleep it off. He was pretty out of it last night. Besides, I think I can deal with the snoring better than I can his attitude." She shot a glance to the rearview mirror for any sign of Cormick stirring. "If Cormick can sleep through it, I'm happy."

Sayer's blonde head popped up from the rear seat. He buried the palms of his hands into his eyes and pulled downward on his face. He stretched his arms forward working the seat in front of him like a cat kneading its favorite cushion. He was making contorted expressions, as if he were stretching every muscle in his face, when his eyes met Dawn's fixed stare in the rearview mirror.

"I have a hard time coming back to the real world," he said.

Sayer looked down at his sleeping brother. He reached down and gently pushed Horace's jaw shut.

"Sayer's awake," Dawn said, "but I think he just killed Horace." There was little remorse in her voice.

The Temptations wrapped up their number and surrendered the airwaves to Van Morrison. Sayer stared out the window and watched the rolling dry hills pass behind him. He felt lonely for the first time in years. God had become his constant companion over the past few days but had not spoken to him since he encountered the three strangers from the north. Had God abandoned him? Were these three interfering with his line of communication with God?

"No, Sayer," the voice called out, "everything is as it should be."

"What was that Sayer?" Dawn asked.

"I didn't say anything," Sayer replied with a confident smile. "God just wanted me to know that things were still cool between us."

Dawn slammed on the brakes, forcing the van to a screaming stop. Cormick was launched from his seat, still in the fetal position, and slammed face first into Dawn's seat. At the same moment, Sayer bounced off of the back of Cormick's seat and landed on the chest of his sleeping brother, forcing an explosive exhale from Horace. The interior of the van erupted into a series of screams and moans that made the sound of the screeching tires barely audible. Dawn skillfully guided the van into the loose dirt and gravel on the shoulder of the road, never easing off the brakes for a second. In the momentarily shocked silence of her passengers, Dawn listened for the voice of God.

"Whoa…" Sayer grunted.

"What the fuck is going on?" Horace yelled as he fought to crawl from beneath his stunned little brother. "Sayer! Get the fuck offa me!"

"My van!" Cormick whined from the floor. He rubbed his neck hard, convinced he had fallen victim to a grievous case of whiplash.

"Shut up! Shut up! Everybody just shut up!" Dawn yelled, sternly, as she shut off the radio. After another moment of silence Dawn asked, "Can you hear me?" She cocked her left ear into the dusty air that poured in through her open window, waiting for an answer.

"I'm blind, not deaf," Angelo said.

"Shhh! Not you."

"It appears you have the undivided attention of us all," Cormick answered.

Dawn continued to listen to the empty air.

"Please talk to me," she implored.

Cormick painfully lifted himself back into his seat and looked back at Sayer.

"Do you know what she is talking about?" he asked in a hushed voice.

"She's trying to talk to God, dude."

"In the middle of the fucking highway?" Horace grumbled as he pulled himself into the set next to his brother. "Couldn't she have waited 'til we hit a rest stop or something?" He was careful to keep his voice low, as well. After the bar fight and his verbal beating the night before, he had gained some respect for—and a little fear of—the school teacher.

Angelo leaned toward Dawn. "We probably won't hear anything now that Cormick's awake."

Cormick stared at Angelo in disbelief.

"Thank you, Angelo. Now my day is complete. The sun has only just come up, and I have already faced death and been completely alienated."

"Hey, no offense man, but let's look at the facts, Cormick. God seems to keep you off of the guest list for all of his speaking engagements."

"He's right, dude. Maybe you should, like, take a walk or something so God can tell us what's up." Sayer smiled warmly at the dejected Cormick.

"I do not believe this. I have taken time from my professional and personal obligations…for what? To hear the voice of God just as all of you have," Cormick implored. "I have transported all of you on this voyage, been pummeled in a tavern, cleaned up your vomit, and held your hands as if I were your babysitter. And now, at the moment that all of you can at long last prove that there is a valid reason for my being here, you want me to 'take a walk or something.'"

Angelo turned toward the sound of Cormick's voice. "Look Cormick, if any of us deserves to hear the voice of God, it's you, man. But the facts speak for themselves. God simply doesn't speak to us when you're around."

Cormick inhaled deeply through his nose, clinching his lips tightly. He pushed himself forcefully from his seat and reached for the handle on the door.

"Fine." His voice had taken on the tone of an angry, pouting child. He slid the door open and stepped onto the roadside. "Fine with me."

"Whoa. And I thought Horace woke up in a bad mood," Sayer said.

"Don't forget to close the door," Dawn called after Cormick with syrupy pleasantry. She smiled and batted her eyes at him for added effect.

"Fine." He slammed the van door shut.

Cormick shuffled around to the back of the van, kicking dust into the air, and stared at the skid marks on the highway. He was sure there was at least half an inch of tread left on the road from Dawn's power braking. The smell of scorched rubber hung in the still air with the dust, making each breath undesirable. He looked eastward across the desert and started walking.

The hills of northern New Mexico were a study of contrast. There were orange and brown eroded mountains that served as a calendar back to the beginning of time. Some were a bleached-out shade of yellow, dotted with hundreds of ugly, round bushes. He did not know what kind of shrub they were, and he could not think of a word to describe their awful color. A bizarre mix of green and black, they stood watch over the pale landscape careful not to grow too close to one another. They reminded him of his companions in the van. Each one stood alone yet would seem out of place without the others.

He walked slowly up a hill as his anger subsided. The people in the van below had become his friends. If cleaning up vomit and getting punched was what it took to protect and take care of them, then that was what he would continue to do.

He found a vantage point on the side of the hill and sat down near one of the unattractive bushes. The Voyager below remained motionless. Wayne, still tightly bound to the roof, grinned up at him with a friendly reassurance. The dent in the van's fender made Cormick's lip curl in painful sympathy as he looked over the vehicle. The Voyager was also his friend, caught up in the madness with him. And the scar from Horace's out of control Bonneville was a wound that would not heal anytime soon.

The side door slid open slowly, and Horace stepped out of the van, raising his hand to shade his dry, swollen eyes from the midmorning sun. He spotted Cormick on the hillside and waved him down. Cormick offered no response.

"Shit, Doc, come down here." Horace stood waiting as Cormick stared blankly downward. "Fuck. If Muhammad won't come off the mountain…" Horace mumbled as he reluctantly headed up the withered hill. "C'mon, Doc. Quit pouting for chrissake."

"I am not pouting," Cormick responded. "I am taking a long overdue respite from all of this. It is becoming increasingly difficult to keep this trip in the proper perspective."

Horace continued up the incline, trying to keep his breathing under control. He had not heard a word of Cormick's response. His ears were ringing too loudly for him to hear much of anything. His mouth was coated with the usual morning film, and running his tongue along the back of his teeth, he felt the gritty dust imbedded in the stickiness of the bile from heaving the night before.

He stopped just short of Cormick and pulled a pint of whiskey from his jacket pocket. "God, I hate the fucking desert." He twisted the cap from the bottle and took a drink, filling his mouth with his liquid breakfast. He swallowed only half, swishing the remainder around in his mouth, then spat it on the ground. "Best mouthwash…" he said as he extended the bottle to Cormick.

"I believe I speak for everyone when I say that I prefer that you start your drinking a little later in the day. I am far from eager to clean up another puddle of vomit and cigarette butts." Cormick squinted up at the unsteady alcoholic wavering in front of him.

Horace pulled a pack of cigarettes from another pocket and lit the first one he could get his shaky fingers on. He looked like an addict desperate for a fix.

"I never asked you to clean up my barf or empty my ashtrays." He brought up a belch from deep inside his gut and forced it forward. Cormick was sure Horace was about to throw up again.

"I did not clean your ashtrays. The cigarettes were actually in the vomit. You must have eaten them between drinks."

Horace pulled the cigarette from his lip and took a good look at it. His tired red eyes were still swollen half shut, making it difficult for him to focus on the cigarette.

He bit off the end of the filter and chewed it slowly and deliberately. It didn't take long for his expression to change from inquisitive to disgusted. He spit the butt into the dirt.

"No wonder I puked. Those things are fucking awful."

"Well, taste and cancerous effects aside, perhaps you should investigate the nutritional value of nicotine-soaked cotton wrapped in colored paper. I would imagine that there are relatively few calories in a cigarette butt."

"Fuck you." Horace pressed the bottle to his lips and, after taking a drink, sneered at Cormick. He swallowed slowly, preparing his comeback. "You self-righteous prick. Are you so high and mighty that you don't have problems like the rest of us? Are you so fucking perfect that you can sit here and look down on us with that smug sense of supe-riority? Do they teach you that in college? Jesus, Cormick. You're a fucking shrink. Your job is to help people who are struggling." He pinched the severed filter of his cigarette and flicked it hard into the dirt at Cormick's feet.

"You know something, Doc? We ain't much. But right now, we're all you've got. We are all struggling to make sense of this moment. Hell, struggling to make sense of our lives. Maybe you should come out from behind your PhD and see us as we are. That would give you the perspective you're looking for." Horace turned and headed down the hill to the van.

"Hey!" Cormick called after him. "I am sorry."

Horace stopped, but did not turn around. He had regret-ted saying anything at all, but if he avoided eye contact for a moment, he figured he could avoid having to deal with apologies and explanations.

Cormick stood up, brushing the dirt from the backside of his khaki pants.

"I deal with people and their problems every day of my life. I do not look down on any of them. If it appears that I am acting in a manner condescending to any of you, I assure you, it is unintentional."

"Okay, I'll buy that," Horace said as he turned to take a few steps up the hill. "But just listen to the way you talk."

"Sorry?" Cormick asked.

"You even talk like you're better than us. You say 'I am' instead of 'I'm,' and 'is not' instead of 'ain't.' You talk like you're Mr. Spock or something!"

"Are you saying that my proper use of the English language makes me sound like a snob?"

"Way to pay attention, Doc. I guess college did some good for you after all," Horace said as he reached for another cigarette.

"Is there anything else? Are there other mitigating factors that appear to enlarge my ego?" Cormick wanted Horace to get everything off his chest now while both men were emotionally open to it. There were relatively few remaining personality conflicts, but he was eager to dispose of them and move forward.

"It's just your whole fucking attitude." Horace lit up and washed the smoke down with a swig of whiskey.

"I am jealous, I suppose." Cormick nodded his head and smiled.

Even though he did not see himself as part of the problem, he was opening up to Horace. He was actually envious of the others. An alcoholic, an unemployed surfer, a blind fisherman, and an assertive woman had found common ground and were working together.

"I am constantly being told by all of you that I am supposed to be here, yet God has chosen to exclude me from his revelations to the four of you. How am I supposed to believe that I am part of this search for the Supreme Being when I am kept from being a part of the one aspect that binds all of you together?"

"It's not our fault," Horace said between puffs from his cigarette.

"I understand that," Cormick said as he snatched the bottle from Horace's left hand. Cormick hoped that the move would assert his control over the situation and that sharing a drink from the same bottle would serve as a symbol of his willingness to create the male bonding that was so obviously missing.

Cormick braced himself for the shock and, in an exaggerated motion, threw back a shot of whiskey. It burned its way down his esophagus like drain cleaner.

"So," Cormick began, his voice was raspy from the pain of the searing alcohol, "tell me what you heard in the van during my absence." He cleared his throat and swallowed in a vain attempt to put out the fire in the pit of his stomach.

"Nothing, really. Nothing important," Horace answered as he crushed the butt beneath his worn out sneakers.

"Horace, second-hand information is all that I am privy to. I feel that I have a right to the same knowledge that all of you share. Please," he implored, "what did you hear?"

Horace lit another cigarette and turned to stare at the van. The others were along the roadside, stretching their muscles for the last leg of the journey. He shook his head and turned back to Cormick.

"We have to go shopping."

"I am not going anywhere until I know what you heard," Cormick said.

"That's what I'm telling you, Doc," Horace said as he

snatched the pint back from Cormick. "God wants us to go shopping."

Horace took a quick drink and turned from Cormick to avoid eye contact. He knew as soon as he spoke the words how ridiculous they sounded to Cormick. But he also knew they were God's words.

"Shopping? God told us to go shopping? Have all of you taken leave of your good senses?"

Cormick reached out and swiped the bottle back from Horace. He drank without hesitation, dumping two quick shots into his system. Cormick could feel he was losing his composure but used the burn of the alcohol to stay focused.

"Slow down there, Doc. You're not a drinker. Three shots for breakfast might be a bit tough on your tender body." Horace reached out to grab hold of Cormick's arm. "Drinking is no way to deal with this."

Cormick looked at Horace and laughed.

"You are...oh, excuse me. I mean *you're* the expert. If anyone around here can tell me which problems are best handled with alcohol, I hope it is you." Cormick turned and headed down the hill. He threw his arms skyward and let his head fall back. "Attention K-Mart shoppers...there is a special on insanity today...!" he called out to the open sky above, which appeared to give its undivided attention as Cormick continued down the slope to the van.

"I am driving," Cormick snapped at Dawn as he threw open the driver's door. He jumped in and slammed the door.

Cormick started the van and revved hard. He looked out the open window at his companions who stood motionless staring blankly back at him.

"Get in the fucking car!" he snapped.

The others bolted for the van without a word. Horace

slowly brought up the rear and slid the door closed as he crawled in next to Dawn.

"He's comin' around," he said with a wink and a smile.

———〜∭〜———

Cormick eased the Voyager slowly forward through the congested traffic of downtown Santa Fe. He had not spoken a word to anyone since taking over the driver's seat after his uncharacteristically profane outburst. To further the deterioration of his mood, the alcohol he had so freely poured into his system had given him a dull headache.

"Bad Karma…" Cormick moaned.

"Whoa, this is, like, the strangest place I have ever seen," Sayer said. "It's like the old west over here…is that building made of dirt?"

"It's made to look like adobe, Sayer," Dawn replied, still upset at having to relinquish her position behind the wheel. "C'mon, Cormick, find a parking space so we can go shopping!"

"Typical woman." Horace reached for his Marlboros, only to find a single cigarette, broken into three pieces, held together by torn paper and a few strands of tobacco. "Christ! Now that is bad karma!" He fumbled with the cigarette, trying to push the pieces back together. "Anyone have some tape or something?"

"There is no such thing as a typical woman," Dawn said.

"Yeah…okay. Whatever you say, honey." Horace only had a passing interest in the conversation. He had bigger problems. "Hey, pull over at the next Circle K, will ya, Doc? I need some smokes."

"And I need to address your sexist attitude," Dawn said, glaring at Horace.

"Look, I just want a smoke." He glanced up from his repair work to give Dawn a serious stare of his own. "You can bitch about my attitude all you want after that."

"No. I'll deal with it now. What is a typical woman?" Dawn asked of the four men surrounding her.

"Like…you know…soft and smells nice…" Sayer responded.

"Nice. Thank you for that, Sayer." Dawn leaned forward. "Cormick?" Cormick continued to stare straight ahead, refusing to oblige either side in the debate. "Angelo…?" She asked.

Angelo remained quiet. His body was completely rigid in the passenger seat. Unbeknownst to the others, he was overcome by bright flashes in the darkness behind his sightless eyes. Unable to clear the intense visions from his brain, he sat silently waiting for what would come next.

Dawn bit her bottom lip and looked back at Horace. He was digging in the ashtray in the armrest searching for a butt long enough to light.

"I'm not going to shut up until someone other than Sayer answers," said Dawn.

"So, whaddaya sayin'?" Sayer questioned.

"Okay. You want an answer?" Horace asked through gritted teeth.

"Yes, I do. No holds barred. Be honest."

"What was the question?" he asked.

"What is a typical woman?" Dawn snapped.

"You know…shopping and shit." He felt that had satisfactorily answered her inane question.

"You're an ass. You were here. You heard what God said. Does that mean God is a woman?"

"No fucking way!" Horace laughed. "God ain't no chick."

"Whoa…dude, what if God were a woman. She'd be a total babe." Sayer looked at his brother with a confused gaze. The concept was well beyond what he could piece together.

"Sayer, you've talked to God, right?" Horace asked. Sayer responded with an eager nod. "Good. Did he have a woman's voice?"

Sayer just stared at Horace. He was unable to define the sound of God's voice.

"Dude…I'm not sure. It was like…it was…"

Dawn thought back to the times she had heard the voice. There was no tone that leant itself to male or female. It was calm and soothing and there was simply no other way to describe it. It was low and quiet and resonated inside her when she heard it.

"I remember how she sounded. God's a woman," Dawn said, refusing to concede her point. "Who knows, Horace? Maybe she's waiting in one of these quaint little shops to give you a fabulous discount on a big turquoise belt buckle!"

Dawn didn't want to sound like Horace's definition of a typical woman. She gave no hint at how excited she actually was to wander the local shops to see what treasures she could discover.

"Shit. I need a smoke," Horace said as he crumpled the empty pack and let it fall to the floor. He shot a quick glance at the rearview mirror to make sure Cormick hadn't seen him litter.

Cormick had been listening to the conversation and was relieved to have had no part in it. He concentrated on the city around him. He had never given Santa Fe a passing thought. He had always pictured it as little more than a stop-over for cowboys, with few amenities. He realized now that he had been way off the mark.

Santa Fe was a consumer's dream vacation. Every billboard beckoned visitors to visit an authentic Native American craft shop or to empty their wallets at a point of interest with live western shows. The intersections were clogged with out-of-state plates, and the sidewalks full of tourists and their shopping bags.

Without warning, Angelo thrust his hands forward and slapped them hard on the dash. His grip on the light blue plastic was tight enough to turn his knuckles white. He drew in a sudden shallow breath, which sounded to the others like he was choking.

"Honey, are you okay?" Dawn leaned forward, placing her hand gently on Angelo's left arm. She was caught off guard at the strength of his hold on the dash.

"We're here," he said breathlessly. "Let me out! Let me out of the van!"

Angelo slammed his hands against the door and fumbled for the latch, his awkward hands flopped about like suffocating fish thrown onto dry land. Dawn lurched forward trying to get a grip on Angelo.

"Cormick, do something!" she cried.

It was too late. Angelo had found the handle and pushed open the door, ready to bolt from the van into the crowded street. Cormick hit the brake, throwing Angelo against the windshield as Horace and Sayer were thrown forward and then back again into their seats.

"Can't anyone drive this fucking thing?" Horace yelled.

Sayer lunged over the seat, past his complaining brother, to help Dawn hold onto Angelo. Tossed back into his seat, Angelo regained his balance and slipped from Sayer's grasp, who then fell chest first on the floor between the front seats as the soles of his shoes slammed against the headliner.

"Dude!" Sayer cried from the floor as the blind man stepped into the heavy traffic. Sayer scrambled from the floor and leapt over the passenger seat landing behind Angelo. He wrapped him up in his arms amidst blaring horns and cursing drivers.

"Chill out!" Sayer called to the traffic behind them that had screeched to a standstill.

Dawn threw open the sliding door of the van and joined them in the street.

"You park. We'll wait for you here," she said to Cormick. With that, she shut the door and helped Sayer lead Angelo to the curb.

Cormick sat motionless in the driver's seat, ignoring the honking and shouting behind him. He watched as the others crossed the street, their arms acting like a human straight jacket wrapped around Angelo. Slowly climbing his way through the van, Horace made his way to the passenger seat, grunting as if each step was a labored task. He plopped down into the passenger seat and handed Cormick the pint.

"Crazy shit, huh? Here ya go, Doc. You look like you could use a little jump start."

Horace held out the bottle until he realized Cormick was too stunned to accept it. He retracted his arm and took a quick swallow.

"Maybe we should…oh, I don't know…drive or something," he said as he looked through the back windows at the cars lined up behind them.

Cormick drew in a deep breath and slowly lifted his foot from the brake. He took advantage of the motionless traffic and guided the van into the right lane. Parking would be difficult. Surrounded by hostile tourists, he searched for a side street with a friendly name.

Marcy... he thought as he approached the next street sign. How unfriendly could a street named Marcy be?

"I can see you're burnt out over this, Doc," Horace said, trying to force a conversation from the uncooperative driver. "Shit, it could be worse."

Worse? Cormick thought to himself. *What could be worse?* He struggled to think what could make the journey even more unenjoyable than it was. A broken leg? A tornado? Another chain-smoking alcoholic feigning empathy? Suddenly, a loud bang sounded from beneath the van and the driver's side dropped three inches. The sound of metal scraping against the pavement cut through Cormick like fingernails on a chalkboard. A flat tire.

"It's worse," Horace said.

A delivery truck pulled from the curb a few car lengths ahead, and Cormick steered for the space near the corner of Washington. Now there was a friendly name. Just seeing the name of his home state made him long for the safety of his condo and the comfort of Allison's arms.

"Umm...Doc? You're not gonna fall apart on me, are ya?" said Horace.

The concern in Horace's voice was genuine, but Cormick did not answer; he remained detached. He tried to focus on the deteriorating situation around him, but he felt like he was drowning in his own thoughts.

Cormick nosed the van in, eased it along the curb, and shut off the ignition. As he stared out the bug-splattered windshield, he exhaled at length and deflated in his seat. Horace was talking, but Cormick wasn't able to comprehend any of it. His thoughts turned to Angelo, the man who had talked him into this ridiculous journey. Through it all, Angelo had been his rock of sanity. But now, he had crumbled like a cookie in the hand of a two year old. The calm assurance that he had given Cormick was gone. If Angelo had lost control, how long would it be before he lost his grip on the situation?

"Well, I'm outta here," Horace said, as he tucked his pint into the pocket of his olive drab field jacket. "I need to track down the others and some smokes. You comin'?"

"Yes…yes. I am coming with you."

"It's a miracle! He speaks!" Horace laughed as he stepped from the van. "We have found God!"

Cormick stepped into the afternoon sun and drew in a deep breath of the dry air as he stared in disbelief at what was left of the tire. The shredded rubber barely clung to the rim, and the front portion of the damaged wheel well rested on the pavement. He felt as bad as the Voyager looked: beaten, broken, and unable to go another inch forward.

Horace walked around the front of the van to survey the damage.

"That's a fucking mess," he said rubbing his backside. "My ass aches. Too much sitting." Cormick just stared at the damage, offering nothing. "Crazy looking town, eh, Doc? Whaddaya think…do they paint or just smear new mud on the walls once in a while?"

Cormick looked up at the architecture that surrounded him. As far as he was concerned, Santa Fe was a city of dirt. Cormick did not care for dirt or even the thought of being dirty. It appeared to him that the entire city had been bull-dozed into separate piles, and people had just painted blue trim on the hills of earth.

"C'mon, Doc…" Horace said pulling him away from the van. "We're on a mission, remember? One of these mud huts has to sell cigarettes."

Cormick turned and followed Horace down the street, shuffling slowly along the cobblestone. His heels seemed to catch every uneven stone.

"Here they are!" Horace exclaimed, happy to be reunited with his baby brother. "Sayer, did you see a place to buy smokes?"

Cormick stepped past Horace and stood in front of Angelo. He wanted to embrace him. He reached out and grabbed Angelo's upper arms. He could feel him trembling.

"That was not a smart decision," Cormick said. "I need you to be strong, my friend. Your welfare is in my hands as I have placed mine in yours."

"Cormick, cut the guilt trip," Dawn snapped.

"Cormick, I'm sorry. But we're here. We're close. Really close," Angelo said. "God is here, Cormick. God is here."

"Okay. I want you to take a deep, calming breath and exhale. Then, can you tell us where he is, Angelo?" Cormick asked.

"He's in the Plaza! Cormick, he's calling me to the Plaza!" Angelo exclaimed without the benefit of a calming breath.

"The Plaza?" Dawn asked. "Is that a hotel?"

"Dude...I see it, too." Sayer said. "It's like a mall but outside. Whoa, what a cool place! Angelo, I totally see it!"

"Where is it?" Dawn yelled, shaking her hands wildly.

"It's over there," Horace said. He pushed through the travelers and pointed to the next block.

"Dude! You had a vision!" his brother exclaimed joyfully.

"No, I read the fucking street sign," he replied as he scratched the graying stubble on his chin. "And there had better be some goddam cigarettes over there!"

Dawn grabbed hold of Angelo's hand and crossed the street with Sayer at her heels. Cormick stopped beside

Horace and nodded in the direction of the others.

"Perhaps God has a pack of cigarettes."

"Think he'll bum me one? If I keep breathing this fresh air much longer, my fucking lungs will explode." He smiled and placed his hand on Cormick's shoulder. "After you… God's waiting for us in the Plaza."

The two men followed the others, keeping pace from behind. They rounded the corner to find dozens of Native Americans sitting under a covered sidewalk. In front of each peddler lay a blanket covered with either pottery or jewelry. The line of merchants stretched the length of the entire block, and it seemed as if busloads of tourists had been dropped off just to gather and gawk at the natives and their wares.

Just ahead, Angelo was leading Dawn and Sayer through the crowd as they both held tightly onto his hands. Even though Angelo could not see where he was going, his mystical radar was operating at maximum efficiency. He bumped into nearly every camera-laden sightseer without stopping. Cormick was struggling to keep up but kept his watchful eye on Angelo. Horace was even farther behind, stopping occasionally to ask for a cigarette.

Without a word, Angelo stopped abruptly, causing Dawn to slam into him. Sayer tried to stop but crashed into the back of Dawn, knocking Angelo to the ground. Angelo's dark glasses flew from his face and onto a blanket of ceramic figures. Cormick continued to navigate quickly through the sea of people, using his shoulder as a rudder to guide him.

"Angelo!" he called out. "Angelo, are you okay?" He knelt down beside his friend.

"My glasses! Where are my glasses?' His hands wildly patted the ground in front of him.

"That Indian dude has them." Sayer pointed to a native merchant who had plucked the sunglasses from the blanket and was holding them in the air so the group could see where they landed.

"Cormick…Cormick, I've lost him."

Cormick looked up at Sayer. "What about you? Can you see where God is?" He knew that any random passerby would think him insane.

"No, dude. When we collided the TV in my brain just signed off."

"Well, then…" Cormick began. "We all got a little excited there for a moment, so we can use this time to calm down and regroup."

Angelo started to cry, still on his hands and knees, as careless strangers pushed by them.

"My glasses…" he sobbed.

Cormick knew that it was not about a pair of sunglasses. Angelo had traveled the farthest, sustained life-threatening injuries, and lost his sight on his quest to find God. He simply couldn't face another setback.

"Angelo," Cormick said in a hushed, reassuring voice, "it will be fine. We will get your glasses for you. You just need to take some time and collect yourself."

"What did I do wrong?" Angelo asked as Cormick helped him to his feet. He wiped the tears from his eyes. "Why did he break contact?"

"We will get your glasses and then we will get the answers," Cormick said. The two men made their way to the merchant who held the glasses in his hand.

"Your friend fell hard," he said smiling.

"Yes. He will be okay," Cormick offered. "If we could just…"

"Hey Chief," Horace interrupted. "Do you have a cigarette?" Horace had been so preoccupied, he had failed to notice the collision.

"I do not smoke," the merchant replied.

"Not even a peace pipe?" Horace snapped.

"As I was saying," Cormick inserted, "if we could just have those glasses, we will be on our way."

"Why does your friend need these glasses?" the smiling merchant asked.

"Look here, Geronimo," Horace barked, "that's none of your goddammed business. Just give us the glasses like the Doc said."

"Horace," the merchant smiled, "Angelo no longer needs these glasses."

"How the hell do you know...?" Horace glared at the man as Angelo opened his eyes to daylight for the first time since his accident.

"I can see!" Angelo exclaimed. "Oh my God, I can see!" He quickly moved his head from side to side waiting for a response from the stunned blurred images that surrounded him.

"Whoa!" Sayer jumped to Angelo's side hardly able to control his joy. "This is, like, a total miracle! This is way cool!"

"Now everyone just take a deep breath and relax," Cormick said calmly as he took control of the situation. "It has been an emotional day, and we must all take a step back and look at this rationally." Cormick wanted to prevent another explosive crescendo of emotions from taking control of everyone. "This is no miracle."

"Cormick, how can you say that?" Dawn asked. "It's just like in the Bible when Jesus healed the blind man."

"I understand how you are feeling, Dawn, but we can hardly compare any part of this situation to the Bible. Healing is physiology not the hand of God."

"Well what do you think instantly healed him? Your deep breath exercises?" Dawn snapped.

"Angelo nearly lost his life in that accident just a short time ago. He suffered severe trauma to the occipital region of his skull. The rather serious concussion and the resulting inflammation…"

"Who gives a shit?" Horace interrupted. "The blind guy can see." He turned to the merchant. "I want to know how this Indian knew my name." He reached out and snatched Angelo's glasses from his hands. "How 'bout it, Tonto?"

"Dude, did you heal Angelo's eyes?" Sayer asked with a knowing smile.

"God healed my eyes!" Angelo cried out. "It's true. It's all true. I knew it. God has great things planned for me! For us! We are the chosen!"

"Angelo, please…" Cormick reached for his outstretched hands and pulled them down to his side. "People are staring." Cormick put his arm around him and turned back to face the others. "Everyone needs to…"

"Take a deep breath?" Dawn said.

"Stay calm and rational," Cormick finished.

"Calm?" Dawn was mocking him. "A blind man has a vision that leads to God and suddenly he can see? And you're telling us that we should just…"

"Yes. Yes, I am, and yes we should," Cormick responded.

"Look," Horace interrupted, "I just want to know two things. First, how does this son of a bitch know my name, and second, where can I get a pack of goddam cigarettes!"

"I know your name because I have been expecting you."

"Whoa! God's an Indian!" Sayer exclaimed.

"I'm sorry to disappoint you, Sayer. I am not God. I am merely your guide." He held out his hand to shake. "My name is Clayton."

"What the hell kind of Indian name is that?" Horace asked.

"You can call me Clayton Mist of the Lake if that name makes it easier for you."

"Well, Mist of the Lake," Horace snarled, "if you're not the one who brought us here, how do you know so much about us?"

"As I said before, I am your guide. I will lead you on the rest of your journey." Clayton motioned to a large middle-aged native woman, who came and took his place on the blanket. Her face was expressionless, and she did not acknowledge the visitors from the north.

"If I may," Cormick interjected, "where is it exactly that you will be leading us? Where is this journey to end if not here in Santa Fe?"

"We must go to the Taos Pueblo," he said smiling. "There, everything will be revealed to you."

"I ain't going anywhere 'til I get a pack of smokes. Maybe then I could deal with Sitting Bullshit here." With that, Horace turned and pushed his way through the crowd. "See ya at the van!"

Cormick grabbed Dawn's arm. "You had better follow him. The last thing we need to do is form a search party to figure out which bar he has crawled into." Cormick paused to make sure Angelo was still under control. "Meet us back at the van as soon as he gets his smokes…um, I mean cigarettes."

Dawn was thrilled to be the one to keep Horace in check.

Cormick was far too spineless, and the others were too easy going. She darted through the crowd after Horace, keeping a safe distance so she could catch him in the act. *This will be fun,* she thought.

Cormick turned to Clayton. It was time for answers. "Pardon me, Mr…?"

"My name is Clayton." The gentleness of his voice seemed to hang in the air and caress Cormick's ears.

"I see. First names. Well I am…"

"Cormick," Clayton said with a soft smile.

"Where is…"

"About 70 miles north of here," Clayton replied.

"Yes. Well then…" Cormick was unsure how to continue. He was being cut off at every turn, each sentence anticipated and answered before he could finish. "As you can imagine there are…"

"Several questions you require answers to."

"Perhaps you would just like to give me some answers, and I could tailor my questions to them," Cormick snapped.

"My friend," Clayton said as he placed his hand on Cormick's shoulder, "you have traveled a great distance in a short time. The end of your journey is almost upon you." He slid his hand from Cormick's shoulder, across his back, and pulled him close, filling Cormick with anxiety. "Sayer and Angelo have no fear. Now the time comes for you to let go of your fear."

"Clayton, our lives have been completely disrupted by this. All of this can be explained as a series of coincidences. I could even go so far as to say that perhaps overpowering psychic phenomena…"

"Cormick," Angelo interrupted, "it's God."

"Totally," Sayer added.

Cormick pulled himself from Clayton's arm and turned to face him.

"I cannot and will not put up with any more of this ridiculous talk." Cormick turned to the others to argue his point but stopped short. Sayer had his hand in front of Angelo's face, his fingers spread wide apart.

"Okay dude, this is what a hand looks like, and these things here are fingers…"

Cormick turned back to Clayton and sighed with resignation.

"Simply put, I do not wish to wait any longer for answers. What would you suggest? Do I have to schedule an appointment with God to get some straight answers?"

"Once we reach the Pueblo, all of your questions will be answered. And much, much more."

"Cormick, it's good to see you, man!" Angelo said as he embraced him. "You look just as worried as I thought you would."

"Angelo, I am very happy that you have your sight back. But you must understand, this is no more a miracle than the sun rising in the morning." He eased from Angelo's embrace and looked directly into his eyes. "If anything, this is the miracle of the human body at work."

"No…no, Cormick, you're wrong. You've trusted me this far. Trust me now," Angelo pleaded. "Man, God brought me here…us here…to do some good. I'm going to make the world a better place. I'm going to be a fisher of men, Cormick." He turned to Clayton. "Isn't that right?"

"Oh yes, Angelo. You will be all of that and more."

"Dude, what about me? Will I get to fish for men, too?" Sayer asked with anticipation.

"The future holds a great deal for you my young friend.

You have only to follow and then you will lead."

"That is enough!" Cormick demanded. "You are talking, but you are not saying anything. I want to know right now what is going on here."

"Soon, Cormick," Clayton said. "This is not the time or the place for this. For now, why not return to your van and wait for Horace and Dawn to join us."

"There is no point in that," Cormick said. "We are not going anywhere anytime soon. The van is in bad shape."

"I don't believe that will be a problem," Clayton said smiling.

TAOS

Horace stepped up to the bar and signaled for the bartender.

"Sell cigarettes here?" he asked and the bartender nodded. "Marlboro Reds and a shot of Jack," he ordered.

The bartender tossed a pack of cigarettes in front of Horace.

"Open a tab?" he asked.

"I'll pay as I go. It's only a matter of time before God sends someone in here to get me," Horace replied. He threw a wadded up twenty onto the bar.

"Well, well, well…" Dawn began as she slid up onto the barstool beside him. "This is a surprise."

"Come here often?" Horace asked as he shook his head. "Christ, I haven't even had a drink yet." He tore the cellophane from his cigarettes and pulled one from the pack. He lit it, taking a long, slow drag. He turned to her and blew a cloud of smoke over her head. "Of all the gin joints in all the towns in all the world…she walks into mine," he said smiling.

"Casablanca. Maybe there's hope for you yet," she said. She turned to the bartender. "Can I get an ice water, please?"

"Go easy now…my bartender back home says that stuff will kill you," Horace said.

"I'll just have the one," she smiled. "I know my limits."

"Did the Doc send you in here?"

"Something like that," she said, still smiling. She sipped

from her straw and looked him over. He was staring blankly into his shot glass, taking an occasional drag from his cigarette. There was not even a hint of a smile through his graying stubble. His face was partially hidden by his field jacket. He looked defeated. Dawn knew he had to be hurting. Between the car wreck, the hangover, and all of the yelling, she knew he had to be in pain.

"Who was that woman last night?" she asked softly.

Horace shook his head, continuing to stare into the pool of alcohol. He had been thinking about Elaine since he got away from the others. He was sure he needed to be alone to sort everything out, but he was surprised that Dawn's presence was so comforting.

"Elaine? She's…she's what might have been," he replied. "But that was a lifetime ago."

"Is that why you drink? To forget her? Or is it to forget a lifetime?" Dawn asked.

Horace laughed and crushed out his cigarette.

"I drink to forget a lot of things…Elaine, the war, my mom, my fucking hemorrhoids. The only problem is, I sober up and all the bullshit is still there staring me in the face." He picked up the shot glass and held it in front of his face. "This numbs the pain."

"Maybe that's why you're here," Dawn said. "God is going to heal you just like he did Angelo. Maybe you're here to be made whole again."

"I can never be whole again." He finally tossed back the shot and signaled for another. He looked away so Dawn wouldn't notice the tears welling in his eyes. "I'm lucky, I suppose. I came home alive. But it still cost me my life."

"Cormick told me about how you were shot…" Dawn began.

"You want the truth about that day? About me getting shot?" he asked. "What the Doc told you is true. I stupidly lowered my gun, and I was shot by a kid. Twice." He lit another cigarette and inhaled deeply. "But I didn't tell Doc everything."

"Maybe that's the problem. Maybe you need to tell someone everything. If you keep your pain inside, it will tear you apart."

"It's not about the pain," Horace said. "It's about the truth."

"I don't understand," Dawn replied. "You didn't tell the truth?"

"After I was hit, I was layin' there, sure I was going to die, and the little bastard came over to me and sat on my chest. He pulled out a knife. He wanted to finish the job, maybe take an ear as a souvenir." He took a drag from his smoke. "I don't know where I got the strength, but I grabbed the knife, and we struggled. I rolled over on top of him and I buried the knife in that boy's chest. Not just once. More times than I could count. Maybe I was screaming. I don't know. And then I slit his throat. I slit it so deep, I almost took his fucking head off. I…I'm…"

"Horace, it was the war. God forgives…" Dawn said.

"You don't get it, Dawn. It's about the truth. That memory haunts me every day of my life. And not just that one. I'm no fucking saint. I killed people. I stood by and did nothing as my friends brutalized women and children. Fuck, I still hear their screams. I burned innocent people out of their homes, sometimes in their homes. Homes made of sticks for chrissake! All they had in this world was fucking sticks, and I took it from them. How is God going to forgive me for that? And the one time that I decide to show a little mercy…

I take two bullets in the chest." He took another drag as his shot arrived. "Two bullets that robbed me of everything I had, just as I robbed all of those people of everything they had. God evened the score."

"Horace, you have your life," Dawn said as she reached out and placed her hand on his. "Cormick told me that you believe that God kept you alive for something. Those bullets took nothing."

"Sometimes I think God kept me alive to punish me," he said, "and those bullets stole my dreams. I couldn't run anymore. I went to 'Nam two months before the '68 Olympics and came back unable to compete in '72." He tossed back his shot and took another drag. "One of the bullets severed my dog tags. They didn't know who I was for months, and I couldn't tell them. While I was in the hospital, they told my Mom I was dead. I can't even imagine what that must have been like for her. There was a funeral and everything. Elaine moved on, and my Mom never recovered." He paused and took a long slow drag from his cigarette. "Those bullets took everything from me."

"No, Horace. You let everything go," Dawn said. "You can't keep living your life thinking about what you've lost. If you do, you'll never be thankful for all you have."

Horace thought for a moment. What did he have? His mother had left him her car, her house, and her youngest son. The only thing he could call his own was the shop he built onto the garage and a disability check. He had lived fifteen years with nothing to show for it or call his own.

"Let's change the subject," Horace said as he slid onto his barstool. "Tell me about you. Who is Dawn Gallagher? Why has a good-looking woman like you left everything behind to find God in the desert?"

"Well, I…" Dawn stammered, flattered by his comment. "I was talked into it by Angelo I suppose. At first I thought someone was screwing with me, and then I met Angelo and Cormick, and…and I knew I had to come." She thought about her comment and laughed. "Okay, wait, not so much Cormick." She paused briefly and thought about meeting the men in the hospital. "I wish you could have been there that first day. I thought Cormick was going to have both of us committed," she laughed. "Besides, what woman doesn't enjoy being surrounded by dysfunctional men?"

"I guess, if that's what you're into, you hit the jackpot with us," he laughed.

"I didn't leave much behind. School is out. My sister is housesitting for me," she said. "It's summer vacation. My friends call me Tourist Extraordinaire. Every summer I travel to another country and immerse myself in the people and the culture. But in all that time, even as I taught the history of the southwest, I have never come here. So I figure, why not take a road trip and see what God has in store for me?"

"You travel alone?" Horace asked. "No special guy?"

"Ohhh…there have been some pretty *special* guys alright," she laughed. "But no one meaningful. Certainly no one as entertaining as you four."

"What about the Doc?" Horace asked. "You two seem close."

Dawn burst into laughter.

"Oh God, no! Cormick? No. Definitely no," she said shrugging. "Too high maintenance. I swear, I don't know if he has spent his life helping people with their problems or absorbing their problems and making them his own." She twirled the straw in her glass as she thought about him.

"Besides, he's in love with some teenage nurse."

"Sayer thinks you're pretty hot. You kinda took his breath away when he first saw you. I have to tell you, you are the first woman I've ever seen turn him down."

"No offense, but your baby brother is a man-child," she replied. "He's nice to look at, but I'm past that stage in my life. I'm almost thirty. When it's time…if it's ever time…I'll want someone strong and stable."

"Angelo owns his own boat up in Alaska," Horace said. "The two of you could hunt polar bears in the off season… vacation in your summer igloo…raise red-headed kickboxing Eskimo babies…"

Dawn laughed. "No Eskimo babies for me! Angelo's nice, but it's just not there." She reached for her water and took a drink. "You're starting to sound like my mother…trying to pair me up with every man I come in contact with."

"No," Horace said lighting up another cigarette, "it's just that you're…well you know…you see yourself in the mirror."

"What is it that you think I see, exactly?" she asked.

"C'mon," he said, "you're a knock out. Thick red hair, green eyes…" he hesitated for a moment to find her staring into his eyes. "You look great first thing in the morning, you're at home in jeans and t-shirts…" He stopped to take a drag and flick his ash. "You're smart, funny…"

She watched as he stared down at the bar. She watched as his thumb flicked at the butt of his cigarette, tapping ashes into the ashtray. Glancing up at his face, she noticed he was biting nervously at his top lip. She could see beyond his facade for the first time.

"Thank you, Horace," she said softly as she reached over and gently squeezed his hand.

"Yeah, well." He continued staring downward. Embarrassed, he struggled to find a way to continue. He looked at her and smiled. "Listen, Dawn...I'm sorry about all that stuff at the house. I'm not the asshole I make myself out to be. Sometimes I get wrapped up in feeling sorry for myself. Sometimes I don't feel like I'm living, I feel like I'm just going through the motions, waiting for it to all be over. Time is too short." He abruptly stopped talking. He realized that he was on the brink of telling her that he had cancer. He couldn't say it out loud. That would mean acknowledging the truth, and he wasn't ready for that just yet. He looked up and smiled at her. "C'mon, have a drink with me."

"I can't, Horace, you know that. We have to get back to the others," she replied. "It's time to find out why we're here. You can't hide out in this bar forever. The answers are waiting for us." Watching as he turned back to staring at the ashtray, she decided to meet him halfway. "Okay, one drink, Horace. One," she said with her index finger in the air, "then we find the others."

Horace smiled and signaled for the bartender.

"Did you give in because you feel sorry for me or because I like your hair?" he asked.

"A little of both. And, besides, you're not the worst looking guy in the bar."

"We will need to find a towing company," Cormick said as the four men approached the van. He had never changed a tire, and this was not going to be the day he learned. "Perhaps we can..." he began before stopping suddenly.

"Dude, what's wrong?" Sayer asked. He turned to see what had Cormick riveted. "Woah! Check that shit out!"

There, in front of them, was the Voyager, exactly where

they had left it but far from how they had left it. Not only had the tire had been repaired, the jagged tear in the front quarter panel existed only in their memories. The van looked as if it had just rolled off the showroom floor.

"What?" Angelo asked. "What's wrong?" Angelo looked around and saw the Voyager for the first time. "Oh, now I see why you were embarrassed."

"The fender...the tire." Momentarily unable to form a coherent sentence, Cormick tried to process what lay in front of him. "It is not possible," he mumbled. He turned to Clayton. "How did you do that?"

"I did nothing," he responded quietly.

Cormick looked at the van then back to Clayton. "That van was undrivable thirty minutes ago. Now look at it. Look! I want to know how you did that!"

"Cormick," Clayton said as he placed his hand on his shoulder, "I know you have many questions, and the answers await you. But your journey is not yet complete. All your answers lie in Taos."

"Cormick, we can't just stand here arguing on the sidewalk," Angelo said. "We've come this far, tough it out, man."

"Dude, he's totally right," Sayer said. "Just chill."

Cormick turned away, biting his bottom lip. He had spent a lifetime not giving in to anger or acting out. Now he found himself in a situation that grew more frustrating every day, and his calm, logical exterior was starting to crack from his growing anxiety. He did not want to talk anymore, and he was certainly done listening to everyone else talk in circles.

The tension broke as Dawn and Horace rounded the corner laughing. Their fun came to an abrupt end when they saw Cormick.

"Back to reality," Horace mumbled.

"Hey bro'!" Sayer said waving.

Angelo walked up to Dawn and kissed her on the cheek. "I knew you were beautiful," he said. He turned and looked at Horace. "And you look just as I thought you would."

"I'm not sure how to take that," Horace replied as a smile spread across his face.

"Enough with the pleasantries," Cormick said. I have driven almost two thousand miles to discover that the destination has moved. I just want to get in the van and go."

"Holy shit!" Horace exclaimed as he turned to look at the van. "What did you do?"

"It was not me. It was our friend here," Cormick said as he turned and came face to face with no one. "Where is he? Where did he go?" Cormick asked as he frantically looked around. "He was just here!" He ran to the corner and slowly spun around looking for Clayton in the sea of tourists.

"Cormick, you heard him," Angelo said. "We have to go to Taos Pueblo. It's not that far. Maybe he is heading there now to prepare for us. Who knows, right?" he shrugged.

Cormick buried his face into the palms of his hands and fought to keep from screaming. His breathing was so staggered that the others wondered if he was crying. As his hands slowly dragged down his face, his fingers pressed deep into his cheeks and seemed to hang on his jawline for a few seconds before dropping to his sides. Facing the midday sun, his eyes still closed, Cormick let his head fall backward.

Horace walked up beside him.

"Remember Doc, take a deep breath," he said as he put his arm around his shoulders. "We know where we need to go, and we'll be there by midafternoon. Hang in there, Doc. We need you."

Cormick opened his eyes and squared his head on his shoulders.

"Why am I needed here? Any one of you could have…" he began as he looked at his friends. "Well, almost half of you could have driven a van down here. Why did you include me? I was happy before I met all of you."

Angelo stepped forward and looked Cormick in the eyes. "Were you really happy, Cormick? Can you honestly say that you were better off on Monday than you are today?" Angelo paused and grabbed Cormick's hand. "Before you answer, let me recap for you. This week, you kissed Nurse Paige, you met four new people, you went on an adventure, you got away from that dick head Dr. Blanton, and you're no longer trapped in that pink office!"

"It is mauve," Cormick wearily responded.

"I know, it's just funny to me that you had that discussion a dozen times this week," Angelo smiled. "Don't you get it, man? This is living. This is what life should be. Life should taste like your favorite ice cream, sound like laughter, and smell as good as Nurse Paige's hair," he said throwing his arms in the air. "You do the same thing day in, day out. That's not life, man. Life is unexpected and unpredictable. This is what God wants you…wants all of us to experience. This is living!" he exclaimed.

Cormick stared at him with a blank look on his face. Angelo had a unique ability to say exactly the right words to him. Cormick had lived his life confident that he, and he alone, knew what was best. But when Angelo spoke to him, he was not so sure he was the only one with the answers. It was Angelo who had the confidence and strength that he lacked.

"We're your friends, man," Angelo continued. "We're

here with you until we all have the answers we seek. We will support you. We have your back. When the chips were down, and you were falsely accused of taking a body, where were your hospital buddies? Who stood by you when you needed someone most?" he asked. "I certainly didn't hear anybody come to your defense."

Cormick took a couple of steps forward and stepped into the street. He briefly envisioned himself walking into traffic but shrugged it off. Instead, he sat on the curb and stared down at the street.

Angelo was right. He really had no friends to speak of, and it had been that way since the death of his parents. He lived a solitary existence, which he never realized was a lonely existence until Allison kissed him. The four people around him told him every day that they needed him, and now he heard something he had never heard from anyone other than his father: they would be there for him when he needed them.

Cormick looked up and stared at the Voyager. Was he looking at a miracle? If it was not, the only other explanation was that it was not the same van. Regardless, he could not believe that either could be true. Yet there it was. How could he reason this away?

Angelo joined him on the curb.

"Listen Cormick, God sent me to you. Man, I don't know why, and I don't know why you can't hear him speak. But I do know this: you're here for a reason, Cormick. You are important to everything that is happening. And, I guess if you really look at it now, you have sacrificed and lost more than any of us to get here. After almost two thousand miles, you are just seventy miles away from understanding everything." Angelo stood up and held out his hand. "Now, c'mon, man. Get up and get us to Taos Pueblo."

Cormick looked at the outstretched hand and into Angelo's eyes. It was the first time the two could really see one another. His eyes looked as if they could see into Cormick's soul. He let out a sigh and clasped the rough hand of his friend. Angelo gave a solid tug and pulled Cormick from the cement.

Angelo wrapped his arms around Cormick and patted him on the back. As soon as he released him, Dawn grabbed him by one side and Sayer the other. It was his first group hug, and he could not believe how wonderful it felt. When they released him, he looked at Horace, who was smoking a cigarette, watching the love fest.

"I wasn't sure if that speech was going to end with crying or a fucking engagement ring," he said gruffly. He glared at Cormick for a second then a broad smile appeared on his face. With the cigarette dangling from his mouth, he gave Cormick a one-arm hug and squeezed his shoulder. "You got the keys, Doc. We're waitin' on you."

Cormick shook his head and smiled. "I suppose another few hours will not kill me."

"Give me the keys," Dawn said, "and I'll have us there in forty-five minutes."

"I will drive," Cormick said. "I have come this far. If I am going to meet God, I would rather it be face to face and not because I died with you behind the wheel."

⸺〰︎⸺

As they neared Taos, Dawn relieved Cormick of his chauffeur duties. The mountain highway had sent him into a near-paralyzed state. Halfway up Highway 68, Cormick was unable to accelerate past fifteen miles an hour and had a white-knuckled death grip on the steering wheel. Cars were lined up for more than half a mile behind the Voyager, all of them honking and exacerbating the panic that had hold of Cormick. It had taken both Sayer and Angelo to remove the hyperventilating doctor from the driver's seat after he had pulled over in a near catatonic state.

"I apologize," Cormick said finally able to sit up after a prolonged period of lying on the floor. "I suffer from severe vertigo and acrophobia. It makes it extraordinarily difficult to operate a motor vehicle in the mountains. I did not realize we would be so close to the edge."

Horace handed him his pint.

"Here Doc, this will calm you down. Any other surprise conditions we need to know about?"

Cormick took the bottle and swallowed.

"Other than being extremely claustrophobic and deathly afraid of guns, not really."

"Jesus, maybe you should get a shrink for yourself," Horace noted.

Cormick nodded in agreement and took another sip before handing the bottle back to Horace. He looked out the window and sighed. To protect his reputation, he had never sought help for his issues. Besides, he was a trained professional and had felt that he was more than competent enough to treat himself. However, after talking to Angelo a few days earlier, he had realized just how much he could benefit from the help.

Everyone was quiet as they headed north through the congested traffic on Paseo del Pueblo Norte, approaching their destination at a snail's pace. The small shops that lined the narrow, winding street and the throngs of tourists strolling on the sidewalks could not distract them from the nervous anticipation of what lay ahead.

Dawn turned down a dusty dirt road and headed toward Taos Pueblo. There were some modern houses scattered along the roadside and the occasional deteriorating adobe structure. A few horses stood watch in the tall yellow grass that danced in the light summer breeze. The travelers were silent as they pulled into a small gravel parking lot outside the entrance to the pueblo. Dawn turned and faced everyone.

"Okay boys, this is it," she said. "Is anyone else scared shitless?"

"No way, babe," Sayer said. "I'm totally ready to meet the big guy!"

Horace shot a questioning glance to Cormick, who simply nodded yes. Horace handed him the pint, and after taking a quick sip, Cormick handed it back. The two men had developed their own unspoken language.

"Now we're ready," Horace said as he slipped the pint into his pocket. "Let's do this."

Angelo turned and faced everyone from the passenger seat.

"God is here. I can feel it." He opened the door and stepped out into the afternoon sun. "We're never going to be the same after this."

THE KIVA

Unsure of how to proceed, they stood at the entrance to the pueblo in silence. As the tourists strolled casually by, they split off into two directions. Some walked over for a better view of the cemetery, but most funneled past the old church and onto the grounds of the pueblo.

"Whoa, this place needs some work!" Sayer exclaimed.

"It's supposed to look like this," Dawn said in awe of her surroundings. "Some of these buildings have been here for centuries. It's beautiful."

"I can't believe we had to pay to look at a bunch of mud huts," Horace grumbled.

"I'm sure the money goes to support the people and property," Dawn replied as she took in the moment. "You know, I've described places like this to students, but being here…wow. Just wow."

"It's breathtaking," Angelo said.

Cormick looked around searching the faces of the people who were milling about in the distance.

"As interesting as the scenery is, does anyone have any idea what we are supposed to do now?" His question was met with silence. "Well?" he asked as he turned around to find the others walking along the old cemetery fence. "It figures," he said as he made his way to join the group.

"Dude," Sayer said, smacking Angelo in the arm, "what is that?"

"I think it's the bell tower of an old church or something," he replied.

Sayer marveled at what was left of the old structure. The exposed adobe brick at the base of the bell tower had withstood almost four hundred years of sun and snow. There were remnants of the original southern and eastern walls weathered by time and the unforgiving elements.

The tower was surrounded by wooden crosses that had been slowly decaying over decades but still bore the names of the dead. Most of the graying markers leaned to the side and looked as if the wind had tried to blow them from the ground. On the east side of the bell tower lay a large pile of crosses that had been pulled from the cemetery, little more than a disorganized heap of firewood.

Horace stared at the remains of the old church.

"It looks like this place was shelled by artillery fire," he noted.

"Could have been the Spanish…maybe Americans… hard to say, really," Dawn said. "The indigenous people in this area have played tug of war with the government for their land for centuries."

"I hate to interrupt," Cormick interjected, "but should we be devoting our attention to other matters? Unless you are anticipating a sudden and miraculous resurrection, I think we should look elsewhere." He walked back to the entry road and looked around.

"Not everybody likes history," Dawn said. "C'mon fellas, let's not keep Cormick waiting."

As they walked toward the compound, they were flanked by a few small adobe houses with brightly painted doors on their left and a church on their right.

"The tribe must have rebuilt the church here," Dawn

noted as she passed, running her fingers along the wall. "Probably as slave labor."

As they continued forward, the dirt road opened into a spacious compound. To their left, set against the backdrop of the Taos Mountains, lay the northern structure of the compound: a multi-unit adobe complex that appeared to be five stories high. Most of the units in the building had doors and windows, but a few of the upper houses had primitive ladders leading to entrance holes in the adobe walls.

"Oh my goodness," Dawn said as she came to an abrupt halt. "I should have brought a camera. There is no way I'll ever be able to describe this to my class."

"I could describe it," Horace said disdainfully.

"Dude, are those carports?" Sayer asked pointing to the wooden structures in front of the complex. The structures were little more than a framework of small tree trunks placed in the ground with smaller trunks placed across the top to form a roof over the posts.

"No…"Dawn replied. "Those are drying racks. I wonder how old they are."

Cormick walked a few steps in front of the group and surveyed the scene. In the distance, the Taos Mountains stood guard against dangers that could approach from the east. In the afternoon sun, the peaks appeared gray, rising above a lush tree line of green and black. Using his hand to cover his eyes from the brilliant sun, he saw a small creek running through the middle of the large courtyard, separating the pueblo into northern and southern halves. There were numerous earthen structures on the south side as well, though none as large as the building to the north.

The details of the ancient architecture escaped his eyes, however. He was looking for the man they had met in Santa

Fe. Clayton had told them to come to the pueblo for answers, and now that he was finally at his destination, he wanted those answers immediately.

"I do not see our friend," he said. "What do we do next?" he asked as he turned back to face the crowd.

"Let's have a drink," Horace said as he twisted off the cap of his pint and took a sip. He held the bottle out to the others to share, but there were no takers.

"Put that away," Dawn demanded in a hushed voice, "and don't even think about lighting a cigarette."

"Too late," he fired back, "I'm already thinking about it." He reached into his pocket, but his pack was gone. "Shit. I must've left 'em in the van."

"Hey bro', you can totally wait a bit," Sayer said. "Give those lungs of yours a break." He breathed in deep. "Just breathe in this fresh air."

Horace took a quick, shallow breath.

"Yeah, it's nice," he said.

Angelo walked over to the church. A small wall extended from the northern and southern walls, creating a small, square courtyard. The east wall had an arched entrance which led to the large wooden doors of the church.

"Maybe he's in here," he said. "After all, where's a better place to find God?"

He led the way as the group followed him to the entry of the church. He pulled opened the doors and walked in. The nave of the church, dimly lit by the sunlight that diffused through the blue stained-glass windows, had old wooden pews on either side. The railing in front separated the sanctuary from where the congregation would be seated.

The wall behind the altar, beautifully painted with imagery that seemed to be a mix of both native and Catholic beliefs, held nearly a dozen likenesses of the Virgin Mary ornately dressed in a variety of colorful costumes. As the others walked down the aisle toward the altar, marveling at the interior of the building, Cormick stood near the door unable to move forward.

He had not been in a church since the death of his parents. It had been thirty years since he suffered at the hands of Father Thomas, but standing there, facing the altar, the terrible memories came back with a vengeance. Oblivious to what the others were saying, he was twelve years old again, reliving the nightmare in his head.

Horace plopped down in a pew and looked around for Cormick. He saw him standing in the shadows by the door, partially lit by the light from the windows.

"Doc," he called. Met with silence, he called out again. "Hey, what's up, Doc?" he laughed as he watched Cormick stand motionless.

The words went unheeded. Cormick remained detached from his current surroundings. As he stared forward, he found himself in St. Peter's, wearing a cassock and surplice, listening as Father Thomas' footsteps behind him drew closer. He was paralyzed by the overwhelming reality of his flashback.

"Cormick," a voice from behind him called as a hand was gently placed on his shoulder.

Startled and completely enveloped in his waking nightmare, he turned, expecting to see Father Thomas. He yelled as he jumped back and was pulled into the present. It was Clayton.

Cormick's frightened outburst got the attention of the others who watched, without a word, as the heavy wooden doors slowly closed behind the backlit figure. As the light behind him faded, they could see it was Clayton.

"Cormick," he repeated as he once again placed his hand on Cormick's shoulder, "It is alright. You're safe."

The others walked toward them, but Horace sat in his pew and took a drink. His head was buzzing, and he wanted a cigarette. He stayed put for a moment, then put the pint in his pocket.

"Shit," he mumbled as he got to his feet and reluctantly joined the others.

As they approached, Clayton raised a finger to his lips, signaling quiet.

"You are in the church of St. Jerome, known to the people of this place as San Geronimo Church. This is a place of worship not a place for us to talk." He turned and started toward the door, motioning the others to follow. He pushed the doors open bathing them in the warmth of the sun.

He led them eastward, where the pueblo opened to the mountains in the distance. The enormous peaks dwarfed everything that lay in the foreground. They silently followed as he guided them across the parched soil.

"Why are we just following this guy?" Horace asked in a whisper. "Where is he taking us?"

"Dude…he's taking us to God!" Sayer replied in a hushed voice. "So awesome."

"Shhhh," Dawn hissed.

They reached an adobe wall, no more than two feet high, at the end of the complex, and Clayton continued past the fence into the field of tall, golden grass. As Angelo followed, Cormick grabbed his arm and pointed to the no-trespassing sign. Several steps ahead, Clayton stopped and turned to face them.

"Those words do not apply to us today," Clayton said with a smile. "Have you really come this far to let two words stop you from what lies ahead?"

"No, I have not," Angelo smiled as he brushed past Cormick. Dawn and Sayer followed. Bringing up the rear of the formation, Horace stopped and looked at Cormick. He shrugged his shoulders and walked by the sign. Cormick cautiously glanced both ways and hesitantly moved forward to join the others.

The group wound its way through the waist-high grass without speaking a word as Clayton moved southward toward a lightly wooded area. Near the tree line sat a single adobe structure. Unlike those on the pueblo, the building had no visible doors or glass-paned windows. There was a large hole in the side of the house about ten feet up from the ground. A ladder, made from the trees that grew just beyond, provided access.

Clayton climbed the twelve rungs and entered the building. He stuck his head out and smiled at them, motioning them to follow. Angelo immediately climbed the ladder followed by Dawn and a very eager Sayer.

"This is where they'll find our bodies," Horace said as he stood at the base of the ladder.

"I do not find that the least bit amusing," Cormick replied.

Cormick watched as Horace scaled the ladder and entered the house. He looked back toward the pueblo and wondered who would venture this way to find their bodies. He looked up the ladder to the entryway. It might as well have been a mile straight up.

Horace popped his head through the hole and looked at Cormick below.

"C'mon Doc, it ain't that high." He could see Cormick

was too scared to make the ascent. "Just one foot over the other, Doc. You can do this."

Cormick reached forward and stepped on the first rung. After a moment, he stepped up to the second, then third rung. He looked around to assure himself he was not too high and stepped up to the fourth, and then the fifth rung.

"So far, so good, buddy," Horace called from the opening. "Almost halfway there!"

Cormick leaned forward against the ladder and climbed to the sixth rung. He looked to the ground and felt a little dizzy. His grip on the ladder tightened. He had never measured in feet how far up he could go before his vertigo overcame him. Unlike the walled stairwell at the hospital, there was no protective railing to hold as he climbed.

"Hey, Cormick," Horace yelled. "Look up at me. Don't look down." His words failed to get the frozen man moving. "Doc, you're not even five feet in the air. It's like sitting on someone's shoulders. A few more steps. That's all you need."

Cormick closed his eyes and took in a deep breath. For his entire career, he believed the deep-breath technique gave his patients a moment to peacefully regroup before going on, but the calming effect was lost on him. He moved to the sixth rung without opening his eyes.

Horace leaned forward and reached to touch Cormick's hand.

"I'm right here, Doc. Look up and open your eyes," he said. "I ain't gonna let you fall."

Cormick looked up and saw Horace smiling down at him. His breathing slowed a bit as he found some reassurance in Horace's words. He stepped up one more rung, and Horace grabbed his shirt to help pull him into the adobe house. Once inside, Cormick nodded a thank you to Horace.

"No sweat, Doc," he said, "the others went down already."

The two men climbed down another ladder to the lower floor. Horace had gone first to reach up and hold Cormick as he made his descent. It was still a struggle for Cormick, but having Horace guide him down made the task easier.

"Hey," Horace said, "whaddaya know...a door!"

Cormick could feel his temper rise like mercury in a thermometer. The door was on the east side of the building and had gone unnoticed as they'd made their approach. He reached forward and turned the knob and discovered a ground-level entrance. He bit down hard on his lip to prevent himself from yelling.

"Bad news, Doc," Horace said. "It looks like we got another ladder."

There was a hole in the earthen floor with two small-diameter tree trunks sticking up from the darkened pit. Horace walked over and looked down. There was a faint light flickering below apparently just a few feet from the entrance.

"I am *not* going down there," Cormick said firmly.

"It's just one more ladder," Horace shrugged. "You've safely climbed up and down two already."

"It is not just the ladder," Cormick said through gritted teeth. "I experience a great deal of emotional distress in small, dark spaces."

"I'm gonna be with you the whole way, Doc. I swear, nothing is gonna happen to you," Horace said, trying to keep Cormick moving. "Now, just like before...I'll go down first and be there with you the whole way." With that, Horace climbed down the ladder into the darkness. "It's okay, Doc. C'mon down," Horace called from below.

Cormick sat on the ground with his feet in the hole.

Placing his feet on the second rung down, he began his slow descent to the subterranean chamber. As he slowly climbed down, Horace offered reassuring words the whole way.

At the base of the ladder, Cormick turned and immediately flew back against the wall. His heart was racing as he felt the walls close in on him. He slid down the dirt wall and closed his eyes. He began to breathe rapidly, and Horace thought he was about to pass out.

Angelo walked up and sat next to him.

"Cormick, take my hand," he said. "You need to breathe slowly, do you understand? You're a doctor. You know what you need to do." He held on tight to Cormick's hand. "Cormick, if you don't take a deep breath, you're going to hyperventilate," he warned. "Now close your eyes and take a deep breath."

Cormick closed his eyes but struggled to take in a deep, cleansing breath. After several moments, he was able to slow his breathing. His heart rate slowed, as well, and though he loosened his grip on Angelo's hand, he did not let go.

"Now Cormick," Angelo said, "you're going to open your eyes when you're ready. We're in an underground chamber. But you're safe, okay? You are not alone. Nod if you understand."

Cormick nodded and began to take in deep breaths. Finally able to inhale and exhale through his nose, he closed his mouth and slowly opened his eyes. It took a few seconds for his eyes to adjust to the darkness.

The chamber was about eight feet across and ten feet deep. At the far end of the kiva, he saw an opening that he assumed ventilated the room. In front of the air shaft, a small wall made of adobe bricks acted as an air deflector.

Dawn and Sayer were sitting toward the far end of the

chamber, illuminated by a fire. Clayton stood between them, smiling at the three men at the back of the room.

"Welcome, gentlemen," Clayton said. "Please, come forward and join us by the fire."

"C'mon, Doc," Horace said. "We got ya."

With that, Angelo and Horace each grabbed an arm and carefully walked Cormick a few feet forward to join the others forming a circle around the flames.

"*Shema e'tewa,*" Clayton said, welcoming them. "This room is my kiva, a sacred place where great truths are shared with a chosen few. Kivas are where the Pueblo people pass on their history, their legends, and their religion. It is not a place where white men are allowed." He knelt in front of the fire and smiled at his guests. "Now…tell me…why have you come here?"

"Is that a joke?" Horace barked as he looked around at the others.

"Yes. It is. That is why I'm smiling," Clayton responded. "I have not made a public speech in some time, but I understand it is best to open with a joke."

"Real fuckin' funny," Horace said.

"Hey bro', watch the language," Sayer interrupted. "It's a joke. Let's just chill and hear the man out."

"The number four is sacred to the Pueblo people," Clayton began. "The Zia sun symbol has four sets of stripes which symbolize the four seasons, the four directions, the four stages life, and the four times of day. And, just as there are four phases of the moon, four elements, and four parts to the soul, the four of you each have a unique destiny to fulfill. The four of you are the chosen few who will receive the great truth."

The travelers looked around at each other, confused

by what they had just heard. Each quickly counted the members of the group. Simultaneously, they turned back toward Clayton.

"But there are five of us," Dawn said.

"That's true. There are five of you," he replied, "but one of you has completed his journey and is now free to go."

Cormick felt his chest tighten as he held his breath. He was the only one who had not heard the voice that led the others to New Mexico. He was the reluctant one, and he was the Charioteer. If they had, in fact, reached their destination, it seemed logical to him that he had suddenly become expendable.

"It is me, is it not?" he asked as he glared at Clayton. "I am the one who is supposed to leave. Is that correct?"

"That is correct, Cormick," Clayton said with a smile. "You have served your purpose well. You have safely delivered your friends to me. But now, you are free to go."

Only the crackling of the fire could be heard as a stillness consumed the kiva. All eyes, which had been on Clayton, turned to Cormick as the other four stared at him in stunned silence. Cormick was focused only on Clayton as if they were the only two people in the chamber. He drew in a loud breath through his nose and, disregarding his claustrophobia, suddenly sprang from the floor into a standing position.

"This is fucking bullshit!" he screamed. "I have fucking sacrificed everything to be here! Have I endured hell to bring these people here, to share in this fucking moment, only to have you fucking tell me that I fucking do not get to learn why we are here in the first fucking place?"

"Woah!" Sayer exclaimed, shocked by the sudden change in the usually calm and reserved doctor.

"Easy Doc," Horace said as he got to his feet. "Let's just fall back and regroup for a minute."

"Fuck you, too," Cormick yelled as he pushed him away. Horace fell to the ground. "And, especially, fuck you!" he said as he pointed to Clayton. "I have sacrificed everything for this moment. My fucking job, my fucking reputation, my fucking car, and, nearly, my fucking sanity to learn why…to understand…" He pressed his palms against his face.

"Cormick," Angelo began, "I…"

"And fuck you, Angelo," he said as he turned to his friend. "I was happy. I had a good life. Some would say I had it all. Then you showed up and fucking ruined my fucking life!"

Cormick looked toward Horace and noticed the half pint had slipped from his pocket and was lying on the ground. He reached down and quickly scooped it up. He spun the lid off and chugged as much as he could handle. Swallowing hard, he fought back his gag reflex and wiped the whiskey from his lips.

"Cormick, you must understand, you are the Charioteer," Clayton said. "It is the literal meaning of your name. This is your fate. It always was, just as it is today."

"Fuck this," Cormick said as Dawn and Sayer sat shocked by the torrent of profanity that flowed from Cormick. "I am the fucking Charioteer?" he said as he took another drink. "Well you are all fucking welcome for the ride!"

"Cormick, please…" Angelo said, "take a deep breath and…"

"Shove your deep breath up your fucking ass, Angelo," he said taking another drink.

"This is the simple truth, Cormick," Clayton said. "You are and always have been fated to take this journey. Beyond this moment, everything you choose will lead you to your destiny. One can't simply…"

"Fuck you," Cormick said and took another drink. "I am so fucking tired of all this bullshit. You know what? I am leaving. I am taking the van and heading back to town." He glared at Horace. "And I am taking your fucking booze."

Cormick turned and stormed to the ladder. His anger gripped him tight, like a clenched fist. He started up the ladder but stumbled as his heart started to race. Focusing on the light above, he forced himself upward through the opening in the floor.

The others raced to the ladder just as his feet disappeared through the opening. They heard the door above open and slam shut as Cormick continued to scream profanities until he was out of ear shot.

Angelo turned to Clayton. "I'm sorry. I have to go," he said. "I have to go after him."

"Cormick has left because his journey has ended and now he goes to face his destiny, Angelo," Clayton said. "Please don't worry about him. He is stronger than he—or any of you—can imagine. He is walking his own path. Do not interfere as he discovers his destiny."

They all looked at each other unsure of what to do.

"Wait here," Angelo said as he scurried up the ladder. He threw open the door and ran into the field. He searched the landscape, but Cormick was nowhere to be seen. Angelo called for him to no avail. "Oh, Cormick," he sighed as he turned and walked back into the house. He slowly climbed down the ladder and looked at the others. "He's gone. And so is our ride and our clothes."

"Shit, my cigarettes are in the van!" Horace cried in horror.

"You won't need those anymore," Clayton said. "Time to quit smoking."

As the commotion at the ladder subsided, Clayton watched as all eyes turned to him in the silence.

"Please, my friends, come join me. There is much to discuss." He motioned toward the fire in front of him.

"I'm not doing anything without Cormick," Angelo said.

"Yeah, this is bullshit," Horace interjected. "We're in this together. Doc deserves to be here with us."

"I understand your feelings," Clayton said. "But none of you are here because you deserve to be here. You're here because you're supposed to be here, and Cormick is not."

"Why not?" Dawn asked.

"Cormick is a man who lives in fear. It is said that the whole secret of existence is to live with no fear. Cormick fears the past and is unable to evolve because it impacts him to this day. He fears the present because he doesn't believe in others and has no spiritual center, and he fears the future because he cannot predict what will be. It is an unnecessary waste of time to fear the future. Fearing for and worrying about the future will not change its outcome. Even death is not to be feared by one who has lived wisely." He paused for a moment and knelt by the fire. "This may be hard for you to believe, but Cormick had to leave to fulfill his destiny. His purpose was to bring you here together, his destiny is significantly greater."

"But how could you treat him like that?" she countered.

"I only told him the truth," Clayton said. "What he needs to learn lies elsewhere. What you need to learn is here."

"What do we need to learn?" Dawn asked. "Why are we here?"

"In time, Dawn," Clayton smiled. "Please, sit by the fire with me."

The four of them looked at each other. Until this moment, they had not realized how important Cormick had been in keeping them together. He had done more than drive them to New Mexico, he had kept them moving forward despite his own objections. His absence left them at a loss. Reluctantly, they walked to the fire and sat on the ground.

"You all have questions," Clayton said. "The answers can't be revealed all at once. But when we are finished, you will have the answers to all your questions and much more. Until then, please open your minds and listen."

"Are we gonna get a smoke break?" Horace asked.

"Time to quit smoking," Clayton replied.

"Not even a fucking peace pipe?" Horace asked through gritted teeth.

The anxiety on his face could not be hidden. Dawn reached out and grabbed his hand, squeezing it tight as she smiled at him. He looked back at her and nodded. He took in a deep breath and exhaled to calm himself.

"For centuries, man has sat at the fire for safety, to eat, and to pass knowledge on to the next generation of leaders," Clayton began. "As you sit around the fire in this kiva, you will receive a higher understanding of the world around you and the undeniable truth of life.

"This pueblo is a place like no other. Here, all things meet and coexist in peace," Clayton continued. "Different religions, beliefs, cultures, and people are not merely tolerated but accepted, honored, and respected."

"My understanding of the history of this area is just a bit different than what you are describing. The people of this area were slaves to the Spanish and overrun by the government," Dawn pointed out. "The entire southwest has a brutal history."

"That is true," Clayton continued. "The earth has been stained with blood and tears." He bowed his head and looked down into the fire. "Mankind has killed in the name of religion and in its quest for land and wealth. And mankind will continue to do so, unless you act."

"Dude…wait…what?" a bewildered Sayer asked. "Is this still about God?"

"Hold on a second," Horace interrupted. "I sure as hell am not going to get involved in any fight with the fucking government."

"And I would never suggest such a thing," Clayton responded. "What you learn here will change the world and set right the course of mankind."

"Well, I'm not here to be part of a cult, either," Horace snapped. "I'm not gonna be one of those assholes who shave their head and beg for money."

"I certainly hope not," Clayton said.

"I'm sorry," Angelo said, "I'm a little lost here. You're doing a lot of talking but saying very little. I was called to be a fisher of men. I just don't see where this is going."

"He is totally right," Sayer added. "I've been walking the beach telling everyone how awesome God is, and I thought he'd be here. I mean, are we going to meet God, or what?"

"I'm sorry, Sayer, but you are not here to meet God," Clayton smiled.

"But it was God," Sayer said. "He called to me."

"It is true that you were called, Sayer, but you are mistaken about the rest," Clayton said.

"Mistaken because God isn't a he?" Dawn asked. "I knew it!" She laughed as she looked at the others. "She called us.

I wish Cormick were here for this!"

"Mistaken because god is just a word made up by man," Clayton said. "It is a vague term used by some men to place the Supreme Being of their faith above those of all other faiths. There are many gods in many cultures. God as you understand him, does not exist."

"That can't be," Angelo cried. "The voice…"

"Okay…stop. Everybody stop," Horace said as he got to his feet. "No more games. We're all here because God called us to Santa Fe. We get to Santa Fe, and you tell us that we need to come here. We come here and you tell us there is no God. I want to know what the fuck is going on."

"I didn't say there is no God, I said your understanding of God is incorrect. If I were to ask you to describe God to me, you would tell me that God is a man who has a long white beard and wears a robe. That is not God. It is nothing more than an idea that makes God relatable to you. As for what is going on, that will take a while," Clayton said as he rose to his feet. "Let's eat first. In the room above, there are beans, bread, and corn. After our meal, we can begin."

"I don't want to wait anymore," Angelo cried. "I can't take this. I need to understand what's happening to us."

"Guys, we should do as he says," Dawn interjected. "We've come a long way, we're tired…hungry…let's get a bite to eat and—as Cormick would say—take a deep breath."

"Beans and corn? Really?" Horace asked sarcastically. "You call that a meal?"

"Hey bro', relax," Sayer said. "We're guests here. I don't know what he's talking about, but we're here now. And he says he's totally going to explain God after we eat. Why are you arguing with him? Let's just go upstairs and eat. What could it hurt?"

Horace knew he was outnumbered. The only person who would have stuck up for him had driven off in a drunken rage. He looked at the others and shook his head. He was going to need help getting through the rest of the day, and the unopened pint of whiskey safely secured in the pocket of his field jacket was the help he needed.

"Okay…one meal and then a lot of answers," he said, pointing at Clayton.

"Be patient my friends, everything comes to you in the right moment," Clayton said as he motioned for the group to climb the ladder. "For now, let's enjoy our meal."

———

Cormick stumbled into the lobby of the Sagebrush Inn. He had chosen the motel simply because it was the first place he found on the right side of the road. Intoxicated from the whiskey he had freely poured down his throat, he feared having to make a left turn across traffic.

"Welcome to the Sagebrush!" the clerk called from behind the desk, startling him.

Cormick stared at her for a moment, squeezed his eyes shut and reopened them as he leaned forward to get a good look at her. He guessed her to be just over five feet tall, and he surmised she was at least five feet around as well. The only thing that prevented her thick, bright-blue eye shadow from spreading up her forehead were two deep-black eyebrows, which appeared to be drawn on with a crayon.

"Circus in town?" he grumbled.

"I don't think so," she said, bewildered by the question.

"Just give me a room, please," he replied.

"Smoking or nonsmoking?" the woman asked.

"Do I fucking look like a smoker?" Cormick fired back.

He pulled his American Express card from his wallet and tossed it on the desk. He was swaying slightly back and forth and held onto the desk to steady himself. He burped but kept his mouth closed. He was drunk enough to forget his manners and just sober enough to be concerned about spilling the contents of his stomach on the counter.

"How many nights?" she asked.

"One. One fucking night." As she ran his card, he looked around the lobby. There were pamphlets neatly arranged on a wire rack behind him, advertising points of interest, tourist traps, and overpriced tours. "D.H. Lawrence lived here?" he asked.

"Oh yes," she answered excitedly. "One of our most famous residents!"

"That is probably what killed him," he said as he turned back to her.

"No…no…I'm pretty sure it was tuberculosis," she said.

"Lady, I am a doctor, and looking around, I feel confident in my diagnosis that this fucking miserable town killed him." He grabbed his card and stuck it back in his wallet. "Unless you ate him."

He heard the man behind him laugh, and he pivoted and nodded to the man with a smile. Turning back to the clerk, he saw he had hurt her feelings.

"I apologize," he said. "That remark was completely inappropriate." Guilt consumed him as he signed the slip and took the key. "I have had an extraordinarily bad week, and I am lashing out. Please forgive me."

"It's Room 214," she said, unable to look at him. "It's the building with the conference center just around the corner."

"Great…where is the bar?" he asked.

"Just to the right," she said as she pointed through the archway.

"Again, I am sincerely sorry about what I said."

Cormick turned and glanced at the man behind him, who was staring right at him. He gave the man an uncomfortable smile and started toward the bar. He stopped just short of the entrance and looked back at the man who was still glaring at him. Something did not seem right to Cormick. The man had laughed at his rude comment but now seemed unhappy with him. He assumed the man had also had a bad week and continued into the bar.

The lounge was empty, except for the bartender, who was leaning against the bar, smoking a cigarette and staring at a baseball game on the television. Cormick walked past several empty stools and took a seat near the far end of the bar. As a matter of principle, for self-preservation, he never sat near the door.

Cormick waited for a minute as he looked at the bartender who was completely uninterested in his only customer.

"Excuse me," Cormick said, "can I get a shot of Jack Daniels? No, wait…I will have that on the rocks. And ice water. Can I get an ice water as well?"

"Sandberg's up," the bartender said as he continued watching the game. "I'll be there in a minute."

"I said I would like a drink," Cormick reiterated.

"And I said Sandberg is at the plate," the bartender snapped.

Cormick sat quietly and waited for the bartender. He looked up at the set and studied the action. Aside from golf, he had never given sports of any kind a second thought. As he waited, he could not understand why someone would be so riveted to such a monotonous game.

The man from the lobby walked in and took a seat near the bartender.

"Well whiskey and a beer back," he said as he tossed a ten on the bar.

To Cormick's displeasure, the bartender poured the order, set it in front of the man, and turned back to the television.

"Why the fuck is Dunston batting third?" the man asked.

"Zim's got a master plan," the bartender said.

"Excuse me," Cormick repeated, "is Sandberg still at the plate? If not, I would appreciate my drink."

The bartender rolled his eyes and poured Cormick his drinks. He walked to the end of the bar and set them down.

"Charge to your room?"

"Yes…214," Cormick replied.

He took a sip of the whiskey, and was pleased to discover the alcohol burned a little less as it cooled on the ice in his glass. He glanced over and noticed the man staring at him. Cormick tried to turn away, but there was something familiar and disquieting about him. He picked up his drinks and moved a few stools closer to him.

"I can see the game much better now," he said to the unconcerned bartender. He looked at the man and smiled. "Hello. This may sound strange, but I cannot help but feel like we have met before."

"Funny, I was just thinking the same thing about you," he replied. "But that doesn't make sense, does it? I mean, two people who know each other show up in Taos and check into the same motel on the same day?"

"Yes, the odds are certainly against that," Cormick laughed. "Are you here on vacation?"

"I have to wrap up some personal business," he replied. "What about you?"

"You would not believe me if I told you," Cormick said as he sipped from his glass.

"Try me," the man replied.

"Honestly, you won't believe me. In a nutshell, I had to chauffeur some people here who—for reasons beyond my understanding—could not drive themselves." He shook his head. "They are here looking for God. Can you believe that? God. In New Mexico." The alcohol had made him more talkative than he normally would have been.

"You'd be surprised what I can believe," the man replied with a smile that was almost a sneer. "I didn't catch your name."

"I am Cormick. Dr. Cormick Proffitt," he said as he held out his hand. "And you are?"

"Russ. Russ Hanrahan," he replied. "Nice to meet you, Cormick. Now, tell me more about these friends of yours."

THE STORYTELLER

Horace watched as the others descended the ladder into the kiva.
For the past eighteen years, he had smoked a cigarette after
every meal. Though he could hardly define what he had just
eaten as a meal, the craving for nicotine was overpowering,
made worse by the bitter aftertaste of the meal lingering on
his tongue. Looking around to make sure no one could see
him, he reached in his pocket for the pint and took a quick
drink. To his dismay, even the taste of the whiskey couldn't
cleanse his tongue.

He peered into the entrance to the kiva. It was darker
than before, an obvious sign that the fire had died down. He
could hear Sayer calling to him in the dark and reluctantly
decided to join his brother and the others in the chamber.
He slipped the pint into his back pocket and started to climb
down the ladder.

As he lowered himself into the darkness of the kiva, he
turned and looked toward the dying light. He could see
everyone standing around as someone added more wood
to the fire. Thinking he was at ground level, he stepped back
into the air and fell, ass first, onto the hard ground, shatter-
ing his precious pint.

"Are you alright?" Dawn asked as she navigated the
darkness to Horace.

"Goddammit," he moaned as he rolled over onto his
stomach.

Dawn found her way to Horace and knelt beside him to help him up.

"Your back is soaking wet. What is it?"

"I hope it's blood," he said.

It was just a split second before Dawn caught the aroma from his clothes.

"It's booze," she said.

"I'd rather it was blood," he said as he got to his knees. "That was all I had left, unless Cochise over there has any firewater."

"Stop it," she ordered. "You sound racist when you say things like that. His name is Clayton." She reached down and grabbed his arm as the flames grew behind her. "Come on, get up. And make sure you're not covered in broken glass."

The pint had fallen free from his pocket, and the broken glass lay on the ground. He kicked it aside and let out a mournful sigh. He stared at the carnage at his feet and imagined the sound of a bugle playing *Taps* for the fallen soldier.

"I don't want to seem like an ungrateful guest," Angelo said as he turned to Clayton, "but I can't seem to get the taste of that cactus out of my mouth."

"Yes, Peyote is quite bitter," Clayton said nodding.

"Well, alright!" Sayer exclaimed. "Now we're talking!"

"Peyote? You fed us peyote without telling us?" Dawn said. "You gave us drugs?"

"I gave you medicine," Clayton replied calmly.

"That isn't medicine," Dawn yelled, "it's an hallucinogenic drug!"

"Peyote is a medicine with many uses," Clayton said. "It has been used for more than fifty centuries, not only to heal illness but to aid in the spiritual journey of those who seek answers. While you're here, it will serve both purposes."

"Who the hell do you think you are?" Horace asked. "Carlos Castaneda? You think we're all going to sit around in the dark and trip with you?"

"Dude, I am so cool with that," Sayer said.

"I am asking you to take a leap of faith," Clayton said, "not unlike that which led you here."

"I need to sit down, guys," Angelo said. "I'm a little scared. I can't believe I traveled this far to break the law. If Cormick were here, he'd shit his pants."

"You aren't breaking the law," Clayton said. "Though the people of this pueblo don't approve of the use of peyote, it is used in religious and healing ceremonies in many places. Now please, don't worry," he said as he sat on the ground next to Angelo. "Join us."

"Gotcha!" Sayer said as he sat next to Clayton. "Come on, bro'. This is gonna be totally cool."

Dawn and Horace looked at each other. Without a word, each could see that the other was gravely concerned about where circumstances were leading them. They were underground in a foreign place and had ingested mescaline fed to them by a stranger. Dawn shrugged at Horace as he slowly shook his head to convey his concern. She sat down and reached up for his hand. Clasping it gently, she lightly tugged at him until he joined her on the ground.

"I'm going to share with you an undeniable truth," Clayton paused and looked at each one of them. "There is only one Great Spirit or, as you would say, God. Regardless of your religion or practice, you—and every living thing in the universe—are connected to the Great Spirit. You share in the image of the Great Spirit."

"I thought you said that our view of God was mistaken,"

Angelo said. "So, now what? God looks like me?"

"Goodness, no," Clayton smiled.

"But you said we were created in his image," Dawn replied.

"That isn't exactly what I said but, in a sense, you were," Clayton said. "But your body is not who you are, nor is it what the Great Spirit looks like. Your physical form is merely a product of millions of years of evolution."

"That doesn't make any sense," Angelo said. "If we weren't created this way but instead evolved into people, are you saying God looks like a prehistoric mammal?"

"You are too wrapped up in the physical world," Clayton said. "You were conceived during a physical act, and you walk around in physical form. But that is not the image of the Great Spirit."

"I don't get it," Sayer said. "When we're born…"

"You were never born," Clayton said. "You were created when all things were created. You have been and always will be."

"You're totally blowing my mind right now," Sayer said.

"Maybe it's the peyote," Horace said.

"I'm sorry," Angelo said, "I just don't get what you're talking about. I was born. I had parents. And I'm pretty sure I'm going to die one day."

"You will not die. Your body will, one day in the distant future, simply give up. It is finite. But you are pure energy. You could call it your soul. Existing at the same time as— and in the image of—the Great Spirit. Your soul is made from that which makes up all things."

"Everyone hold on," Dawn said as she looked at her companions, each of whom appeared to be glowing. "Oh, my goodness," she said as she placed her hand on her chest.

"I think I can see your auras. It's...it's beautiful. Can anyone else see this?"

"It's just the peyote," Horace repeated even though he was amazed at what he was witnessing.

"It's like the northern lights," Angelo replied.

"I see it, too," Sayer responded. "It's awesome!"

"Then we are ready to begin," Clayton said as he tossed a log on the fire sending glowing embers skyward. "Behold! The stars!" he said rising to his feet and throwing his arms upward.

They watched as the sparks hung above their heads like constellations in the night sky. It was as if they were sitting around a fire in a field, staring up at the heavens. No one spoke. Their shared vision had them captivated.

"You have been told that in the beginning there were the heavens and the Earth. This is not true," Clayton said. He brought together his outstretched arms, as the lights came together, compacting them until only one small, glowing ember could be seen in the darkness. "This was the beginning." He pointed at the insignificant light. "Here is the Great Spirit. Here lies all that you are. Here, in the beginning, is all that ever was and will be."

Clayton smiled as he looked at them.

"In that barely visible light, is the universe in its entirety. All matter that exists today once existed in that little speck of light." He looked up at the light. "Today, you would call this the bottom of a black hole. But that is not an adequate description. All the matter pulled into it has been compressed by a force a gravity beyond your capabilities to comprehend. Uncounted planets, stars, and even lives, crushed into their original state of pure energy. This is the beginning and the end."

He closed his raised fist tight and took in a deep breath. "Behold! Creation!" he exclaimed as he threw open his fingers.

The light exploded outward, startling the others as the blinding light forced their eyes closed. As they felt the light dim, they opened their eyes to a star filled night sky.

"As the heavens opened, energy and matter moved outward, separated by unfathomable distances yet interconnected. The energy that fuels the sun exists in you. All life is joined as one by the energy of the Great Spirit," Clayton said, as he looked down at them. "God is not an old man with a white beard. We are merely fragments of the greater whole. Call it God, Yahweh, Allah, Vishnu, or the Great Spirit, it doesn't matter. There are many names, but only one truth."

"The Bible doesn't say anything about the big bang," Angelo said. "God created the universe in six days."

"Are you sure?" Clayton asked. "Do you believe that everything could be created in six days? Buddhist teachings tell us that the universe expands to a stabilizing point before collapsing in upon itself. The Qur'an tells us that 'the heaven We created with might, and indeed We are its expander.' It also redefines the six days as six separate and distinct time periods. Moses wrote of the creation of all things in Genesis. All philosophies have the same message but express it differently."

Clayton brought his hands together above his head and slowly moved them outward, expanding the heavens.

"Today, we know the universe is expanding and will one day contract." He waved his hand through the air, leaving only the light of the fire.

"What happens then?" Sayer asked.

"The process repeats itself," Clayton said. "All matter will one day be pulled inward and concentrated into a single point of immense energy only to explode outward again." He reached up and poked his finger into the darkness. "Let there be light," he commanded as a bright light appeared beneath his finger. "Our sun is considered a god in some cultures because it makes all physical life on Earth possible. To worship it is not a sin, it is just a lack of understanding."

"What are we supposed to worship?" Horace asked.

"I'm not sure that worship is the right term," Clayton replied.

"What is the right term?" Dawn asked.

"Honor…respect," Clayton answered. "The Great Spirit is in you as it is in all things. The energies of humans and nature are interconnected. They have been flowing together forever."

"Aside from watching the drug induced light show," Horace began, "what do you want from us?"

"Tonight, I want you to understand creation," Clayton said, "and I want to guide you to the understanding that, regardless of who is writing or passing on the knowledge, the story is the same."

"I can see they're similar," Dawn said, "but I think it's a pretty broad interpretation."

"In legend handed down since the beginning," Clayton began, "it is said the sun and the moon mated and gave birth to man. It is said that man fell from the stars into the sacred Blue Lake above us in the mountains. Mankind lived in the underworld to gain understanding and knowledge before emerging. When he emerged, he found plants and animals and knew that their energies were intertwined with his own."

"How exactly does that correspond with the Bible?" Dawn asked.

Clayton turned and walked away from the fire toward a small, circular hole dug in the floor of the kiva. "This is a *sipapu*. It is a representation of where our ancient ancestors rose from the underworld."

He knelt and spread his arms as faint images of ancient Native Americans rose from the sipapu and faded into obscurity moments later. The four sat without speaking, overwhelmed by the vision. There was no fear and no interruption. They sat in awe watching the images unfold and fade before them.

"As it is in the legend," Clayton continued, "the Bible tells us that God created man from the dust of earth and breathed life into him. All holy books and legends tell the same story as does science today. Mankind is born of the stars, risen from the earth and the seas, and evolved to his present form today. All holy texts detail the course of evolution. This is the undeniable truth."

"Wait," Sayer interjected, "if that's true, why are all those TV preachers so mad about evolution?"

"Evolution is outlined in the Bible, it is an account written thousands of years past. In it, God creates the Earth and the oceans followed by plants and sea life, mammals and, finally, man. Isn't that evolution?

"In the Qur'an is reads, 'Allah has created every animal from water. Of them are some that creep on their bellies, some that walk on two legs, and some that walk on four. Allah creates what He wills for, truly, Allah has power over all things.' It goes on to ask us, 'What is the matter with you, that you are not conscious of Allah's majesty, seeing that it is He Who has created you in diverse stages?'"

Clayton stood and drew in a deep breath.

"As for the men you see on your television, they will tell

you that they believe in the teachings of Jesus, but they do not. Their actions betray them."

"I don't think you're going to sway Christians toward evolution," Angelo said. "I see what you're saying, but Genesis doesn't exactly describe evolution."

"But it does," Clayton smiled. "It is from the perspective of a man who had no knowledge of science. Ask yourselves this: How can these writings describe scientific fact centuries, even millennia, before the facts were discovered?" He sat in front of the fire, poking it with a stick. "We were there. We were all there, as we are here today. The infinite energy of our very being existed at the point of creation. It is not God who revealed to Moses the details of creation and evolution. It was Moses's recollection. Moses, just like you, was never born and will never die. Energy can neither be created nor destroyed."

"Gotcha!" Sayer said. "I totally get it." He sprang to his feet. "I feel it, dude," he walked over to Angelo and knelt beside him, "and so do you!"

"I'm not sure I..." Angelo began.

"Dude! Take my hand and close your eyes."

Angelo did as Sayer asked. The peyote was creating bright, lightning-fast flashes of color against the back of his eyelids.

"What am I supposed to feel?" he asked.

"Just let your mind roll," Sayer said.

Angelo sat completely still as Dawn and Horace quietly watched. Within seconds, the lights slowed before giving way to darkness. Holding Sayer's hand, he felt a pulsating heat slowly move up his arm and spread through his entire body. The black emptiness gave way to images of plants and animals. Each one pulsated with the same energy he felt from Sayer. He pictured himself on his boat in the Bering Sea. From the wheelhouse, he watched as his crew, and even the crab, radiated the same pulsing light.

"Oh my God," Angelo said as he threw open his eyes and looked up at Clayton. "I'm sorry. I'm so sorry."

"You have nothing to apologize for," Clayton said as he reached over and placed his hand on Angelo's shoulder. "The crabs are there to nourish you."

"But the dead loss," Angelo said, "I feel their pain." His eyes welled with tears. "It's just my job, you know."

"In legend, man first ate only plants, nuts, and berries. It was the deer who came forward and sacrificed himself to feed man and strengthen his energy. This is the cycle of life. The deer gave itself to the hunter. While the energy from the deer was released to either join the Great Spirit or be reborn, man used the deer to create energy for his body. The pain you feel is the animal not fulfilling its purpose."

Angelo stared at the ground, shaking his head. He had spent years harvesting crab. He watched as his crew would throw them onto the sorting table, then either stomp them into the tanks or carelessly toss them overboard. He had never felt guilty about his job, until now.

"Don't feel bad, Angelo," Clayton said. "Guilt is unnecessary and a waste of your time."

"What did you show him?" Horace barked. "Sayer, what did you just do?"

"You're not gonna believe it, bro'!" Sayer stood up with a large smile beaming from his face. "I feel God…I mean, the Great Spirit in me. I totally understand it now. It's time for a bottom turn, and it's gonna be totally choka!"

"Okay," Dawn began, "now I don't know what *he's* talking about."

"It's surf slang for awesome," Horace said. He turned back to his brother. "Sayer, what did you do to him?"

"Dude, I don't know. I just knew I could do it!" Sayer said excitedly. "It's crazy, bro'. I know we had some peyote, but I don't just see your energy, I totally feel it."

"What's happening to my brother?" Horace asked.

"Nothing is happening to him," Clayton said. "Sayer is as he always was. The energy inside of him is stronger than that of most people."

"What does that mean, exactly?" Dawn asked.

"As energy burst forward in the beginning of time, it was not evenly divided," Clayton said. "The center of the energy remained the most powerful. That is God. That is the Great Spirit. Sayer's body contains powerful energy as well."

Angelo raised his hand as he shook his head. "What are you saying? Sayer is God?"

"No…" Clayton said. "The amount of energy in Sayer makes it possible for him to do things most people cannot. It allows him to use more of his brain."

"I'm calling bullshit," Dawn said. "He's the smartest one here?"

"None of you are any smarter than the other," Clayton responded. "The knowledge you have gathered up to this point is from what you have been taught and what you have experienced. The knowledge you gain tonight, and in the coming days, is what you have always known."

"Hold on a fucking second!" Horace said as he got to his feet. "The coming days? How long are you going to keep us here?"

"I'm not keeping you here, but you will stay," Clayton said. "Tonight, you will sleep and dream of everything I have shared with you. Tomorrow, I will begin with Horace."

"Begin what?" Horace asked. "What are you going to do with me?"

"I'm going to make you whole again." Clayton smiled.

———ⲘⲘ———

Horace lay awake, staring at the timbers that made up the ceiling above him. The wood grain seemed to wave back and forth in the faint flickering light of a small oil lamp on a table in the corner. He knew the peyote wasn't helping matters. Without nicotine or whiskey, he found it a struggle to close his eyes and rest. He let out a heavy sigh and tossed the wool blanket aside.

"Still awake?" Dawn whispered.

"Yeah, I'm having a little trouble focusing," he replied.

"You'll never get to sleep if you try to focus on it," Dawn said. She sat up and looked across the room at Sayer and Angelo sleeping soundly on their blankets. "Those two sure don't seem to have any problem."

"Maybe they have thicker blankets to lay on," Horace answered. He rolled his head to the side to face her and promptly forgot what he was saying.

It had been years since he had been this close to such an attractive young woman. She was lying on her back, facing the ceiling. He gazed at her as if he were memorizing every contour of her face. Her high cheekbones, lightly dusted with freckles, created lines that made her always look like she was smiling. He wanted to reach out and lightly caress her supple cheek with the back of his index finger. But after seeing her fight, he was sure she could easily break that finger if he tried it. He turned his head and stared at the timbers again. His confidence had eroded in the lonely years following the war and was shaken even further by her beauty. They shared the same planet but lived in vastly different worlds.

Dawn rolled over onto her side and propped her head up. "Do you want my blanket?" she offered.

Horace turned back to face her. "I don't think it would help," he said. "Besides, if I took your blanket to make myself more comfortable, my mom would spin in her grave."

"We can't have that," she smiled. "But it is 1990. Women can be chivalrous if they want. Heck, we can even vote and everything."

"What I mean is…"

"I know what you mean," she interrupted, fearing she had embarrassed him. "It's sweet. Really. I know a lot of guys who wouldn't think twice about satisfying their needs first and the needs of a woman second."

"You know a lot of guys?" he asked with a sly smile.

"Okay," she laughed, "you know what I mean." She paused and shook her head. "I don't know what it is with men today. I'll go on a date with a guy and by the end of dinner, he's already talking about sex. It's gross. I can tell you one thing, that's not the way to get laid. So…needless to say, I go on a lot of first dates."

"What do want from a date?" Horace asked.

"I want to talk. I want to be flirty. I want sexual tension to overwhelm me to the point of breathless anticipation."

"Maybe you should date older guys," he offered.

She looked deep into his eyes as the smile returned to her face.

"Maybe I should."

They lay there, staring at each other without a word, facing off in a flirtatious game of chicken. Horace blinked first.

"What do you think about all of this?" he asked, changing the subject. "I mean, God is energy, evolution is creation, black holes…" he trailed off.

"I don't know," she replied, shaking her head. "It's a lot to take in. Logically, it makes sense, I guess."

"Why does he keep talking about the Qur'an?" Horace asked as he propped himself up.

"It's part of the lesson," she said. "I think I believe him. I mean, I haven't read the Qur'an, and I don't know much about Buddhism, but it can't just be a coincidence that the expanding universe was described centuries before we even came up with the theory. I had a professor who once talked about 'genetic memory.' He said that everything that has happened since the beginning of time is stored in our DNA. So what if it's all true? What if our bodies and our energies carry all of that history?"

Horace rolled onto his stomach and propped himself up on his elbows.

"I didn't go to college. I feel a little stupid when I don't understand what you guys are talking about." He quietly stared at the blanket he was lying on then started to laugh. "Speaking of people that make me feel stupid, I wonder where the Doc is."

"I hope he didn't go far," she said. "He has all of our clothes. I'll bet he's at a nice hotel, ordering room service, telling the employees to take a deep breath." She laughed as she pictured Cormick wearing a hotel robe and fuzzy pink slippers, lying poolside with cucumber slices on his eyes, and a towel meticulously wrapped around his head like a turban.

"He wouldn't skip town, would he?" Horace asked. "He left here pretty fucking pissed off."

"I don't think so," she replied, "but can you imagine if he had been here the whole time? Sleeping on sheepskin and wool blankets? Sitting in the dark…high on peyote? He's neurotic enough already."

"How do we find him?" Horace asked.

"He'll find us," she assured him. "He knows where we are. Cormick wouldn't just leave us out here without clean underwear. Trust me, he'll come back once he calms down."

"Well, when he does, he better at least bring me my cigarettes."

"Time to quit smoking," she said with a smile.

THE KEEPER OF THE HOURS

Horace awoke to the brilliant, rising sun beaming in through the window. The sunlight hit him directly in the eyes, causing him to turn away until they adjusted to the light. After a moment, he looked over at Dawn, who was quietly sleeping. He was comforted by the peaceful sound of her slow, deep breaths. He lay there for a few minutes just to look at her.

The wall of calm he felt collapsed when he realized he didn't have a cigarette. He sat up, tossing his blanket aside. On the far side of the room, Angelo and Sayer were still asleep, lightly snoring in unison. Their host was noticeably absent.

He got up and climbed down the ladder into the kiva to look for Clayton, but the room was empty. The overpowering desire for nicotine had him biting the side of his tongue. He was going to have to find a cigarette somewhere even if it was only a discarded butt that he could salvage one precious drag from.

He scaled the ladder back to the main floor then immediately went to the ladder that led to the second story. He stopped a little more than halfway up, popping his head out of the hole like a gopher. Clayton was nowhere to be seen.

"Dammit…" he muttered as he made his way down the ladder. He looked around for a moment then walked past the sleeping trio and out the door.

The sun had just begun to clear the Taos Mountains in

the distance. He took in a deep breath to mimic the feeling of taking a hard drag from a cigarette. Just as his lungs filled with the dry desert air, it exploded out again sending him into a coughing fit. He hacked hard forcing a brown glob of mucous into his mouth. He spit it out and could feel residual saliva on his bottom lip. He wiped it away and, as he lowered his hand, a dark stain near his thumb caught his attention. It was blood.

"Fuck…" he groaned as he wiped the blood on the side of his jeans.

Horace's doctor had prepared him for this moment and for the painful weeks, maybe months, that would inevitably follow. But seeing the blood he had coughed up unnerved him more than he had anticipated. He shaded his eyes and looked at the sunrise again. He wondered how many more he would see.

He could hear water streaming over rocks just a few yards away. The lush green tree growth to the southeast gave away its location. He figured that a lake, high in the mountains above, fed the stream. If that was the case, he could get a cold drink of fresh water and wash up. He made his way toward the tree line and discovered crystal clear water rushing by.

He knelt beside the stream and cupped his hands in the current. As he drank the cold water from his hands, he could feel it make its way through him. Unaware until that moment how dehydrated he was, he repeated his actions four more times, using the last handful to wash his face before running his hands through his hair. He rocked backward and sat down beside the stream, watching it race past him. He took in a deep breath and coughed hard, expelling more thick phlegm and a trace of blood. He turned from the creek and spit it into the grass.

"You don't sound well," Clayton said from behind him.

"Fuck!" Horace was startled and fell to his side. "Are you trying to give me a heart attack?"

"Not at all," Clayton said as he walked to the water's edge and sat beside Horace. "But it doesn't sound like your heart is the problem."

"It's nothing a cigarette couldn't help," Horace replied. He coughed again as more mucus filled his mouth. Concerned that Clayton would see the blood in his mucus, he swallowed hard. The taste was awful.

"You really should spit that out," Clayton said.

"It's not a problem if you like oysters," Horace quipped.

"It is a problem if you are coughing up blood," he replied.

"Just a little lung butter," Horace said. "It happens when no one has a fucking cigarette to give me."

"Time to quit smoking," Clayton smiled.

Horace shook his head. "You're a broken fucking record."

Horace knew Clayton was right. His doctor had told him that so often, that he quit going to his appointments. He was dying. What damage could the cigarettes do that they hadn't done already? Cigarettes and alcohol were part of his life, and he intended to die as he had lived.

"A man who smokes like you and drinks like you is going to destroy himself," Clayton turned to him. "If you weren't meant to be here, in this moment, you would be dead already."

"Look, I've been playing with house money for years," Horace said. "What difference does it make if I die today or ten years from now?'

"Ask your brother," Clayton said. "What would his answer be?"

"What the fuck do you know about it?" Horace fired back. "You don't know shit. You have no fucking idea what it's like to avoid looking in mirrors so you don't make eye contact with yourself. All my friends back home pity me; most of the guys in my platoon are dead, almost half of them from drugs or suicide after they got home safe. My life is empty. Nothing makes me truly happy.

"Every time I do something nice for someone, it doesn't make me feel good; it's an act of atonement for all my sins: sins that God could never forgive me for. Even though I never meant the things I did in war, I still fucking did them! It took years to go a day without crying or a night without waking up screaming. Booze lets me get through one more day…one more night without losing my fucking mind." He looked at Clayton. "You don't know me. You don't know my pain."

"That is not true," Clayton said as he turned toward the creek. "Look at the water. It was once in the sky. It came a great distance, turning to snow as it fell to Mother Earth. The sun warmed the snow to feed the sacred Blue Lake high in the mountains, which, in turn, creates this stream."

"What a great story," Horace said. "And they all lived happily ever after. Now if you'll excuse me…"

"This stream is Red Willow Creek. The water that flows down this path has supplied these people with fresh water for a thousand years. They bathe in these waters; newborn children are cleansed here. This water has kept countless animals and crops alive. Asking nothing in return, it has given life ever since it first began flowing."

"Is there a point to this?" Horace asked.

Clayton got to his knees and dipped his hand in the water. He pulled it out and let the water fall from between his fingers, leaving a single droplet in his palm.

"It's a long journey for that snowflake. It falls with no direction. It travels miles over rocks and waterfalls just to reach this point. It has no idea that it has a purpose." He moved his open palm to Horace. The last drop of water had turned to a snowflake. "Like you, it has endured much to be here, in this moment, exactly as it is meant to be." He blew gently into his palm, and the snowflake took flight and fell into the stream. "And like you, it has no idea how much it will mean to someone downstream."

"I have nothing to give anyone," Horace said. "And before you say anything, I'm not feeling sorry for myself. It's just a fact." He looked at the creek, and sighed. "I'm not living. Hell, I'm barely existing. There is not a single fucking thing I can contribute to society." He looked up at Clayton. "As for your little snowflake trick, I'm sure the peyote has me highly susceptible to the power of suggestion."

"Neither of those things are true, my friend," Clayton said quietly.

"Oh, bullshit," said Horace. "I had it all once. Until the war, I had the love of a good woman. Hell, I was going to the Olympics. Do you understand? The fucking Olympics! There was a time when I had something to offer, but that time is long gone. Everything I was died in a jungle a long time ago and half a world away from here."

"Everything you were made you who you are today," Clayton said as he placed his hand on Horace's shoulder.

"Who I am today?" Horace repeated.

He leaned forward and caught his reflection in the water, making eye contact with himself. He looked old and tired. As the water rippled along the shore, he could see his father's face. The memories of the time he spent with his dad flooded his brain. He had been a good man, and Horace knew he would be heartbroken to see the man his son had become. He stared silently for a moment as a tear ran down his cheek.

"I'm an alcoholic," he said as he pressed his palms against his face. "I'm an angry fucking drunk. I am irredeemable." He wiped his eyes and stared off into the trees. "I can't go a day without a drink. I can't function without whiskey and cigarettes."

"Yet here you are," Clayton said.

"Yeah…here I am," Horace said as he took in a deep breath, coughing as he exhaled. "And all I want right now is a drink."

"Why do you drink like that, Horace?" Clayton asked.

"I drink to forget," he replied.

"Tell me, after all of this time, what is it you have forgotten exactly?"

Horace lifted his head and stared into the trees.

"Okay…it's the pain. I drink for my pain."

"And has your pain eased at all?" Clayton inquired. "Or does drinking just keep it alive inside of you? Alcohol doesn't ease the pain, it only delays the moment when you have to face it. Horace, you are drowning, and no one can save you if you don't want to be saved. Living this way, you will pull anyone who tries to save you to the bottom. Do you want that for Sayer? Do you want that for Dawn?"

"What's she got to do with it?" Horace asked.

"Don't let the image of what you once thought you might become take control of your life. Focus instead on who you are today and what that will mean for you—and others—tomorrow."

"Fuck this," Horace said. "You don't know me. You can't

even begin to understand me."

Clayton stood up and turned to face his dwelling. He held his palms just at the height of the grass as it swayed in the wind.

"I know you have nightmares from killing that boy. I know the screams of young girls, raped by your brothers in arms, haunt you in the quiet times. I know you blame yourself for the loss of your mother, and another man for the loss of a woman. I know that you are desperately lonely and have no idea how to change that. I know that cancer is consuming you from the inside out." He turned back to Horace, who was staring at the ground. "I also know that, no matter how difficult the past has been, you can begin anew anytime you choose."

"How do you know all of that?" Horace asked without looking up.

"As I said, you and I—like all living things—are forever intertwined like the snowflakes in the creek."

"Let's say that's true," Horace said as he got to his feet. "Let's say I believe you. Then what? What am I to do? If you know I have cancer, you know that I'm going to die. My tomorrows are limited." He looked toward the house where the others lay sleeping. For the first time in years, he realized that he did not want to die. "Let's say that today I could start fresh. How do I begin?"

"Time to quit smoking," Clayton smiled.

"Again, with that shit?" Horace asked.

"Horace, if you could start anew today…would you? Would you stop killing yourself with cigarettes? Would you stop drinking to the point of death? Would you be able to forgive yourself?" Clayton asked.

Horace took in a deep breath as he watched Dawn

step out of the house into the brilliant morning sun. She stretched her arms upward, arched her back, and yawned. He watched every movement, amazed by her. She caught sight of the men and, smiling broadly, gave them an exaggerated wave. Horace raised his hand and waved back. The two of them silently gazed at each other.

"Yes," Horace said. "Yes, to all of it."

"It's good to see you smile," Clayton said. "How often can a man experience a beautiful dawn twice in one morning?"

Horace motioned for her to join them by the creek. She nodded and went inside to get her shoes.

"Hey," he said turning to Clayton, "is it possible we could make some coffee? Maybe brush our teeth?"

"Anything is possible, Horace," Clayton said, grinning. "But first, drink from the creek one more time." He motioned to the water. "Only this time, drink the water from my hands."

"That's a little weird," he said as he watched Clayton kneel beside the creek.

Horace looked back toward the house, but Dawn was not on her way yet. He took in a deep breath and knelt in front Clayton. He drank the water from his cupped palms.

"That will ease your cough," Clayton said.

"A drink from the creek is going to keep me from hacking?"

"For now," Clayton responded. "Let's go back to the house. I will start a fire for breakfast, and you and Dawn can return to the creek together for water."

"Wait…" Horace said. "Last night you said something about making me whole again. What does that mean?"

"It means that today you awoke and, without even knowing it, began your life anew." He placed his hand on Horace's shoulder and gave him a reassuring smile.

"Is it possible I could begin my new life with some clean underwear?" Horace asked.

"It's on the way," Clayton said as he turned and walked toward the house. "Come, we would do well with some breakfast."

—◊◊◊—

Sayer stared in awe out the window toward the mountains. Outside of the occasional competition near the volcanic peaks in Hawaii, he rarely saw anything on land so majestic. He thought about the Pacific Ocean back home and realized that he had taken it for granted. He understood it was a powerful, living thing, much more than just a place to play or white noise to help him sleep. He knew he would never take it for granted again.

"Hey man, what are you looking at?" Angelo asked as he stepped up beside him and peered out the window.

"Dude, those mountains."

"Yeah, they're big ones," Angelo said, "like the mountains back home."

"No dude...just that one to the right," Sayer pointed to Old Mile Peak. "I totally had a dream about that mountain last night. It knows my name." He continued staring out the window. "There's something out there."

"Are you sure it wasn't the peyote?" Angelo asked.

"No, dude, that mountain called to me," Sayer said. "It was the same voice I heard back home. But the dancing zebra...now that had to be the peyote."

"Dancing zebra? You obviously had more than me," Angelo laughed. "Wait...you heard the voice? What did it say?"

"It didn't really say anything." He turned to Angelo. "But it's calling me."

"I'm jealous," Angelo said as he turned back to the horizon. "I miss it. Is that crazy? I miss the voice in my head that almost got me locked up in a loony bin."

"Dude, I'm gonna tell you something, but you have to promise me that you won't tell the others and that you won't be mad," Sayer implored.

"Out of all the people on the planet, Sayer, you are probably the last person anyone could ever be mad at," Angelo laughed. Looking at Sayer, he saw that whatever he was about to say was no laughing matter. "Hey, what is it?"

"I hear it all the time," he replied. "But not just the voice that I heard on the ocean…I hear the voice of everything." He walked over to the old handmade chair in the corner and sat down. "I hear every living thing."

"What does that mean?" Angelo asked. "Shit…what does that even sound like?"

Sayer shook his head and smiled.

"It sounds beautiful."

Just as he was about to go on, the others came in from the field, with Clayton leading the way.

"Yo, Clayton…what's up with that mountain over there?" Sayer asked as he got to his feet and returned to the window.

Clayton joined Sayer and Angelo at the window.

"Those mountains are part of the Sangre de Cristo range, which is Spanish for blood of Christ. They are holy mountains, they protect the most sacred shrine of the Taos people." Turning to Sayer, he smiled then walked to the door, motioning for Sayer to follow. "Come with me, Sayer."

The two men stepped out into the morning sun and walked beside each other through the field.

"It's not the mountain that calls you, Sayer. It is *Ba Whyea*," Clayton said as he slowly walked through the grassy field.

Sayer stopped in his tracks.

"What is Ba Whyea?"

"Today it is known as Blue Lake," he replied. "Last night, I did not go into detail for everyone because the knowledge that lies on the mountain is yours to discover and share. That's why the others can't hear its call."

"Why me?' Sayer asked. "The voice called all of us. Why am I the only one who can hear it now?"

"Sayer, you are a larger part of the whole. I can't tell you everything you need to know. Some things, you must learn for yourself. Though I will always be with you, there are things you must learn alone."

"But my brother…" Sayer began.

"Horace has his path as you have yours," Clayton said.

Sayer looked toward the fertile elevations standing guard over the pueblo.

"Dude, I have never climbed a mountain," Sayer said. "How will I know where to go?"

"How did you know to come here?" Clayton said as he looked toward the mountain. "You will know the way. You can be there just after the sun sets." He turned toward the house and saw the trio standing in the doorway. "Do not share this with the others. This is your path and yours alone. Take water from the creek. There is bread and dried venison inside."

"I'll go," Sayer said. "I know it's what I'm supposed to do. You know, I haven't second guessed anything. I've followed God…the Great Spirit…without even blinking. So why am I so nervous?"

"Everything is about to change for you, and you are about to change everything." Clayton started walking back to the house. After a couple of steps, he stopped and turned his head to the side. "Take care, my friend. Don't fear the way forward." With that, he continued making his way back to the others.

"Horace and I need time alone in the kiva," Clayton said as he stepped past the others and into the house. "The pueblo has opened for the public," he mentioned to Dawn and Angelo. "Join them. You never know who you'll see." He started down the ladder. "I will light a fire, Horace."

"What about Sayer?" Angelo asked.

"He said he's going for a walk," Clayton replied as he disappeared into the chamber.

Horace looked at Dawn and shrugged. "I guess we need time alone." He walked to the ladder and started his descent. Halfway down, he stopped and turned to her. "Hey, see if one of those shops sells deodorant, will ya? I can't afford to lose any more friends."

Horace stepped off the ladder and heard broken glass crunch beneath his feet. He looked down, but the darkness hid the fragments of what remained of the bottle he had dropped the night before. Staring at the ground in the darkness, he felt the need for a drink squeeze him like a fist.

"You don't need that," Clayton said as the flames illuminated his face. He was looking down into the fire. "You never did."

Horace stared at him for a moment then back down at the ground. The glow from the fire was reflected in a few of the shards next to his foot. The way the light hit them, they reminded him of tears. It was only a matter of seconds before he quietly shed some of his own.

"Why do you cry?" Clayton asked without looking up.

"So much wasted time," Horace said as he waved his foot over the broken glass. "So much fucking wasted time."

"You have wasted nothing," Clayton said as he looked up at him. "Time is merely how you measure your physical existence. No other living thing on this planet is concerned with time. You need only to be concerned about today. Mourning yesterday accomplishes nothing."

"That's not what I mean," Horace answered. "My life…"

"Is what it is supposed to be," Clayton said. "Instead of living the days ahead in remorse for what you have done in the past, make the choice to walk a new path in the present and apply the lessons you have learned to your life in the days ahead. Please, come join me."

Horace sniffled and wiped the tears from his cheeks. He struggled to take a step away from the broken bottle. He closed his eyes and moved toward the fire, fighting the urge to look back.

"That bottle represents a part of your journey to this moment. You don't need to fear it or regret it. You only need to leave it behind and move forward."

"Let me guess…it's twelve steps to the future."

"No…" Clayton smiled, "but you should write that down."

"You know, there was a time when writing was my passion," Horace said as he neared the fire.

"It still is," Clayton replied.

"No, those days are gone," Horace replied as he sat down. "I have no passion."

"I would have to disagree with you, my friend. I see the way you look at Dawn," Clayton said as he walked over and handed a bowl of liquid to Horace. "Here, drink this."

Horace brought the bowl to his nose and gave it a couple of sniffs.

"Smells like shit!" he exclaimed as Clayton motioned for him to drink. Horace pressed the bowl to his lips and drank. He winced and forced it down his throat, fighting his gag reflex. "Tastes like shit," he said in a strained voice. "Fuck. Is that more peyote?"

"Yes, it is. You said you wanted to begin anew, so this is how we proceed," Clayton said.

"By making me vomit?" Horace cried. "I thought you said this shit wasn't allowed on the pueblo."

"It's not. But as I said last night, there are tribes that use this as part of a healing ceremony," Clayton said. "Drink what you can." He returned to the far side of the fire and sat down. "Tell me, why did you stop writing?"

"The war," Horace said as he took another sip from the bowl. "Christ, is there anything to make this taste better?"

"No. Keep drinking," Clayton said. "Why do you believe the war stopped you from writing?"

"Because it was war," Horace fired back. "Because it's the ugliest thing to be a part of." Horace plugged his nose and took another drink. "They say you're a man at eighteen. But you're not. You're just a kid. At that age, you're innocent. You're just out of school. Fuck, you haven't even lived in the real world, yet. Then they ship you off to someplace you only just learned about, to kill people you've never met."

Horace put the bowl down and let his head rest in his palms.

"I lost myself because I killed people. Because, with one flick of my finger, I made sure some other boy would never see his mother again." His eyes welled with tears. "Because I am a murderer."

As the tears fell from his eyes, Horace's body began to

shake, and the sound of his mournful weeping echoed in the kiva.

"I'm sorry. I don't know what's wrong with me," he said, shaking his head. "I can't remember the last time I cried and now I've done it three times this morning."

"You're in pain," Clayton said. "You've been in pain for a very long time. Crying will help. As will writing."

"I can't!" Horace raised his voice. "Why are you pushing the issue?"

"Because that is what you're here to do," Clayton said. "You will change the world with your words."

"And how the fuck am I going to do that?" Horace asked. "I have nothing of any value to say to anyone."

"Horace, that is not true," Clayton responded. "You just need to believe."

"In what?" he demanded.

Horace got to his feet and walked toward the ladder. He stared at the rungs, wanting to escape to anywhere, a bar, his home, the past. Anywhere was a better option than where he was standing. But he was unable to make the climb. He watched his shadow, cast on the wall in front him, dance in the fire light. The shadow took his shape, and his face appeared in the darkness. He saw himself as a youth, a soldier, and a drunk. The portraits seemed to appear as one, but were distinctly different. It was a struggle for him to keep his eyes on the blurry images. Overcome with emotion, he was unable to look any longer. He bowed his head.

"Give me something to believe in," he said.

"I will," Clayton said. "Come back to the fire. Sit with me."

Horace hesitated but turned and slowly walked back to Clayton.

"I need to believe in something...anything...before I

die." He sat down and looked at Clayton, his eyes pleading him to ease his pain.

"You have to forgive yourself first," Clayton said. "You've spent more than half of your life waiting to die. You've done everything you can to speed up the process. Remember what I told you. You are and always will be."

"I'm not sure I can forgive myself," he replied.

"Forgiving is easier than you think. Forgetting is not," Clayton said. "You remember what you heard in Vietnam when you thought you were going to die. You remember what you saw. You told Cormick it was a warm forgiving light that called you by name as you lie bleeding on the ground."

"How the fuck do you know that?" Horace asked.

"I was there," Clayton said.

"You were where? In my living room? In the jungle?"

"I have always been there," Clayton said. "I am the voice you heard. I am the light you saw."

"Bullshit," Horace replied.

"You interpreted what you saw as light, but it was energy," Clayton said as he leaned toward him. "You interpreted it as forgiving because in that moment all was revealed to you. In those brief minutes, you understood that there is no such thing as right or wrong. You and that boy each had a lesson to learn. You were brothers. You existed in the same place at one time, and you will again."

"I know the difference between right and wrong and…"

"No, you were taught a concept," Clayton said. "As it is with east and west, right and wrong are merely designations created by man."

"I fucking killed people," Horace shot back.

"That boy was going to end your current physical existence," Clayton said. "You acted to end his, instead. The energy of his being—his soul—exists today."

"Okay, wait…" Horace stammered as he tried to grasp what he was hearing. "If I knew everything then, how come I didn't remember it when I woke up?"

"Before the point of conception, you exist in a state of total awareness," Clayton said as he stood up and walked to the opposite side of the fire. "In our true state, we choose the lessons we wish to learn. This can only be done as a physical being. We seek out the energy that was closest to us before all things began because we are drawn to the fragments of ourselves. When those factors align, we choose a physical body that is being conceived, and we live that brief life. In doing so, we sacrifice our knowledge of all that lies beyond the physical world.

"You were born and were instantly overstimulated by your physical surroundings, forgetting the knowledge of all things. That is what happened to you when you awoke in the hospital after you were shot. For a time, you were with all things. When you awoke, the pain you felt overcame the peace and knowledge once again."

"If you're the light…the voice we heard…are you God?"

"There is no God. There is only the greatest part of the whole," Clayton said. "Mine was the voice that called you here. But it was a chorus of voices that reminded you that you are here to learn and teach far more than you had when you were shot."

"A chorus of voices?" Horace asked. "What fucking sense does that make?"

"When you chose to be Horace Jordan, you chose his future. You chose to fight in war and to poison your body because you needed to learn about pain. But you also chose to surf the waves of the ocean so that you could experience the excitement. You chose to write—and you will again—because you were aware that the times ahead would absolutely require it. And you chose your family because your energies—your souls—have been linked since the beginning of all things. You have chosen each other time after time and will again and again. That is the chorus of voices. I was there, as was your father, your grandparents, and your children."

"I don't have any children," Horace said as he thought back through the one night stands in his life. "At least, I don't think so."

"You always have, and you always will," Clayton said. "Souls...spiritual energies...are inextricably tied to one another, forever. Would It surprise you to know that your brother was once your child?"

Horace thought for a moment as he stared into the flames.

"No, I suppose not. After Dad died, I tried to do the best I could."

"The two of you have been together since before the sun rose above the mountains," Clayton said, "as have you and Dawn."

"Please don't tell me she was once my mother," Horace said.

"Okay, I won't tell you," Clayton said.

The two men stared at each other in silence, before Horace started to laugh. He felt the peyote playing with his mind. He saw faces in the fire. He turned to Clayton and noticed that he had begun to radiate light.

"Fuck," he said, "this is a little out there for me."

"And it is only the beginning," Clayton said. "You've

already begun to forgive yourself. The cigarettes and alcohol were the physical toxins in your life. Your self-loathing is a spiritual toxin. Within a very short time, you will be rid of all three."

"And I'll still be dying," Horace said. "If you know everything, you know I don't have long."

"Let me worry about that," Clayton said. "The peyote is going to help you see your illness. You will understand where your sickness comes from and how to treat it. It is part of a healing ceremony that dates back thousands of years. You will see that you have longer than you think."

"And then what?" Horace asked.

"And then you will do all that you have come here to do," Clayton said. "When you are ready, lie back with your arms at your side. Then we can begin."

"How will I know when I'm ready?" Horace asked.

As he spoke, the wall behind Clayton faded into the shores of the Pacific Ocean at Huntington Beach. He saw his parents waving him toward the water. They were so young. It was more than a hallucination. It was a distant memory of the three of them together in 1956. He could hear them calling for him, and he could smell the warm sea breeze blowing in across the thundering waves as the tide fought to pull away from the shore. He turned to survey the horizon and saw Clayton standing beside him in his yard, smiling at him.

"It appears you're ready," Clayton said.

⸺⸺⸺

Dawn and Angelo followed the tree line on the banks of Red Willow Creek to the pueblo. As they approached the main structures, they saw dozens of tourists filtering through the entrance and into the compound. Noticing that the majority of the sightseers had stopped at the entrance to the church courtyard, they decided to blend in but walk the grounds without the help of a guide. Angelo scanned the north side of the complex.

"I don't think any of those shops are selling anything we need."

"Let's not rush to judgement," Dawn replied. "I'm probably going to need something in at least one of those little shops. You know…to use as part of a lesson plan next year."

"Oh yeah, lesson plan," Angelo laughed. "I'll believe that when you quit staring at the sign that says JEWELRY." He looked across the creek at the smaller south house. "There's shops over there, too. It looks like there may be more of them over there and less people. Why don't we start there? I haven't had enough coffee to deal with anyone who wears black socks with their Bermuda shorts." He motioned with his head toward an old man in the crowd.

"You don't think socks and sandals go good together?" Dawn laughed. "With that fashion sense, you'd think he was from Alaska or something."

"Easy now!" Angelo laughed. "Besides, I'm from Seattle."

"Nobody's perfect," Dawn quipped. "Listen, I'm going to eavesdrop on the tour. Who knows? I may learn something. I'll meet you over there in a few." She started to walk toward the church. "If you find coffee over there, cream and sugar!" She turned and waved, her fingers fluttering like hummingbirds.

Angelo walked across the sunbaked earth toward the middle wooden bridge. He stopped at the bank and stared at the crystal-clear water rushing past on its way to the Rio Grande and listened. He missed the sound of the waves on the ocean. He had spent his entire adult life traveling from the Puget Sound, up the Pacific, to the fertile fishing grounds of the Bering Sea and back several times a year. He missed riding the slow roll of the waves, and he missed hearing the voice of God.

He crossed the bridge and surveyed the shops that made up the facade of the south house. As he read the signs, it was clear that the coffee and toiletries he sought would have to be found outside of the reservation. He looked back toward Dawn, who was standing next to the tour guide. He couldn't hear her, but it seemed she had hijacked the tour. Laughing to himself, he shook his head and continued forward.

He walked to the closest structure which had a sign offering water near an open door. The room was no bigger than ten feet deep and ten feet wide. There were old tables displaying all manner of knick-knacks from peace pipes to clay figurines. An old native man stood smiling and nodding behind a glass display case full of silver and turquoise jewelry.

"The sign out front said water," Angelo said as he motioned to the door. "But if there's any coffee…"

"Only water," the old man replied. "If that is what you thirst for."

"Well, like I said, coffee is actually what I thirst for."

"Only water," the old man repeated. He walked from behind the case to the table against the back wall. He picked up a small clay figure of a woman sitting with a small child in her lap. Her mouth was wide open. "This is a storyteller. This is how we pass knowledge to the next generation."

"You make pottery to pass on knowledge?" Angelo asked.

The old man stared at him for a moment.

"No, we tell the ancient stories to our young. We share

our history and our traditions without books."

"Oh…very nice. I really just wanted to get some water," Angelo said.

"Thirty dollars," the old man said.

"For water?" Angelo asked, astonished at the cost.

"You're not very bright, are you?" The old man held out the storyteller. "Thirty dollars."

"Yes, it's very nice," Angelo repeated. "I'm not really interested in souvenirs. But I'm very interested in some water.

"Be mindful of what you thirst for," he replied with a smile. "Thirty dollars."

The two men stared at each other without blinking, waiting for the other to give in. Like two gunfighters facing off in the old west, they stood in the silence, completely expressionless. But the old man was far more experienced at the game.

"Okay…thirty dollars," Angelo said as he bent to the will of his opponent. He reached for his wallet and pulled out the money. "Worth it, I guess. I mean Indian pottery and all."

The old man walked back to his glass case and began wrapping the figure in old newspaper. He tied it up with a length of twine and handed it to Angelo. Again, they found themselves in a silent standoff.

"So…thank you," Angelo said. "Now about the water…"

"All out," the old man replied without so much as a smile.

Angelo looked at him, wondering if he was kidding.

"Uh…okay," he said as he turned to the door. "Well, thank you."

He reached into his pocket and pulled out his sunglasses. Putting them on, he stepped back into the sun and looked around. He didn't see Dawn and he didn't see another sign offering water. Back toward the creek he spied a log that had been cut in half to act as a bench. From there he could watch all three footbridges as well as the entire southern compound. It was the perfect place to wait it out.

He sat on the edge of the log and stared off into the east at the Taos Mountains. He counted nine separate peaks but wasn't sure if they were nine separate mountains. Except for one peak that was completely barren, the dense vegetation near their tops made them appear black. Below the tree line, the sparse green vegetation showed the same pale brown baked earth as the pueblo. He looked down at the ground to compare the color. There were grey rocks deeply imbedded in the ground and several small withered yellow plants. At one time, the area had been the floor of an ancient sea, teeming with prehistoric aquatic life, but now it was merely dust beneath his feet.

At that moment, a dragonfly landed on the parched soil in front of him. Though he knew what it was, he had never seen one before. He took off his glasses and slowly leaned forward for a closer look. It was barely a shade darker than the dirt it sat on, the perfect camouflage from predators. He marveled at the insect, watching intently as its orange and black eyes darted back and forth. Its head seemed to make rapid movements to the right and left.

"You are a fisher of men," a quiet voice called out.

His jaw fell open and his breathing stopped as he stared at the insect. He was sure he had seen it move its mouth when he heard the voice. He leaned in for closer inspection, watching the bug dart its eyes back and forth again.

"You are the Angel Messenger," the voice said again.

He was sure he had heard the dragonfly talk. It moved its mouth. He heard the voice. There was no other explanation. He remembered the connection between all living things Clayton had discussed the night before. He bent over, his face just a foot from the insect.

"Tell me what I'm supposed to do," he implored. "Tell me where all of this is leading."

"You will…"

At that moment, a dirty tennis shoe crushed the dragonfly into the dirt, and a shadow was cast over him. His lungs deflated as he exhaled in horror. He jumped up and shoved the man in front of him.

"Angelo!" Cormick called from his right.

Angelo turned and looked at Cormick then back to the man in front of him. He was angry and devastated to the point where he couldn't feel his relief at seeing Cormick.

"You just killed that dragonfly!" Angelo exclaimed.

"You want to fight me over a dead dragonfly?" the man asked. "No offense, but I used to smack skinny hippies like you around just for fun."

Cormick stepped between the two men and grabbed Angelo by the upper arms, forcing him to make eye contact.

"Angelo, it is okay," Cormick said. "Are you okay? How are the others?"

Angelo stared at Cormick until tears filled his eyes. He dropped back down onto the bench and covered his eyes.

"He killed the dragonfly," he cried. "He killed the dragonfly."

"I am sure it was an accident," Cormick said, comfortingly, as he knelt beside his friend. "Russ, please tell Angelo it was an accident."

"I'd like to, Cormick," Hanrahan said, "but it seemed as good a place as any to stomp on a bug."

"You son of a bitch!" Angelo yelled as he jumped up,

knocking Cormick backward into the dirt.

"Easy boy," Hanrahan warned.

"Angelo, please," Cormick said as he got up and dusted himself off. "This is Russ. He is staying at my hotel. When I told him what I was doing here, he was very interested in learning more."

"Yep, that's true," Hanrahan said. "I know a guy who is long overdue to meet God…face to face."

"Cormick, can I talk to you for a minute?" Angelo asked as he wiped the tears from his eyes. "Alone?"

"Certainly," Cormick said as they stepped away. "Please excuse us. This will just take a moment."

Angelo shot a glance at Hanrahan then turned his back to him.

"Cormick, this isn't right. You just can't bring people here to meet God. What are you thinking?"

"It is not like that," Cormick responded. "I was in the hotel lounge, and we struck up a conversation. He asked why I was in Taos, and when I told him, he was quite interested in learning more. It is that simple." He looked back at Hanrahan and motioned that it would be another moment. "I saw him at breakfast and told him I needed to bring you and the others your belongings, and he offered to ride along."

"I don't like him, Cormick. I don't know what it is, but something isn't right with that guy."

"Why, Angelo? Because he stepped on a dragonfly?"

"Cormick, that dragonfly was a living thing. It was about to tell me…" he stopped himself before he said too much.

"Are you telling me God came to you as an insect?" Cormick asked.

"Look, I don't want to be a dick, but you remember what Clayton said last night. The knowledge we receive here is for the four of us."

"Yes, I remember quite well what was said last night," Cormick snapped. "I remember that I was excluded from learning anything beyond the fact that I am little more than a chauffeur for the rest of you. I remember being asked to leave that cave because, for reasons beyond my understanding, I am somehow unworthy of understanding why we made this journey in the first place."

Angelo reached out and placed his hand on Cormick's shoulder.

"It's not like that. You don't understand."

"That is correct. I do not understand." Cormick turned away and walked back to Hanrahan. "I have your stuff in the van. I could not help but notice that Horace left his cigarettes. I am sure he is suffering some sort of vile nicotine fit at this very moment." He looked around the pueblo. "Where is he? Where is everyone?"

"I don't know where anyone is," Angelo said. "They're all around here somewhere."

"I'm gonna take a look around," Hanrahan said as he glanced about. "I'll meet up with you at the van in a while."

Hanrahan stared at Angelo with an evil smile on his face. He wanted to hit him for crying over a dead bug but couldn't risk giving himself away. He had been lucky so far. Angelo was sightless during the altercation in the bar, and Cormick had been too terrified to get a good look at anyone, but Hanrahan remembered all of them. He had shaven off his full beard which had been enough to keep Cormick from figuring out who he was. He gave a half-hearted salute to the two men and walked toward the first open door. He would do a house by house search if necessary, but he was going to find Horace Jordan.

Angelo knelt on the dusty ground and looked at the dragonfly that had the life stomped out of it.

"I don't care where you found that guy, Cormick. He's not a good man," He looked up and shook his head, "but I'm glad to see you."

Cormick sat on the bench and watched as Hanrahan entered and exited the small shops in the south house. It seemed odd that he appeared to be searching for something rather than exploring the adobe monument, but he shrugged it off and turned his attention to his friend.

"So…did I miss anything? Did you find the answers you were seeking?"

Angelo slowly got up and sat beside him. "I've definitely been enlightened," he sighed. "And if you're friend there hadn't killed that dragonfly…" he looked back at the impression in the dust left by Harahan's foot. The dragonfly was gone. "What the hell?" he muttered.

"Enlightened how?" Cormick asked. "You have to tell me something, Angelo. I need answers…just like you."

"I'm not sure what I can tell you. Not because I don't want to, I just don't have all of the answers yet." He looked at Cormick, wishing he could give him the answers he needed. "I can tell you this…my perception of God has dramatically changed. God is inside of us; inside of everything." He smiled and looked around at the pueblo, squinting from the bright sun. "I know why we're here, I just haven't figured out why I'm here, yet. Does that make any sense?"

"I suppose that makes as much sense as everything else," Cormick sighed. "Listen, I am staying in town about ten miles from here. I am not leaving without you…any of you. I promise." He put his hand on Angelo's shoulder. "There appear to be no pay phones here. I am concerned that you will not be able to reach me if you need me. I was thinking I could drive up here every day to check in on you."

"I hope you brought me some clean panties," Dawn said as she approached them from the foot bridge.

Cormick stood up and nodded. "Is it possible you could just call them underwear?"

"Come here," she said with outstretched arms. "Give me a hug!" She pulled him close and squeezed tight. As he began to pull away, she put her lips next to his ear and, breathlessly, whispered, "Panties." When he pulled back she smiled at him. "I was afraid we wouldn't see you again, Cormick. You were pretty upset."

"I apologize for the way I acted," he said. "My outburst…"

"Don't sweat it Cormick," Angelo said as he got to his feet. "Any one of us would have reacted the same way."

"Perhaps," he replied. "Nonetheless, I was wrong. I acted like a petulant child. The emotional stress combined with the alcohol…" He took a couple of steps toward the creek and bowed his head. "No. No, that is not correct. I was angry."

"No one can blame you," Dawn said. "I promise, you will be the first to know everything."

He turned back to them and tried to smile, but his eyes betrayed him. "I must admit, I find that I am a bit lonely. I have grown accustomed to the chaos that comes with spending time with all of you. Perhaps we could drive into town and have some lunch."

"We can't," Dawn said. "We'll have to get back soon. I'm sorry."

"I see," Cormick said dejectedly. "Well, as I said, I have your things in the van. You can take what you need, and I will keep everything else safe." He turned and looked toward the entrance to the pueblo. "I am parked just outside the gate."

"What about your friend?" Angelo asked.

"Cormick!" Dawn exclaimed. "You made a friend?"

"Is that so hard to believe?" he asked as he started toward the van. He stopped at the bridge and looked around. "He is here somewhere. We can get your things, and I will wait for him in the van."

"You could wait here," Angelo said.

"There is nothing for me here," Cormick said.

THE ANGEL MESSENGER

Angelo made his way through the compound toward the decaying adobe wall to the east that kept tourists from wandering onto the private land of the reservation. He had filled Horace's army duffle bag with what he hoped was enough clothes to get everyone through the next few days. Dawn followed close behind with a bag of the essential toiletries needed to keep the group happy in their close quarters. Angelo stopped at the wall and looked out over the field ahead.

"Isn't it odd?" Angelo asked as he turned to Dawn. "This is the third time we'll cross this wall. With all these signs telling us to not to go any farther, no one tries to stop us."

"We were with Clayton the first time," she responded. "Maybe if you're with someone from the tribe, they let you pass."

"Maybe," Angelo said as he stepped over the wall. He held his hand out and helped her over the wall. "Still… seems odd."

"I feel bad leaving Cormick behind," Dawn said as the two continued forward. "I feel like I'm betraying him. Did you see the look on his face? It was like walking away from a sad puppy at the shelter."

"I don't see what harm it would do to have him around," Angelo said. "I get that four is a mystical number, but Clayton has to know we'll tell Cormick everything." He took a few more steps then stopped and turned to face her. "You know…I once had this Japanese guy fishing for me that told me that the word for four and death are pronounced the same in his language. That doesn't fill me with a lot of confidence right now."

"I could have gone the rest of this trip without hearing that," she replied.

They walked side by side without another word until they reached the house. As they rounded the corner, they saw Clayton standing alone in the field staring at the mountains in the distance. Angelo unshouldered the duffel bag and let it rest against the earthen wall of the house as Dawn headed inside.

"Well, you were right," Angelo said as he walked over to him. "You never know who you're going to run into."

"And how was Cormick?" Clayton asked, continuing to stare off into the horizon.

"He was Cormick," Angelo answered. He stepped up beside him and stared at the peaks standing watch over the pueblo. "He's a good man, you know. Would it really do any harm to have him here? He sacrificed a lot to make this journey."

"Did you ever stop to think that he is still on his journey?" Clayton turned to him. "As you are still on yours?"

"And what is my journey?" Angelo implored. "Where does this end for me?"

"It never ends," Clayton said. "This is about the infinite. It is about all that is and ever will be."

"Okay then, what is my purpose?" Angelo asked.

"Again, you're talking in finite terms," Clayton responded. "You have more than one purpose. For example, as a captain, you guided your boat to fertile fishing grounds, feeding tens of thousands of people you will never meet. You paid your crew a wage that allowed them to keep their families healthy and happy. You accomplished many things at once. A few days ago, you thought your purpose was to answer the call you heard on the ocean. But what have you accomplished along the way? You became a friend to a man who had none. You think you ripped Cormick from his world, but you freed him. And now, Cormick will serve his purpose."

"So, that's it?" Angelo asked. "I set things in motion for others?"

"Everything we do sets in motion events we cannot see and may never be made aware of. You have had, and will continue to have, a profound impact on the lives of countless others."

"That sounds a lot like karma," Angelo said as he turned away and watched the tall grass bend in the summer wind. He took in a deep breath of the warm, dry air and slowly exhaled. He laughed, knowing Cormick would have been proud of him for taking a deep, calming breath. "I'm just impatient," he said. "You've made me realize that I have a place in the universe. I feel like I'm awakening. Does that make sense?"

"Yes, but you will need to be patient. The true awakening is not today, but in the future," Clayton smiled. "Be mindful of what you thirst for."

"The old man…he said the same thing. But I don't understand," Angelo said.

"Show me what you bought from the old man," Clayton said.

Angelo walked to the duffel bag and dug around for the clay figure. He pulled it out and unwrapped it, then handed it to Clayton.

"This is a storyteller," Clayton said. "This one is the singing mother. She is passing knowledge and tradition to the next generation. She holds a child to show how close we become when sharing our history. It is what binds us all."

"Like in the kiva," Angelo said.

"Yes," Clayton nodded. "In the kiva, you experience an intimate connection with the story. Sharing knowledge this way allows the storyteller to create a lasting bond with those who are listening. When we are in the kiva, you feel my excitement as I reveal the truth to you. You get swept up in more than the story. You feel the emotion."

"Is that it, then?" he asked. "Are you trying to create a bond between yourself and the rest of us?"

"The bond should not be with me, but with all of you," he smiled and looked back at the mountains, "and with all living things."

"Your story of creation…" Angelo began.

"It is *the* story of creation," Clayton corrected him.

"Sorry…the story of creation…about how all living things come from the same place and are made of the same stuff. Is that the message I should be sharing?"

"In part, yes," he responded. "Look to the mountains and listen. What do you hear?"

Angelo turned to face the mountains. "I don't hear anything. It's so quiet."

"That is why all of you came here. The physical world is a very noisy place. In the coming years, the world will be even noisier. So many people talking, but no one actually listening." He shook his head and sighed. "Coming here to the pueblo will help you hear beyond the noise. Face the mountains again. Look to that peak," he said, pointing to where Sayer had gone. "This time, close your eyes and listen."

Angelo did as he was told. He stood silently and listened to the wind rustle the dry grass as it blew across the open field. In the distance, he heard a bird cry out. He began to hear sounds he was unfamiliar with. He opened his eyes and turned to Clayton.

"What was that?" he asked.

"Life," Clayton smiled.

"I don't get it," Angelo said. "Life makes a sound?"

"All life makes a sound," he answered. "As the human race has continued to evolve technologically, it has stopped growing spiritually. Mankind is out of touch with his soul and the soul of his world. In ancient times, we knew much more than we know now. We shared the earth with all living things. There was no religion, only the belief in the Great Spirit. Man was one with his world. Over time, what I say to you will become clearer. Then you will become the storyteller."

"I saw a dragonfly today," he said.

"A reminder of why you're here," Clayton said.

"Some asshole crushed the life out of it," Angelo said with disgust.

"Did he?" Clayton asked. "Remember, life is energy. Energy is matter. The dragonfly is not dead. Listen for it, and you will hear it again."

"This morning, Sayer told me he could hear every living thing. Will that happen to me, too?"

"If you allow it. Everything you need will come to you when the time is right and not a moment sooner," Clayton said. "Sit by the creek. Listen to the natural world for a while. I will be inside with the others."

"Isn't this for everyone?" Angelo questioned. "If we're not all together, how will we all learn what we need to? I mean, our conversation…shouldn't they hear what you just told me?"

Clayton turned toward the house and started walking away. "They will. You'll tell them. You'll tell everyone. You are the Angel Messenger."

———\\\———

Inside the house, Dawn had already changed into khaki shorts and a clean t-shirt. Unable to find Horace, she descended the ladder into the dimly lit kiva to look for him. Horace was lying, eyes closed, on the ground in front of the fire. She quietly walked over and knelt beside him. She was unsure if he was awake, so she said nothing. Instead, she reached for him and gently cupped his cheek in her hand and ran her thumb across his cheekbone.

Horace opened his eyes slowly and saw Dawn smiling down at him. It took him a moment to realize it was not a hallucination. Silently, he gazed into her eyes. He welcomed her touch and said nothing as he tried to preserve the moment.

"Hey, sleepy head," she whispered. "How are you feeling?"

"I wasn't sleeping," he said. "And I feel good. The best I've felt in years." He looked her over and noticed she had changed her clothes. "You saw the Doc?" he asked.

"Yes," she replied. "He's doing better. He brought your cigarettes and apologized for drinking all of your booze. I guess he tied one on last night," she laughed. "Can you imagine…Cormick…drunk in a bar?"

"Poor Doc," he said, "this has really done a number on him." He rolled his head and stared up at the ceiling. "Do me a favor. Throw my cigarettes away."

Astonished, Dawn sat up quickly. "What did you just say?"

"Time to quit smoking," he said. He sat up and crossed his legs as he faced her. "It's time to quit killing myself. Clayton made me realize...no, that's not true. I realize that it's time to move forward."

"Just like that? You're quitting cold turkey?"

"We did this thing...he called it a healing ceremony. I drank some peyote and he helped me see...I saw..."

"It's okay," she said. "Take your time."

"I'm going to tell you something that I haven't told anyone." He took in a deep breath and bowed his head. "I'm sick, Dawn," he said, making eye contact with her. "The alcohol, the smoking...it's done quite a number on me. But I went through this ceremony...I became aware...Aw, fuck..." he struggled to find the words to describe what he had seen.

"It allowed me to see what's killing me. It's me, I'm killing myself. I've been poisoning myself for years, doing everything I can to make death come just a little bit quicker. But now, I realize that the real poisons are my feelings of anger and loss. I wasn't numbing myself all these years, I was trying to feel something...anything."

"I'm not sure I understand," she said.

"I have cancer," he said as he lowered his head again. "Lung cancer. I came down here with a very short amount of time left." He looked up and saw her expression had changed to one of deep sadness. He reached out and grabbed her hand. "Let me finish," he said. "I'm not going to die. Not for a while, at least."

"Now I really don't understand," she said.

"This is going to sound really strange, but I left my body today," he said. "I saw everything...my whole life. I saw inside my body. Dawn, I saw the cancer. I know now that we make ourselves sick, and we can make ourselves well."

He stood up and walked toward the adobe air deflector.

"I was drafted and missed my shot at the Olympics. I saw things in the war that made me cold and empty but did nothing about it. I killed strangers and suffered in silence. I came home to people I knew calling me a baby killer, and a country that wished I would've never returned. And I lost my parents without the chance to tell them how much I loved them." He shrugged as his eyes filled with tears. "I kept all of that inside. That was the real poison. That's what was killing me. That was the real cancer."

"Lung cancer is real cancer, Horace."

"I know," he replied. "I'm sick because I poisoned my body and my soul. I…the me inside this body…is living this life to understand grief. It's a lesson I can't learn outside of my body."

"And now what?" she asked quietly. "What happens now?"

"Now I can heal myself," he said. "And I forgive myself." He walked around the fire and sat beside her. "It's true. Everything he said is true. We are pure energy. I know that now. I floated above my body. It was like in 'Nam when I got shot. I saw myself. I saw everything today as I did then. But this time, I understood." He smiled at her and took her hand in his. "We have the power to do anything. Dawn, have you ever heard someone tell you that if you say something out loud…say something to the universe, that the universe responds?"

"I'm sorry," she said as she shook her head. "I've never heard that."

"Maybe it's a sixties thing," he said as he sat back and crossed his legs again. "Try this…we know that the universe exploded into existence, right? That energy shot out into a

million different directions. But all those…I don't know…
those fragments of energy weren't the same size. So, what
if Jesus had more of that energy? Maybe, he could heal the
sick, right? If we have that same energy…if we are made of
the same stuff, why can't we do it?"

"You're not Jesus, Horace," she replied as she reached out
and cupped his cheek. "You're high on peyote."

"I don't think I'm Jesus," he laughed. "But what's stopping
us from being like Jesus? Think about it. He was a man. But
he could do amazing things. Back then they called it the
power of God. What if it's just the power in all of us?"

"Alright, who are you and what have you done with
Horace?"

"It's me," he said. "I think it's true. I think we could
change the world!"

"How are we going to do that?" she asked.

"By revealing to the world the undeniable truth," Clayton
called out as he climbed down the ladder.

"I'll repeat my question," Dawn said as she turned to face
him. "Just how do we do that? Who's going to believe us?
Christians? Buddhists? Hindus? Don't misunderstand me.
I believe you. But that's because I'm here living it. To people
out there, we'll sound like New Age wackos."

"And how did Jesus sound to the people of his time?"
Clayton asked as he walked past her to the far side of the
flickering flames. He grabbed two small logs from behind
the deflector and placed them in the fire pit.

"If Jesus is the yardstick we're going to measure ourselves
by, we're going to come up a few feet short," she retorted.

"That is the dogma of religion pulling at you," Clayton
said.

"The Bible says…" she began.

"The Bible is a very good book, as is the Torah, the *Tanakh*, the Qur'an…" Clayton pointed out. "I could go on."

"If we go out into the real world and start saying we're just as good as Jesus, there will be a lot of people who will want to bring back crucifixion," Dawn argued.

"Others have thought the same thing throughout history. Do you think those who wrote the books of the Bible ever imagined that they would be the authors of texts that have lasted for thousands of years? Or the men who transcribed the Qur'an? Do you think they had any idea what those words would come to mean?"

"What are you talking about?" Horace asked.

"I'm talking about you, Horace. You are no different than any of those men. You carry the same knowledge inside of you that those men did. You feel the power of the Great Spirit; the energy that exists in all of us. You have come to believe that you can change the world. You have the words. Commit them to paper."

Horace stared at him in disbelief, then started to laugh.

"Look, you've made a believer out of me. Really, you have. But if you're asking me to write a Bible…"

"No, the Bible has been written," Clayton said. "But the truth is being revealed to you and will continue to be revealed to the four of you, individually as well as together. Look inside yourself, Horace. You know this to be true."

"I know that the message that I will carry from here is a powerful one," Horace began, "but to write…I'm just not good enough. Maybe I never was."

"The men who contributed their words to the Bible did so because the message was so powerful they had no choice," he replied. "You don't realize it yet, but that is what's happening to you."

"But it's not like someone just sat at a typewriter and banged out a novel," Dawn interjected.

"For centuries, there was no Bible," Clayton said as he sat by the fire. "It is a compilation of stories written over more than fifteen hundred years. It was written in many languages. Because of that, it contradicts itself, sending a mixed message of strict adherence to a vengeful God and the promise of salvation through belief in a single man. The message, the truth, is lost to the reader.

"Christians believe that God used Moses to write the first five books of the Bible. The Jews accept these books as the Torah, the holiest books of the Tanakh. Genesis begins with Moses sharing his divine revelation: the universe coming into being, evolution, and nature's connection with the energy that connects us all. But Moses also had a duty to his religion. The Old Testament quickly devolved into a book of war and Jewish law. Passage after passage tells us that women are little more than property, and those who are not faithful adherents to what is considered the one true religion deserve enslavement and death. This is not the message that was intended."

"There's a world full of people who aren't going to be happy to hear that," Dawn said.

"The world is full of people who are not going to be happy," Clayton replied. "Jesus knew this. He set out to reform Jewish traditions, to remove the lust for money and power from the temples. He brought the message that I am sharing with you. Christians call him the son of God; Muslims call him a prophet. But he was just like us."

"There is no way Muslims believe in Jesus," Horace said.

"Horace, have you ever read the Qur'an?" Clayton asked. "Would it surprise you to know that in doing so, you would read about Abraham, Moses, and Jesus just as you would in the Bible?" He smiled at Horace, who sat quietly without a response. "As I told you, there is only one truth. Different men have interpreted it differently, and they and their followers then refuse to accept any other way of thinking. Religion closes minds. Spirituality opens them."

Clayton got to his feet and looked at the fire.

"These flames give us light. They give us warmth. But they have often been used to destroy the truth." He shook his head and began to slowly walk in a circle around them. "At the beginning of the Dark Ages, three centuries after Jesus was gone, there were more than three hundred versions of the Bible and a Christian sect for each one of them. Not all that were written became part of the Bible as we know it today."

"Wait a minute," Dawn interrupted, "I know most of what's in it. What didn't make it?"

"Everything else," Clayton replied.

"Thanks for narrowing that down for us," she quipped.

"People forget that Jesus was not a Christian. He had no desire to create a new religion. He wanted us to believe in ourselves and the beauty of the universe. The last thing he wanted was to be worshipped," Clayton said. "He wanted us to see that all living things are connected. He told us that life is everlasting, just as I have told you. He told us that we don't have to be in a temple to know the Great Spirit—the energy from which we all are made—we have only to seek and share the knowledge for the betterment of mankind." He stopped and sat on the ground beside them.

"But the church fast became everything that Jesus had fought against. It needed money to grow and power to convert entire populations. Without offerings, the church suffered. It set about editing the Bible to create a dependence on religion over spirituality. In doing so, the message changed from one of spiritual unity and growth to one that threatened eternal pain for those who did not bend to the theocracy. Do you believe for even a moment that Jesus would want anyone tortured and killed simply because their beliefs differed from his? If, as we are told, 'God so loved the world,' would that God then create a hell for souls to burn in for all eternity?"

"No…" Horace said. "No, he wouldn't. But how would I even begin?"

"Dawn will help you," he grinned. "Who better than a history teacher to help you put things in perspective?"

"I can do that," she said as she placed her hand on Horace's thigh and smiled. "Just think, I'll be there to grade your work. I'm a stickler for proper sentence structure."

"I'm scared," Horace said. "I wouldn't know how to begin. I mean, how do you even start to write a book on spirituality?"

"It will come to you," Clayton said. "Think of what you have learned already. Think of the eagerness with which you shared it with Dawn. Through your writing, you can share it with the world."

"Will it take fifteen hundred years?" he asked.

"Try to be optimistic," Clayton said. "The Qur'an was revealed to Mohammed in just twenty-three years. And you'll have the others to help you."

"What about Sayer?" Horace asked. "What's his role in all of this?"

"I think you know the answer to that already," Clayton said.

THE CARPENTER

Sayer stood at the headwaters of Rio Pueblo de Taos, peering through the darkness at the still water of Blue Lake. The mirrored surface of the lake reflected the radiant glow of the full moon above, providing enough light to survey his surroundings. He had made the journey in just under twelve hours, guided only by intuition. He was now counting on that same intuition to guide him to shelter.

He was ill prepared for the cold of the night air. He had carried the bread and venison for his journey in a wool blanket. Emptying what was left of his supplies onto the ground, he wrapped the blanket around his shoulders. Even though there was no breeze, the elevation of the mountain lake presented climate challenges he had not anticipated. He blew a warm breath into his hands and briskly rubbed them together as he glanced around for a place to warm up.

He gathered up his food and walked the shoreline flanked by large pine trees standing watch over the sacred lake. His experience in the forest was limited to a few camping trips with friends when he was younger. He tried hard to remember something—anything—about being in the woods but drew a blank. Turning toward the lake, he realized that, as long as there was a body of water nearby, he had a safe and familiar place to turn to in case of trouble.

"Sayer…" a hushed whisper called to him from the lake.

He turned to face the water, but saw nothing. He listened intently for his name to be called once again. Just above his head, perched on a low branch, sat a spotted owl, silently staring down at him. At first, he thought the owl was asleep but soon realized that its dark brown eyes were fixed on his every movement.

"Did you call me, little dude?" He said as he grinned at the owl. He hoped the owl would ask, "Who?" so he could answer back but was greeted with silence. "Bummer," he said as his hopes were dashed at the owl's refusal to play along. Instead, the two quietly faced off in the dark.

"Sayer..." the voice called out through the trees.

Sayer looked back toward the lake, and a faint light in the trees nearby caught his eye. As he started toward it, he could see it was the faint flicker of a small fire. He crept through the tree line, keeping the safety of the lake in sight.

He reached the campsite and saw a man sitting by the fire with his back to him. As he watched, crouched behind a tree, the man lifted his arms into the air and called out to the stars. Though he could hear the man speaking, he was unable to understand a word. He hesitated, unsure whether to ask the stranger to share the warmth of his fire.

"Sayer," the man called to him as he lowered his arms. "Come join me by the fire," he said as he continued to face forward. "Have something warm to drink."

Surprised he had been discovered, Sayer stood up and looked around wondering if someone behind him had given him away. He had been quiet as he approached, but immediately realized that he was not as stealthy as he thought. He considered the invitation for a moment as apprehension gave way to curiosity and the desire to keep warm. He stepped though the underbrush and made his way to the fire.

"You made good time," the man said as he turned around

to face him.

"Whoa! Clayton! What the…How did you get here before me?" Sayer exclaimed as he looked around the campsite. "Dude, if you drove, I totally could have used a ride."

"I didn't drive," Clayton said. "Here, take a drink of something warm." He offered a beaten-up tin mug.

"More peyote?" Sayer said with a broad smile as he nodded with approval.

"Hot chocolate," Clayton said.

"That's a bummer," Sayer replied as he grasped the mug and took a sip. "Hate to tell you, bro'…this tastes almost as bad as the peyote." He sat on a log on the opposite side of the fire and took another sip. "Why couldn't we just hike up here together?"

"You needed the time, Sayer. You needed to feel and be a part of the energy in the natural world," Clayton said.

"Yo, Clayton, I do that all the time back home. I'm all about being one with nature." He took a drink and looked intently at Clayton. "But seriously, dude…how did you get up here?"

"I've always been here," Clayton answered.

"But you were in your house this morning," Sayer countered.

"Are you sure of that?" Clayton asked.

Sayer sat quietly replaying the day in his head. "Yes," he said at last. "I'm totally sure of it. Unless this is a trick question."

"It's no trick," Clayton responded as he poked a stick into the fire, setting embers free into the night sky.

Sayer watched as their orange glow faded and suddenly turned black, becoming indistinguishable from the night sky.

"Those glowing cinders are like all things in the physical world," Clayton said without looking up. "They burn bright and beautiful, but their time is short. They will fall back to the earth and fertilize the soil in which another tree will grow and perhaps, one day, be used once again in a fire to warm two old friends."

"Are we old friends?" Sayer asked.

"Take this stone," Clayton said as he reached across the fire, handing Sayer a black and white translucent stone.

"What is it?" he asked as he took the crystal and studied it.

"Merlinite. It brings magic into your life," Clayton said. "This stone is one with the four elements: earth, water, air, and fire."

"What am I supposed to do with it?"

"It is your companion," Clayton said. "You will need to keep it with you always."

"I knew this girl who was into crystals," Sayer offered, "but I've never heard of this one."

"This stone is used by shamans to travel between worlds and to see the past and the future together at one time. It will allow you to accept the divine knowledge into your physical body," Clayton said. "Holding this stone will realign the emotional lessons you have learned since birth and set you on the one, true path."

"Gotcha…" Sayer said. "But crystals? Not a lot of people believe in that."

"A lot of people don't have to," Clayton said. "It was once believed that crystals were living things, taking a single breath every century or two. The truth is, crystals are matter created by energy. Just as you were. You are related to that stone every bit as much as you are to your brother, to the owl that watched you, and to the tree it sat in. Remember, all things come from the same place. You are one with the universe, Sayer."

"Okay…I guess. But how can I see the past and the future at the same time?" he asked.

"Everything exists at once," Clayton said.

"That's trippy, dude. Are you sure we don't need peyote for this conversation? Because, seriously, you're kinda blowing my mind right now," Sayer said as he ran his fingers through his hair.

"When did you learn to surf?" Clayton asked.

"What? When I was little," Sayer shrugged. "What does that have to do with anything?"

"You've always known how to surf," he responded. "You have always had the ability to do anything and everything. You knew this until seconds before your birth. But during those traumatic moments your physical senses came alive, reprogramming you, in a manner of speaking. But your knowledge wasn't lost. It was merely hidden by the overwhelming stimulation of the world around you."

"Whoa…so wait…what?" Sayer was very confused.

"The metaphysical properties of the Merlinite will help you to understand, to see your past lives, to heal others," he said. "Sayer, you are on the edge of a great discovery and not a moment too soon."

"Why?" Sayer asked. "What's going to happen?"

"The world needs you Sayer. Great changes are coming. The world is moving faster, getting louder…you will set right the trajectory of mankind."

"Okay…hold on a sec," Sayer said as he got to his feet. "I'm just a beach bum, dude. No one will listen to me."

"They were listening already," Clayton answered calmly.

"You just didn't have the whole message. But you will."

"I don't know, bro'...seems sketchy," Sayer said.

"Sayer, you are the only one who accepted the reality of hearing the call to come here," Clayton said. "Do you know why that is?"

"Dude, I totally believe you...I believe it all," Sayer said, "but I don't think that the world is going to listen to me. I'm not smart," he admitted as he hung his head. "People will ask me questions...they'll know I'm not smart."

"Sayer..." a hushed voice called, echoing across the lake through the still night air.

Sayer looked over the lake and turned back to Clayton. "Hey, how did you do that? I didn't see your lips move."

"Because I didn't say anything," Clayton smiled.

"You're not the voice I heard?" Sayer asked.

"Ba Whyea calls you," Clayton said.

"I don't understand," Sayer said. "I thought you were the reason we came."

"*You* are the reason you came," Clayton said. "Please, sit down. I'll tell you everything," he said as he motioned to the log. "The people of this place understand the sacred bond between man and his world. This is their Garden of Eden. The lake gave them life, and it continues to do so today. Their entire belief system is centered here, in Ba Whyea. For them, God exists here."

"But if there is no God," Sayer began, "how am I supposed to convince people to believe in God?"

"If you leave here and tell the world that there is no God, they will turn from you," Clayton said. "Your words will carry no weight. But if you leave here and help them understand the true nature of God, they will listen and they will believe."

"If the lake called me, then why are you here?"

"Squeeze your crystal tight in your hand and close your eyes," Clayton said. Sayer complied with his wishes. "I am the lake, Sayer. I am the spirit of the lake. I am known by many names. People of this land have known me as *Poshayanki, Poseyemu,* and here at the lake I am known as *Piankettacholla.*"

As Clayton spoke, Sayer listened while visions of ancient native tribes filled his head. Suddenly, he was unsure if he was listening to Clayton or walking among the people in his vision. He could hear them. He felt the sun on his back and even smelled bread baking in the hornos.

He saw a young girl. She was poor and an outcast in her world. He listened as she talked to her grandmother about giving birth to the son of the Sun. Sayer watched as her child grew to be a great hunter. In a matter of moments, he learned that the boy was considered the mediator between heaven and Earth, and when Sayer looked at the face of the man who had grown from that child, it was Clayton.

"Whoa!" Sayer yelled as he opened his eyes. "Where was I? Were you even talking? What did I just see?"

"You saw my life," Clayton smiled. "One of them, that is."

"You've lived others?" Sayer asked.

"Countless other lives, as have you," Clayton said. "I told you earlier that God, Allah, Yaweh, *Kaang,* the Father of All Spirits, the Sun God…are the same great concentration of energy. Is it so hard to believe that Moses and Muhammad are one in the same? That Jesus, Buddha, and Piankettacholla are the same as well?"

Sayer sat there dumbfounded at what he had just heard. He replayed it slowly in his mind, carefully listening to every word as it repeated in his memory.

"Dude, are you telling me that you're Jesus?"

"No," Clayton said.

"Okay…that's good," Sayer said, "because I'd totally be trippin.'"

"I *was* Jesus," Clayton said.

Sayer let his face fall into his open palms and shook his head. He lifted his head up, stared at Clayton for a few seconds with his mouth wide open then let his face fall back into his palms, where he once again shook his head in disbelief.

"This might be one big wave too many," he said.

"Sayer, give me your hand," Clayton said with his arm outstretched. Sayer reluctantly put his hand in Clayton's, and allowed himself to be pulled to his feet. "Walk with me to the lake."

The two men walked side by side to the lake without a word. In less than a minute, they were at the shore. There was a low mist covering the surface of the lake, thick enough to obscure where the water caressed the land. The bright moon above illuminated the fog in a ghostly white light.

"Put the crystal in your pocket," Clayton said.

"Why?" Sayer asked.

"Trust me," Clayton said as he turned back and looked over the mist. "This is my home. This lake, Ba Whyea, is holy to the people of this pueblo. They believe that this is the sipapu from which their ancestors emerged into the world. I brought them the message of evolution many centuries ago. Over time, without a book to refer to, the meaning was altered. Rather than life emerging from the seas, they came to believe it was from Ba Whyea. I brought the message many times only to have it altered by poor translations and religious and political influence. It is the same message every time. This time, there will be no misunderstandings."

"Am I supposed to bring people here? To see you? To hear the message?" Sayer asked.

"No," Clayton said firmly. "This is their sacred place. They have fought to regain this land. It is the center of the lives." He put his arm around Sayer and continued walking through the mist. "But you won't be far from here."

"If I can't bring people here...if they can't see you, hear your words," Sayer said, "how can you be sure they'll believe me?"

"You'll show them this," Clayton said.

Sayer looked at him, then turned his head to survey his surroundings.

"Show them what?"

"This," Clayton said as he outstretched his arms, clearing the mist from their ankles.

Sayer looked down and discovered he was standing on the surface of the water. Startled, he let out a gasp and immediately sunk nearly twelve inches underwater. He ran to the shore and turned to look at Clayton who was shaking his head.

"Dude! How did we do that?" he cried. "Why did I sink? How are you...?"

"Sayer," Clayton began as he set foot on the shore, "we did that because the energy that created us is more powerful than the matter we are made of. You sunk because you let your perception of the world control your emotions. If you hadn't looked down and thought you couldn't do it, you would still be doing it."

"Can you teach me to do that?" Sayer asked excitedly.

"You already know how," Clayton smiled. "Sayer, you're going to develop the power to do many things." He put his hand on Sayer's shoulder. "I need you to remember something. It's important," he said to an eagerly nodding Sayer. "No matter what happens, I will be with you always. I am in all things, as are you. When the time comes, and we cannot physically touch each other, I will still be here for you as your teacher, your guide. Do you understand?"

"Totally," Sayer said.

"There is some land north of this pueblo. On it is an old adobe home with a small kiva beneath. It is yours. If anything happens, go there and wait for me."

"Gotcha," Sayer said. "But dude, is something going to happen?"

"Something always happens," Clayton said. "It won't be long before you are one with nature and can begin teaching others the undeniable truth about our existence." He waved his hand in front of the landscape. "This is heaven, Sayer. We sacrifice ultimate knowledge to be born here. In our natural state, we can't laugh or cry, love or hurt…" He paused and looked up at the starry night sky. "This is our classroom and our playground. This is where we learn. Every living thing on this planet is here for every other living thing. You, Sayer…you will remind everyone of the reason we are here."

Sayer nodded and returned the smile. "Hey, Clayton… why me?"

"You are the Carpenter," Clayton said. "You will build the movement that changes the destiny of mankind. It will take time, but you will show them the way. Besides, I was a carpenter once. I have a soft spot for them." He reached over and patted Sayer on the back. "Let's dry your feet at the fire and get some sleep. We're going to need our rest."

"Sounds cool, dude," Sayer said. "Hey, you didn't bring any peyote up with you by any chance?"

"You won't need that anymore," Clayton said.

—⟋⟍⟍⟍⟍—

Sitting alone on the edge of his bed, Cormick stared at the television. Images came and went on the screen, but all of them failed to grab his attention. For more than an hour he sat there, recalling the events of the past week and thinking of his companions. He carefully replayed every moment, second guessing each decision he had made. Though he did not want to admit it, the psychiatrist in him told him what he already knew to be true: he was depressed.

After leading a near solitary existence most of his life, he had discovered loneliness for the first time. Year after year, he had avoided personal attachments and kept acquaintances rather than friends. But that had all changed the night Angelo arrived at Vancouver Memorial. He realized that he was not better than everyone else, he was just like them. He needed people in his life.

He turned to the nightstand and stared at the phone. He wanted to call Allison, to hear her melodic voice tell him that everything was going to be okay. But he could not bring himself to pick up the receiver. Afraid that she would gain insight into the despair he was feeling, he decided that the call could wait one more day. The pain was his to bear. He saw no benefit to burdening her with his negative emotions. He was convinced that she was attracted to his well-crafted unemotional facade, not the vulnerable man he was inside.

"What do you think?" he asked Wayne, propped up in the corner of his room for safe keeping. "Should I sit here and wallow in misery, or should I venture to the lounge and wallow in whiskey?"

Wayne stood there silent, smiling at him. Cormick

regarded the surfboard as the smartest traveler on the journey. He smiled, kept his mouth shut, and remained aloof
and emotionless. Cormick was envious of his inanimate
roommate. Just a week earlier, the two had a lot in common.

"Santa Fe…" a low, deep voice called from the television,
immediately grabbing his attention, and forcing him to
catch his breath. He saw an image of a pueblo-style home
then a stark room with an old wooden table and deer antlers
mounted on the wall above it. "For centuries, men have
been mysteriously drawn to it. Santa Fe Cologne for men…
discover the mystery of its attraction."

He let out his breath, and shook his head.

"I bet that stuff stinks," he mumbled as he turned back
to Wayne. "Okay, wallow in whiskey it is," he nodded as he
grabbed his room key and headed out the door and into
the hallway.

When he reached the exit, he paused and considered
what he was about to do. Alcohol was not going to solve
any of his problems. He knew that when he awoke the next
morning he would still be lonely and have unanswered
questions. The only difference would be a hangover. After
weighing his options, he pushed the door open and started
toward the hotel lounge.

"Fuck it," he said.

He entered the bar and saw nearly two dozen unfamiliar
faces. He surmised that the couples sitting at tables were
sightseers and tourists who had packed the worst of their
wardrobes into their Winnebago and set out across the
southwest to fill their suitcases with useless trinkets and col-
lector throw pillows, leaving in their wake empty beer cans
and fast food wrappers to decorate the landscape. At the bar
sat seven or eight men, most of whom were fixated on the

game on the television in the corner. At the far end he saw the profile of a familiar face and began walking toward him.

"Well hello, Russ," he said as he sat on the stool beside him. "I thought you were moving on today." He looked up at the bartender. "Jack Daniels please, and a glass of ice water."

"I checked back in," Hanrahan said. "Unfinished business."

"Yes, I did as well. Why the map?" Cormick asked. "If you are attempting to plot your escape from Taos, there is only one road in or out of this desolate place," he laughed.

"I need to get on that fucking reservation," Hanrahan said as he studied the map.

"We were just there," Cormick said as he turned to the bartender and held up his room key. "Charge it to my room." He took a sip of the whiskey, and winced as it burned its way down his throat, forcing him to tightly shut his eyes for a moment.

"We were in the tourist area," Hanrahan snapped. "Jesus, pay attention. The reservation is almost a hundred thousand acres."

"Why not just go there?" Cormick asked.

"I tried today. They got no-trespassing signs everywhere. I climbed over the fence and almost got scalped by some seriously pissed off Indians." He looked up from the map. "Are you going to drink that or just sip on it like a little girl?"

Taken aback by the harshness of Russ' tone and embarrassed by his inability to drink like a man, Cormick grabbed the glass and lifted it up.

"I am going to drink it, of course."

He tossed the entire contents of the glass into his mouth and swallowed hard, while doing his best to control his gag reflex. He slammed the glass down hard on the bar, inadvertently signaled the bartender to pour him another. Hanrahan shook his head and turned back to the map.

"There has to be a back way…" he mumbled as he ran his finger along the map.

"I am afraid I do not understand," Cormick said as another shot arrived. "Why are you so interested in getting on the reservation?"

He looked at the shot and turned to Hanrahan who was glaring at him. He grabbed the shot and drank it. This time he gently set the glass on the bar and reached for the cool, healing powers of the ice water.

"It is important to stay hydrated," he said as Hanrahan looked on with disapproval.

"What does it matter?" Hanrahan asked. "I've got some unfinished business to take care of." He turned and signaled the bartender for two more. "And what about you, shrink? You don't want to get on that reservation? You don't want to find those fuckers who turned their backs on you after all you did for them? I'll tell you what…if I was you, I'd get on that reservation and I'd teach those miserable fuckers what it means to betray me."

"Well, I do not believe I was betrayed, per se," Cormick said. "It was my job to get them here safely and…"

"And what?" Hanrahan demanded. "Sit by yourself in a bar while the four of them laugh at you? Are you really this pathetic?"

"Well, no," Cormick began. "I do not believe anyone is laughing at me."

"Look. You see this?" Hanrahan asked, pointing at the map. "This is a ski resort. I figure we can drive up here and hike down to the reservation. If we get to Blue Lake, we can follow this river right onto the reservation. Then all you have to do is find that adobe house you were in and bam!" he yelled as he slammed his hand down on the bar.

"Bam?" Cormick questioned.

"You know, we find them," Hanrahan said, regaining his composure. "Don't you want to see those guys? Maybe tell them how they mistreated you?"

"Why is this so important to you?" Cormick asked.

"Hey, I'm here to help you, buddy," Hanrahan said, with a sly smile. "Look, we can leave in the morning and be on the mountain in less than an hour. We can hike to Blue Lake and then we got him."

"Him?" Cormick asked.

"Them…I said them," Hanrahan replied. "You know, your friends."

"I cannot go on that mountain," Cormick said. "I think it would be best…"

"Why not?' Hanrahan asked.

"I do not make it a habit of sharing this with people, but I have a paralyzing fear of heights," Cormick said as he bowed his head. "I am afraid that if I were to get up there, I may not be able to come down."

"Look Cormick," Hanrahan began, "you've already helped me in ways you can't even imagine," he laughed. "Now I'm gonna help you." He raised his glass to Cormick. "Here's to unfinished business."

Cormick followed suit and the two men gulped down their whiskey. Cormick watched as Hanrahan turned back to the map. Something wasn't right; he felt uneasy as he studied Hanrahan's face.

"Listen, Russ, I appreciate the help. But I am not sure I should do this," he said. "It simply does not feel right… sneaking onto the reservation, going where I am not supposed to be…and I am truly unable to function in high places. I think it would be best if I waited for my friends here in town."

Hanrahan stood up and folded his map.

"I'll be at your room in the morning. Dress warm, it'll be cold up there." He waved to the bartender. "My drinks are on him." He shot Cormick a menacing glance and walked away.

Cormick turned toward the bar and signaled for another drink. "One more, please. Then I would like to close out my tab."

He looked out the window and caught sight of his reflection. He stared at himself in the darkened glass. He was almost unrecognizable. Unkempt hair, two days of stubble on his face, wrinkled clothes, and sitting alone in a hotel bar in the desert. He had become a stranger to himself.

"I am going home tomorrow," he muttered.

He shook his head and sighed. He had reached his limit. As soon as the sun rose, he would drive to the pueblo to tell the others that he was leaving them the van, and that he was flying home.

———∿∿∿———

"Hey," Dawn whispered, "are you asleep?"

"No…" Horace moaned. "Can't sleep. I'm worried about Sayer." He stared up at the wooden timbers that made up the ceiling above him. "All I can get out of Clayton is that he went for a walk and…" He rolled his head to the side and saw her staring at him.

He had lost his train of thought and lay speechless as he stared her. Even in the dim light from the oil lamp in the corner, her eyes sparkled. She was smiling. The natural lines of her face made it appear as if she was always happy, and that always made him glad to see her.

"And what?" she asked lyrically as she propped herself up on her elbow and looked at him.

"And my God you're beautiful," he whispered.

"What?" she asked, surprised by his blunt statement.

"You are beautiful," he repeated. "Your hair reminds me of the sunset over the Pacific in late summer. When I look you in the eyes, I feel, I feel like all my pain is gone. I remember when you walked past me in the bar. I remember the look on your face, how your hair was styled, the deep red lipstick…that moment and countless others over the past week are frozen in time for me. It's like my brain is taking snapshots of you every time I see you." He gazed deep into her eyes and thought for a moment that her beauty would reduce him to tears.

Dawn stared at him for a bit and slowly sat up, never turning her eyes from his. She scooted next to him and laid down with her face just inches from his. She ran her fingers through his hair and slid her palm down his cheek. Slowly, she moved her face to his until their lips brushed against one another. She moved her head slowly, rubbing the side of her nose against his, delicately kissing him. She leaned into him, until her cheek glided against his.

"Hey guys," Angelo called out. "I'm still awake."

Dawn slowly pulled back and looked at him.

"So…that must be what it's like to have kids."

"Don't get me wrong, I love a good show," Angelo called from the dark. "But I'm not sure this is what our host had in mind."

Horace rolled over on his back and let out a sigh.

"We weren't going to have sex," he lamented.

Dawn leaned in and whispered in his ear. "Don't be so sure."

"Sayer's up at Blue Lake," Angelo said. "He told me he heard the mountain calling him."

"So, he went?" Horace said as he sat up. "You let him just disappear into the woods?"

"Hey man, relax," Angelo fired back. "Sayer wanted to go and Clayton let him. He heard the voice and went. It's as simple as that."

"Is there shelter up there? What if he gets lost?" Horace asked. "Where's Clayton?"

"He said something about a Night Chant ceremony," Angelo answered.

"Horace, I'm sure he's okay," Dawn said as she placed her hand on his. "If you want, we can go after him in the morning. There's nothing we can do right now."

"Hey, man," Angelo began, "we all got here in one piece because we followed the voice. It's not going to be any different now. We'll all go up in the morning and find him."

Horace closed his eyes and rubbed his forehead. Images of Sayer being eaten by a bear and falling off a cliff filled his mind.

"Shit," he said. "I'm worried." He shook his head and let go a mournful sigh.

"Sayer is a big boy," Angelo responded. "He can take care of himself. Search your feelings, you know it to be true." Angelo stopped for a minute and broke out into laughter. "Oh man, I sound like Obi-Wan Kenobi!"

"I'm really worried," Horace said as he turned to Dawn. "I'll go up tomorrow at first light. I'll make Clayton show me the way."

Dawn reached out and grabbed his hand. "We're going with you. We're in this together."

"No…no," he said. "I don't want anyone to get hurt. Besides, I can probably move faster without worrying about you."

Dawn sat up and leaned back. The severity of the look on her face betrayed her emotions.

"We just had a moment. Don't fuck it up by being an asshole."

"Whoa, whoa, whoa!" Horace said in defense. "I just meant…"

"Oh, I know what you meant. We both know what you meant," she scolded as she motioned toward Angelo. "I'm a woman, so I should stay behind. News flash: I can take care of myself."

Horace let his head fall and shook it from side to side.

"I'm sorry," he said quietly. "Sometimes I see myself as that eighteen-year-old kid who can do anything." He turned his head slightly toward her. Embarrassed, he struggled to keep eye contact with her. "Truth is, I'm already worried about my brother. I don't want to worry about you, too. I'm not sure I can keep both of you safe."

Dawn's face softened as he spoke. She watched as he hung his head and softly spoke. He cared about her, there was no mistaking that. She reached forward and touched his cheek. When he turned to face her, she briefly pressed her lips against his and pulled back to look at him. Eleven years her senior, addicted, and terminally ill, Horace Jordan was not the man she saw herself with when she pictured the perfect life.

"Nobody's perfect," she whispered.

"Don't worry about me!" Angelo called as he laid back

down and covered himself with his wool blanket. "I'll be fine. I may run into wolves and badgers, but I got this."

Dawn turned to him and laughed. "I'm sorry, honey, did you want a kiss, too?"

Angelo sat up and shrugged. "Couldn't hurt," he said.

Dawn snuggled in next to Horace under his blanket. "Horace, do me a favor…kiss Angelo goodnight."

SANGRE DE CRISTO

Forced awake by the stomach acids burning his esophagus, Cormick sat up in bed and swallowed hard. But it was inevitable: he was going to vomit. He tossed the sheets aside and ran to the bathroom. He slammed his palms down on either side of the sink and launched a torrent of thick, yellow bile into the basin. He raised his head briefly, but his diaphragm convulsed again as another explosive splash of his stomach contents filled the sink.

He raised his head again and looked at himself in the mirror. The face that confronted him was still a complete stranger. His blood-shot eyes were swollen and tears streamed down his cheeks. A thin trail of sticky mucus flowed from each nostril, coating the stubble on his upper lip and a mixture of bile and saliva glistened on his chin.

He turned on the faucet and splashed cold water on his face, washing away the signs of the violent reaction his body had suffered from his liquid dinner. He tossed back a capful of mouthwash and swished it around in his mouth before spitting it into the drain. He looked at himself again and immediately knew that the decision he had made to leave Taos was the right one.

He stepped into the shower, turned on the water, and let it wash him clean. As he stood under the jets of hot water, thoughts of Allison filled his head. He imagined how tender her touch would be if she were there with him as they gently washed each other. He had never thought of, let alone done something so sensual. But that was the old Cormick Proffitt.

He realized he had lived his whole life in fear. Driven by doubt and anxiety his entire life, he made a commitment to live life as his companions did: with passion and joy. He wondered if that had been the point of this journey for him. Ripped from his comfortable day-to-day routine, he had been forced to live with strangers who followed their hearts and enthusiastically embraced adventure. Starting that day, he would be like them.

He toweled himself off and got dressed as the sun began to rise over the Sangre de Cristo Mountains in the east.

"It is a new day," he mumbled as he stared out the window. Tonight, he would be in the arms of the woman he loved. "No more wasted time," he whispered as his breath fogged the glass.

The peace was shattered by a fierce pounding on his door. Startled from his trance, he made his way to the door and looked out through the peep hole. Russ Hanrahan was standing in the hallway. He opened the door just as Hanrahan raised his fist to pound on the door again.

"Are you ready?" he asked as he forced himself past Cormick.

"About that…" Cormick began as he shut the door. "I have decided to cut my vacation short and fly back home tonight."

"Bullshit!" he barked in response. "I need you to show me where that house is. I told you last night that we're going up there. I found some old Forest Service roads that can get us to Blue Lake. We can hike down from there."

"I do apologize," Cormick said. "Really, I do. But as I said, I am not comfortable trespassing on native lands. Instead, I am driving to the pueblo to tell the others that I am leaving," he said as he sat down to put on his shoes.

"Listen here, you little pussy," Hanrahan growled. "We can do this one of two ways…but either way, you're taking me to that house."

Cormick looked up to ask him to leave and found himself staring down the barrel of a gun. He sat frozen, unable to focus on anything beyond the muzzle, which was just inches from his head. He slowly raised his hands and leaned back in the chair to put some distance between himself and the gun.

"Okay, just take it easy now," Cormick said quietly.

"I'm done taking it easy," Hanrahan said. "I've spent two days trying to pretend to give a shit about you, but right now, I'm sick and fucking tired of listening to you talk." He pulled the hammer back on the pistol. "And now, I have to shoot you. You could've just done what you were told and left here alive, but now…" He shook his head and smiled.

"Just take deep breath," Cormick said, "and put the gun down. We can talk this out. There is no need for bloodshed." He stared at the barrel of the gun. The opening seemed as big as a cannon. He feared that he was going to die as his father had. He hoped his father had not seen it coming and been spared the terror that he was enduring.

"Don't worry," Hanrahan said, "I'm not going to kill you here. Oh no…first you're taking me to that fucking house."

"I do not understand," Cormick said. "All of this so you can learn about the voice my friends heard? If you just ask them, I am sure they will…"

"You really are an idiot, aren't you?" Hanrahan interrupted. "I'm not here for any Jesus bullshit. I'm going to kill Horace Jordan. And then, I'm going to kill you."

"Horace?" Cormick said, trying to comprehend what was happening. "Why not put the gun down, and we can talk about this. Whatever it is that you believe Horace did, I am sure we can find a way to work through it."

"You know, shrink, I've been looking forward to killing Horace my whole life. But now, man...I can't wait for you to be dead, too." He motioned for Cormick to stand up. "Now, we're gonna leave here, and if you even cough in the wrong direction, I'll use this .45 caliber paint gun to spray your fucking brains all over the wall."

"Russ, listen, you do not have to do this," Cormick pleaded. "It is not too late to just let this go. I can help you and Horace work out your issues. All you have to do is put the gun down."

Hanrahan slowly eased the hammer down. "Maybe you're right," he said, nodding.

Then, without warning, he turned the gun, holding the barrel in his fist and swung hard at the side of Cormick's face. Cormick fell against the wall and dropped to the floor as the white-hot pain from the impact on his temple momentarily blinded him. "Now get up!" Hanrahan demanded. "Oh, one more thing," he said as he bent down to look Cormick in the face, "if you do anything to warn anyone, I'll kill everybody in that house and make you watch."

—~∧∧∧~—

Horace walked to the creek as the sun crested the mountains in the distance. He knelt beside the rushing water, scooped up a handful, and splashed it on his face, rubbing the moisture into his skin. He reached in for another handful to quench his thirst. Looking down, he could see his hands shake; a clear sign his body was detoxing.

"Going to Blue Lake today?" Clayton asked from behind, startling Horace.

"Where have you been?" Horace asked as he jumped to his feet. "What were you thinking sending Sayer up that mountain?"

"I didn't send Sayer, he went on his own. He went because he was called by the Great Spirit," Clayton said. "And now you go on your own. I can't stop you just as I could not stop Sayer."

"I want you to take us up there," Horace fired back.

"I will guide you. We'll take horses. A walk of that distance takes almost two days." Clayton answered as he drew closer to Horace. "I promise your brother is safe. At this moment, he is sitting beside a warm fire, talking to the forest."

"Talking to…? You know what, never mind," Horace said. "If it takes almost two days to get up there, how did Sayer get there in a day?" Horace asked as he pointed up at the mountain. He turned back to Clayton. "Umm…horses?"

"Remember, all living things are created from the same energy," Clayton reminded him. "Don't fear the horse and it won't fear you."

"Fuck, I could really use a drink," Horace said.

"That is not something you could use," Clayton said. "That is something you desire. There is a difference. Lay down."

"What?" Horace asked.

"I asked you to lay down," Clayton said.

Horace stared blankly at the face of his companion. He replayed the conversation to see if he had missed something that led to the odd request. After a few seconds, he looked around for a dry place next to the creek and did as he was told. Clayton walked around Horace and knelt between him and the creek. He placed his hands on Horace's chest and pressed down on his rib cage.

Suddenly, Horace felt as if he couldn't breathe. Feeling like he was fighting for every breath, he tried to sit up but was unable to move. He exhaled loudly, and he felt like his lungs were being pulled out of his body through his chest. When he reached the point where he thought he was going to blackout, Clayton removed his hands, and Horace forcefully inhaled as his lungs began to feel normal again.

"What the fuck was that?" Horace groaned, rubbing his chest as he sat up.

"A second chance," Clayton said. "Every human being is the author of their own disease. It's time for you to write something else. Author your health instead." Clayton turned and washed his hands in the creek and briskly rubbed them together. "Health is the greatest gift we have. When we are in our true form, we choose the bodies we will inhabit and the lives we will live. As I said, you chose this life to learn about loss and pain. Now you can make your lessons your teachings."

"What do you mean by a second chance?" Horace asked

"Your cancer is gone, Horace," he replied as he stood up. "You will live a long and healthy life. Be mindful of what you have received today and say out loud that you will not smoke or drink again. In doing so, you'll make it true."

Horace stood up and looked at Clayton.

"I will not smoke or drink again," he said. "Is it true? No cancer?"

"Yes, it's true," Clayton smiled.

"I thought the healing ceremony..." Horace stopped talking and smiled at Clayton. "Thank you. Thank you for my life."

"Life is full of suffering, Horace. Without it, we can never truly know happiness," Clayton said. "I only took your cancer. I can't erase the pain and the loss that you hold so dear. And there will be more pain and greater loss. Free yourself of the burdens of the past. You'll be better prepared for the burdens of the future." He turned and looked up at the mountains. "It's time. Everyone should fill a canteen from the creek and bring a blanket. I'll get us four horses."

Horace watched as he walked away.

"Great," he mumbled. "We're the four horsemen. Nothing apocalyptic about that."

———⟋⟋⟋———

Sayer stood at the edge of the cobalt-blue lake with his eyes closed. He listened intently as the wind caressed the trees as it made its way across the mountain tops. The wind carried with it the sound of the forest. He could hear a family of mule deer grazing in the distance; the low, twittering sound of a raccoon as it paused from eating berries; and the owl, quietly breathing as it prepared to swoop down and make the raccoon its midday meal. He could hear everything, and it was beautiful.

He opened his eyes and surveyed the scenic wonder of the landscape. The California shore had been his home for his entire life. If he had been asked—just a week earlier—to name the most beautiful place on Earth, it would have been wherever there was good surfing and small bikinis. But that was no longer his truth. Here, in Taos, he could silence the white noise of the crashing waves and the laughing and screaming from the people on the beach that was a constant assault on his ears. Here, there was peace.

He looked to his right side and saw a grey fox sitting

next to him. The animal was motionless and looked completely relaxed.

"Nice doggie," Sayer called as he waved to the animal. The fox offered no response.

Clayton's hand came down on Sayer's left shoulder and caused him to turn away from the fox.

"Dude, you scared me," he said. "I think that fox…" he turned back and pointed to where the fox had just been. "It's gone now."

"That was *Letaiyo*," Clayton said. "He is many things, a runner, a trickster, and an omen. What message did he bring you?"

"Umm…he didn't say anything. He just stared at me."

"Close your eyes Sayer, just as you did before Letaiyo appeared to you. Clear your mind and listen to the sounds of the forest."

Sayer did as he was told. He closed his eyes and took in a full, cleansing breath, exhaled, and slowed his breathing. He could hear a spotted skunk making its way through the underbrush on the other side of the lake and listened as a hawk circled high above. He opened his eyes and turned to see the fox sitting exactly where it had been, staring at him.

"Letaiyo…" he whispered. "What message have you brought me?"

Sayer closed his eyes again and heard human footsteps crackling in the underbrush. He listened as faint echoes of yelling voices were carried in the wind, and then he heard an explosion. He opened his eyes and looked at the fox. Letaiyo stared back at him then slowly hung its head.

"Dude," Sayer said as he turned to Clayton. "I think it was a bad omen."

"Sayer, try to remember that words like good and bad,

right and wrong are words man uses as moral definitions to create oppression, and mete out justice."

"Someone is going to die today," Sayer said. "I can feel it." He crouched down and placed his open palm on the ground. "Yesterday, I felt the peace…even love…today it feels different." He stood up and brushed the dirt off his hands. "The energy I feel today is turning my stomach."

"Because today, the people closest to you are feeling afraid. Today, fate becomes destiny."

"I don't want my brother to die," Sayer said.

"As I said, no one can die because no one is born," Clayton reminded him. "One cannot live his life fearing death. We were all created with the universe. Don't look for loved ones you've lost in the faces of others, look for their energies, their souls. That's how you'll recognize each other. You are energy in the form of matter. Matter is finite and will become energy, and the cycle repeats itself."

"Gotcha," Sayer said. "It's still sad."

"Yes…but there is no escaping the inevitable." Clayton looked toward the sky and closed his eyes. "You are going to change the world, Sayer. That too, is inevitable." Clayton lowered his head and smiled at Sayer. "I have to leave for a while. Get yourself something to eat. You'll need your strength for the journey down the mountain."

"Wait! Where are you going? I don't want to leave, yet," Sayer said. "There's so much more to learn!"

"You will see me again very soon," Clayton said. "In the days after you leave Ba Whyea, go to the land north of here. I will see you there. Together, we will build a grand kiva. And then you will build a bridge for mankind that leads to the undeniable truth. You will strengthen the bond between man and nature."

"I need time," Sayer responded.

"When you say *I*, that is your ego. When you say *need*, that is your desire. Remove ego and desire and see what you're left with." He smiled at a confused Sayer. "You will understand soon," Clayton said as he turned and started walking into the woods. "We have an eternity," he called out as he disappeared into the forest.

—⁓⁓⁓—

The afternoon sun and the thinning air were taking a heavy toll on Cormick. Hanrahan had ordered him to park the van at an abandoned campground outside the reservation fence. The hike was taking significantly longer than his captor had anticipated.

Hanrahan was directly behind him. His gun had never left his hand. Cormick knew he couldn't negotiate with, or outrun, a bullet. So, he continued forward, looking for any real opportunity to diffuse the situation or escape. Looking ahead he could see that they were approaching a cliff. The startling reality of the elevation caused him to struggle for breath as the entire landscape seemed to spin and rock. He fell backward but managed to turn to land on his upper arm.

"Get up, goddammit," Hanrahan said, aiming the gun at his head.

Cormick opened his eyes and stared up at the sky.

"I need a moment," he said breathlessly. "We are too high…I have vertigo…"

Hanrahan held the gun on him and considered firing. But he didn't want to attract any attention. Not yet, at least. He lowered the gun and made his way to the edge and looked down. They weren't on a cliff, they had crested the mountain. Hanrahan was looking down on Blue Lake.

"We're at the lake," he said as he made his way back to Cormick. "I'll tell you what," he said as he grabbed Cormick by the hair and yanked his head up. "I'll give you five minutes, then we're gonna make our way around the tree line and down the mountain. Got it?"

Cormick nodded as Hanrahan walked to the edge once again and looked around. On the opposite shore, he caught sight of smoke from a campfire. He pulled out his binoculars and peered down at the fire. Unable to believe what he saw through the lenses, he moved them from his eyes, squinted at the fire, then pressed the binoculars against his face again.

"Fuck me," he laughed. "I can't believe my luck! Sayer fucking Jordan." He turned to Cormick. "Decisions, decisions…" he said as he shook his head. "Stick with Plan A or kill you now and make him take me to his brother?" Hanrahan walked over to Cormick and sat on his chest. "You know," he began as he tapped the gun against Cormick's cheek. "I'm not up for a fight. I'll just kill him on the way to that house. Then I'll kill Horace." He smiled as he dragged the gun up Cormick's face.

"You do not have to kill anybody," Cormick reminded him as he struggled for breath from the pressure on his chest.

"Oh, but I do," he replied as he got to his feet. "Get up. Listen close. We're gonna walk down to just above where the river starts. I saw a good vantage point on the rocks. And, shrink, if you even fart, I'll blow your fucking brains out."

Cormick nodded as he got to his feet. He followed Hanrahan's directions for three hours through thick underbrush, doing his best not to make a sound. He had reached a point of hopelessness. He had no self-defense training and had no idea how to disarm an attacker. Hanrahan was single-minded in his purpose; there was no way to reason with him.

Cormick considered the fate of his four friends. Though he had no idea how many bullets the gun held, he was confident it was enough to kill them all, and he knew it would be his fault. He had brought them here. He had befriended Hanrahan and led him to the pueblo to find his target. Now, he would be responsible for the deaths of all of them.

He had carried the guilt of his father's death since childhood. Even though he knew that his mother's illness had set the tragic events in motion, his father had died trying to keep him safe. The remorse he felt by staying home that fateful morning had stayed with him for three decades, and now he realized that he would die as he lived: afraid, alone, and responsible for needless loss of life.

Cormick had been able to make the slow descent through the trees, but as they neared their destination, he could see that he was not going to make it. The lake was still and quiet, but the headwaters of the river began as a waterfall. To get to Sayer, the two men would have to cross the top of the falls with the deep lake on one side and what Cormick considered a certain death on the other.

"Get down!" Hanrahan demanded as he pushed Cormick to the ground. He threw himself on top of Cormick and aimed the gun in front of him. The two men watched silently from a distance as Clayton appeared on horseback, immediately followed by Angelo, Dawn, and Horace. "I'm going to Vegas after this," Hanrahan whispered. "I'm so lucky my fucking dick is hard."

Cormick was unsure what to do. If he yelled now, he faced certain death. But if he was quiet for a little longer, maybe Horace could save them all. He had never realized how weak he was. Men like Horace Jordan had put their life on the line for total strangers, and now, here was Cormick, unable to risk his own life for his friends.

Hanrahan turned to him and pressed the gun against his head.

"Looks like you get to watch after all," he whispered. "We're gonna crawl across the top of the falls and get to that cave over there in the rocks."

"I cannot cross here," Cormick said. "You must believe me, I am physically incapable…"

"I don't give a fuck what you're capable of," Hanrahan said. "When they reach that little bitch at the fire, we're going."

From about two hundred yards away, they watched as the riders neared the campsite. Hanrahan motioned to Cormick, who crawled on his belly into the frigid lake. The current pushed hard against his body, and he fought to keep from being washed over the edge. He kept his face turned toward his friends to avoid seeing the sheer drop just a few feet away.

The cold water made breathing difficult, and it became a struggle to move his extremities. He wondered what would kill him first, a bullet or hypothermia. Halfway across, he thought of his mother and how she had held him high above the foyer all those years ago. If she had let go, his father would be alive and his friends would be safe. All he had to do was yell at his friends and let go. But he couldn't do it. Terrified, he continued across until he reached the shore.

Hanrahan crawled out of the water and grabbed Cormick by the collar.

"Get moving or I'll drag your ass there."

Cormick got to his hands and knees and crawled away from the ledge toward the small rocky shelter. Finally reaching a point where he felt stable, he stood up and walked the final few feet. The cavern was dimly lit by sunlight, which he assumed was coming from above. To his horror, he discovered the opposite was true. Centuries earlier, the cavern had been directly in the path of the flowing water, which had eroded a portion of its floor and created a spillway. Standing in the cave was tantamount to standing at the top of the falls.

Cormick immediately flung himself backward against the wall of the grotto with his arms outstretched. Within seconds, he was on the brink of hyperventilating. He turned his head away from the large hole toward his friends in the distance. He was almost completely immobilized by fear.

"You're pathetic," Hanrahan said. He put his hand on Cormick's throat and squeezed until he could hear him fight for breath. He released him and stepped away. "You can't even move to defend yourself," he laughed. He walked to the entrance of the cave and aimed his gun at Horace. "Bang," he whispered. He knew he couldn't hit anything at that distance. All he had to do was wait for the cover of darkness.

At the campsite, Sayer jumped up and held his arms in the air welcoming everyone.

"Hey bro'!" he shouted. "Welcome to my summer home at Ba Whyea!"

The group dismounted and Horace walked over to his brother and embraced him.

"I was scared shitless, Sayer," he said. "I should have known you would be all right." He tussled his little brother's hair. "I should have known," he smiled and looked around. "What have you been doing up here?"

"Oh, you know…hanging out with…" Sayer looked at

Clayton as the others dismounted. "Bro', let me just tell you this, I've learned a lot up here. I don't want to go."

"Sunny can't feed that fucking cat forever," Horace said. "We'll have to go sometime."

"No dude, I'm not going back," Sayer said. "My place is here, now. I don't want to live that life anymore. All I did was surf, screw, and smoke pot. I could be doing so much more."

Horace shot a glance toward Clayton then back at Sayer. "Well, we can talk about that later," he said.

"Hey guys," Angelo said, "I think I just saw someone over there." He craned his neck toward the falls and shaded his eyes, attempting to get a better look. "Geez, I hope it isn't bigfoot," he laughed.

Sayer looked toward the headwaters of the river. There was Letaiyo, sitting on the bank of the lake staring at him. Sayer turned to Clayton, his constant smile replaced by a look of fear.

"Clayton…no," he whispered.

Dawn walked to the water's edge to get a better look.

"I don't see anything," she said as she walked back to the group. "We're all exhausted. Let's relax a little while and get something to eat."

"There it is again," Angelo said. "I can't make it out, but something is over there. I swear I saw the sun reflect off something for a second." He took a couple steps away from the group. "You know what…I'm going over there."

"I'll go with you," Horace said. "I need to walk off the ride up here. My ass is killing me."

"Hey bro', I don't want you to go," Sayer said. "In fact, you both should stay here."

"I'll go," Clayton said. He looked at Sayer and smiled. "You stay here, Sayer. Fate becomes destiny."

Clayton walked away from the group along the shoreline.

"Hello, old friend," he said as he passed Letaiyo. He continued along the edge of the water toward the cave as the others watched.

Suddenly, a shot rang out, reverberating against the peaks that surrounded the lake. Birds rocketed from the trees and the horses scattered into the dense woods. Everyone turned toward the cave in stunned silence. They watched as Clayton stopped in his tracks, then fell backward into the lake.

"Clayton!" Sayer screamed.

"Get down!" Horace commanded.

Sayer bolted toward Clayton, only to be tackled by his brother. "I said get down, goddammit!"

"We have to help him!" Sayer cried.

"I'll help him," Horace said. "I need you to stay here. I need you to get Dawn out of here if I don't get back. Do you understand?"

"But Horace…"

"Sayer, I'm not asking you." He put his face down and took a deep breath. Lying there, he remembered what it had been like in Vietnam. But the odds weren't even this time. He was unarmed. "Look, it could just be a hunter that fucked up."

"Horace, please be careful," Dawn implored.

"I'm going with you," Angelo said. "If it was a hunter, why didn't he come out of the woods to see his kill? Right? If we come at him from opposite sides, there's a better chance we can take him down."

"What if there's more than one?" Dawn asked.

"Clayton's not moving," Horace said. "Sayer, get Dawn

into the woods and stay low." He looked at Angelo. "You saw the reflection in that cave…I want you to make an arc through the woods and come up from behind the cave on the west side. I'll go through the brush along the shoreline."

"Got it," Angelo said.

"And Angelo, for the love of God, don't get shot."

"Right back atcha," he replied as he took off into the woods.

Keeping his eye on the entrance to the cave, Horace crawled through the brush doing his best not to disturb a single branch. Images of the war flashed through his mind. He remembered how the bullets felt as they hit him in the chest. At first, it felt like he had been punched, then it burned. He prepared himself for worse. This time, he would not be caught by surprise.

He stayed in the undergrowth as he neared Clayton, who was floating on his back in the lake with his feet still on the shore. He watched to see if his chest was moving, but there was nothing. Clayton was dead. He wanted to call out to him to be sure but couldn't risk being heard. It was still several yards to the cave. He knew that if the shooter had a scoped rifle, he'd be dead as soon as he stood up.

"Horace," a voice called from the cave. "I'll trade you. Your life for the life of your friends," Hanrahan said as he stepped from the cave. "I can see you, Horace." He slowly walked toward Horace's position. "Come on, Horace. We both know how this is going to end."

"Russ?" He asked.

"That's right, it's me. Get up."

Horace took a deep breath and got to his knees. He raised his hands above his head and cautiously stood up to face his nemesis.

"What are you doing here? Why are you…?"

"I followed you," Hanrahan said. "It wasn't easy, you got a good head start. But thanks to your doctor friend, I found you." Hanrahan took another step closer and aimed the gun at Horace's chest. "I'm gonna finish the job that little gook started. Then I'm gonna kill your friends."

"Wait!" Horace said, trying to buy Dawn and Sayer time to put some distance between themselves and Hanrahan. "You said you'd let them go."

"I lied," Hanrahan said as a smile spread across his face.

"Hey!" Angelo called as he sprang out of the woods.

Hanrahan turned and fired as Angelo jumped toward the entrance of the cave for cover. Horace bolted toward Hanrahan and tackled him to the ground. Horace landed on top of him. He tried to grab the gun as Hanrahan grabbed his throat and squeezed hard. Horace gritted his teeth as Hanrahan applied more pressure to his jugular and pushed his chin upward. Horace struggled for air as he desperately tried to pull Hanrahan's hand from his neck. On the threshold of losing consciousness, Horace released the hand that held the gun and tried to use both hands to free himself. Hanrahan swung his hand upward, smashing the gun into Horace's cheekbone, knocking him sideways to the ground.

Hanrahan stood up and aimed the gun at Horace's chest. Angelo charged directly into him as he pulled the trigger. Horace felt the impact of the bullet as it ripped through his shoulder just under his clavicle. Hanrahan fell to the side knocking the gun free as Angelo began to swing wildly at his head.

Reaching into his boot, Hanrahan pulled his knife and drove it deep into the side of Angelo's thigh. Angelo reared up and screamed as he rolled off Hanrahan toward the lake.

Horace and Hanrahan rose simultaneously and dove for the pistol. With the weapon firmly in his grasp, Hanrahan hammered the butt repeatedly into Horace's wound as they wrestled for control, until the pain forced Horace off him.

Still paralyzed with fear, Cormick had witnessed everything from the cave. Unable to move, he watched helplessly as Angelo pulled the knife from his thigh and writhed in agony next to the lifeless body of Clayton. Hanrahan stood at the top of the falls and aimed the gun at Horace.

"Get on your knees," Hanrahan said, trying to catch his breath. "Beg for your life."

Out of breath and losing blood, Horace did as he was commanded.

"You can't kill me, Russ," he said. "I was never born."

"What the fuck is that supposed to mean?" Hanrahan asked.

Cormick flashed back to his mother holding him over the railing. As a helpless child, he had been powerless to stop her from almost killing him. If he had fought back at that moment, his beloved father would be alive. He felt a surge of anger unlike anything he had felt before rising inside of him. *No more fear. Deep breath,* he thought. Using all his strength he pulled himself free of the wall of the cave and bolted toward Hanrahan. Caught off guard, Russ swung around and fired, the bullet whizzing by Cormick's ear. He charged into Hanrahan with his head down, and at the point of impact, wrapped his arms around him, sending both men over the falls.

Stunned, Angelo and Horace stared in silent disbelief of what they had just witnessed. They both rose to their feet, never taking their eyes off the cliff. They slowly walked to the edge and looked down past the rushing water into the abyss several hundred feet below.

"Cormick…" Angelo whispered as tears began to stream down his cheeks.

"Thanks, Doc." Horace said.

Dawn and Sayer emerged from the woods, running toward them. Dawn tightly embraced Horace. Crying, she pulled his head down and kissed his cheek repeatedly. Horace held her and continued to stare into the dense woods below. She pulled back and looked at his shoulder.

"Are you okay?" she asked, her voice trembling.

"Yeah…I'm used to being shot," he smiled as he looked at the bloody hole in his shoulder. "That's gonna leave a mark."

Sayer threw his arms around the two of them.

"I don't know what I would've done…"

"I love you, too, Sayer," Horace said as he kissed his brother's head.

"Cormick?" Dawn asked, her eyes pleading for good news.

"The bravest man I ever knew," Horace said. He drew in a deep breath. "I'm gonna need a doctor."

Angelo continued watching the water surge past him and cascade downward into an opaque mist far below. The others turned to head back to camp but stopped immediately. Clayton was gone. His body had been just a few yards away minutes earlier, and now there was no trace of him.

"What the fuck?" Horace mumbled.

A fine mist slowly rose from the lake and settled on the surface, obscuring the water from their sight. Sayer walked to the shore where Clayton had been and fell to his knees. He leaned forward and gently pushed his hand into the haze. He closed his eyes and smiled. Nodding quietly, he got to his feet.

"He's not gone," he said to the others.

"Where is he then?" Dawn asked.

"He's here. He's in all of us," Sayer said as he turned and made his way back to camp.

———·\\\\·———

After nearly two days of hiking down the mountain, the four emerged from the tree line with Sayer leading the way. Each of them had their wool blanket draped over their shoulders. The left side of the blanket Horace wore was soaked with blood. He was light headed and leaned on Dawn for support as he stumbled forward.

The grassy expanse that led to the pueblo was a welcome site. Out of food and weakened by the journey, they moved slowly through the tall, yellow grass on their way to Clayton's adobe home. They hoped to get Horace and Angelo to the hospital, then return to the house to collect their belongings and find a nice, clean motel. It had never occurred to any of them that running water and mattresses were luxury items.

Several yards ahead of the others, Sayer stopped and looked around.

"I don't get it…" he mumbled. Thinking he had come down the wrong side of the mountain, he scanned the horizon for the house. It was nowhere to be seen.

Angelo limped up beside him. "Where's the house?" he asked. "I can see the pueblo. The house should be right here."

Sayer didn't respond. As the grass bowed in the wind, he could see something ahead. He continued forward until he came upon the ruins of an adobe structure lost to history hundreds of years earlier. The decaying mud walls had been battered by the elements for centuries, returning to the earth from which they were made. Looking over it carefully, he realized he was standing in Clayton's home.

Angelo walked up beside him and looked around. "Is this it?" he asked. "What happened to it?"

"Everything exists at once," Sayer said, remembering the words of his friend. He turned to Angelo. "Dude, this is how it always looked."

"How is that possible?"

"Everything is possible," Sayer replied.

In the distance, a crowd began to gather at the east wall of the pueblo. As tourists and onlookers pointed at them crossing the open plain, tribal police jumped the barrier and ran toward the four survivors.

"Stay where you are!" one shouted as he pulled his gun. "Don't go any farther!"

Three officers surrounded Angelo and Sayer, as the fourth ran to Horace and Dawn.

"Get on your knees! Now!" the officer screamed. "Hands behind your head!"

The two men complied, lifting their arms, as their blankets fell to the ground behind them. While one officer held his gun on them, the others moved behind them and threw them to the ground. Almost in unison, they dropped on Sayer and Angelo, each with one knee firmly in their backs. They pulled their arms behind them and clamped handcuffs tightly around their wrists.

"You're under arrest for trespassing on tribal land," the officer with the gun yelled.

Unable to go on, Horace slipped from Dawn's grasp and dropped to his knees in the tall grass.

"I'm not gonna make it," he said. He fell to his side on the parched earth and rolled onto his back. With the sun caressing the side of his face, he stared up at the bright blue sky. Dawn leaned over him, eclipsing the sunlight. She was crying and saying something, but he could only hear his heart beating, and his own labored breathing. Though he could see the panicked expression on her face, he could only silently smile back at her.

The officer threw Dawn to the side and cuffed her wrists behind her back. Incapable of moving, Horace continued to gaze upward. He heard the sound of his cherished Pacific Ocean echoing in his head as the moments of his life filled his mind. He knew he was dying, he had been through it before. This time, he wasn't afraid. As his eyelids slowly closed, the warm, azure sky above slowly faded from blue to black.

EPILOGUE: GENESIS

Angelo sat on the old wooden porch staring at the Taos Mountains in the distance. It had been almost a year since Cormick died, but he thought of him every day. Only now was he able to reminisce about him without breaking into tears. He sat in the same spot every morning to watch the sun come up over the mountains. For him, the light was akin to Cormick's soul rising to watch over him. Warm and nurturing, the two had a lot in common.

Sayer's sprawling desert ranch was his new home. He had retired to the desert of northern New Mexico, turning the command of his prized vessel over to a new captain. He had found peace in being just the owner of his boat. He had other work to do now.

Sunny came around the corner carrying the cat she had rescued from Sayer's home in Huntington Beach. The large brim of her woven sun hat bounced playfully as she made her way to the porch and sat beside Angelo.

"Do you miss it?" she asked, as she gently stroked the cat. "You know, the ocean?"

Angelo laughed. "You know, when I was young, there was this song that had the line, *the desert is an ocean with its life underground*. I didn't get it until I got here. This was all ocean once," he said as he looked around. "This ancient sea is just as peaceful. Maybe more so. This place tells the story of us."

348   RIC LEONETTI

"I don't miss it," she said. "I have everything I need here. I have Sayer," she smiled as she watched Sayer walk past in the distance. "He's a new man…my man. And he's going to do great things."

"Yeah…yeah he is," Angelo nodded. "Does he miss surfing?"

"Do you miss fishing?" she countered.

Angelo paused and looked back at the rocky peaks in the distance, then down as a dragonfly quietly landed at his feet on the weathered wooden porch.

"I'm still fishing," he said. "I'm a Fisher of Men."

Sayer had finished digging out his grand kiva. He stood above the twelve-by-twelve hole admiring his handy work. It had been an arduous task, but it was worth it. The kiva was only the beginning. With guidance from Clayton, he would set about taking the message of the true nature of man to the world.

Dawn walked up beside him, carrying a ladder she had made from some of the smaller trees on the property.

"It's finished," she said. "What do you think?"

"It's totally awesome!" Sayer exclaimed. He took the ladder and lowered it into the kiva. He climbed down and looked around. "I'm almost done with the vent," he said, looking at the tunnel he had started. "Sunny is making bricks today for the deflector. I just need some timbers, and then I can build my house!" He climbed back up the ladder to Dawn. "Nice and sturdy! Good work."

"You know, Sayer, I really had my doubts about you at first. But you are an incredible human being."

"Nah…" he said. "I'm just a human being. It's my soul

that's incredible. But, so is yours. So is everybody's. And it's time to teach people that."

"I hope they listen," she replied.

"When I was a little grommet, I thought church was a drag. You know why? Because it is." He raised his hands and slowly turned in a circle. "The Earth is our temple. This is what will make people understand. Inside their hearts... their souls, they'll know we're telling the truth."

"We're not going to win any debates with fundamentalists," she said.

"There's no debate," he replied. "It's the undeniable truth. How can anyone debate that?"

—⟡—

Horace walked to the window and gazed at the Taos Mountains. The sun had risen just above the peaks, beginning its long journey across the cerulean sky. Thin wisps of clouds dotted the sky like brush strokes from Monet himself, creating a fleeting masterpiece, showcasing the beauty of the world around them. Dawn quietly approached him from behind and put her arms around his waist. She gently nuzzled her nose on his neck and breathed him in.

"I love you," she said.

Horace turned around and wrapped his arms around her, looking deep into her eyes.

"Nobody's perfect," he said as he smiled and softly pressed his lips against hers. He reached down and placed his hand on her baby bump. "How's little Cormick doing in there?"

"He's moving a lot," she said. "Probably trying to tidy up my uterus."

"With any luck, he chose us to help him in this life. We

can teach him it's okay to be a little messy this time." Horace took in a deep breath and looked down at her belly. "We already know he's brave." He bent down and kissed her stomach. "Be patient, Doc. Only a month to go." He stood up and smiled. "How's the work going out there?" he asked.

"Sayer is finishing his kiva," she said. "I'm taking Angelo shopping. Need anything?"

"I have everything I need right here," he replied.

She gave him a quick, playful smooch and pulled away. "Yes, you do," she said. "Including pen and paper." She motioned to the desk beside the window. "You're my only student right now. I'd be a total failure if you didn't get at least an A minus." She turned and started to walk out of the room. "I believe in you," she called as she disappeared down the hallway.

He faced the desk and looked down at the legal pad. At first, the blank pages were overwhelming. Filling them seemed as daunting a task as swimming across the ocean. He pulled out the chair and sat down. Taking in a deep breath, he picked up the pen and rested the ball point on the paper.

In the beginning, he wrote, *all things existed as one…*

Made in the USA
Middletown, DE
06 May 2017